false pretenses

OTHER BOOKS AND AUDIO BOOKS
BY CAROLE THAYNE:

A Question of Trust

false pretenses

a novel

carole thayne

Covenant Communications, Inc.

Cover image by Mel Curtis © 2004 Photodisc/Getty Images

Cover design copyrighted 2004 by Covenant Communications, Inc.

Published by Covenant Communications, Inc.
American Fork, Utah

Printed in Canada
First Printing: June 2004

10 09 08 07 06 05 04   10 9 8 7 6 5 4 3 2 1

ISBN 1-59156-519-7

To my mother, Jeanne Thayne, for being the example and for creating a home where creativity could flourish.

Acknowledgments

Thanks most especially to my writing friends Helen Cannon, Julie Dymock, Kathy A. Herbert, and Anne Stark for helping me shape this novel. Thanks to my friends and family who read drafts, offered encouragement, and kept my spirits up through the process—especially my mother, Jeanne Thayne, and my brother and his wife, Brian and Norma Thayne.

Thanks to the many friends, family, bookstore personnel, and unknown readers who embraced my first novel with enthusiasm and who passed the word along. Thanks also to Alan Smith and my friends in Grouse Creek, including all the numerous part-timers for their support and response to my writing. Special note of thanks to Jason Kimber for letting me steal his joke. Appreciation also goes to Uncle Jim Sheridan, whose real-life job and personality inspired a chapter in this book.

Thanks to my editor Angela Colvin and to Covenant Communications. And last but not least, thanks to my always kind and supportive family, my husband Mick Warburton, our daughter Ginger, and our son Trevor and his wife Joanna.

chapter 1

---

nerve

Sunny watched the man come in and take a seat at the end of the counter. She'd seen him before at church, but never in her diner. After more than twenty years, she'd just started going back to church some months earlier. At some church function or another, something about the man had bothered her, but she couldn't remember what it was. She took the pencil out from behind her ear and stood in front of him. He wasn't too bad looking—dark, graying hair, green eyes, wire-frame glasses, broad chest, and probably wasn't much older than she was. She glanced at his left hand and noticed he wasn't wearing a ring. Men, decent men, available men, were a rarity in the small Montana town. Who was she kidding? Even men her own age never gave her a second glance anymore—she was over fifty. Nevertheless, she tried to smile at him. Surprisingly, it seemed to work because he looked right into her face with a gaze that seared right through her.

"What can I get for you today?" she asked, after a pause.

"Actually, I came to issue a calling."

"Calling? What are you talking about?" She leaned closer to him, and rested her elbows on the counter, hoping that no one could hear what he said.

"You are LDS?" the man asked.

"So what if I am?"

"I'm the new branch president, Jack Heath."

"That explains it, then. I haven't had a Church calling in . . ." She cocked her head to the side and thought for a minute, ". . . twenty-nine years, come Thanksgiving time."

"Yes, I know that," he answered.

"I've even lived with a man—several actually—before I married."

"That was before you were baptized, doesn't count."

"I cheat at cards."

"Well, as I heard it, you don't play for money, so I don't think that's too serious." He grinned.

"And I'm a vegetarian," Sunny added.

"A vegetarian?"

"Yes." A bell tinkled, signaling that someone had walked through the door. It was an elderly couple she didn't recognize. She nodded a greeting. "Take a seat anywhere. I'll be right with you," she said loudly.

"I don't think being a vegetarian is a problem, let alone a sin," the president continued.

"Still, I thought you should know, because of all the ham."

"Ham?"

"Sure, you know, every branch party, picnic, dinner, fund-raiser. There's always ham. "

"You can change that. We don't need to eat ham—change it to something else. Back to that call—"

"And I smoke."

"That's not a problem."

"It isn't?"

"Not as long as you quit. I need you to be Relief Society president."

"Are you out of your ever-living mind?" Sunny felt faint.

She was so loud that two of her customers looked over. "Sunny, bring me some more coffee, would ya?" one called.

Sunny motioned to the branch president that she'd be back, then she walked over to the customer who had shouted for her. She poured a little too much in Ned's cup and it spilled on the booth table. "Say, your hand is tremblin'. Careful now. Did Jack say something to upset you? You look like you seen a ghost."

"Something like that," Sunny answered, then walked over to the jukebox. She flipped the side open where she could bypass putting quarters in and chose three more songs, the first being "Your Cheatin' Heart." The second two were from the Grateful Dead and Joan Baez. She always made sure she mixed country with the songs she really liked. She glanced over to the end stool at the counter and hoped it would be empty. It wasn't.

"Sunny, could you bring me a potpie and a tall glass of milk?" President Jack Heath shouted.

Sunny turned the order in and then asked the cook, Marty, if he would deliver it to the man at the end of the counter himself.

"To Jack? Why? You do it." Marty wiped his hands on a towel.

When the potpie was ready, Sunny let it sit under the hot-lights for a full three minutes. Finally the new branch president hollered, "Sunny, the pie, it's getting cold!"

"Okay." She grabbed it and slammed it down in front of him.

"Milk?"

She retrieved a tall glass out of the plastic carton and pressed it under the machine spout, again spilling it over. She set it in front of the man and shook the excess liquid from her fingers.

"What happened to the old branch president?" she asked, annoyed. "We had an understanding."

"And what was that?"

"He never bothered me about anything."

"Well, you must've missed church last week—he moved. And I'm not bothering you, Sunny. If you want to blame someone, you'll have to blame the Lord. He's the one who wants you for Relief Society president, not me. Believe me, I argued with Him. Told Him just what you told me, about the smoking, cheating—all those things. Left out the vegetarian thing. He still wants you. Your name rose above the others like cream to the top."

"Who else was on that list?" Sunny demanded.

"Well, I'm not going to tell you that."

"What about Andrea Wood?"

"No car. No phone."

"Annabel?"

"She's eighty-eight. Besides, she's been Relief Society president for the last eleven years. She needs a break."

"I know, that new young woman, uh . . . lives at the end of Willow Lane."

"Moved already."

"What about Cindy Abel?"

"Need her for Young Women's president."

"Like cream to the top, huh?"

"Definitely," he countered.

"Are you sure you want me—even with all my faults?" She glanced up at the cook's window and could see two more plates there. "Excuse me a second."

"Actually, it's the Lord who wants you." Jack looked out over the top of his wire frames.

"Yeah, you said that. Maybe then," she said to the branch president. "If you're sure."

A broad smile formed on his face. He stuck out his right hand. "We'll expect you then, Sunday at 10 A.M." He drank the last of his milk, then stood up. "Oh, and I expect you don't know we'll be meeting here."

"In my café?"

"It's the only place. When President Anderson and his family moved, they sold their place. New owners aren't LDS, so I didn't figure we could keep meeting in their large basement. Now your place is the only one I can think of."

"But where will we sit? I'm open on Sundays." Sunny glanced around her diner in a panic.

"Oh, I guess I should've told you that you'll have to start closing down on the Sabbath, at least in the mornings, if not altogether."

"You just wanted me to be president so you could use my place. You're a sneaky weasel. I don't think I'll do it." As she followed Jack out to his truck she started to get mad. *Where did this man get the nerve?* She couldn't believe it. *He must be completely crazy, either that, or—*

"As I mentioned, you're going to have to quit smoking. This week is general conference, so you'll have an extra week. I'll drop in next Saturday to see if you're ready to be set apart on Sunday."

"You said you wanted me, even with all my faults."

"The Lord takes us however He can get us, but doesn't expect us to keep all our vices. And I'd like you to start with kicking your smoking habit. Then we'll work up from there."

Sunny was really irritated at that point. "I can't do that. If I could quit smoking then I would've by now! You think I like smoking? Do you think I like the fact that I'm puffing away years of my life? Do you think I like coughing, not being able to taste my own delicious food? Do you think . . . ?" It wasn't like Sunny to yell, but who did this self-righteous man think he was? She could feel her face getting hot. The elderly couple was looking through the window, aghast. She glanced at them and realized they were still waiting to order. "It would take a miracle for me to quit smoking," she said coldly, lowering her volume.

"Then I'll be praying for one," Jack said before backing his pickup away from the café. Sunny stood in front of her diner until he disappeared from view, then headed back inside. She was fuming. *And what does he mean work up from there, what else is there?*

"What'd Jack say that made you so mad?" Ned asked.

"He asked me to be Relief Society president. Not only that, he said he would be holding church in the Lazy Moose."

"Oh yeah—he's a Mormon, isn't he? Folks in town like to call him Jack Mormon, doesn't seem to bother him none," Ned added with an amused smile. "But what's that got to do with you? You're not a Mormon." Ned said taking a sip of his coffee.

Sunny sat down in the booth next to Ned and put her head on the table. "Yes, I am."

"That so? I thought Mormons didn't smoke. And what kind of president does he want you for?"

"I'll be like the spiritual leader of all the Mormon women in the branch."

"Jumping Jehoshaphat! That's funny—you?"

* * *

Sunny always sat in the far west booth after closing, smoked, and looked out the window. She liked to watch as the sun dropped behind Horseshoe Mountain and the windows across the street glowed as if a fire burned behind them. She could see the main part of town, less than a dozen businesses all dedicated to the tourist trade—motels, cafés, and souvenir shops. This time of year the streets quieted earlier, but in the middle of the summer the town buzzed until early morning. Usually she smoked two cigarettes before heading home, but today, she kept smoking, one after the other, piling the snuffed-out butts until they overfilled the glass ashtray, creating a pile of burning embers on the table. President What's His Name was all she could think about. He'd never even spoken to her before this day, except maybe at the July Fourth picnic last year. Now that she thought about it, he'd been the one who'd said he admired her for protesting the logging that was going on in the forests around town. She was surprised, since few locals agreed with her on her "issues." His admiration was especially confusing . . . Sunny suddenly remembered what had been nagging her about him. She'd heard a rumor that he was trying to develop a recreation area, complete with hundreds of cabins on the shores of Trout Lake. The idea was repulsive to Sunny.

Sunny watched the smoke fog the window, snuffed out the last cigarette in her pack, and thought back. She wished that she'd never started smoking. Most smokers were smokers before they converted to Mormonism, but Sunny didn't start until after her husband Shane had died. The last thing she cared about at the time was doing the right thing—doing the healthy thing in the "healing" process. Even though her conversion to the Church was somewhat less than it should have been, she wished she could have, would have tried harder to keep going to church.

* * *

She'd met the missionaries in a village outside of San Francisco in the late '60s. Really it was a hippie commune. On the day that the two elders showed up, she had been furious with her boyfriend. They'd been living in his van. He was in his late twenties and she was barely nineteen. They'd just shared a joint, then she'd walked to the outhouse. When she came back, he was with another girl. She could still envision the girl's red springy hair contrasting with his—greasy, blond, and straight. In her mind, she'd told herself that this free lifestyle was what it was all about, but seeing the two of them together made her sick. She didn't say anything, but started stalking away from the commune, not sure if she was just going for a brisk walk or going for good, when two young men—short hair, white shirts, ties, and black name tags—drove up in a blazing orange Pinto. When they saw her, they stopped and one stuck his hand out an open window to shake hers. She asked them for a ride and they said that they weren't allowed to give her one.

"So who won't allow you?" she'd asked. "You look like adults to me."

"We are representatives of Jesus Christ and we are teaching about His gospel."

"That's cool, but Jesus would give a girl a ride when she's trying to shed what you would call an immoral lifestyle. If you'll excuse me, I think I'll start jogging." She started running and they turned the car around and caught up to her, matching her pace.

"You're running from sin?" the driver shouted.

"Maybe," she'd answered.

"We've decided to make an exception—hop in."

By this time her boyfriend had realized she was gone, started the van up, and was coming up behind them.

"Can't you drive this thing any faster?" Sunny asked.

"It's a Pinto," one of the missionaries explained.

"He's got a ten-year-old Volkswagen. Besides that, he'll run out of gas before you hit the main highway," Sunny said desperately.

The driver pushed the pedal to the floor and they bounced along the rural road at close to forty miles per hour. The commune disappeared from focus in the rearview mirror. She wasn't sure what she would do if her boyfriend caught up, or what he would do, but she no longer cared. She lay down on the floor of the car, hoping he couldn't see her. When she climbed up and sat on the backseat, they were out on the main highway near 'Frisco, and she could see the van sputtering to a stop behind them.

"We really don't know where to take you. You have family? Friends?" one of them asked.

She'd snorted a laugh. "Just left my best friend back there. He seemed to prefer some redhead to me. You can just drop me off anywhere. I'm used to living on the street—anywhere would be cool. The Haight District is hip, lots of free food, actually free everything. I can hang out there."

The missionary in the passenger seat turned around then. Freckles plastered his otherwise pale face. He wore black-rimmed glasses and had strawberry-blond hair. "We aren't allowed to even drive through that area," he said with wide eyes.

After turning back around, he mumbled something to the driver. "We've got a place we can take you to."

They finally pulled up in front of a home. It was the epitome of what she had been trying to avoid with her free life. The house was a white, sprawling rambler with a green, manicured lawn and beautiful trees and flowers. It had a two-car garage, and children sucked Popsicles on the covered porch. She didn't want to get out of the car, and wouldn't have if it hadn't been for the four-year-old. A girl not much bigger than a Kewpie doll tugged open the door and shoved a yellow puppy into Sunny's lap. The puppy licked her face and romped out of the car. Sunny jumped out after it and watched the missionaries speed off. *The nerve of those two*, she thought. The Pinto protested with a loud backfire.

The next evening, the two young men, elders, she learned, showed up in the spacious family living room, with its exposed beams and cathedral ceiling, to teach her the gospel. After nearly a month of nightly visual aids and spiritual prodding, she was baptized. She remembered that it was family prayer, kneeling around a table with this family who had taken her in—no questions asked—that had converted her. Every time that happened she'd felt a warmth she hadn't felt before.

As Sunny now thought about her life, Shane, his death and their all-too-brief life together, took front and center in her mind. Shane had always told her that she was his Sunny Day, his reason for living. When he died, she'd promised him that she would go on giving as she always had. "Cast thy bread upon the waters . . ." She'd always done that, but the promised return hadn't happened. When would she "find it after many days"? Many days seemed to have passed her by and her bread hadn't been returned to her, not in the way she would have liked. She was always giving—it was part of her nature—as natural as breathing, and she couldn't be selfish even when she tried to be, but she was still alone—she still missed Shane and her stillborn child. When could she put it all behind her? Maybe accepting this calling would be the answer. Maybe now she could quit smoking, could give it her all, and her bread would come back to her. Before Sunny headed home that night, she stepped back into her kitchen, away from the windows, and dropped to her knees, praying for a miracle. For so many years she'd convinced herself it wasn't possible to quit smoking—not worth the effort to try and then fail. One thing was sure, she couldn't possibly do it on her own. When she started her clunky VW Bug late that night to head home, she couldn't have known that her prayer for a changed life would be answered in the form of a redheaded young woman from Idaho.

chapter 2

kelli's choice

Kelli took strands of her dark auburn hair and deftly braided a white ribbon through it. Then she held up the plastic mirror in an attempt to see the effect. Only part of her hair was reflected in the small oval, but the contrast was just what she wanted. Even though she needed to keep her hairstyle simple, it was still her wedding day and she hoped to look pretty. But vanity was to be disdained and Kelli tried not to linger in admiration. Her hair had always brought attention to her. It was smooth, thick, straight, and because of the color, it stood out. Her dress was a thin, simple peasant style, nearly worn out. She slipped it on. Still, it was white and would serve its purpose.

Kelli never imagined that she would be preparing for her wedding day by herself. After her parents died, she'd always thought that her Aunt Jenny would be the one to help her dress for the most special day in her life. Then, after she met Stacey, her big brother Sam's girlfriend, and Sam had confided to her that he planned to make Stacey his wife, Kelli assumed Stacey would be there to help too. But none of them knew, could know, about this day. It had to be kept secret. A fleeting feeling of sadness washed over Kelli. Then she tried to replace it with the joy she should feel. *I'm doing the right thing,* she told herself. She told herself that over and over, hoping to believe it. The fact that it wasn't a temple wedding bothered her, but she wasn't sure what God really wanted from her anymore. She felt her hand tremble as she held the mirror up to her face. *Just one more glance,* she promised herself. She was startled to see her chalk-white complexion peering unsmilingly back at her. Pulling the mirror away from her face, she checked her hair once more. *Just right,* she thought. Kelli suppressed her feelings of disappointment. She wasn't worthy to want more than was being offered. It was sinful for her to fall in love with Kevin. It wasn't up to her to decide for herself. She knew now that though her whole life she'd dreamed of her wedding day, she had been wrong, selfish to even think of herself. Kevin wasn't to be her husband; instead she would be required to marry a much older man. It would bring her salvation though. It was right. Or was it? Kelli felt sick every time she allowed herself to think deeply about what she was about to do. She set the mirror down, smoothed her dress with her hands, and walked out for the ceremony.

The weather was perfect. The evening sun had lowered in the sky and spread an unusual warmth across the compound. The cloudless sky was deep azure with white cumulus clouds painted across the horizon. Richard's wives, his children, and the rest of the group all sat waiting on rough pine benches that formed a semicircle. The self-proclaimed Prophet Daniel was there too. He was younger than Richard. He had intense blue eyes, and smooth blond hair to his shoulders. A small beard accentuated the look. Other than his clothes, he looked biblical. Kelli knew that he was the spiritual leader of this community, as well as another group in Montana. Unlike Richard, the man she would marry, Prophet Daniel dressed casually in jeans and a sky-blue polo shirt. He stood in front of the group with his head bowed as if in prayer. Richard was dressed in an expensive, pin-striped suit with a silk shirt. He probably owned it, Kelli thought, because he transacted all the business dealings for the growing church.

Richard took Kelli's hand and together they walked toward the prophet. Kelli tried not to think about what she was about to do. She'd already made the choice. She would live with it—but his hand made her cringe. Again, she asked herself how she could live with a man she didn't love. Did God really require her unhappiness for penance? Her mind raced. Maybe this wasn't the answer. She glanced around the small audience, searching for Kevin's face. At first she couldn't see him, but she finally spotted him and tried to catch his gaze. Kevin was looking past her, his thoughts apparently miles away. If only he'd look up and give her a reassuring nod, she could go through with the ceremony, but his gaze was fixed. Maybe he didn't love her anyway. She had believed him when he'd said God wanted her to marry Richard. She had believed the prophet when he said women couldn't choose for themselves. But now she wasn't sure.

She tried to force her feet to move toward the prophet. But with each step, her heart raced and she felt so dizzy that the sagebrush, junipers, and aspens swirled together with kinetic energy. *Is this how I'm supposed to feel on my wedding day?* She grabbed onto the lapels of Richard's jacket to steady her stance, but then slid down to the ground on all fours. She could feel the earth beneath her spinning out of control. Clutching her midsection, she threw up in the dry grass.

When Kelli woke up, Andrea was sitting on the edge of her bed, stroking her hair and giving her sips of water. "What happened? Am I married?"

"No—we'll postpone it until tomorrow," Richard said from the corner of the room with an impatient glare on his face. He twitched angrily. Kelli had never seen him like this. "I had to cast Satan's spirits from your soul, Kelli. You were possessed."

"But I didn't feel—"

"Whenever we attempt to do something good, something very right, Satan will use his influence over us. You must fight that, Kelli. Tomorrow we'll try again. I know this marriage is right for you. It will bring you the salvation that you seek—the absolution you desire and need. Trust me. It's what God asks of you to absolve you from your sins."

Kelli tried to think. Her thoughts during the past weeks had been cloudy. *This isn't how it's supposed to be. Something's not right.* Kelli thought back to what had brought her to this polygamist group in the first place. She'd just broken up with her boyfriend and wanted to meet new people. A national seminar for young adults promising to teach inner peace, self-awareness, and success would be just the right place, she'd thought. But instead she found herself wishing she hadn't come. Instead of inner peace, the conference had focused on having a good time. Socializing was the last thing she needed. During the four-day conference she found herself wandering away from the group more and more—sitting by herself, reading, praying, hoping someone would come along and help her with her problem. For years now she'd been successful at burying her burden. She doubted anyone suspected that she was crippled with guilt at causing the accident that killed her parents. Until recently, she thought she was over it, but then, when

Justin pushed her for a more serious commitment, she crumbled and fled the relationship, just as she had from Brian the year before, and from Zach the year before that. Despite her misgivings, Kelli forced herself to go to the seminar's closing social, a dance, and tried to forget her problems for one night.

It had been a night to remember. Kelli was sipping lemonade from a paper cup and watching couples swaying to enchanting dance music, when Kevin suddenly appeared. He held his hand out. "Care to dance?"

Actually, truth be known, Kelli didn't care to dance; instead she'd hoped to blend into the crowd. But Kevin had singled her out several times during the conference, hoping to get to know her better, he'd told her, and now he gently grabbed her free hand, waited for her to put her cup down, and led her out to the middle of the floor. Before she knew it, she'd momentarily forgotten her problems and found herself enjoying Kevin's company. He was so easy to be with. It might've been his eyes that convinced Kelli that she wanted to get to know him better. They were dark brown with specks of green, and they seemed to suggest gentleness and intelligence. His charismatic personality was a bonus and she was flattered by the attention. After a couple of dances they'd walked away from the group, sat on an expanse of green grass, and looked up at the stars and a silver moon. She'd been surprised to learn that Kevin's religious beliefs weren't exactly mainstream LDS—or mainstream anything for that matter. He told her his church lived according to the lost biblical teachings, such as polygamy, animal sacrifice—that sort of thing. Kelli remembered laughing at first. "A joke, right?" she'd asked. She'd never met a polyga-mist, but knew they didn't look as normal as Kevin did. He didn't dress any differently than any of the guys she'd dated. That's why she was so surprised when he hesitated, then said, "Well, I'm not married yet, but some in our group are polygamists. You really can't judge until you get to know us. It's nothing like you hear about. Come see. It'll surprise you, I promise. Our group works very hard to better the world. You seem like someone who's open enough to see what we're all about. Besides that, if I want to date you, I need to get permission."

"Do you?"

"Need permission or want to date you?" he asked.

"Want to date me?"

"Yeah, I'd like to. I've been watching you all week. You're deeper than the rest of the people here. They're all just about having a good time—you seem to want more."

Kelli considered that. *It's probably because none of them have killed their own parents,* she thought darkly. Still, what did she have to lose? She was curious about what made Kevin tick. She'd always been interested in other cultures and religious beliefs. She'd never really thought much about polygamists, but still, it would be educational. They were misled of course, wrong certainly; but this Kevin seemed okay. Maybe she could get him to see why he needed to convert to Mormonism. He could be her missionary project.

"Well okay," she agreed, "but we can't date. We'll just hang out some. You tell me what you believe, but only if I can tell you what I believe."

* * *

Kelli slept after her panic attack. She was vaguely aware of voices and people coming in and out of the room. Occasionally, she recognized Richard's voice, but usually she couldn't identify the speaker. Once in a while, she'd feel a cool rag swabbing her forehead, and a warm, smooth hand on her head.

Finally it was dark and there were no more voices and no more people coming in and going from the room. The room itself was just large enough for a single bed, a chair, and a trunk. Richard's wives lived in this trailer on the nights that it wasn't their turn to spend with him. He, and whoever's turn it was, would spend the night in a trailer some distance from the others. Kelli sat up in bed. She wasn't wearing the wedding dress anymore, but instead was dressed in flowered cotton pajamas. They felt good on her skin. She lay back down and pressed her nose into the down pillow. She couldn't remember changing clothes and wondered who had dressed her. *Not Richard,* she hoped. No, probably it had been Andrea, who had been so much like a mother to her. Time had a way of folding on top of itself and she wasn't sure how long she'd been living with the group. At first she'd just come to listen to Kevin and walk in the hills with him. Then the lines of friendship had blurred. She remembered trying to teach Kevin about the Church, but somewhere along the way, he was doing more of the teaching. At first everything he said seemed terribly wrong, but little by little, it began to make sense.

Her mind shifted to the present. Richard said the marriage would be rescheduled for the next day. When would that be? Maybe a few hours from now? And even though she had been anxious to start her new life, now she was beginning to feel strangely nervous about the upcoming event. *But isn't this the way I'm supposed to feel on my wedding day? Wedding jitters, cold feet. Everyone feels this way—that's all it is.* Before she joined the group, she often prayed whenever she was scared, and she would feel comforted. But after she met Richard, she realized she wasn't worthy to ask God for His comfort. Her sins had come crashing into her mind, parading her guilt daily, and only her leaders could offer her the comfort she sought. At first it was Kevin who had prayed for her, but then Richard. She would listen to his words and know that she was unworthy. All she could think about was her desire to feel whole. Kelli sighed and thought about her proof that she was repentant. The next day she would marry Richard and she would be, if not happy, content—absolved. She was determined.

chapter 3

an accidental parent

Sam had always struggled with parenting the two young people he was responsible for. He'd often wondered how a rough-and-tumble cowboy who'd made plenty of mistakes himself could keep teenagers living the way their folks would want them to. Only occasionally did the unfairness of his situation sneak up and remind Sam that he'd rather be irresponsible himself—hang out with the guys, ride off in the hills without a care in the world rather than make sure his two younger siblings had food on the table and did their homework. "Life isn't fair," he remembered his dad often saying when one of them had whined about something. And now, just when Kelli and Brandon were grown and Sam thought his worries were behind him, this new concern about Kelli had emerged.

Sam tried to remember when it first dawned on him that he'd have to grow up in a hurry. It was six months after the accident. Sam had sat down on the kitchen chair, held the heel of his left boot, pulled it off, then his other one, and set the pair by the back door. He'd glanced at the clock again. It was after one in the morning. He'd just gotten back from a date, his second in two weeks with Cara. Heather was already history, married to one of his best friends. Just an hour earlier, Sam and Cara had been dancing together; he could still smell her perfume. He stood in the window and peered out into the inky blackness. Brandon, seventeen, wasn't home yet. Sam had quietly gone down the stairs, opened Kelli's bedroom door, noted her form, listened for her breath, then trod back up the stairs, turned off the lights, and gone to bed.

He hadn't been able to sleep in the stifling heat. The windows were open to let in the night air. He hadn't bothered undressing; he'd figured it would be easier that way when Brandon got home. The ceiling above him had swirls in the plaster that he could barely make out in the dark. Sometimes, when he was a young boy, he'd gotten up early on Sunday mornings and lain on top of this bed between his parents, trying to find scenes in the swirls, the way he did with clouds. He could still find the elephant with her outstretched trunk, and the dragon blowing fire, he realized with a smile. A faint sound caught his attention and he raised his head off the pillow. He'd stepped out into the kitchen and peered out the window. He could barely see Brandon's car rolling across the gravel drive, lights out, motor off. What was he up to? Sam watched his younger brother stagger across the sidewalk and fumble up the steps. Sam opened the front door just as his brother fell across the threshold.

"Shoot," Brandon mumbled, "thought you'd be asleep."

"You're crocked."

Brandon laughed. "Sure am, big brother."

Sam had helped his brother down to his room, pulled his boots off for him, laid him on his bed, and pulled his quilt up to his chin. Brandon laughed again. "Thanks, bro. Hope you had fun with your lady friend," he slurred.

Without turning on any lights, Sam had fumbled his way back through the darkness and into what had been his parents' room. He'd waited until six months after they'd died before moving out of the room he had shared with Brandon all of his life. Before slipping back into bed, he slammed his fist into the framed photo of his parents as he passed it, causing the glass to crack as it crashed against the dresser. "Shoot, Mom and Dad!" he said out loud. "I didn't sign up for this. This wasn't in the cards. I'm not supposed to be worrying about this kind of stuff for at least another fifteen or twenty years."

Sam had climbed back onto the bed and drifted to sleep. In the morning, he'd gone downstairs again and sat on the edge of Brandon's bed.

Sun had streaked through the small basement window and cast a ray across Brandon's face. He shielded his eyes. "Man, would you close that blind?"

"How ya feeling?" Sam asked.

"I've been better."

"Sit up. We need to talk."

"Oh come on. You aren't my dad. If you start in on me and give me a load of crap, I think I'll puke."

"Go ahead, just clean it up when you're through. You've got a choice here. You can live here with me and Kelli and help out, or you can pack up your things right now and go live with Granny, or even Aunt Jenny. But if you choose to live here, you'd better not ever come home plastered again. If you want to drink, I guess that's your business, but you won't do it while you live here."

"What gives you the right? You drank when you were my age. Everyone knew it."

"Yeah, you're right. I did a few times. And it was stupid." Sam glanced at the digital clock on the dresser. "It's time for church. You coming?"

"No way."

"You guys going to church?" Kelli shouted from upstairs.

"Just a minute, Kell," Sam responded, then he lowered his voice to speak to Brandon again. "You want to hear Dad's sermon or . . ."

"Don't bring out the dead baby story. I've heard all about the baby who would've been our uncle if the drunk driver hadn't killed him. I don't need to see his picture in the photo album again. Got nothin' to do with me. I promise, I won't drink and drive again."

"Not good enough if you want to live here. There is no way I'm taking the chance that you'll drink in front of Kelli. I need your help, Brandon. This isn't fun for me, you know."

"Could've fooled me, with your holier-than-thou attitude."

"Well, I'm taking Kelli to church. By the time I get back I'll expect you to be packed and out of this house."

"You're such a hypocrite."

Sam hurried to finish getting ready for church, and was still angry when he and Kelli stepped through the chapel doors. It was almost more than he could stand to sit there through the meeting, listening about a God who had abandoned him, leaving him with a burden he wasn't prepared for. More than anything he wanted to get in his truck, drive up in the hills, and take a walk to think things out, but today he'd sit through it all—for Kelli. She needed him to. He put his arm around her and she smiled.

After sacrament meeting, Sam slipped away between meetings and hurried home. All he could think about was Brandon, how he couldn't take it if Brandon really did leave. Maybe he was wrong to have come down so hard on him. He needed him home more than anything. Sam got into his pickup and zoomed back to the house, hoping Brandon hadn't had a chance to pack his bags and leave.

When he got there, Brandon was rubbing butter on some potatoes and sticking them in the oven.

"Brandon, I'm sorry. I was wrong. You're right. I'm not your parent and I had no right—"

"Don't worry about it. What're you doing home anyway? You shouldn't be home yet for another hour or more."

"Just didn't want you to leave. I need you here."

"I wasn't going anywhere. I know better than to let your hot head run me out of a comfortable bed. And . . . I'll think about what you said."

* * *

Sam's thoughts were jarred to the present again. After ten years he was still the parent. Kelli had been such a responsible teenager, and now he didn't understand what was going on with her. Sam was in the middle of taking bids on a Brangus bull when he saw Stacey and Herman take their usual seat on the fourth bench of the auction arena. Sam acknowledged his friends with a quick wave of his hand, and a huge smile, then continued to babble in the mesmerizing language of a livestock auctioneer.

Stacey, with her bright smile, cheered him. He'd hoped that she would come. For the last six months they had been dating, but with her living nearly sixty miles away from Burley, Idaho, in the remote town of Grouse Creek, he didn't see her nearly as often as he wanted to. The responsibility of being both a father and mother had consumed the last ten years of his life, and even though both Brandon and Kelli were grown and on their own, they had taken much of his life away from him. He had all but given up dating in his twenties. He'd found it too difficult to juggle being a supportive parent—attending honor nights, basketball games, rodeos, church functions—and finding time to date. Girls were interested initially, but when they discovered that they would have to play second fiddle to the needs of two teenagers, they would vanish and send him an invitation to their wedding receptions. By the time Brandon had married, and Kelli had finished college and landed a decent job, it seemed all the girls were already taken. He was thirty-one years old now. There were a few women he'd met who were on their second go around, but none who had interested him. Then, where he'd least expected to meet someone, Stacey Willis had shown up one day at the livestock auction with his old friend Herman from Grouse Creek.

Herman was a longtime rancher in his mid-eighties with whitish-gray wispy hair protruding from his cowboy hat. Fifty years earlier he'd been accused and acquitted of murder, but the suspicion had lingered until recently. Finally, with the help of Stacey and Sam, his name had been cleared and they were now all good friends. It had also opened the door for Herman to be reunited with his fiancée of fifty years earlier. Sam was pleased to have brought some happiness into the old man's life, just as Herman had brought Stacey into his life.

Thinking back, he wondered why he'd fallen for her so fast and so completely. She was a pretty twenty-five-year-old with her almost-black hair now to her shoulders, a quick smile, dark skin, and walnut-colored eyes, but he'd known lots of pretty girls. It wasn't her looks that had captured him, but rather her personality—her fiery spirit and her intensity. It didn't take him long to realize that his first impressions of her were right. And now, just when he'd finally planned on asking Stacey to marry him, his parenting responsibilities were getting in the way yet again. He'd been calling and calling Kelli, leaving messages every day, but she never returned his calls. It was so out of character for her that he knew something must be terribly wrong—his gut told him.

Sam temporarily forgot what he was doing and the auction stalled. He noticed Marv from Elba trying to get his attention, waving his wide-brimmed cowboy hat frantically.

"Sold!" Sam blurted. He turned to see if Mel was coming yet.

Sam leaned back in his chair. "Mel, you ready to take over? I've got a lot going on. I was hoping you could spell me for the rest of the day."

Now a red Hereford was on the auction floor, pacing.

"Go on, now." Mel grinned, "I seen her come in and take her spot on the fourth row. When you goin' to tie the knot? Hobble yerself to her permanent like?"

Sam put his hand over the microphone. "Careful Mel—don't want you asking me for her now. But thanks for the encouragement. So anyway, we'll see you later." Sam slipped out of the chair behind the microphone, and Mel immediately jumped in and went to work, waving Sam away with another wide grin and a flip of his hand.

Sam took the back stairs, and when he reached the bottom Stacey was standing there waiting for him. "Boy, am I glad to see you today. I wasn't sure you'd make it," he said. Sam kissed her quickly and grabbed her hand. "Let's eat. I really need to talk to you about something."

"You look serious," Stacey said.

"Yeah."

Herman trudged alongside, and the trio sat down in a booth with red vinyl seats in the small café adjoining the auction building. It was only open on Thursdays—auction days.

Sam smiled at a waitress, a young woman probably not yet twenty, but expecting what Sam knew was her second child. "Usual, Sam? Herman?"

"Yeah," Sam answered.

"Tell that cook to cut back on the onions this time. I've got my lady comin' tonight," Herman said.

The waitress raised an eyebrow. "You joshing me, Herman?"

"No sirree Bob."

"Well, that's something, now isn't it? How is it you found yerself a woman that'd have you after all these years?"

"Livin' right—I suppose." Herman winked.

The waitress grinned and turned to Stacey. "We've still got some of that turkey meat Sam ordered in for you."

"Thanks, Chelsea. A turkey sandwich would be great, and—"

"Tall glass of orange juice?" the waitress asked.

"Yes. Thanks again," Stacey said, with an appreciative smile.

Sam loved the woman sitting next to him. For days he had been carrying a ring in his jeans pocket. He stuck the tips of his fingers in his coin pocket and felt the circular band. It was his mother's wedding ring, a simple silver band embedded with a double row of tiny diamonds. He'd been hoping for some wonderfully spontaneous moment to pop up so he could give it to her, but this wasn't it.

"You had something serious to tell me?" Stacey asked.

"Yeah, it's Kelli. Something's up with her. She won't answer her phone, so yesterday I called her at her office. They told me she up and left weeks ago. Didn't even give her two weeks' notice." Sam took his black felt cowboy hat off and set it on the seat next to him.

"That doesn't sound good."

"Yeah. Anyway, I'll understand if you two can't run up to Twin with me. I tried calling you this morning. Must've been on your morning run. Herman, I tried calling you too—"

"Now you know I've got more irons in the fire than 'bout anyone my age. Can't be wait'n around all mornin' to answer the tellyphone. But if Stacey's willin' to make the journey, then so am I. She's got the car keys anyways. And as spry as I am, it's a long way to hoof it."

"We can go with you," Stacey agreed.

* * *

Stacey scooted all the way across the bench seat of Sam's pickup to be next to him. She had to straddle her legs around the gears so Sam could shift. It was more awkward, but he liked her so close he could smell her—a fresh blend of clean laundry, spring air, and baby powder. Herman sat next to the window, rubbed the stubble on his chin, and hummed "She'll Be Comin' Round the Mountain."

It was early April, and the farm ground sprawled out in all directions from the highway—a mosaic of spring green and shades of furrowed earth. Huge circular patterns could already be seen from the automatic pivoting irrigation lines. Water cascaded from the sprinklers in iridescent arches.

Sam watched the road intently, sometimes almost forgetting that Stacey and Herman were with him. In spite of his early troubles with Brandon, Kelli had always been his biggest worry. The fact that she had been in the car when their parents died, and she had lived, seemed to have damaged her beyond what he could do to help her. He knew that deep down she was burdened and hadn't healed. He suspected that besides feeling an enormous sense of loss, she probably felt guilty that she had lived. Why wouldn't she? He too had felt guilt for not being there when the accident happened. Most people assumed Kelli was doing great. She'd continued excelling in school clear through graduation—always smiling, and was even a student-body officer. And in church . . . well in church she always went the extra mile, Sam recalled. A do-gooder. *Man, she must've volunteered for every service project imaginable,* Sam thought. This assured everyone that Kelli was doing well, but Sam could sense something underneath the facade, her lackluster moods at the end of each day signaling despair. He'd tried to help her, get her to open up, but she always kept a piece of herself away from him.

"What ya thinking about? Kelli?" Stacey asked.

"Yeah."

"I wish me and my brothers had the kind of relationship you two have. We hardly even talk. Last time I called home, I found out my youngest brother is getting married. He didn't even tell me he was dating anyone. Of course, I imagine it's my fault that we aren't close. I'm the older sister. But you, you're amazing."

"If I'm so amazing, then why don't I know where she is? Why did she quit her job?" Sam asked.

"It's your caring that is so amazing. It's what I love about you. People come first in your life."

Sam nodded. "Well, I'd rather have a friend than a ten-dollar bill—that's for sure. Wouldn't you?"

"What's that? You payin' your friends money?" Herman mumbled, cocking his head so he could hear better.

* * *

Herman waited in the truck while Stacey and Sam knocked on the door of Kelli's apartment. The next-door neighbor stuck her head out the door. "Hey, Sam, how are you today?" she chirped. "Kelli going to be gone long?" The young woman flipped her straight blond hair, her highlights catching the late afternoon sun. She seemed to be there every time Sam showed up, and always wore short shorts, no matter what the weather or time of day. Sam knew she thought he was cute. Kelli had told him that. Kelli had tried to get him to take her out for a favor, and he'd even said he would, but that was before Stacey had shown up in his life.

"What do you mean?" he replied.

"Took off. Saw her leave a couple of weeks ago with a suitcase. Thought you'd know where she went."

"Well, I don't. Mandy, is it? She seem like she's been acting strange to you lately?" Sam fumbled in his pocket for the key to Kelli's apartment, accidentally pulled the ring out, and quickly stuffed it back in.

"Like, yeah, she has, but I thought she told you everything. Kelli never stops talking about her 'older brother Sam.' It's always Sam says this, and Sam took me to dinner, or Sam has a girlfriend. At least until a few weeks ago."

"Yeah, what then?" Sam asked.

"She started giving me stuff. Good stuff, clothes mostly. Come to think of it, by then she hardly even mentioned you anymore."

Chills went up Sam's spine when Mandy said that. *Good stuff?* he thought, his panic rising. He pushed open the door and the three of them went inside. Immediately Sam noticed the white piece of paper lying on the pale blue bedspread and he grabbed it. A box with "For Stacey" scrawled on it in black marker sat on the bed.

"Shoot, this is serious," Mandy said. "She's giving away her favorite boots."

Stacey shot a worried glance at Sam. He sat down on the edge of the bed and read the letter.

Dear Sam,

I am happy and finally doing something important with my life. For a while I can't contact you, but I want you to know that you have nothing to worry about. I am in good hands. Don't try to find me—I'll contact you later, I promise. I don't think I've ever thanked you for giving up so much of your life for me. I love you, Sam
Kelli
P.S. Take whatever you want—give the rest to charity.

"Where could she possibly be that she wouldn't want to tell me about? Mandy, she must've told you something."

"Not really, I mean, I did think it was strange that she broke up with this really hot guy she'd been dating," Mandy said.

"Justin?"

"She didn't really tell me what was going on. I mean, sure, I asked her. I was like—if you aren't going with Justin anymore—like mind if I hook up with him? I mean, you know he kind of looks like Ben Affleck and—"

Stacey reached out and touched Mandy's arm as if she was trying to push a fast-forward button on a tape machine. "So anyway, she said I could have him. She even gave me his phone number so I could call him. I did once, but he didn't seem interested in getting to know anyone new yet. Seemed a little bitter about the whole thing."

"You still have his number?" Sam asked.

"Sure. Somewhere." Mandy leaned toward Sam.

"How long does she have the rent paid for on this place, you think?" Sam asked.

"Till the end of the month, I imagine . . . got a few more weeks on it. Kelli always paid one month ahead."

"Mandy, did you ever see anyone here? Any other guy? Someone she met recently, maybe?" Stacey asked.

"No. Well, there was one guy who's been hanging out here a lot, but it seemed like she didn't want me to meet him. She avoided ever introducing us. And she's been gone a lot more than usual. I mean, lots of times I'd get up around seven and notice she was already gone—her car I mean. She doesn't have to be to work until nine, so I thought, you know, like weird. But anyway, later I'd ask her about it and she said she liked to drive the long route, to clear her head—think and pray."

"Pray?" Sam asked.

"Oh, you know how Kelli is. I mean, I swear that girl is an absolute saint."

"Yeah, she's that," Sam agreed. Sam grabbed the boots off the bed. "Want them, Stace?"

"No, leave them for her. We'll find her."

Mandy looked longingly at the boots. Sam took them off the bed and slid them underneath.

"You don't think she . . . ?" Mandy asked.

"Committed suicide?" Sam completed the sentence.

"Well I didn't want to ask, but . . ."

"No, in the note she says she'll contact me, and I don't think she meant telepathically."

Sam locked the apartment door and pulled it shut behind them, tugging on the door to make sure it was tight. "You got that phone number?"

Mandy disappeared into her apartment and came out with a curled Post-It Note. "Saved it, just in case, you know. What about you, Sam? Got another brother somewhere as cute as you are? Want to come in to make that call?" She turned and placed her hands on her hips.

Sam colored and turned his head away, surprised that she would flirt with him right in front of Stacey; especially when she should be worried about Kelli. "No—no one available. But I'm sure you don't have any trouble finding dates. Pretty as you are," he added as an afterthought.

"You'd be surprised. Around this town the only guys that hit on me are married or drunks."

"Well, don't sell yourself short."

"You mean that, Sam?"

"Sure I mean it. The phone number, please?

Stacey laughed when they got back in the truck. "It must be tough being you."

Sam chuckled. "Must be tough being you. I'm sure you get the same thing wherever you go."

"No—not like that. She really wanted to get you into her apartment."

"Why do you think I didn't go in? Even as badly as I wanted to borrow her phone to get this number called." Sam stuck the Post-It on the dash of the truck.

"Well, you're in luck, Cowboy, 'cause I just bought this." Stacey reached into her canvas carryall and pulled out a cell phone. "I know what you're thinking—they don't even work in Grouse Creek, but they do sporadically between here and there, and being stranded somewhere sort of scares me. I'm hoping if I live right, I'll only be stranded where the cell picks up reception and I can call for help."

"Well, hot diggity, give me that thing," Sam said.

By this time, Herman's head was slung backward, his eyes were closed, his mouth was open, and a labored breathing sound escaped him.

"No, no. I'll dial the number, then hand it to you. I know technology is beyond you yet," she teased playfully.

Stacey held the phone to Sam's ear while he shifted gears. Sam could tell by the tone in Justin's voice that he was hanging on to some bitter feelings toward Kelli. He'd obviously thought things were going well enough to push for a stronger commitment, then Kelli suddenly fled the relationship. So with nothing more than Justin's promise that he'd call if he heard anything new, Herman, Stacey, and Sam headed back to Burley.

chapter 4

secrets

Kelli had been given a reprieve. The Prophet Daniel had business with a small band of believers in Montana. So Richard and Kelli wouldn't be married until his return. Kelli tried to suppress her rush of relief. She still felt like she probably just wasn't ready, so she tried to find a place she could think—prepare herself. There was a hollow a short distance from the trailers that had a small cluster of aspens. Aspens surviving in this dry country were a sure indication of water and, sure enough, Kelli discovered a small gurgling spring. The spring was probably the reason the group had settled there, but she found it a beautiful spot to just visit.

Kevin, the reason she had joined the group in the first place, had been forbidden to see her. She missed him, and she often replayed in her mind the events that had led her to him and the group. After the seminar, Kevin had begun dropping by Kelli's apartment regularly after her work, and had engaged her in invigorating discussions. Finally, he invited her to meet the group, the Church of Faith, and on weekends she often visited the compound. Even though she was well versed in scripture and doctrine, he could refute everything she said. She'd been no match for his vast grasp of ancient doctrines and obscure writings she knew nothing about.

Within weeks of visiting the Church of Faith, she'd felt like she wanted to belong. It wasn't any specific doctrine that finally won her over, but more the idea of isolation. Here she could get away from the constant reminders of her family and what she had done to them. Here she could find a way to serve and help others. She liked how the group, especially the women, really loved children. Maybe, she reasoned, if she made a real difference in someone's life, she could be absolved. Eventually, she hoped she would be able to feel comfortable again with her own family. At the time, even though she still didn't want to believe in modern polygamy, she found herself more and more wanting to be with Kevin. He wasn't exactly a polygamist, and besides, he was so different than anyone she knew. She liked how he despised worldliness. Kelli was trying to despise it as well. She didn't deserve nice things anyway. She wanted to be selfless. In truth, she wanted to suffer. This could be the answer to her prayers. When she was with her own family, as much as she loved them—especially Sam—her guilt overwhelmed her and she found herself wanting to get away from them. They were constant reminders of her shame, and they couldn't help her. It was realizing that her family couldn't help her that probably had the most influence in her decision to join the group. Here she could forget.

She remembered the day Sam had arrived home from his mission to Germany. The ride to the airport to pick him up was grim. Kelli was wedged in between Heather, Sam's girlfriend, and Brandon, her other brother. Heather didn't say anything the entire trip, but stared straight ahead. Heather's parents, the Wilkensons, were in the front seat, and they continually turned around to make pleasant chatter about how much fun it would be to have Sam home, and how everyone must be excited to see him. Brandon volleyed the small talk back to the Wilkensons without a miss, protecting her, she knew—trying to make sure no one said a word about the . . . what was the expression? She tried to recall. *Oh yeah, the elephant in the room.* Or in her case, the elephant in the car that no one was talking about.

But for Kelli, that elephant would continually weigh her down beyond what she could possibly bear. She was hoping that when Sam emerged from the plane he would banish the elephant, just as he had other unpleasant things in her life. Kelli had held her tears back, even after the doctor confirmed that her parents were dead. Of course she knew they were, because she had been safely buckled in the backseat of the car during the horrific accident. She also knew that she had urged her dad to hurry. Always notoriously late, they'd leave at least five minutes later than they should have, and then try to make up for lost time on the road. Already in the season she had missed being able to play the first quarter of one church basketball game because she'd been late. Then, on the fateful night, because of her pestering, her dad had floored the gas pedal, and both her mom and dad were dead, killed when an elk bounded out onto the road.

Kelli remembered exactly what she had said to her father that evening in the car.

"Can't we go faster, Dad? I *hate* being late to every game!" she said angrily. "Why are you guys *always* late?"

"I know. I'm sorry, honey, but I'm trying to get you there now, aren't I?" he said with a smile, stepping on the gas a little.

"We should be careful, Deloy." Her mom spoke a little more tensely as the car sped quickly down the road.

They were the last words spoken between them before the car slammed into the elk—unkind words on her part, words that made her parents die because they were trying to please her. They were killed on impact, and she was alive and well with only minor scratches. This was her painful secret. The secret she could not—had not—told anyone. The secret she was finding increasingly difficult to live with.

When Sam had stepped off the plane, he beelined right past his girlfriend and bolted toward Kelli. It was then that she had let the tears flow unchecked. He'd held her until nothing was left for her to cry, and the crying turned into uncontrollable trembling and gasps for breath. She was fourteen years old, but felt like she was nothing more than a rag doll, completely without muscle or will.

Sam didn't cry, not then, and not the next day at the double funeral. In fact, Kelli could only remember seeing Sam cry once, when he was about ten years old and she was only three, and that had been because of his Irish Setter puppy. She and Sam were playing catch in the front yard when she heard tires screech. Sam dropped the ball he'd been tossing to her and ran to the road. It surprised her now that she could still remember the look on Sam's face when she trailed after him and found him sobbing over the still body of his puppy. But that had been the only time she'd seen him cry, and even then she'd suspected it was because of the suddenness of the accident, his emotions spilling out before he could stop them.

That was the one thing that had bothered her about Sam. He didn't cry, or couldn't cry. But now she knew something else; that he couldn't take away the enormity of the burden she carried. She kept the secret that she had killed her parents and no matter what anyone else told her, she knew it was true. That truth had turned her even more toward God. For a brief time, she'd wished she were Catholic. She had even found a priest in town to talk to, at the Little Flower Catholic Church in Burley, a small white stucco building with colorful stained-glass windows and white crosses on each corner and at the apex. She'd waited until daily mass was over and then had gone inside. She hoped she wouldn't see anyone she knew as she watched the small group of people slowly disperse. She really hadn't known what to say to the priest, so she told him that she wanted to be absolved. She confessed her secret sin, hoping that he could tell her exactly what penance she needed to perform to be forgiven. She'd liked the idea of penance and absolution, and hoped he'd tell her that she needed to have her arm cut off—her right arm, since she needed her right arm to play basketball. Losing her arm would have won forgiveness, she was sure, but the priest hadn't suggested that. Instead, he asked her if she were Catholic, and she remembered saying she could be. She liked him for not laughing at her then. Before sending her on her way, he'd asked her for the name of her Mormon bishop. When she returned home, she'd barely had time to put her jacket away before her bishop stopped in to see her. He kindly told her that she would feel better in time, and set up a counseling schedule to help her with the grieving process. But all of them had missed the point. She had killed her parents and needed to be absolved, in some way.

It was then that she turned back to her own religion and tried to insulate herself in a cocoon, layer upon layer, from pain, sin, and the world. Mormonism became something deep within her, something that was as much a part of her as her heart. That was it—it was her heart. Religion kept her alive. She felt that if she could do everything right, perfectly, or as close as was humanly possible, then she could be absolved. She thought with Sam it was different. For him Mormonism seemed to be something he wore as easily as he did his cowboy hat. For Sam, as for any real cowboy, he wasn't fully dressed without his hat. Being a Mormon was just a part of what he was, a part that after some struggle, he never seemed to question. After their parents' deaths, he continued as though nothing had happened. He took on the responsibility of taking care of her and her brother. Usually, he went to church, but sometimes he dropped Brandon and Kelli off. She wasn't sure what he did then. Instead of her parents sitting in the stands while she played church basketball—and later high school basketball—it had been Sam. Sure, she appreciated him for that, knew that he'd sacrificed a lot of his own needs for theirs; but looking back, it'd all seemed so easy for him. It was probably because he hadn't felt the guilt that she had—probably because he was halfway around the world when the accident happened.

Kelli's thoughts strayed back to Kevin. After she'd gotten to know him and the group he belonged to, she thought he might have the answers. After months of persistent visits to Kelli's apartment, then weekends at the compound, Kelli made the commitment to move in with the polygamous group for a trial run. After she'd been there for two weeks, Kelli and Kevin stood before Prophet Daniel and asked for permission to marry, the prophet bowed his head, put his hands out palm side up, and was silent. When he opened his eyes again, he said, "No. You're to be given in marriage to Richard Ellstrom." Kelli remembered the shocked feeling. She'd glanced at Kevin.

"But—" Kelli began.

"You are not in any position to decide for yourself. I believe you sincerely desire absolution. I've asked God what He demands for you to be forgiven for your unworthy behavior and this is God's request, not mine. Surely you won't question God's will? Richard is a worthy man. He can be your spiritual guide in a way Kevin isn't ready to be."

Kelli felt like she couldn't breathe. Her throat felt as tight as if a rock were lodged in it. She wanted to cry.

"You're excused, Kelli. I'll be praying for you so that you can come to accept the peace we desire for you."

After she left the room, instead of walking away, she paused to listen. Kelli heard Kevin speaking to the young, bearded prophet.

"Please listen," Kevin began. "I was sent out to recruit someone with property and money, with the promise that she would be mine in return. I've done that. I've been duped and she's been duped."

"God doesn't dupe people, Kevin. This is the punishment God has chosen for you for your rebellion, your worldliness. In time, Kevin, with true submission to God's will, you'll be granted the desires of your heart. Not now. Now, if you'll excuse yourself, I have matters to attend to."

"But . . ." she heard Kevin protest. "Richard is a selfish . . ."

"You are out of line," the prophet's voice rose.

"I'm . . . sorry."

"Oh, and one more thing . . ." It was the prophet's voice again. ". . . You aren't to have any contact with the girl. She needs to prove she's one of us. That can only happen if she's asked to do something difficult. I don't need to remind you that she was raised among the godless Mormons. Her heart can easily be turned back. A word to the wise: if you're seen with her, you and she both will be punished severely."

Kelli had moved away from the door when she heard the doorknob click, then sat around the corner and pretended not to have heard. She was startled by the anger she saw in Kevin's face.

"Oh, you're still here."

She stood up. "Can we talk?" she asked hopefully.

"No. It's over. It would be . . ." Then he whispered, "dangerous for both of us. I'm so sorry, but I won't be talking to you ever again."

* * *

Kelli wondered if she had ever hurt this much in her entire life, and then she remembered that she had. This pain was nearly as unbearable as when she sat at the cemetery while their bishop dedicated the grave of her parents. Of course it made sense to her now. She needed to feel this much agony if she expected to ever feel whole again. This was her penance, to marry someone she didn't want and didn't love. Someone much older, and already married spiritually to two other women. This one thing, this sacrifice, would bring her the absolution she needed and would free her from her guilt.

She and Kevin had never really spoken since that day. Kelli sighed and looked around her at the beauty in the hollow. Taking time out for a walk was an unusual treat and she enjoyed feeling the warm sun on her back. Just as she got there she heard a groaning and a thumping sound. Her first impulse was to yell, thinking it was someone in danger, but she held back and tiptoed closer. She could see Richard, who she hadn't even known was home, beating a teenage girl with his fist, and then kicking her with his heavy shoes. Kelli was horrified and held her hand over her mouth to keep from giving herself away. *This can't be real.* The girl was his own daughter, Mary Rachel, curled in a ball with her arms wrapped around her head and whimpering like a puppy. With each kick, Kelli found it more difficult not to run to the girl, but she held back. He continued kicking Mary Rachel until she begged him to stop. "Stop, please stop. I'll do it."

"Don't defy me again. Your salvation depends on it." He growled at her.

Kelli kept very still and watched as Richard stalked away. He didn't even glance back at the girl writhing in pain. Although Kelli was ashamed of herself for not trying to stop the beating, somehow she knew that she would also be beaten if she let her presence be known. A dreadful feeling crept over her. The girl stayed in a fetal position for a couple of minutes, sobbing and rolling in pain. Finally she wiped her eyes, stood up painfully, and limped back toward the commune.

Kelli was amazed by the bravery the girl had shown. Whatever it was that Richard wanted her to do, the girl had resisted until she had nothing left. Kelli's whole body trembled with fear and her breathing was rapid and shallow. *I need to pull myself together. I can't face Richard.* Kelli had no idea how long she sat under the tree thinking, but by the time Kelli's shaking stopped, her head felt clear for the first time in a long while. She needed to feel whole again, but these people didn't have the solution, and even if they did, she knew she couldn't risk being hurt. Finally, she stood up and started walking back to the trailer house. She knew she had to leave. How had she been so wrong? She was in shock, stunned. But she was used to feeling one way and acting another, so she pulled herself together quickly. She would act as though nothing were wrong. Her safety depended on it.

"Kelli," Richard greeted her when she stepped inside the trailer. "Out for a walk?"

"Yes," Kelli said as cheerfully as she could muster. Richard sat in a recliner, and a young girl was bouncing on his leg, like she was riding a pony. Kelli had often done that with her grandpa and smiled at the memory.

She glanced around for Mary Rachel, but couldn't see her anywhere.

"Later, when the rest of the family gets in, I have an announcement to make. I think everyone will want to hear. It's very exciting news," Richard said.

They all, except for Richard's two oldest children, gathered in the largest room of the double-wide trailer. Kelli knew the oldest daughter was married to one of the other brethren. Mary must've been in her room, recovering. The two other wives and Kelli sat on the floor near Richard's feet.

"We've been very honored as a family, and everyone will be pleased to know that I heard from the prophet today and he's on his way back. He's asked for Mary to be his fourth wife, and she has, of course, agreed to it."

Of course. When you're beaten within an inch of your life you'll agree to anything, Kelli thought angrily. Richard wasn't the kind of person she had thought he was. She had come to believe this pious man had the answers, but now a scripture popped into her mind: *No power or influence can or ought to be maintained by virtue of the priesthood, only by persuasion, by long-suffering, by gentleness and meekness, and by love unfeigned.*

Kelli forced a smile and nodded her approval. Richard's first wife began to weep quietly. Kelli wondered if she knew about the beatings. *She probably doesn't. She's much too motherly and loving.* But, then, Kelli had been fooled by Richard; maybe she had been fooled by the woman as well. Now she wasn't sure whom she could trust.

Kelli's chance to get away didn't come for several days. The car, her car, was community property now, and the only time she would have access to it would be when she took some of the children to a dental appointment in Burley. One of Richard's wives would be with her though, and slipping away would be nearly impossible, but she would find a way.

The next day Mary Rachel emerged from the bedroom she shared with two of her siblings. Everyone had been told that she had been suffering from a bout of the flu the night before. Kelli put her arm around her and felt the girl jerk in pain.

"What happened to you?" Kelli asked.

"Fell. Fell off a big rock I was climbing on."

"Heard you are marrying. Do you really want to?" Kelli whispered.

Kelli saw a look of despair flash across the girl's face, before it turned placid. "Of course I want to. It's an honor to be chosen," Mary Rachel said mechanically.

Kelli wanted to throw her arms around her and tell her they'd escape together, but she was afraid the girl would either accidentally or knowingly betray her. She didn't know if Mary Rachel could help but tell; Kelli thought about how she had been turned from her normal way of thinking by the society's teaching in just a few weeks, and this girl had been hearing it her whole life. Mary Rachel had learned from an early age that she had no right to think for herself or to defy authority, and if she did, Kelli now suspected that beatings were often common fare.

chapter 5

missing

Sam sat in the straw next to the wet, newborn foal. Its mother, Starbuck, had just given birth and seemed startled to find the small breathing colt next to her. Immediately, the mother began to lick the foal and Sam began to stroke and rub the colt's nose, mouth, and legs. Sam knew that if he did this, the colt would bond with him, just as he would his mother, Starbuck. The foal was a buckskin with a blaze of white between his eyes. Sam watched as the colt struggled to his feet on wobbly legs, and smiled as the colt navigated toward his mother's udder. That first drink was important, giving the colt a head start with his immune system. The colt staggered like a drunken sailor with every move. But he was sturdy and would soon be running alongside Starbuck in the pasture. Sam stroked the foal's withers as it nuzzled underneath the mare's belly. Finally, Sam could hear a slurping sound as the foal's mouth located the nipple and began sucking. Sam would spend the next few mornings imprinting and desensitizing the colt, readying him for the more intense training that would follow. Sam felt that the best horses were handled from the day of their birth, just as Sam's grandpa had taught him, and he would do the same with this colt.

When Sam stepped back into his house, the phone was ringing. He let the machine pick it up as he took off his outer chore clothes on the back porch.

"Sam, if you're there, pick up. It's important." He could hear his brother sigh then pause. "It's about Kelli . . ."

Sam launched toward the phone with his coveralls bunched around his knees. "Yeah?"

"Uh, this isn't good . . ." Brandon began. "I got a call today from the renters. You know, the Masons, who are renting our house that Kelli used to own."

"What do you mean *used to*?" Sam started pushing his coveralls off with his foot, but they caught, tripping him and sending him to the floor. "Whoa!" he shouted as he hit the floor with a loud thud.

"Sam? You okay?"

The phone had flown from Sam's hand and crashed beneath the kitchen table. He crawled over to it with his coveralls now around his feet. "Sorry, about that," he panted. "Go on."

"What happened to you?"

"Never mind, just get to the punch line."

"I guess she sold it. I didn't think she would ever sell the house we grew up in, but I guess she did just that . . ."

"Shoot, she wouldn't."

"Yeah, and since I own the farm next to it I had always planned on buying it myself someday, or at least building there. That way with you owning Grandpa's place we'd all be close again. It would've been great. And worse yet, the new owners, whoever they are, have put it up for sale again. Realtor said they already have interested buyers. The renters figured we knew all about it. They just called to find out how long they could stay. Since they couldn't get hold of Kelli they tried one of us."

Sam felt that gnawing in his stomach again. "Justin—that's Kelli's ex—has been doing some checking around. He said someone saw her drive right through Oakley and then keep going. That's the last anyone—"

"She had the legal work done for the sale of the house and then quit her job, right?" Brandon asked.

"Where would she go?"

"Is there anything past Oakley? I mean anything at all?" Brandon interrupted.

"Almo, but that isn't the road she was seen on. The next town south is forty-five miles away, a little speck of a town—Grouse Creek. She couldn't be there because that's where Herman and Stacey live. They would've seen her. Herman says it's such a small town you know whose checks are good and whose spouses aren't. Besides that, it wouldn't make any sense. Doesn't fit in with the clues."

"Could Justin be wrong?"

"Yeah, of course, but he seemed pretty sure. Brandon, did the renters give you a name? Of the person she sold the house to, I mean." Sam pulled himself off the kitchen floor and sat down on a chair, pulled his coveralls off, and tossed them against the back door.

"No, they didn't know. But I'm guessing it wouldn't be hard to call the Realtor and find out—"

"I'll drive by there on my way to work and see what realty company is on the sign." Sam said.

Brandon was quiet, but Sam could hear his soft breathing. "What ya thinking? You mad at her?"

"Mad, no. Hurt, yeah. How could she do this to us? That's our childhood home, Sam. You remember how Mom used to cook up those great big oven pancakes, puffed up four inches above the pan in the old Hotpoint and—"

"Brandon, whatever Kelli did . . . it had to be something that she couldn't help. Kelli has got some deep issues; something has been brewing beneath her cheerful facade ready to explode. I failed her—we failed her. I should've seen this coming and done something sooner. And lately, well, you know my thoughts have been elsewhere . . ."

"Yeah, I know. I remember what it's like to be twitterpated. The house doesn't matter, Sam, not in the long run. We'll find Kelli."

* * *

After work, Sam pulled away from the Burley livestock yard and headed to Twin Falls. Kelli had been missing for more than two weeks now, and her promised letter to him had never arrived. He had filed a missing persons report, but found the whole process somewhat disheartening. Adults could vanish if they wanted to and it was obvious that Kelli had wanted to vanish. Even her bank account had been closed.

Sam drove to the bank where Kelli had worked. The bank manager, a fiftyish well-dressed woman in a pale yellow suit, recognized Sam as Kelli's brother. She told Sam that she had been very concerned about Kelli, particularly after she'd issued Kelli a check for over ten thousand dollars. The check represented her entire savings and what was left from the life insurance money Kelli had received.

"I tried to find out what she needed all that money for, but she was very quiet on that matter. She sat right here at this desk, told me she was quitting—effective immediately—and then asked me to close everything out. The thing that bothered me the most was the man I saw."

"There was a man with her?" Sam asked.

"Not with her so much. I didn't see him until after Kelli had finished doing all the paperwork. But I was so disturbed by it all, I mean . . ." she paused and tapped her pencil on the edge of her desk. "I guess you would say I followed her right out the door and watched where she went. I like Kelli—she has always been such a good employee and I was worried. I'm still worried. Anyway, she walked out the door, check in hand, and I could see an older gentlemen waiting for her at the end of the block. I knew it couldn't be her father, so . . ."

Sam forcefully held his gray felt Stetson on his lap; he was tense and ready to spring to his feet. "What did the man look like?"

"He was a long ways off, but I could see that he looked to be, oh, probably around my age. Wore a suit, gray or blue. His hair was thin, but not gray. Brown, I think."

"Anything else?"

"No, I'm sorry. I should've followed, but there's no law against—"

"Yeah, no law against running away from home when you're twenty-four years old, is there?" Sam fiddled with the brim of his hat.

"No. Anyway. I'm sorry I don't know more. Good luck finding her. I know she thinks so much of you. We know all about you—how you used to interrogate all her dates, your bull riding, your girlfriend . . . now what's her name?"

"Stacey. Thanks for talking to me." Sam held his hand out to shake hers and then left the office as she wished him luck again.

Sam's next stop was the Realtor's office. A young woman about the same age as Kelli sat at a computer. Without glancing up, she asked, "How may I help you?" as she continued typing.

Sam cleared his throat and leaned onto the counter. "Uh, yeah. The name is Sam Carson. Your office has a house for sale that, until recently, belonged to my sister. I need to contact the new owners. Just wondering . . ."

The girl had short dark hair, styled to look messy. A style that bewildered Sam, but one he was noticing more of lately. The girl looked up and flashed Sam a huge smile. "What's the address to look for?"

Sam told her, and as the girl looked, he started flipping through a Rolodex file on the counter and glanced around the office walls, which were plastered with real-estate fliers.

"Kelli Carson? Yeah, here it is. It looks like the current listing agent is the same one who handled Kelli's sale. You know, Kelli Carson sounds familiar. I think I might've known her from high school—gorgeous redhead, right? If I'd known she had such a good-looking brother, I might've tried to get to know her better. What's she up to anyway?"

If only I knew, Sam thought, wondering how much he should tell her. "Well, she's uh, she's uh . . . missing."

"Missing?" she asked in a genuinely concerned tone. "Let me write down the current owners for you." The young woman grabbed a business card from off of her desk, jotted something down, and then handed it to Sam.

"Angie Baker," Sam read aloud. Flipping the card over, he read her hand-written note, "Enlightened Enterprises." He cocked his eyebrow at the unfamiliar name. "Got an address for this company, or a phone number, anything?"

"Actually, no. We've handled sales for them before, and they always insist on contacting us for some reason. I'm just a gopher around here, but I'll try and dig something up. Maybe you can meet me for dinner sometime and I'll let you know."

"I'll uh, get back to you on that," Sam said touching the brim of his hat as he turned to go.

"Let me put my home number on that, then, 'cause you can call me anytime, cowboy, anytime." Angie bounced up out of her chair, grabbed the card back, and quickly wrote her home number on it before slipping it back to Sam.

Sam took out his wallet and slipped the business card inside as he laughed, then he waved as he left the office.

chapter 6

timely appointment

Kelli was used to acting. She'd done it convincingly ever since the accident. She knew that most people thought she was a well-adjusted, happy person. So waiting four more days for a chance to get away from Richard, fooling him into thinking she was still dedicated to him, to his church, was easy. What was more difficult was leaving behind children, especially Mary Rachel, barely sixteen, with the very real possibility of more physical and definitely mental abuse.

She worried until it was finally time for her to drive what had been her car to the children's dental appointments in Burley. She had four seat belts besides hers, so four of Richard's children piled into her car. The rest rode with Andrea, Richard's first wife, in a van. It was strange being back in Burley after living in the compound, and she worried that someone who knew her would see her. The dental office was on 15th and Normal Avenue. She'd gotten there ahead of the van and marched the children into the office. The receptionist knew the children and nodded for them to take a seat. "And will Dr. Atkins be seeing you today? You're new aren't you?"

New. New wife? Did everyone know the situation? "Uh no—I just had an appointment awhile back."

"Still, would you like us to set up your records here, like the others have?"

"No, not this time." She felt her face burn with embarrassment, shame, and guilt.

Kelli picked up a magazine and began to thumb through it. The rest of the group came in through the door with a clamor. Andrea sat down next to Kelli and began to chuckle.

"Oh, it feels so good to sit down, doesn't it? Can you believe how much work there is to do, how it never ends?" Andrea asked.

"You know what they say, 'a woman's work is never done,'" Kelli said as lightly as possible.

"Isn't that the truth, even when there are so many of us to help each other. I don't know how the rest of the world does it. Without sister wives, I mean."

"Well, they don't have as many children for one thing, and there are some conveniences that you—I mean we—don't have at the compound," Kelli pointed out.

Kelli noticed that Mary Rachel had been playing with the children, but she was gone now. Kelli hadn't seen her go back for her appointment, but she might have missed her.

"Still, it would be hard," Andrea continued. "Things have been so much better since you've joined us. You have such talent in teaching the children, and Richard plans to use your accounting skills to help with the books."

"Thanks." Kelli wondered if she was allowed to look at magazines, but she continued to thumb through *Time* magazine.

Finally, Andrea nudged her. "Keep an eye on things. I just need to use the rest room." Kelli waited until she heard the door close. She told the playing children that she'd be right back, that she just had to get something out of the car. They didn't give her a second glance. Her palms were sweating and her face felt hot. She jumped in the car. Without even looking to see if the road was clear, she started it and sped away, then opened the window and let the spring air whip her long hair. She took a back road to the freeway, just in case, and headed northeast, not knowing or caring where she would end up. She had reached Pocatello before she heard Mary Rachel sit up and buckle her seat belt.

Kelli startled, then laughed and squealed with delight. "I'm so glad you came. I didn't dare tell you. How did you know I was leaving?"

"I had a feeling you would when you asked me that day if I wanted to get married. I guessed you knew that I didn't get those bruises just from falling. But I didn't know for sure until I saw your face redden and you started to fan it with the *Time* magazine. And, by the way, it's a sin to read *Time*. Didn't they tell you that?" she laughed nervously. "You won't take me back, will you?"

"Heavens, no. We're accomplices. We're in this together now. Free, free, free at last," Kelli added, beaming. "I feel like we're Butch Cassidy and the Sundance Kid, don't you?"

"Who?" Mary asked.

"Oh yeah—you wouldn't know, of course. But I hope our story turns out better than theirs did."

"Why, what happened?"

"Well they were outlaws, and in the movie they escape to Bolivia, vowing to live a clean life, but then . . .'"

"Then what?"

"They're killed in a hail of bullets surrounded by hundreds of Bolivian police. The movie stops with a freeze frame on them running out of their hiding places and you hear the guns. And even though you know they've been killed, you are left with this ounce of hope that somehow they've survived. There are lots of legends about them claiming they did make it out alive."

"I'm coming up there," Mary climbed into the front and buckled up. "I hope we escape and that we won't die in a hail of bullets."

"No, we won't," Kelli said. "At least I hope not."

"I feel so guilty about everything." Mary Rachel admitted.

"Tell me about it," Kelli quipped.

"I was chosen to marry the prophet. To go against that is unthinkable."

"He isn't a prophet." Kelli realized that of course Mary would have doubts. She was turning her back on everything she knew. Kelli had done that, too. "It'll be okay—I promise," Kelli assured her.

Kelli realized that she could only drive as far away from the dentist office as one tank of gas would take them, and then that would have to be their destination, wherever it was. She would leave it up to fate and the gas tank. Montana called itself "Big Sky Country," and to her, "big sky" represented the kind of freedom that she wanted a taste of. In Big Sky Montana she could escape her past and become a different person, someone who hadn't done the things she'd done. One tank of gas could get her there, but then what? Kelli hoped she would be able to simply leave the guilt-ridden Kelli at the

Montana-Idaho border. She watched nervously as the needle dropped closer to the empty mark with each passing Idaho town. The flat scenery looked way too much like Burley. Her quick calculations showed that she couldn't make it past Rexburg. Just before she got into town, her heart started thumping so fast it seemed to keep pace with the fast tempo of the country music on the radio. She felt sweaty and hot, even though the air was cool. She couldn't stay here. The new Kelli could not live in Idaho.

"We'll be needing gas, looks like," Mary said.

"I don't have any money. We're stuck here." Kelli felt her throat tighten.

"You didn't plan this out very well did you?"

"How could I under the circumstances? I didn't exactly have time to stop at an ATM. 'Course, I don't have money in the bank anymore anyway. I don't even have an account—I gave all my money and even my house to the Church of Faith. Got any good ideas? We can't stay in Idaho."

"Good thing you brought me along then."

"What?" Kelli glanced at Mary as she pulled twenty dollar bills, three of them, out of her skirt pocket.

"Hallelujah, Sister Mary Rachel! Where'd you get that?"

"Out of Mother's purse when I was packing the car for her. Don't worry, I didn't take enough that it'll be missed."

They pulled over at the Fall River Trading Post. A painting of mountains adorned the cinder block wall. Plywood silhouettes of moose were lined up by a buck-and-rail fence. The sky was blue and if Kelli squinted, she could see the Teton mountains hovering above the flat valley like a mirage.

chapter 7

white crosses

After Sunny prayed for a miracle she headed home. It was dark when she drove through Trout Haven. Most of the businesses in town were shut down for the night, except for the Miner's Saloon. There the lights shone brightly and she could hear music, even with her windows rolled up tight. In April, Montana nights were still frigid. She fumbled with the heater and pushed the switch up to high. *I've got to get a decent car with a decent heater,* she thought. She was nearly to her turnoff when she saw a car parked on the side of the road. Someone must have run out of gas, she decided. She slowed down, just in case the driver was in the car. But then, not seeing anyone, she sped back up again. As she slowed again to make the turn, she saw movement in her rearview mirror. Someone was near the car, outside. *Way too cold for that!* She turned around and pulled up behind the car, leaving her lights on. She wasn't foolish enough to just jump out. *Who knows what kind of person would fake a breakdown just to hit me over the head with a crowbar,* she thought. Locals would know she'd have all her money from the day's take with her. She was always mindful that one of these days someone might try to knock her over the head and steal it. Easy pickings. She locked her doors, then unrolled her window a crack and shouted. "Need me to call a tow truck?" Now she could see a dark form crouching in the grass near two white crosses. It was unusual for people to stop at the roadside memorials, but at night it was completely unheard of. The person didn't answer her, and now Sunny could hear sobbing.

"You hurt?" she shouted. Nothing. *Doesn't that beat all?* Sunny finally got out of her car and cautiously walked over to the figure. She had her can of mace in her hand, just in case. *A woman alone can never be too careful,* she knew. When she got close to the figure, she could see that it was actually a young woman sobbing uncontrollably. Sunny bolted to the girl and knelt by her. "What happened? How can I help?"

The girl didn't answer, but pointed at the crosses. Sunny didn't know the people who had died in the accident marked by the crosses but knew that the crosses had been there all the years she had lived here. This girl couldn't even have known them—she would have barely been born. Sunny nudged the girl to her feet. "We'll just leave your car where it is and come back after it in the morning, okay? Anything you need out of it?"

"Backseat," the girl said between heaving breaths.

The girl didn't resist Sunny leading her to the Volkswagen. Then Sunny went to the car and looked in the backseat. She was surprised to see another young girl, or young woman—Sunny couldn't quite tell—curled in a ball on the seat, asleep. She opened the door and tugged on her arm. The girl jumped at her touch, shouted something, and sat up, shivering visibly. "Come on," Sunny said. The girl followed and got into Sunny's Volkswagen once she had seen that her friend was doing the same.

"You're sure lucky I came along. This highway gets plenty of drunks and crazies driving it this late. If someone else had spotted you—who knows? Besides, it's freezing out here. Were you meeting someone or something and they didn't show?" Sunny turned and looked at the young women. Neither acknowledged her in any way. She was surprised at how ill prepared they were for cold, wearing nothing more than thin jackets. Sunny pulled out and drove a little farther, then turned down her lane. Her cabin was nothing more than a run-down miner's shack, but Sunny had worked hard on the place and had made it comfortable and warm. It was just one large room with a partition at one end for a bathroom. The kitchen area took up most of the living space since Sunny liked to cook. A woodstove stood right in the middle of the cabin, and Sunny's double bed was on the west wall. A sofa covered with an East Indian Batik faced the large picture window that Sunny had framed in herself.

The older girl's sobbing had subsided and Sunny led her to a kitchen chair. The younger girl sat down at the table on her own.

With the light shining on the younger girl's face, Sunny noticed that there were bruises around her eyes, and her lip was swollen. "I've got some vegetable soup with homemade noodles already made. And some sprouted wheat bread. No matter how bad you're feeling, you'll feel better when you've eaten."

Sunny watched the young women eat and was pleased that they practically devoured what she had set in front of them. After eating three bowls of soup and two pieces of bread, the older girl indicated that she didn't want anymore. The younger of the two cleared the dishes. She looked in worse shape than the older girl, yet she smiled and immediately filled the sink with warm, soapy water and started washing.

Sunny found a warm nightshirt and some fuzzy socks for the older one and helped her change. She tucked her into her own bed and sat down next to her. "My name is Sunny, Sunny Day. I know it's funny, but don't laugh." It didn't seem necessary to say, as the young woman didn't even smile or look up at her. "My given name is Debra, but in the '60s that just wouldn't do, so I named myself Sunny. Don't tell the locals my real name, I'm sure they don't know. Well, Jack probably does, he's the new bishop—er, branch president. Branch presidents are . . . well I'll tell you about that sometime."

With that the older girl turned and looked at Sunny with large vacant eyes. "Mormon branch presidents?"

"Yeah, Mormon. You aren't a Mormon, are you?"

"Sort of," the girl whispered and put her head down.

"That is exactly what I am—sort of a Mormon. We'll get along good then. You don't mind if I smoke, do you?" Sunny asked.

"Mormons don't smoke. Besides it does make me sick—the smell I mean. Gives me migraines."

"That's okay. I quit anyway as of today. I just thought I'd have one last one before I quit for good, but maybe it can wait."

"Yeah, that would be better."

"Were you two heading up to Bozeman or over to Yellowstone?"

The girl sat up in bed now. She glanced around her surroundings as if noticing them for the first time. "Kelli. My name's Kelli."

"Oh, Kelli. Well that's nice. Last name?" Sunny could hear the other girl humming as she washed the dishes. Kelli looked away. "Okay—no last name? Running away from somewhere?"

"I like this place. Everything you need right here. You can practically reach anything you want right from the bed. Oh, but . . ." Kelli broke off.

"What?" Sunny asked.

"This is your bed, isn't it?"

"Well yeah, but I can sleep on the sofa for the night. Back in the '60s I got used to sleeping anywhere, and you really look like you need a little comfort. And your friend can sleep in here with you. Head to toe."

Kelli's eyes filled with tears again.

"You must have some luggage in your car. We'll go back and get it tomorrow."

Kelli shook her head.

"No luggage?" Sunny asked.

"No."

"Then do you live close by? Big Sky or Belgrade?"

"No."

"Where do you live then?"

"Nowhere. I don't live anywhere."

Sunny realized a change of subject was in order, or the end of the conversation perhaps, and she was already getting fidgety and desperately wanted a smoke, even though she'd thought she'd smoked enough cigarettes to last her the rest of her life. "The branch president told me to quit smoking—can you believe that? And he wants me to be Relief Society president," she finished as she got up to leave.

Frigid air slapped Sunny in the face as she stepped onto the front porch. She reached down to get a cigarette out of her thick socks, where she kept them, and then remembered she'd smoked the last one before she'd left the café. *Now what?*

When Sunny came back inside her cabin, she was shivering uncontrollably. She rummaged through every drawer in the kitchen looking for a stray cigarette, but couldn't find a single one.

Sunny sat back down and thought. *These girls are in trouble and one thing I'm good at is helping people out of trouble, even if it gets me into more trouble. I'll just quit smoking and focus on helping them instead. Resolve, that's what I need.* She walked over to the bed and could hear Kelli breathing quietly.

The younger of the two dried her hands on a dish towel and came and sat down on the sofa. "She was fine most of the way. Giddy with excitement even, and then the farther north we drove the more she started crying. I have no idea what's wrong with her," the younger woman said. "Seems like it had something to do with those crosses on the sides of the road. There was one curve just before we got here, it must've had five or so crosses. She started crying then. But when she saw those two together, she completely lost it."

"Are you her younger sister?" Sunny asked.

"Sort of."

"Lots of sort-of's around here. So are you also sort of a Mormon?"

"Not really."

"Look—something happened to you. I mean your face. Are you two running away from someone?" Sunny asked.

"Yeah, sort of."

"Well, I'll find another shirt for you to wear, and then I've got to hit the sack. You can sleep in there with your sister can't you? Oh, and what's your name?"

"Uh . . . Marsha."

Sunny tossed Marsha a pair of socks and a flannel shirt from her pine bureau. Then Sunny snuggled under a heavy quilt on the sofa.

In the morning, Sunny woke with a start. Kelli was still sleeping, but the other girl, Marsha, was gone. When Sunny set her bare feet down on the cold plank floor, she shivered. She hopped over to the wood box, grabbed some small logs, and tossed them on the still hot coals in the wood burning stove. The fire sprang to life as Sunny jabbed it with the iron poker. On the kitchen table, Sunny could see a note. She read it out loud "Thank you so much for your kindness. I'm so sorry for what I had to take and I promise I'll return all of it with interest. Marsha."

"Just my luck, that little bedraggled rug rat . . ." Sunny bolted to the kitchen counter where she'd left the deposit bag. The checks were stacked outside of it in a pile. Sunny reached in and at first thought—in startlement—that all two hundred and seventy-one dollars were still there. She pulled the cash out and stacked the various denominations. Marsha had only taken forty dollars. After examining her belongings, Sunny decided the girl had also taken a quilt, a change of clothes, and a loaf of bread.

Sunny stood next to her bed watching Kelli sleep. Then she went to the bathroom and got ready for her day. Saturday. Her morning help at the café would already be doing food prep. After all these years, she trusted Marty enough to let him work some mornings without her careful attention to detail. She called it attention, he called it nagging.

Finally, she heard the girl rustling her covers. Then she sat up. "Where's Mary Rachel?"

"Uh—Mary, or Marsha, or whatever you want to call your sort-of sister, flew the coop. Don't plan on seeing her again, since she helped herself to some of my things." Sunny watched Kelli. "You ready to tell me what's going on yet?"

But Kelli was pulling off her nightshirt. She hurried to put on her now-dry clothes and then bolted out the front door.

"Good luck." Sunny yelled after her. *I hope she finds her sister,* she thought. *They're adults. Well, at least one of them is. They'll be fine. They've got money now and a few things. Wherever they were planning to go they'll get there and I won't have to worry about them ever again.* She had the nagging feeling that she should have gone after the young women. Something was wrong—one had been beaten, and the other . . . what was she running from and why was she crying so much of the time? *It's not your problem,* she told herself. As Marty kept telling her, she didn't have to take care of every stray dog and cat in Montana, or people for that matter. Every time she got involved in someone's life, her own spiraled out of control. She wouldn't let it happen this time.

Sunny had an enormous headache. Too much nicotine—then none. She'd have to stop at the store on the way to the café and buy some cigarettes. Maybe she would quit tomorrow, but she knew the only way to get rid of the headache now was to smoke again. When she rounded the corner, she noticed with relief that the car, the girls' car, was gone. They were on their way. Everything was fine. Suddenly Sunny realized everything wasn't fine. The oldest one, Kelli, was sitting cross-legged in the grass next to the white crosses.

She slammed on her brakes, rolled down the window, and asked, "Want a job?"

Kelli pulled herself up out of the tall grass, walked to the car and got in the passenger side. "They're dead."

"Yeah, they're dead. Been dead a long time, honey." Sunny said, pulling back out on the highway.

"Ten years."

"No, Kelli, it's been lots longer. At least twenty. Really."

"I killed them," Kelli mumbled.

"Why would you say a thing like that? You probably weren't even born when those two kids were killed."

Kelli didn't say anything then, just stared ahead.

"Where do you think your sister went?"

"I don't know."

"Well, get in the car. We'll sort it out together. Meanwhile we'll put you to work at the café. Ever waitress?"

Kelli just sat with her knees pressed against her face and didn't say anything. Sunny passed the grocery store, deciding she'd have to wait until after work to buy her cigarettes, and parked behind her café.

chapter 8

searching

In the years after the accident that took their parents' lives, Sam grew more comfortable with his role as a parent. Even helping his sister find a dress for a school dance became second nature for him. Before her first dance, Sam had sat on a black vinyl chair and waited for Kelli to come out of the dressing room. They were on her fifth dress. The first two were cut too low, the third was too puffy, the fourth too orange—it made her look like a pumpkin, she'd said. When she stepped out this time, Sam smiled. "Wow."

Kelli had turned, allowing Sam to admire. "That's it. You look like—well, you look beautiful." Her black satin dress was the perfect contrast to her smooth auburn hair. Sam wished their parents could see her. Her first school dance.

When Kelli had come back out of the dressing room in jeans and a T-shirt, Sam could see that her face had fallen. "It's expensive. We can't afford it."

"Let me see." Sam fingered the dangling tag. "Get it. And buy a piece of jewelry to match. Go over and look at the rack on the counter." Putting in a few extra hours at work would make up the difference—not a big deal. He never could stand to see Kelli's crestfallen face. Anyway, she deserved it. She'd always done everything she could around the house, was a great student, and always gave a hundred percent. Besides, he could never fix what had happened to her while he was on his mission—he'd never be able to make it up to her.

When her date had come to pick her up, Sam hauled him into the living room and sat him down on the sofa. He pulled a chair in front of the boy and stared into his eyes. Sam believed the eyes were the window to the soul—and he was suspicious about this boy's soul since his long, dark brown hair hung in his eyes. Though the top half of the cut was shaggy, it was almost shaved all around the bottom half of his head. The haircut alone, even if the boy's eyes hadn't been covered, annoyed Sam. Kelli's date wrung his hands nervously, and tried to avoid Sam's stare as Sam peppered him with questions. Kelli had been told to wait in the kitchen. "Do you drink? Smoke? Use drugs? Do you understand what the word 'curfew' means? Do you respect women?" If there was one thing Sam couldn't stand it was the attitude that some high school guys had adopted—the "I own you" attitude. If he'd ever been that way, being responsible for Kelli had changed him in a hurry. After the boy had stammered, "No, no, no," and then "Yes" to the last few questions, Sam hollered, "You can come in now, Kelli." Sam watched the look on the young man, Kent Abel. If Sam detected any leering when Kent saw Kelli, Kent would be history.

Sam was satisfied that Kent was all right. Not worthy of Kelli, certainly not, but then what high school boy could be? He'd shaken the boy's limp hand vigorously and sent him out the door. "Remember—midnight. No exceptions."

Kelli had shot him an, *Okay, enough is enough* look, and walked over to her side of the car. Sam was appalled as Kent began to open his own side. "Kent!" Sam shouted.

"Yes sir?" Kent turned abruptly.

"The door, Kelli's door," he yelled, then mumbled quietly, "Strike two."

The first strike had been the haircut. Basically, Sam just hadn't liked it, but figured it must have been the popular thing. It was just a date, he'd told himself, not marriage or anything like that. He would let it slide.

* * *

Sam set the business card in front of Detective Hacker in Burley. "Does that name, Enlightened Enterprises, mean anything to you?"

"Sure, polygamous group—that's the generic name they use for all their businesses and holdings."

Sam felt like he'd been socked in the stomach. He felt his body tense with disbelief. His muscles twitched in uncontrollable spasms, imperceptible to anyone else. This was impossible, absolutely impossible for Kelli to willingly join a polygamous group. She knew better. She loved the gospel, had a testimony . . . how could this be?

"Are you sure?" Sam sat down in the chair and pulled it closer to the detective's desk.

"Sure, we've been watching that group closely. We don't really know where they're located, but they meet around town now and again. We haven't yet figured if they are way out of the way in some canyon somewhere, or if they are right under our noses blending into the community. There's a splinter group up in Montana as well. This group here, they're smart. Do things the legal way and they keep quiet. Ever since news on Tom Green started hitting the talk-show circuit years ago and Utah charged him with child rape and welfare fraud, all the polygamists have been more careful. They've gone underground even deeper than they were before." Detective Hacker picked up a piece of paper. "I told you I'd let you know when we had something on your sister."

"Yeah?" Sam felt his heart thump in his chest.

"Her car was spotted in Montana," Detective Hacker said.

"Spotted? Why didn't they stop her then? At least let her know we're looking for her, that we love her . . ."

"Well, rookie cop pulled the woman over who was driving the car. He didn't run an I.D. on her until after he'd let her go. But he said the woman driving looked more like a kid, not twenty-four, and that her hair was blond. The car could've been stolen?"

"Yeah, anything's possible." Sam tapped the piece of paper. "It looks like my sister has signed her house to this group and—"

"Oh, I hope not. Like I said, this is a smart group. There is only one legal wife, the others just live there, you know. Nothing is ever put directly in the man's name. Occasionally they recruit—persuade money and properties away from people. They own lots of businesses, legitimately too. You'd be surprised what's in their name, mini-marts, chemical companies, all kinds of things. They often keep the businesses in several different names, harder to track and so forth. But every so often, best we can tell, they get seemingly average women to join up and give them property. The women they recruit are usually young, vulnerable, impressionable—pleasers usually, and trustworthy. Was Kelli . . . ?"

"Why did you say 'was'?"

"Just a slip of the tongue," he offered apologetically. "*Is* she any of those things?"

"Yes—all, and completely miserable."

"Then she was the perfect recruit." Detective Hacker shook his head. "I know your sister is probably the victim here, but legally, as of yet, we have to go on what we've got. I'll keep digging and try to find something we can legally prosecute this group on. If we could find the compound we might find your sister as well."

"How is duping young women into signing away their life savings legal? And in this case a house. That's got to be a crime."

"It is very hard to prove," Detective Hacker said, pushing his glasses higher on his nose.

"Why?"

"Okay, look at it this way. Does anyone in your church ever donate property or money to your church?"

"Uh, yeah, but that's different," Sam answered.

"Is it?"

"Of course."

"Look, I'm on your side, but I'm just trying to show you why these things aren't as simple as it seems."

"But it's a cult," Sam protested.

"Some people think your church is a cult, Sam."

"But they are polygamists!"

"Yeah, well find me something I can prosecute, and believe me we'll go after them just like the state of Utah went after Tom Green. 'Course they got him on welfare fraud and there isn't any of that with this group. They keep their noses clean. My own opinion is that it's despicable what these men do to women, but the reality is that they aren't forced, Sam. In your sister's case, I sincerely doubt she was forced to do anything. It's perfectly legal to give away anything you own."

"Yeah, you keep saying that." Sam stood up to leave. "Well, thanks for your time. And by the way, where was her car last seen?"

"North of Bozeman, Montana."

I'll find that conniving dirtbag and when I do . . . Sam thought. Then he remembered something Justin had said. Someone had seen Kelli driving south through Oakley. Sam would drive every single dirt road, and even cow trail, between Oakley and Grouse Creek until he found them.

* * *

The next morning, Saturday, Sam stepped through his back door after checking on his new colt and noticed the answering machine light blinking. He pushed the button. Stacey's voice was upbeat. "Are we still on for tonight?" Sam pulled out a chair and the metal leg screeched across the linoleum. He called her back.

"Hey, I hate to do this to you, but I'm hoping you'll say yes to an alternative plan."

"What, branding calves?"

"That'd be great fun, but no. What would you think of just driving around all day with a good-looking cowboy?" Sam asked.

"Who'd you have in mind?"

"Uh . . ."

"It's so much fun to tease you. Does this have anything to do with your sister?" Stacey asked.

"Yeah—I can't think about much of anything else."

"Sure, Sam. I'll meet you."

* * *

They began on the dirt road south of Oakley. After passing the reservoir, the road narrowed and every time there was a turnoff, they took it. The first two went to rock mines. Workers at these places only had campers and small trailers to live in. Still, Sam and Stacey snooped around, but never saw any women or children. Another turnoff dead-ended at an old ranch house. Sam figured it was part of the Cold Creek Ranch. Just beyond Emery Creek, really a bone-dry gravelly creek bed, they followed a winding road until Sam saw a small wood sign on a fence post, stating they were in Nevada. The country hadn't varied much—dry, windswept sand, junipers, sagebrush, and desert plants struggling for survival in the harsh environment.

Sam stopped the pickup and put his arm around Stacey. "This is pointless—miles of uninhabited land and never-ending miles of wandering dirt roads. They could be anywhere."

"We'll keep looking. We can keep driving each road until we've covered them all," Stacey answered supportively.

"That will take forever. I think maybe we need to research this out some more. I'm just so frustrated! Why would a normal girl like Kelli join up with a bunch of polygamists?"

Stacey gazed at Sam sympathetically. "They must've offered her some kind of solace, something no one else has offered her. You said yourself she's miserable. Miserable people do desperate things—seek extreme measures to find comfort."

"Yeah, I guess you're right, but why couldn't I see how bad it was—fix it before this?"

"Sam, you're only human. You can only offer help, but she . . . well, I don't know."

"Anyway, we might as well pursue something else. What'd ya bring in that cooler you put in the back?"

"Find a picnic spot and I'll show you," Stacey said cheerfully.

"I think I see one."

Sam turned down an almost-invisible road. A tiny patch of green stood out like a postage stamp on an otherwise drab landscape. He headed toward it. The faint road was new and was really just a trail of mashed weeds leading to an open valley. "Someone must've pastured their herd back here. It'd be an okay place. Grass isn't too good, but with that natural spring, well, I imagine in a wet year, it'd do."

He parked the truck at the end of the trail and ran around to Stacey's side and held the door open for her. "Not much of a date. Most of them have been absolutely pathetic lately, I know. Someday I'll make it up to you."

"Sam, when are you going to believe that I love you, and that means the whole package? I knew from the first that if Kelli or Brandon needed you, I'd be left on the back burner to simmer. I'm okay with that."

"You are something." Sam hugged her and then grabbed the cooler. "Let's carry it up to those trees."

Stacey had put together a small feast with roast chicken, potato salad, fruit, and drinks. "Besides, after we find her, I can be put on the front burner again, right?"

"Right. That's if you can stand the heat," he joked.

Sam turned the conversation to his new colt. "You need to come and see him. I'll let you name him for me. I've been so busy that I haven't come up with anything yet. Usually, I call everyone I know when I have a new arrival. I get suggestions from the whole family, then decide. This time, I didn't even call Brandon."

"Or me."

"Didn't I? I thought I did."

When they were through eating and gathering things back up, Sam held his hand out to pull her up, but instead she suddenly stopped moving and pulled him back down in the grass.

"Okay. I'm game," he said, giving her a kiss. He leaned in again.

"No. Look around." Stacey shoved him away gently. "They didn't just pasture cows here."

Sam studied the area and then could see what Stacey meant. Looking closely he could see several flattened impressions in the weeds—not where cattle had lain, as the shapes were too mechanical, and rectangular. "You're right. Trailer houses were set up here. Stacey you're a genius." Sam leaped over squatty sagebrush plants and ran until he reached the flat land. He examined the area, searching for anything the group might have left behind.

"Anything?" Stacey said behind him.

"Nothing."

chapter 9

kelli's initiation

After Kelli had witnessed Mary Rachel being beaten and had determined to leave, she'd had to continue pretending that everything was fine. The most difficult part was continuing to allow Richard's overtures toward her. How foolish she had been to believe that this group had the solution to her problems. Kevin had avoided her altogether, and to think she'd believed Daniel with the flowing blond hair was actually a prophet, and not just some power hungry man who fed off the vulnerability of others. He had no line of authority. Gullible, that is what she'd been. *But why?* she wondered. How had she been deceived?

Kelli had been in the middle of a math lesson with the five- to-eight-year-olds. She sat at a long table with the six children around her. They were sorting beans into sets of five when Richard poked his head into the schoolroom. He gestured for her to come with him and she left the children to finish their task, stepping outside.

"The children like you. You can see now how much we needed you here, how much God needed you to help the children, to teach them in the way you have—making everything simple and easy to grasp," Richard said.

"Thank you."

He grabbed her hand. "Walk with me to the spring."

She felt nervous suddenly. What would he do to her there? Would he find a reason to discipline her the way she knew he had others who hadn't been completely obedient? "What about the children? They'll wonder what happened to me," she said, keeping the panic out of her voice the best she could.

"They saw me and know that God's will comes first, and—"

"God wants you to take me to the spring?" Kelli asked nervously.

"Yes. I need to teach you."

Kelli felt her heart race. She knew she couldn't run, and there was nowhere to run to anyway. Mary Rachel had confided to her that the spring was the "teaching place" at this compound. At other settlements it was located elsewhere; in a thick grove of pines, or against an overhang. The teaching place was where you were taken if you needed to feel God's wrath. Usually the wrath of God was merely a severe tongue lashing, but sometimes it ended with physical punishment of some kind. Kelli feared the physical punishment. In Kelli's home, her parents had never used physical force—had never even spanked her. Seeing the disappointment in their faces was enough to set her straight.

Richard sat down on a large pale-colored slab near the spring. He pulled her down and smiled at her. "I trust you are doing better— that you've managed to push out Satan's will and submit yourself fully to God's will."

"Yes." Kelli forced her lips to smile.

"Good, I'm glad to hear it. Andrea will need help with the children in town tomorrow, and I'm hoping you are ready to help. It will be a test for you—the first time back among the Godless gentiles. You'll be able to show us that you're ready for a strong commitment, a total submersion into the fold. I've heard from the prophet and he will be back tomorrow. Sometime soon he'll take Mary Rachel, so we'll need you more at home. We can be married after you help Andrea in town."

"Yes, I'd like to help," Kelli said, knowing that would be her chance to get away.

Now Richard leaned over and kissed her on the lips. This had only happened a couple of times and it made her very uncomfortable. He kissed her again and the taste of his lips on hers repulsed her, but she tried not to show it. He couldn't suspect her disillusionment with the religion or with him.

He tried to pull her closer to him and kiss her again. "No," she protested softly. "We aren't married yet."

Finally, he pulled away. "No, we aren't, because you let the devil control you. You aren't ready to submit yourself completely. And until you do, you'll never be able to have the forgiveness you desire."

"But—"

"But at least you passed this test. Tomorrow you'll be watched closely."

He stood up from the stone slab and strode briskly away.

* * *

Kelli shuddered at the memory. When Sunny pulled her Volkswagen Bug up to the Lazy Moose Café, Kelli felt safe for the first time in weeks. This woman with the graying, blond hair wound on top of her head in a bun was cheerful and every bit the sort of person that her name announced her to be. The feeling of safety would be fleeting, she knew, but for a few minutes she would bask in Sunny's warm rays and not think about what she had left behind. Kelli wiped the tears from her eyes and allowed Sunny to lead her into the small café. A handful of people were already sitting in the booths, sipping their morning coffee, eating breakfast, and visiting with each other.

"Saturdays begin a bit more slowly around here, but within the hour we'll have a few more customers—locals and travelers alike. The real tourist season doesn't begin until Memorial Day, but we still do okay until then. When the season starts though, you'll be busier than you could possibly imagine."

Kelli looked at the man back in the kitchen. He wore a white apron that covered his ample stomach. He looked close to Sunny's same age, had steel-colored, butched hair, and a ruddy complexion. "Had a hard time getting up this morning, Sunny? How do you expect me to cook and wait tables at the same time?"

"Hold on, Marty. I was busy recruiting help for the upcoming season." Sunny gestured toward Kelli. "Marty, this is Kelli. Kelli, this is Marty Bilkowski."

"Great, but it's kind of early for that, seeing how we don't get busy for more than a month, yet." Marty sounded gruff, but Kelli figured it was just an act.

"I've decided to cut back my hours and Kelli will help me do that."

Kelli forced a smile. "I'm excited about working here. It'll be a nice change."

"Oh, and what did you do before?" Marty asked.

"Uh, bank work. Accounting," Kelli said.

A puzzled look crossed Marty's face. "You'd rather be a waitress?"

"A server," she corrected. "Yeah."

"Well good for us then. Maybe you can get Sunny's books straightened around then. She could really make a go of this place if she didn't pour so much money down the drain on those blasted causes of hers."

"I only hired you to cook, Marty, not give advice. Keep it to yourself," Sunny warned.

"Yeah, yeah, yeah. The thing I can't understand is you buying that expensive cat food and dumping piles of it around town for all the strays to eat. I mean, that is—"

"Uh, Marty. We've been through that before. I've got some new help to train."

Kelli had to admit that she was intrigued by Marty's last statement and wondered what kind of a person Sunny was.

"Okay," Sunny said. "Andy Jacobs just walked in. Now, usually I just put his order in as soon as I see him, 'cause it's always the same, never varies. But today you take this pad and go ask him for it."

Kelli flipped her long hair behind her ears and walked over to the table. She'd been a server before and knew all she had to do was be friendly and take the orders. "What can I get for you today?" The man's brows knitted together and he pursed his lips. He ignored Kelli and turned toward Sunny. Kelli glanced back at Sunny as she was wiping the counters, avoiding looking up.

"What gives, Sunny?" the man shouted.

Sunny continued to swish a red rag over the counter and then she bent over and disappeared from view.

"May I take your order, please?" Kelli tried again.

"Ask Sunny for it," he grumbled.

Kelli walked back to the counter. Sunny appeared with a tray of ketchup and mustard bottles and began wiping the goopy tops.

"He said to ask you for it."

"You go back there and tell him I can't remember it and he'll need to tell you in detail, so Marty can get it right."

Kelli tried to smile when she walked back to the man, but she could feel tears forming in her eyes. "Sunny can't remember your order and she said for you to give it to me in detail so the cook can get it right."

The man shuffled his feet under the table. He shook his head in disgust and glanced toward Sunny. Then he pulled out the menu. "You the summer help?"

"Yes, and I'd like to take your order."

"I hate summer help," he complained, under his breath.

"What's that?"

"Nothing." Now the man had the menu open. His stubby finger pointed to the Sunny Day Special. "Now this is the part you need to write down. Get it right, 'cause I won't be saying it every single time I come in here. I want the two eggs fried, yolks broken, but not cooked through hard. They still gotta be like, I don't know, cottage cheese, soft but cooked through. Can't be any part running out on my bacon like a bleeding pig. And the bacon has to be cooked thorough, but not greasy. Dark brown, the color of a bay horse, but not black. Not black. I don't like black bacon, but limp is even worse. Even though it don't say anything about bacon on the menu, you know being a vegetarian place, Marty makes it for me. No limp edges or soggy middles, neither one. My toast should be golden, but not brown. More the color of the sky just before setting time. Butter spread to the edges, not just plopped into the middle like an ice cube. I don't want to have to wait for the butter to melt before I spread it. Well that's it—did you get all that?"

"Yes sir, I think so. I mean . . ." Kelli was still jotting down the various shades of color. "Now, just to be sure, was it the toast you want dark brown or—"

The man slung his head back. "No! The toast should be golden, like the sky as the sun sets—bacon brown, brown like a chestnut horse."

"I thought you said a bay horse."

"Yeah, a bay, that's what I said."

"Okay." Kelli didn't even try to smile.

"Oh and bring me a cup of coffee with just enough cream to lighten it to the shade of mahogany."

"I'll bring you your own cream," she retorted, more annoyed now than embarrassed or hurt.

Sunny was smiling when Kelli returned with two pages of notes for the man's order. "A good way to break in the new help. If you can handle him, the rest are easy."

Kelli flung in the order at Marty, and Marty tossed the papers back to her. "Keep them for your scrapbook. I know how to cook the order."

"Why didn't you tell me?" she said, still annoyed, but with the hint of a surrendering smile on her lips.

Marty chuckled. "Initiation."

chapter 10

beginnings and endings

Sunny had met Shane, her husband, after she moved from California to Utah to attend Utah State University. One of the missionaries, Elder Watkins, was from Logan and arranged a place for her to start her new life. She loved the atmosphere of Logan—the mountains so close you could touch them, smell them even, and the campus with buildings similar to a small Ivy League college, and then the people. Some of the people on campus were even interested in the same kinds of things she was—Mother Earth, peace, activism—and, of course, plenty of students belonged to her new religion. The man she would marry had spotted her at a peace rally. He told her later that he'd gone to the event to see "what kind of idiots think protesting something as huge as the Vietnam War in little old Logan, Utah, would have any effect on Washington." So he sat on a curb and watched. There she was holding her sign high, shouting with such enthusiasm that he thought even Washington might be able to hear her. At least that's what he'd told her when he sidled up to her and asked her if he could bring her a sandwich or something from the hub.

"Cool," she answered, "but be sure it doesn't have any meat on it, and that the bread is one hundred percent whole wheat."

He laughed, but disappeared into the building, emerging later with a sandwich stuffed with so many vegetables that she handed him the sign and sat down on a bench to eat, having to hold the bulging bread with both hands. She watched him carry the sign at first apprehensively, but eventually, he was grinning and shouting at the top of his lungs, "Make love—not war." His hair was cut almost as short as the missionaries' who had baptized her, and he wore wire-rimmed glasses, suit pants, and a pin-striped dress shirt. During the weeks that followed he showed up at every peace rally with his own hand-lettered sign, duct taped to a yardstick. Finally, after one month of meeting her at protests, he'd asked her on an official date.

* * *

Sunny's first week without smoking was probably no more horrible than it was for every other smoker who had quit cold turkey. She endured a week of headaches, tension, irritability, and urges so strong that she was tempted to give in on numerous occasions. And every time she reached down to grab a smoke out of her sock, Kelli would suddenly appear from nowhere. Remembering Kelli's migraines and the example she felt she should set for the distraught girl, Sunny would stick the cigarette back into the pack she kept in her socks. By the third day, Sunny thought she'd climb the walls of her cabin and the café. Then, just when she thought she couldn't take it another second, she reached for her cigarettes only to find them gone. She searched the cabin and found nothing. Finally, Kelli spoke up. "You aren't looking for your cigarettes are you?"

"I . . . uh . . . am."

"Well, when you were in the shower, I threw them away."

"Why would you do that?" Sunny paced the floor.

"Because the branch president told you to quit and I know you have to quit, right? So carrying around cigarettes is like an alcoholic carrying around a bottle of wine. You set yourself up for failure when you do that. Instead I bought you some gum. Put these in your socks." Kelli tossed a large pack of Juicy Fruit to Sunny and she caught it.

"Gum? You think gum is going to work?"

"Sure. Put them in your socks. You'll feel the pack down there, and every time you have an uncontrollable urge to smoke, put a stick of gum in your mouth."

Sunny felt like her eyes would bulge out of her head if she couldn't smoke. Besides that she couldn't think. A thick cloud had replaced her brain, she was sure.

"Besides," Kelli went on. "If any of us, Marty included, see you with a cigarette, we've vowed to take it from you. And we are all bigger than you are. We can stop you."

"That so?" Sunny was intrigued by this. Everyone wanted her to succeed. She had visions of her lighting a cigarette and Marty and Kelli knocking her down and stuffing gum into her mouth.

On the tenth day, smoke free, Sunny and Kelli readied the café for church services. Church started in less than a half hour. Even with the "closed" sign in the window and the shades drawn, a handful of locals had shown up for their morning coffee, Danish rolls, and Sunny's famous muffins. Marty came even though Sunny had told him they'd be closed.

They slid all the tables to the far side and set the chairs up in rows.

"Okay folks, hurry up with your eating." Sunny shouted over the din of clinking silverware. "We'll be holding Mormon church services here shortly. You are welcome to stay if you'd like, but you can't eat during it. From here on out this will function as a church on Sundays, so we'll be closed at least until dinnertime. Then maybe . . ."

With her brief announcement, a few people started eating faster, but the volume of talking rose several decibels. Ned walked over to Sunny and put his arm on her shoulder. "I'll shoo people away for ya, if that's what you really want, but you'll lose business over this, Sunny. Most of us prefer your place over Molly's. I mean your place is just, I don't know, more sunny." Ned smiled at the pun. "But if people get in the habit of going there on Sunday, they'll keep right on going during the week as well. I'm telling you this as a friend."

"Thanks, I appreciate that, but, yeah, shoo people out of here for this week anyway. I'll try and talk to Jack and see if he can't work something else out." Sunny knew Ned was right. This church thing could kill her business.

She put the final chair in place and watched the last of her customers walk out the door, nearly bumping into President Jack Heath as he came in. The branch president was wearing slacks which bunched above his brown cowboy boots. His white shirt wasn't ironed and he wore a tie with Disney characters on it.

"This will be great," he announced as he set his armload of books down at a booth. "I've got lots more stuff in the truck. Uh, can you help me get it?"

Sunny noticed he was speaking to Kelli who was dumping some coffee cups into a plastic bin. "Oh, President Jack . . . whatever your last name is, this is Kelli, my new waitress and . . ."

Kelli turned and Sunny detected tears in her eyes. But without acknowledging the man, Kelli set her dishes down and followed him out the door. *That young woman's got some serious problem going on,* Sunny thought. By the time Jack and Kelli emerged again, Sunny had placed a small table at the front to be the pulpit for the speakers. She grabbed one of her potted pansies and set it on the table.

"Sister Sunny Day, I trust I can officially extend that calling I talked to you about."

"What made you so sure I could quit smoking?"

"Because you're the right one for the calling, that's why."

Sunny smiled. She was starting to feel better. The urges came less often, her head didn't feel so foggy anymore, and she was actually starting to think life might get better for her. "Yeah, go ahead and extend the call. I've quit," she said, chomping on her gum.

"Great." President Jack Heath glanced at his watch. "It's after ten, I expect our congregation anytime now. Had to make quite a few phone calls to let everyone know we'd be meeting here. We all sure appreciate this, Sister Day."

Sunny groaned. People started walking through the door and Sunny watched them one by one. None of them were regulars at her diner. They started filling in the seats from the back first. Sunny and Kelli took their seats on the front row. Sunny wore a wraparound skirt, a yellow peasant blouse, and thick wool socks with a pack of gum sticking out of them. She wore sandals year round, but didn't shed the socks until July.

President Heath stood in the front at ten minutes after ten and began to speak. "Welcome to our first meeting in our new facility. As you know, it was general conference last week, so this week is fast and testimony meeting."

Sunny could hear pans chinking together in the kitchen and realized that Marty was still in there. Before long the smell of baking pie wafted out from the kitchen and teased their senses. Kelli nudged Sunny and whispered, "This is new for me."

"What, church in a café?" Sunny asked.

"Yes, that and the smell of blueberry pie during fast meeting. It must be driving everyone crazy."

"Huckleberry pie," Sunny corrected. "Maybe next time they'll find somewhere else to meet."

Only about twenty people were scattered among the chairs. With so few in attendance, nearly everyone would be expected to bear their testimony, but Sunny wouldn't—no way. Nearly everyone had borne their testimony, including all five of the Danielson children, even their two-year-old bouncy toddler who could only manage a giggle and a, "Love Mommy and Jesus" before his older sister dragged him kicking and screaming back to his seat. There was a really long pause at that point. Then President Heath stood up. Sunny assumed he'd done so to close the meeting, but instead his eyes bore down on her and he said, "I think it would be fitting to hear from our new Relief Society president and the woman who has so graciously offered us the use of this fine facility—Sister Day."

She gasped, then became indignant. *Where will the nerve of this man end?* Sunny wondered. Finally she stood when she noticed that everyone was staring at her, waiting for her to speak. Without walking to the makeshift podium, she turned and faced the audience. Most were looking at her with such warm expressions that she was taken aback. She smoothed her skirt and began, "I don't know what to say." She began to sit back down, but she felt Kelli grab her hand and push her back up. "Well, okay then," she began again. "If the Lord really wants me to be Relief Society president, then I guess I'm stuck. And the only way to get unstuck is to move forward. So . . . I'll do my best to do a good job and I guess that's all I have to say." Sunny was about to sit down again, but happened to glance at the branch president. He was smiling and nodding as if to encourage her to go on. "I think, I mean, I believe in the gospel of Jesus Christ, and I know He can work miracles in our lives if we work to make them happen."

When Sunny sat back down Kelli whispered, "I wish that were true."

"It is," Sunny said, surprised at her own words. And for the first time in a long time, she actually believed it.

The president closed the meeting and asked Sunny where they could hold a combined Sunday School class for twelve on up, and Primary classes for the six children of Primary age. They decided that, for the time being, Primary could be held in the women's bathroom, where there was a small lounge area left over from when the restaurant had been someone's home. The others would stay where they were in the main café area. Afterward, Relief Society was held in the kitchen with Marty busy cooking what Sunny knew, by the smell, to be her famous stew. When she had taught him to make it even Marty told her he was surprised that stew without meat could taste so good. Sunny hadn't prepared a lesson, and there were no teachers called, so the five women in attendance each took a turn reading from the Bible. The whole thing lasted less than a half hour. But by now, even Sunny's stomach was rumbling for food, and she'd eaten breakfast, having forgotten all about fast Sunday.

By the sounds of the noises from the main room, priesthood meeting was over as well. Sunny was relieved it was over. By next week they'd surely find somewhere else and she'd go back to her old life. But then she remembered she'd promised to do her best job to everyone in the congregation, and Sunny kept her promises. She was doomed.

Marty came out of the kitchen carrying a large tray of empty china bowls. "If you all are done with your meeting, Sunny wanted me to announce that you're all welcome to stay for dinner. On the house— the Sunny Day Stew, with her secret dumplings. Pie afterward."

Sunny began to protest, but then saw the looks on everyone's faces as they immediately found seats at the counter. "Sure, eat up," she announced. "Now if you'll all excuse me, I've got some business to attend to." Sunny hurried to her office. It really wasn't an office; only a storage room away from sight. It had been her place to smoke, but now she wasn't sure what she'd do in it. Without turning on the lights, she stumbled to the chair she knew would be in the corner, and pushed another stick of gum into her mouth. Within the hour, President Heath and his counselor would set her apart as Relief Society president. The thought overwhelmed her. After she'd sat in the dark for a while, Kelli peeked in the door. Light from the adjoining room illuminated Kelli's outline and her face almost glowed. For a second Sunny thought she looked like an angel.

"Uh, President Heath sent me to find you. He said to tell you that he didn't really expect you to feed everyone, but what a treat. Everyone loves it. Can I come in?"

"Sure."

"It smells like smoke in here. You haven't been . . . ?"

"No, but you're right. Let's go out back and get some fresh air."

They stepped outside and Sunny took a deep breath. She'd forgotten that pine trees had such a pungent odor. Her senses were enlivened.

Sunny said, "You ready to talk?"

"I've done some very bad things . . . unforgivable things."

"We all have. And Kelli, nothing is unforgivable. At least not anything you could've done."

"Well, this is," Kelli said.

"Maybe the one you should be talking to is Jack—President Heath."

"I don't think so."

"Well, even Relief Society presidents can't . . . you know, resolve that kind of thing. Besides, I haven't been set apart yet."

"I know, but . . . you said you knew miracles can happen. I need one."

"I thought so." Sunny's heart ached as Kelli started crying again. *Tears spring from this girl like water from an irrigation sprinkler.*

"Can I come out?" Jack poked his head out the door and stepped outside. "Kelli, could I ask you to start teaching Primary and lead the singing?"

Kelli swung her head from side to side in the negative and her crying became louder. "Uh, Sunny, would you mind leaving us alone? I think I need to talk to Kelli. Uh, what's your last name, Kelli?"

Sunny stepped back into her café. Nearly everyone was gone, except for Marty and President Heath's counselor, Brother Danielsen. Marty and Brother Danielsen were seated at a booth conversing. Two women, eighty-six-year-old Annabel and a woman about half that age, were washing dishes in the large stainless-steel sink in the kitchen. Annabel was singing, "Put Your Shoulder to the Wheel," with her arms immersed nearly to her shoulders in soapy water. The other woman was busy drying bowls and setting them into a drainer. Sunny began putting dishes away.

"Would you mind if we put the recipe for your wonderful stew in our monthly newsletter?" the younger woman began. "By the way, I'm Sister Danielsen, and I write the monthly newsletter."

"Well, yes." Sunny said.

"Oh, great. Write it down for me, then, before I leave."

"I mean, yes, I do mind. It took me years to develop that recipe and it's what my café is known for." Sunny hadn't remembered that being so nervy was part of being a Mormon.

"Oh." She looked dejected. "I can see that. I wasn't thinking about this being your business and all. Sister Jenkins liked to pass out her recipes at Relief Society and I just assumed you would, but of course not. It's different, I can see that."

"Good." But Sunny could see that she didn't see that—that she was still waiting for her to change her mind. Sunny put the last dish away and the two women shuffled out of the kitchen. They waited for Brother Danielson to finish his conversation, then walked out the front door. Sunny could see the heads of the children waiting in the station wagon out front.

"Marty, I don't normally give away free food, and you complain about me feeding all the stray cats in town. What was that all about?" She served herself a bowl of stew and sat down in the now-vacated booth.

"Okay, about the free food. You'll see."

President Heath and Kelli came back inside. The man's smile had faded, but Kelli had stopped crying and was wiping her eyes with one of the checkered napkins.

"Well, Sister Day, we've made it through our first day of church meetings, but . . ." He sat down at the booth. Marty stood up, and Jack stood up again to let him out.

"I'll see ya tomorrow, Sunny. You've given up on the idea of opening back up this evening haven't you?" Marty asked.

"Yes, I'm beat."

"And as I was saying, our workday has just begun," President Heath said.

"We've got lots to do, Sister Day. The Abbots are all sick with the flu and I thought we could take them some of your soup, and Sister Hernandez hasn't been coming out, so I think we ought to go out there and see what's going on, and then there's . . ." He went on until Sunny's eyes had nearly popped from her head. "Anyway, we've got lots to do," he said, ignoring her shocked expression. "I don't want to alarm you, but after the Hansens moved out, if we can't get our numbers up, we may become part of a Bozeman ward. I really feel that's why I was impressed that you were the right one for the

Relief Society president. I'm sure you'll make a real difference." Without another word, President Heath began dishing up the stew into take-out cartons and handing them to a stunned, but quickly surrendering, Sunny.

chapter 11

identity crisis

Kelli hadn't told the branch president anything. She'd wanted to, but every time she opened her mouth, nothing came out. President Heath had handed her a checkered napkin. She'd blotted her face and stared at the bear-proof garbage dumpster.

"Do you want to tell me about it?" he'd asked.

"I'm just so ashamed," Kelli mumbled.

"We all do things we aren't proud of."

Kelli looked down at her hands and noticed that they were twisting the red-checkered cloth. She hadn't even noticed. Her knees were quivering. This was a new sensation for her. Kelli glanced up at the president. Not at his face, but at his tie. *Mickey Mouse, Donald Duck, Goofy?* And then at his rumpled shirt. *This man is supposed to be a spiritual leader. What a joke,* she thought in frustration.

"Where did you get that tie?" she asked, not sure she could talk about herself yet.

"This? Oh—hmmm. I think Davey, he would've been eight at the time, gave it to me."

"Oh, well I like it," she said, already repentant of her earlier thoughts. Lately she hadn't felt in control of her thoughts or emotions, she realized with hopelessness.

President Heath laughed. "Do you think it's appropriate attire for a branch president? I wasn't sure. My wife . . . well, being a president is new to me."

"Your wife, was she at the meeting?"

"No." President Heath sat down on a tree stump and motioned for Kelli to sit down on one nearby. "Kelli, I don't even know your last name, but I want you to know that whatever you've done, it doesn't change your worth in the sight of God. You are loved. He loves you. Our Savior loves you. Nothing can change that. Repentance washes away our sin. You start fresh, anew."

Kelli began to cry again. As much as Kelli wanted to believe this man, she couldn't. She knew that somewhere in the scriptures it said, "But unto that soul that sinneth shall the former sins return." She could never stop sinning completely, so this huge sin, her burden, would continually come back to stain her soul. Richard had pounded that in her mind, and now, even though she knew Richard didn't have the answers, she wasn't sure this LDS branch president did either.

"You look skeptical. But when you're ready to talk, I'm ready to listen. And in the meantime, you've got to start praying again."

"How did you know?" While they'd been talking, Kelli had heard cars leaving the parking lot and everything had become very quiet. Most of the branch members had gone.

"'Cause that's what sin makes us think—that we aren't worthy to pray. But nothing could be further from the truth." President Heath stood up. "And while you're at it, put a prayer in there for me—this job is going to be tougher than I thought. And say a word to help Sister Day out too."

When she stepped back into the café, Kelli was surprised when Sunny told her to take her VW home when she was finished. "Don't worry about me, I'll get Jack to drop me off after he's through with me."

"You mean you trust me to take your car home?"

"Of course."

Tears sprang to her eyes. Then Kelli thought about Sam—someone else who trusted her. How could she ever tell him what she did? And Brandon—what would he think? She'd killed their parents, sold the family home, lost the money saved for her . . . she'd done too much to ever face them again. She started Sunny's car and drove the few miles through town, resolved never to let Sam know where she was. She could start a new life here. No one ever needed to know about her past—not Sunny and not President Heath. Even with her stained soul she could start fresh—just as the president had said. Here she could be someone else completely. Now she regretted that she had used her real first name. But at least she could change her last name.

She could get on the computer—somewhere in this town there had to be one—and simply create a new identity: open a new bank account, make a driver's license . . . she figured it might all be accomplished with a good computer, a laser printer, and a laminator. Her classes at the university would be put to good use. Even as she made the plans, she was filled with guilt for considering something illegal. But then anger took over—if she didn't protect herself, no one would. The thought made Kelli worry anew about Mary Rachel, but what could she do about her? After all, she'd stolen Kelli's car.

As Kelli rounded the bend toward Sunny's, she turned her head so she wouldn't see the crosses. Those crosses were keeping her from forgetting her past. She wouldn't look at them. Snowflakes were forming on the windshield, but she couldn't figure out how to turn on the wipers. In the spring snowstorm, the windshield was completely covered in a light blanket of white by the time she pulled up to the small house. Kelli rolled down the window, leaned forward, and wiped it with her hand so she could see where to park the car. The sky was darkening as she stepped inside the house. Finding the room as cold as the outdoors, she grabbed logs out of the wood box on the front porch and carried them inside, opened the woodstove, and set them on top of the hot coals. She stoked the fire as she'd seen Sunny do. Why had she never learned to build a fire? Sam and Brandon had always done it.

Sam. Whenever she thought about him, she felt sad again. He would be worried about her. Still, if he knew the truth, what she was, what she'd done . . . He would . . . what? Hate her? No, not hate exactly, more pity, and be disappointed. She couldn't bear that—the disappointment on his face would be too much for her—the opposite of what his face had looked like when she'd come home from school and announced that she had won the position of student body vice president. Then he'd looked pleased, happy for her, proud. She'd spent her whole life trying to keep him proud. Kelli made up her mind. She would try to get word to him somehow and let him know that everything was okay. She would at least do that much—when she could figure out a way that her contact wouldn't be traced.

After the fire was blazing, Kelli sat down on the sofa and watched the snowflakes fall against the window pane. At first, the flakes fell

softly, but within the hour the flakes became small and hard and hit
the window straight on. She worried about Sunny and the branch
president. She thought they'd be through with their Church work by
now. Finally she decided to take a hot bath. She needed something
new to wear. When Kelli had some free time she would find a place to
buy some clothes of her own—she already had enough money saved
from the tips that she'd earned. But for now, knowing Sunny, she
wouldn't mind her going through her drawers and finding a fresh
outfit. Kelli laughed as she looked for something. Almost everything
Sunny owned could be wrapped around, draped, drawn, or tucked on
any size body. And all the blouses were large and billowy, definitely a
one-size-fits-all style. Kelli found a denim drawstring skirt and a
blouse with tiny blue moose printed on it. She laid them on the small
table next to the tub. She found a box of Epsom salts and poured the
white crystals in as the water flowed into the tub.

Lying as low as she could in the water, she had just about fallen
asleep when she heard laughing and the door slam. Kelli stepped out
of the tub, patted her skin dry, put Sunny's clothes on, then stepped
out from behind the partition with a towel around her hair.

Sunny gasped when she saw her and stared wide-eyed. "Oh."

"I hope you don't mind. Borrowing more of your clothes."

"No, of course you can. It's just that for a second, I thought I was
looking at myself twenty-five years ago. It just was like a glimpse into
my own past. Jack and I visited sick people and old folks and then we
helped this tourist who'd slid off the road. Jack has a truck with a
winch. We've just been so busy—anyway, it was almost fun."

"It was fun," Jack agreed. "Thanks to Sunny. People warmed right
up to her. I heard no one has ever gotten past the front porch of the
Ralsons'—a part-member family. But Sunny did. She's perfect."

"Well, I don't know about that," Sunny protested.

Kelli now wondered again about the branch president's wife. Why
hadn't she come to church, and how would she feel about the two of
them being together all day?

"Kelli," President Heath began, "I'm going to rescind my call for
you to teach the Primary children. I know you didn't accept it
anyway, but I don't want you to feel any burden of guilt about that. I
see now that it isn't the best thing for you. And besides, not having

any records on you yet, it was premature anyway. What we really need you to do is accompany us, the two of us, on these goodwill visits. It won't be an official call, but you'll be on the Lord's errand. You will do that for us, won't you?"

"Well, I don't know. Why would you need me?" Kelli asked.

"I'm in a bit of an awkward position. Actually, both Sunny and I are." He sat down at the kitchen table. Sunny was already over in the kitchen area, pulling fixings out of the fridge. Kelli noticed she was filling a teakettle with water and had it on the stove. "Can you sit down here a minute?"

Kelli sat down at the table and Sunny came over and set a teacup in front of her, then poured a yellowish liquid into her cup. She set another cup in front of the branch president and tilted the kettle to pour, but he put his hand out to stop her. "Don't worry," she said, "it's herbal." Jack moved his hand and she continued to pour. Then Sunny returned again with hot split-pea soup and muffins.

"Wow, thanks." Kelli said, trying to remember if anyone had ever taken such good care of her. Sam had tried, and eventually they'd all learned to cook pretty well. But not like Sunny. Food, good food, just sprang from her with so little effort. How could she accept so much kindness?

"So, what do you say?" the branch president asked.

"You mean you want me to go with you because it's what? Awkward? What do you mean by that?"

"The two of us will be together a lot. Sunny probably doesn't know this about me either, but I'm widowed. Of course, if I were still married, it could be more awkward. But somewhere along the road today, I remembered that Sunny is also widowed, and well, it just doesn't look too good for the branch president to be with the most eligible woman in the branch all day on Sunday—people might wonder about why I called her to this position, and general speculations about us could start. I thought if you came along, it would help squelch the rumors."

Widowed? Kelli glanced at Sunny, but she was looking at President Heath.

"I didn't know. You poor man. I just assumed you were divorced." Sunny sat down in one of the remaining two chairs with her own cup of tea. She seemed awfully fidgety and Kelli wondered if she were still getting the urges to smoke.

"Well, that too. A long time ago. No kids in that marriage, luckily. I should've seen it coming. I'm to blame for much of the problem—typical man, I guess. Absorbed in my own work, not noticing that Carol was being more and more distant. She got tired of being left home alone so much and found someone else to fill the void," Jack said, taking a bite of his muffin. "I was building a log home at the time, and one of my subcontractors didn't show, so I went home early one day. Anyway you know the scenario—there this man was sitting at my kitchen table, eating a pork chop. Pork chops, the way Carol used to fix them, are my favorite. But that sort of cooled things off between us, you might say. She left and I've never heard from her again." He paused. "But Kathy and I had two children together and I don't see them as often as I'd like."

"Oh? Where are they?" Sunny asked, curious.

"They're with their grandparents in Laurel. With Belgrade having the closest high school, we just couldn't see having them on the bus for three hours a day, like some of the other kids in town. So this works out better for them, especially since it's only been a year since their mother died—they really need stability right now. Thought I'd see them more this summer, but then they both got involved with jobs, friends, and whatnot. When they're a little older and on their own, then maybe we can get together more. I was hoping they'd be around to help me out with that resort I'll be starting soon."

"So you *are* the one planning that monstrous devastation next to Trout Lake."

"I don't think 'monstrous devastation' is the official name, but yes."

Sunny groaned. "Last year, at the Fourth of July picnic, you told me you admired my protest of the overdevelopment in the area."

"Oh, but I do. I admire anyone who has the nerve to go against the majority, especially when she doesn't have a chance at winning."

Kelli could see Sunny's face flash with anger. "I don't think I can work with someone who has such little regard for the environment. If you'll excuse me, I need to step outside for a second."

The door slammed shut. "That poor woman. It's freezing outside," the president said glancing out the window. "So, what do you think?"

What do I think? About his kids, his widowhood, divorce, Sunny, helping him out, developers, what? She had never turned down a Church calling, always going the second mile, but that was before she changed her identity. Now she was Kelli . . . not Kelli Carson. She would change her name to Kelli . . . um . . . Brewer. What would Kelli Brewer do? She looked intently into the man's face. He seemed to really need her. "I guess I could help out a little." The new Kelli would help, but not like the old Kelli—eager to please. This Kelli would hesitate and weigh everything carefully.

"Great." His face beamed. "I knew I could count on you. You have something special about you that is indefinable, but your actions show your faith in God."

Kelli winced. Her misguided *faith* was what had gotten her into trouble. Her trust in someone she shouldn't have trusted. "I don't know." Tears sprang to her eyes again. It would be harder than she thought to bury Kelli Carson.

chapter 12

making connections

When Shane had shown up for his first date with Sunny, his hair had grown to just over the tops of his ears and collar. He didn't comb it as neatly anymore, and when he'd stood on Sunny's porch in October to take her on a hike up the Crimson Trail, he wore split and frayed jeans, army boots, and a Jimi Hendrix T-shirt.

"So what do you think?"

"I don't know," Sunny grimaced. "Where's the suit pants? It just isn't you."

"I'll be anything you want me to be, Sunny Day, anything."

"I just want you to be yourself," she said.

The next time she saw him, he wore boot-cut Wranglers, a western-style shirt with pearl buttons, a stamped belt, and a Stetson cowboy hat.

"What do you think?" he asked, turning around on her front porch for an inspection.

"Is this who you are?" Sunny asked, in hesitation and humor.

"Yup, I'm from Montana."

"What happened to the slacks?"

"Only on Sundays."

"Well, it suits you. Does this mean you slaughter cows and eat them?" she asked.

"We'll worry about that another day."

He grabbed her hand and they walked across campus to a poetry reading. She sipped herbal tea and he drank a root beer. She stared intently, entranced by the cadence and voice of a guy with a long ponytail and a tie-dyed T-shirt reading Allen Ginsburg, Walt

Whitman, and poetry of his own. But whenever she glanced at her new boyfriend, Shane, he wasn't even looking at the poet, but rather was staring hypnotized at her, all the while spinning his cowboy hat on his finger.

* * *

Sunny was surprised when she walked through her door to see the back of a young woman she didn't recognize. She had short, brown, curly hair and sat at the table.

"Hi," the young woman said, turning to face Sunny.

Startled, with recognition seeping in now, Sunny asked, "What in heavens name did you do to that gorgeous auburn hair?"

"I didn't like it," Kelli answered. "Here, thought you might want to know who I am." She handed Sunny a driver's license.

"Kelli Brewer," she read. "How'd you make this?"

"I didn't make it. I had it done in Bozeman, at the courthouse. It took awhile, but now, there it is. That's who I am. You asked, now you know," Kelli said in a tone that indicated that should be the end of it.

Sunny could tell the card was a fake. The plastic on it was too thin. Still, it would probably fool most people, but not a police officer. And even though Sunny had wondered who the young woman was, she hadn't asked since that first day. She figured whenever this frightened girl wanted to tell her, she would.

"Okay, well Kelli Brewer, anything else I should know?" Sunny asked.

"No, that's pretty much it."

"Kelli, Kelli Brewer."

"Yes."

"I've been thinking. Wondering really if we shouldn't be worried about your little sister, Mary Marsha Brewer—is that her name?"

Kelli answered slowly. "Mary isn't my sister exactly and . . ." Kelli sighed and put her face in her hands. Sunny had a bowl of freshly baked rolls on the table and some real butter. "I'm getting fat," Kelli said, changing the subject. "I've probably gained three pounds since I've been here."

"My food is very healthy. If you've gained three pounds it's because you were too thin." Sunny was sure Kelli hadn't gained an ounce by the looks of her thin frame. She looked as if a puff of wind could send her spiraling in any direction.

"Smoking. That's what kept you from ballooning up. If I stay here, I'll be as big as a house. I won't be able to fit through the front door," Kelli puffed out her cheeks to show Sunny how fat she was.

Suddenly Kelli began sobbing. Sunny picked up the bowl of rolls, covered them with a cloth napkin, and put them away. "Who is Mary, or Mary Rachel?"

"She—she—she—would be my husband's daughter," Kelli blurted.

Sunny was confused. That would make the husband much older than Kelli. "I knew there had to be a man in this somewhere. Always is. So she's your stepdaughter?"

"Not legally. Not really, no. Not at all."

"Kelli?"

"But I am worried about her too. I don't know where she would've gone. And as long as she's in that car, she's in danger. She doesn't have any knowledge of how the world is, not really." Kelli looked deep in thought.

"Danger?"

"They might find her, beat her again," Kelli sobbed.

"Who, Kelli? We can stop them if you tell me who."

Then Kelli's chin began to quiver. "Sunny, there is one thing."

Kelli was calm again. This young woman was a yo-yo of emotions. "What?"

"There is someone I want to let know I'm okay, but I don't want . . ."

"Yes."

"I just can't think of a way to tell him without giving him a clue, you know, where I am."

"Who, Kelli, your husband?"

"No, I'm not married."

More confusion, but Sunny tried not to show it on her face. "We'll think of something. But you need to trust me more. What else can I do to show you that I want to help you? I . . ." But now Sunny quit talking and looked at the unsmiling Kelli. How sad she felt for her. She knew what pain was. Sometimes when she'd wake up in the morning, pain washed over her senses, suddenly and without warning. Or the slightest thing would remind her of her losses, and there would be the pain again, like a gnawing hole in her heart, ripping at her and reminding her of what could have been. If her baby had lived, she would only be a little older than this lovely young woman. She remembered the doctor setting the still form of an infant girl, too small to live, on her bare stomach. And although she'd looked perfectly formed, her tiny lungs were too underdeveloped to even take a breath. She and Shane didn't try to have any more children after that. He'd wanted to, but her heart couldn't take it. Then, by the time she was ready, it was too late. It wasn't just the loss of an infant, it was the loss of a whole future unrealized. So instead, she embraced the entire world as her offspring and tried to save every damaged or hurting soul she came across—it didn't matter if it was human, plant, or animal. Sunny even tried to protect Mother Earth from the ravages of the human race. But when it came right down to it, she knew her efforts were as vain as they had been in trying to stop the Vietnam War.

"We all have pain, Kelli. Pain so deep, it'll swallow us whole if we let it. When my husband died of cancer at age thirty-one, I thought I'd been swallowed by a whale. But I wasn't spewed out of that whale all at once like Jonah was. I stayed in there a long time, made it my home—a dark, dingy prison. Eventually, I took a step out, a little at a time. Then I started my own diner, began to feed people, and in time I felt like letting people's light back into my life. But it was while I was trapped by grief, unable to look beyond myself, that I took up smoking. The day they closed the casket on my husband's face, I stopped at Joe's Service Station and bought my first pack."

"I'm sorry about your husband. What was he like?"

"Funny and kind and absolutely wonderful. I wish the whole of humanity could have the chance for his kind to grace their lives," Sunny answered, remembering Shane's wry grin.

"I know someone like him. My broth—I mean the person I want to get in touch with."

"Let's call him," Sunny said quietly, trying to ease into the suggestion.

"We can't. He'd put a trace on it."

"So? If he's so wonderful, why won't you let him find you?"

"Because I don't deserve him. I've done something terrible to him, to them," Kelli whispered.

"My guess is it won't matter. What's the number?" Sunny's mind raced with Kelli's possible transgressions.

"No!"

"We'll call him on a cell phone—much more difficult to trace."

Sunny watched Kelli's face light up as if she hadn't thought of this before.

"Do you have one?"

"No, I don't. But Jack does. Let's drive over there right now and call."

Kelli and Sunny stepped out into the night. A cold wind slapped Sunny in the face and she sprinted to the VW Bug. Kelli pulled her thin jacket around her and hunched down in the seat. Sunny started the car and let the cold air from the defrost clear the windshield. When the circle grew just large enough to see out, she drove down the lane. As they passed the white crosses, barely visible in the dark, she glanced at Kelli and noticed her face pressed into her knees. Kelli moved her face almost imperceptibly and peeked out at the crosses.

"Somebody die who was close to you, Kelli?"

Kelli was as silent as the spring snow on the trees around them. Sunny looked out on the scene, wanting to change the subject, and saw a fairy wonderland of lacy branches etched in white, sparkling in the headlights as Sunny navigated their way to Jack Heath's home. It had been snowing each night, but by early morning the snow would be melted and the forest would transform itself to green, sunlit foliage and hope of new growth.

Jack's home was made of logs. *Of course*, Sunny thought. She'd never been here before, but many times she'd seen the sign reading, "The Heaths," with four painted pine trees carved in it. Jack was wearing a woolly tweed sweater, bifocals, and holding a paperback book when he opened the door. He glanced at his watch. "Did we have appointments tonight that I've forgotten?"

"No, no. We just came to borrow your cell phone," Sunny said.

"Sure, sure, what a nice surprise. Make yourselves at home."

Sunny suppressed a laugh. Books, magazines, papers, and junk mail were strewn all around the living room. The sink was completely filled with at least a week's worth of dishes, and dirty socks and mismatched work boots were heaped by the door. Jack shoved a pile of stuff off his couch to make room for the two of them to sit down.

"Do you not do one solitary thing for yourself?"

"Hmmm. You don't mince words, do you?" Jack started rummaging through papers on the table, then the counters, and then started fishing in the couch cushions. "Can't seem to recall where I left that phone. Ahh, I've got an idea."

With that, Jack went to his regular phone and made a call. For a second, Sunny thought he was calling someone to see if they knew where it was, but then she heard Beethoven's Fifth, a tinny, high-pitched sound. "Follow that sound, would you? And find the phone," he directed.

Sunny laughed again, followed the sound, and found the phone in the wood box next to a blazing fire. "Here, Kelli."

Kelli took the phone and disappeared into another room. Suddenly Kelli called out of the room, "If you think it's bad out there, Sunny, you ought to see it in here. Pee-yew!"

"See what you've created, Sunny? She's already a chip off the old block." Jack moved the pots and pans that were piled on his kitchen stove, found a teakettle, dusted it off, filled it with water, and turned on a burner. "I'm going to make you a drink that is going to change the way you think about life."

"Oh really?" Sunny asked, intrigued.

"Really. Just sit down over there by the fire, and in a few minutes I'll bring it over to you. You can't watch me—secret recipe. As secret, even, as Sunny Day Stew with dumplings."

"Sister Danielson told you then, about my not sharing the recipe," Sunny said.

"Of course she told me, and I told her I understood completely, because I have a recipe like that myself . . . 'Course she asked me for it as well."

Sunny smiled and started sorting through the piles of junk. Clutter was something she couldn't stand. She found it impossible to form a worthwhile thought if things weren't neatly in place. By the time Jack came over carrying a tray with three mismatched cups on it, she had completely cleared off the sofas.

"Now we can have a conversation," Sunny said, sitting in the middle of a firm cushion.

Jack set the tray down on a log coffee table, then brought her cup over, handing it to her with a "Ta-da."

She took a sip. Then another. *Chocolate with . . . what?* She couldn't tell, but she had to admit it was very good. "Mmmm, excellent Jack. Who would've thought that a barbaric ravager of virgin forest lands could concoct such a wonder?" She liked teasing Jack. Probably because he didn't ruffle at all—ignored her barbs like she'd just given him the compliment of a lifetime.

"Do you really mean it? I mean that it's good," he clarified, at least acknowledging she'd spoken other words.

"Very good. If I was blind and couldn't see my less-than-ideal surroundings, I'd think I'd been transported to a street café in Tuscany."

Jack sipped his drink as well. "What's with Kelli?"

"Yeah, the appearance change, I know. She cut off that gorgeous auburn hair, dyed and permed it. She's calling her brother, I think. Tried not to tell me, but she slipped up."

"How's she doing? Find out anything?" he asked.

"No, but I don't think she remembers that cell phones keep the phone numbers dialed in their memory," she whispered.

"I take it she doesn't want us to know."

"Not consciously, but if that brother of hers is the kind of person I think he is, then he is the only person in the world that can help her through whatever she's going through."

"Not true, Sunny. Don't forget the Lord. 'Trust in the Lord with all your heart . . .'"

"'And in all thy ways acknowledge him, and he shall direct thy paths.' I know, but sometimes it takes a human hand to put you on that path, don't you think? Whatever happened to that poor kid must've been something awful. You know those two crosses at the edge of town?"

"Sure, I was here when those two teenagers were killed. Driving too fast to make the curve. Terrible tragedy."

"Well, that's where I found her the first time, crying next to those crosses like they were her two best friends. Saying she killed them."

"We know that isn't true," Jack said, putting another log on the fire.

"Right, and then she mentions a husband, but then claims to not be married, not really, and that the girl that was with her wasn't really her sister in the legal sense. And did I tell you, Jack, that her face was bruised, the other girl—Mary, I think her name is. And now Kelli says if they find Mary, they'll beat her again."

"Who?" Jack looked puzzled and took another sip of his chocolate. "A lot of things don't add up."

"No, they don't, and I don't know who they're running from," Sunny agreed.

"By the way, how have things been at the diner?" He smiled knowingly.

"You wouldn't believe it, but business has been up. All those people that Marty gave free food to have been coming in regularly, and they're bringing their friends. That was Marty's plan all along. He knew if people got a taste of my stew and his pie they'd want more. Now if I could just get this recipe, I could retire young," she said, indicating the hot chocolate.

"Oh no, we don't want that. You're the caretaker of the entire town, and even strangers like Kelli. I wish there were ten more of you here."

"What a nice thing to say." Sunny was pleasantly surprised at the sincere compliment. But then she got a playfully wicked glint in her eye. "But if there were ten of me, I'd put you out of business, President Heath. Me and my mighty army of me would stop you from your evil destruction of God's land."

"'And God created the earth for the use of man,'" he countered.

Before Sunny could answer, Kelli emerged from the bedroom. Her face was streaked and puffy but she had a sparkle in her eyes. The first genuine glimpse of joy that Sunny had seen since the girl first came three weeks ago. It was fleeting, but unmistakable.

"Sit down here and have a drink of the honest-to-goodness very best chocolate I've ever tasted." Sunny slid over and Kelli sat down holding the cup. Her hands were visibly shaking as she drew the cup to her lips.

Jack and Sunny watched carefully, hoping to detect a clue to her thoughts.

"Well, what did he say?" Sunny prodded.

"That it wasn't my fault," Kelli answered.

"And you believe him, of course," Sunny said.

"I don't know, but it was so nice to hear. And by the way, I erased the number I dialed on your phone."

Jack shot Sunny a furtive glance and shrugged.

chapter 13

phone calls

When Sam was in high school, his mother had pled with him not to get involved in bull riding, but he did anyway. And when he was awarded "High School Champion Bull Rider" for the state of Idaho, she wasn't in the arena to see him receive the giant shiny belt buckle he still wore. Every time he left home to ride in a rodeo, his mom retreated upstairs and shut the door to her bedroom. He knew that she'd be in there praying. She often said, "Sometimes the only thing you can do is pray." His dad was different though. Once he saw that Sam was serious and had the talent to win, he had encouraged him. "What could possibly happen?" he'd said to Sam's mom. "It's Sam, for Pete's sake, he has the luck of the Irish with him." His dad had sat proudly on the first row of benches and cheered for all he was worth. Sam could still envision the three of them—Brandon, who also rode bulls a few years later, Kelli, just ten, and Dad. His dad wasn't much of a cowboy, but he'd dress the part for the rodeo, and he could've passed as one, if it hadn't been for the way he cheered. His cheers came across more like he was at a football game than a rodeo. "Defense, son!" Sam remembered him shouting while the other spectators yelled things like, "Spur 'em for all you're worth!" and "Hang on there!" with a few cuss words thrown in for emphasis.

If Sam had the chance to do it over again, he still would've ridden the bulls, that was a given, but he would've tried to help his mother understand his choice. He felt bad that he'd ignored her feelings and continued on riding the bulls without acknowledging her worry. Now he finally understood.

* * *

Sam had just stopped in front of the police station to quiz the detective again when he felt a twinge and a tingle go up his spine and settle at the back of his neck. He put his hand there, then turned off the radio, listening to the traffic hum by and thinking. And the thought that came to him was that he should go home as soon as possible. He didn't speed, but weaved through the clogged traffic, and headed south until he hit the highway and could pick up the pace. Instead of feeding the animals as he usually did, he went straight into the house and checked the answering machine— nothing. He looked around, hoping to get an idea, but none came. He'd started pulling out some leftovers from the night before when the phone rang.

"Hello." He didn't hear anything on the other end but a faint breathing sound. "Kelli?"

"Yes, it's me. I promised I'd let you know," Kelli whispered.

"It's been too long Kelli. Where are you?" Sam's heart thumped in his chest as his whole body stiffened. "Are you all right?"

"Sam, forgive me. I didn't know. I didn't know." He could hear her gasping and crying.

"Kelli, if you're talking about the accident, it isn't your fault. Wasn't your fault. You can't go on blaming yourself. Wherever you are, we need you home. We want you here."

"I killed them. We were late for the game and I insisted Dad drive faster," she squeaked.

That was the first time Sam had heard this. He paused, thinking. "Kelli, listen to me. I don't care if you told him to jump off a cliff or even to put a gun to his head. Dad was an adult. You were a child at the time, just fourteen. No one blames you—not me, not Brandon, not Mom and Dad, not anyone."

"God knows the truth, though. Isn't that what Mom and Dad always said? You can fool people, but you can't fool God."

"Especially God doesn't hold you responsible. Kelli, I'm sorry I didn't know what you were going through. I should've known."

Her breathing became more labored. When she finally spoke, she was whispering. "That isn't all Sam, I've done something else terrible, something awful, I'm so embarrassed. I've compounded the sins, and they return—they return."

What is she talking about? "The house? We don't care about that. All we care about is you." Sam said a silent prayer that she would believe him.

"Bye, Sam. I just wanted you to know. And let Brandon know how sorry I am."

"Wait, are they treating you well?" *That filthy rat*, he thought.

"The best. Bye, Sam."

"Don't hang up—" He heard a tiny click. He pushed *69, hoping to find out the number she'd called from, but the mechanical voice announced, "The last number to call your number is unavailable." *All this time she's been carrying that burden. I can't believe it. None of this would've happened if I'd helped her sooner!* Sam slammed the food he was holding down on the counter, then dropped his head into his hands in frustration.

* * *

Sam had just drifted off to sleep and was dreaming about chasing a man in a suit down Oneida Street. Sam had a lasso and was watching the loop go around the man's neck, but then the lasso turned into a noose and the man in the suit stood on a plank, like in a western movie, when the man's cell phone went off suddenly— ringing, ringing, and ringing. Sam then woke and could hear his own phone ringing. He rolled out of bed and stumbled to the hall to answer it.

"Sorry, Sam, to wake you, but I couldn't sleep. And I couldn't wait until morning to tell you."

"Who's this?" Sam could barely make out the clock at the end of the hall. It read 1:23 A.M.

"Lisa Lynn."

"Oh. Yeah, go ahead." Sam blurrily recalled phoning Lisa, Kelli's best friend growing up, to see if she'd heard anything from Kelli lately.

"Well, I ran into this friend of mine, you know, from college, and he asked me how Kelli was doing. I told him I hadn't seen her for a while. I didn't tell him what you told me and how worried you were.

Then, real casual, he said, 'Oh? 'cause I saw her the other day.' I grabbed him by the collar and shook him a bit and he started yelling for me to stop. Of course, then I realized what I was doing and did stop, but then I had to convince him I wasn't crazy before he'd tell me that he saw her going into a dentist office in Burley. You know that one on Normal Avenue."

"So that means she's still close by. Yeah, okay. Good work. Thanks. Anything else?" Sam asked sleepily.

"Said she was with a pack of kids, so that works out, you know, with the polygamy thing you were telling me about. But there's no way I can believe that, Sam, so I wondered if she's been abducted like and brainwashed. I heard once about this rich girl that was abducted by terrorists or something, and then later she became one of them—robbed banks and stuff 'cause she was brainwashed."

"Patty Hearst?"

"Sounds right."

"Yeah, I think you're right about part of that—but Kelli wasn't abducted, at least not technically. She actually called me to let me know everything's okay. But everything's definitely not okay. Anyway, I'll check it out tomorrow and let you know what I find out."

* * *

In the morning, Sam called his work and told them he'd be late. He was doing that a lot lately, either that or leaving early. He hoped they would be patient. Only Mel really knew what was going on, and he was trying to cover for Sam the best he could. Since Sam was the manager and auctioneer, and much depended on his talent and knowledge, things were starting to suffer and he was getting worried about losing his job.

A few people were waiting to be seen when Sam walked into the dental office. He walked straight to the efficient-looking woman behind the front desk and pulled out the most recent photo he had of Kelli.

"Hi, I'm wondering if you've seen this woman here. Would've been in the last couple of weeks." Now Sam wished he'd pinned Lisa Lynn down more on a time period. He'd been so groggy, he'd forgotten to ask.

The woman took the photo and examined it carefully. "Is she a patient here?"

"Probably not, but she brought a bunch of kids in with her for—"

"Oh, sure, now I remember. Caused quite an uproar for the Ellstrom family. Mrs. Ellstrom said she, that girl, was the hired help, but she left them high and dry, even took off with one of their cars. I offered to call the police for them, but the Ellstroms shy from publicity. You know, I think they're part of some religious group. Said they'd rather take care of it themselves."

"Did they go after her, then?" Sam asked, now excited to think Kelli might have left the group.

"Well, now, how could they? Mrs. Ellstrom must've had a dozen kids here."

"Did you see the car she was driving?"

"No, I didn't. Are you going to catch that girl? You don't look like a police officer."

Sam started fishing through his wallet and pulled out a card for the Burley Stockyard. "Listen, I'm writing my home number on here as well, and if you think of anything, would you give me a call?"

"Well, are you representing the Ellstroms or the girl?"

"The young woman has been listed as missing. I'm her brother and I'm helping the police department find out as much as they can about her whereabouts. So I'd really like to talk to the Ellstroms also. Could you tell me an address or phone number where I can contact them? If I find the girl, I'll find their car as well."

The woman digested this information while staring at Sam. He was impressive in his boot-cut slacks, polished black boots, pin-striped western vest, and silk neckerchief. His attire, paired with a boyish grin, gave him a look people warmed up to easily. The woman behind the counter paused, looked around the room, stood up and leaned in closer to Sam. He leaned over the counter as well, until his face was just a hair's breadth away from her face. "We don't have a phone number or address, you know, because I suspect they're polygamists. It's none of our business as long as they pay. And they do. They always bring enough cash with them to cover everything. That's why Dr. Atkins likes them so much. But this time Mrs. Ellstrom didn't have enough money and she complained that the girl in the photo stole some of it as well. Now, the only reason I'm saying anything at all is because I want to do everything to help the police out, and you seem honest, and like you really care about the girl. So you know, when Mr. Ellstrom came in, he was madder than a rooster in a cockfight. It sounded like maybe one of his daughters was gone too. He had to come retrieve some of the kids, you know, and I thought I overheard him mumble something like, 'When I get my hands on her,' but then Mrs. Ellstrom grabbed his arm to quiet him. At the time I didn't make much out of it, but you know, you've got me thinking."

Sam lifted his hat and nodded a thank you. "Call me, now, if you think of anything else. I'll pass this on to the police." The woman held the business card in her hand and nodded.

chapter 14

images

Kelli had been living in Trout Haven, Montana, for over a month now. Mid-May promised to be warmer than April. Yellow glacier lilies blanketed the spongy forest ground surrounding Sunny's home. Several mornings each week, Kelli would follow a distinct trail up Horseshoe Mountain. At first she could only go about a half mile before the snow banks covering the trail were too deep, and she'd have to head back. She liked to see the melting snowpack peeling away a little more each day, revealing the new spring growth beneath. Hope—that's what spring always gave her. Now she hiked much farther before snow sent her back down, but still couldn't reach the saddle that intrigued her so much. *Obviously that's where Horseshoe got its name,* she'd mused. The morning hikes were therapeutic, and before beginning her day at the Lazy Moose, she needed this rejuvenation, this reminder to keep on living.

Sunny made her feel that she was more help than she was burden, but Kelli suspected it was just her warm nature that made her act so. Kelli resolved again that she couldn't go on wearing Sunny's clothes, which in Kelli's opinion didn't flatter Sunny in the least, and looked even worse on her. Taking an afternoon off, Kelli drove Sunny's car up to Bozeman. The drive was beautiful. Large granite cliffs towered above one side of the road and a river flanked the other side. Fly fishermen dotted the golden Gallatin River. She was watching the fishermen when a dark shape caught her attention. A large moose lazily wandered into the road and Kelli slammed on her brakes as the moose made it slowly across the road and to the edge of the river.

Eventually, the valley opened up again to a vast flat spot that reminded her so much of the area around Burley and Twin Falls that she shuddered. At Belgrade she got on the freeway again and exited in Bozeman. Bozeman, just a few miles away from the flat Belgrade area, was surrounded with low mountains that swelled up like green waves. She wandered up and down the streets until she found a strip mall. Not sure what kind of clothes the new Kelli Brewer wore, she spent an hour just browsing. Then she finally settled down to business in a western-wear shop called Horsing Around. In Twin Falls she'd spent a lot of time coordinating stylish, sophisticated outfits. Here she decided to go for the opposite. Not that cowgirl clothes weren't stylish—they probably were in Montana, she figured—but blending in was the important thing. She chose snug-fitting Wranglers, a couple of T-shirts, a skirt, and some dressier blouses with ruffles. She picked out a pair of cowboy boots. She was wearing the skirt, the ruffled shirt, and the boots, admiring herself in the mirror, when she heard a voice behind her.

"Quite a disguise," the male voice said.

Kelli felt her heart jump. "What do you mean?"

"Sorry, I didn't mean to scare you, but I saw you go in and, well, you look like a completely different person. I don't mean to embarrass you, but where in the world did you get the clothes you had on?"

"You didn't like them?" She tried to laugh, sound casual.

"Well, don't take offense but they make you look a lot like this hippie lady that runs a café over in Trout Haven."

"Oh, that's okay. Those are her clothes. I left, I mean, my clothes had an unfortunate accident, so . . . that's why I'm here."

"She your mom?"

She had already said more than she wanted anyone to know, so Kelli started to get uncomfortable again. "No, but anyway, I've got to go." She kept the new outfit on and carried the clothes to the counter. She was surprised to see the same young man move behind the register.

"Oh, you work here?"

"Yeah, guess you want me to ring up the clothes you have on."

"Please."

"What's your name and phone number?" he asked.

"Why?"

"Uh, company policy."

"Well, if that's your policy, then I'm not buying anything here." She turned to change back into Sunny's clothes.

"Wait. They just like to track who shops here, but it's not mandatory. Thought I might call you sometime—get together for a drink or dance or something."

"Oh, well go ahead and ring everything up then."

"Not interested?"

Kelli thought a second. She looked at the young man. He was skinny, had short hair and one of those mustaches she despised, sort of like a U-shape around the mouth. She didn't know what they were called, but they seemed to be popular among the cowboy crowd. The old Kelli wouldn't even think about going out with him, but would Kelli Brewer?

No, the last thing Kelli wanted was to start any relationships. That much she knew. "I don't know. I'm really busy. I work at the Lazy Moose in Trout Haven. If you ever get down that way, stop in for a visit."

"You work there, huh? That place doesn't serve much meat, though, does it?"

"No meat—well, only to special customers, but give it a try. You'll be surprised."

"That lady you work for—she's wacky. But maybe I'll get down that way sometime and look you up."

* * *

When Kelli got back to the Lazy Moose, she was still wearing her new skirt and blouse. She sat down at the counter and waited.

"What can I get for you?" Sunny asked as she set a menu and a glass of ice water in front of her.

"I was thinking of toast, the color of a Montana sunset, eggs the texture of a baby's behind . . ."

"Kelli! What in the world? Didn't recognize you. With your new haircut and those new clothes, no one would."

Kelli laughed and pulled herself off her stool. "I'm ready to give you a break, if you'd like."

"Sure, go ahead and take the man that just sat down in the last booth." Kelli grabbed an order pad and walked to the booth.

"Howdy." She'd never said "howdy" before, but she thought it worked with her new image and disguise. "What can I get for you?"

"Bring me the Sunny Day Special. Is that good?"

"Sure, it's very good."

"All right, and then I'm wondering if you could help me out. Take a look at this photo. Seen this girl around?"

Kelli glanced at the snapshot and recognized Mary Rachel. She hoped she didn't say no too quickly for him to notice.

"Well then, mind sending over the other workers, see if anyone's seen her? My client thinks she's in danger. She was last seen with a woman with red hair—attractive, nice smile, dimple on one side . . . left I think. I've got a photo of her also."

Kelli pulled at her short, dark, springy curls. "Haven't seen her either," she said, suddenly feeling sick and walking away as naturally as possible.

As soon as she was out of sight, Kelli bolted to the bathroom and dropped to her knees, throwing up in the bright pink toilet. She held onto the sides of the bowl and felt her head spin, the paisley-painted walls convulsing toward her. Then she stood up slowly, feeling light-headed still. She washed her face with cold water and pulled at her hair again. Not red, not auburn, but brunette. She didn't look anything like the woman the man had described. Sunny had said so.

Sunny was suddenly in the bathroom. "You okay? You didn't turn the order in and I saw you bolt in here."

"Oh, sorry. Will you turn this into Marty?" She took the order out of her pocket and handed it to her. "Sunny, that man had a photo of Mary Rachel. I don't know what to do, but I'm afraid I might have messed up. I don't know what to do. I don't know . . ." She couldn't seem to gel a single thought.

"I'll take care of it. You sit down a minute and then come back out when you're feeling better. I'm sure it's not as bad as it seems."

"Oh, and please tell Marty not to say anything," Kelli said.

"No need. He would never rat on anyone, even if he thought you and Mary had committed the bank robbery of the century."

chapter 15

warnings

During the spring, after knowing each other a year, Sunny and Shane were married in Logan. No one in her family could attend the ceremony, but that was okay with her. They lived back east and Sunny wasn't close to them, especially after she'd run away to join the hippie movement. After Sunny was baptized a Mormon she had tried to reconnect with her family, but as far as her mother was concerned, being a Mormon wasn't any better than being a flower child.

But Shane's family was ample enough for her to share. It was one of those families that seemed to just go on and on. Besides his parents, four brothers and two sisters, there were aunts and uncles, cousins, and shirttail relatives scattered in nearly every town in Utah and Montana—a huge Mormon family with pioneer heritage. While his family liked her well enough, it was clear they thought the marriage was doomed. Just days from the marriage, Shane's mother sat them down on Sunny's royal blue, threadbare sofa. The look on her face said, *I hate to tell you this,* and an article clipped from *Reader's Digest* about how statistically, mixed-race marriages didn't fare well was in her hand. It didn't matter to her that both Sunny and Shane were Caucasian. In her view, with Sunny being from California and Shane from Montana, they may as well be from the deep Congo and Tokyo.

"It isn't that we don't approve of you Sunny, but we just want Shane to be fully aware of what he's getting into," his mother said kindly.

Shane laughed, put his arm around Sunny, and gave her a lingering kiss on the lips right in front of his mother.

"Gee Mom, by the look on your face, I thought you were here to deliver bad news. All I can say is, it's a good thing Sunny's mom doesn't listen to that kind of stuff, because all the country songs, all the old Westerns, really don't paint cowboys out to be that great of a catch. What's that new Willie Nelson song . . . ? That's it—'Mommas Don't Let Your Babies Grow Up to Be Cowboys.' Mom, I'm lucky, really lucky, that Sunny will have me at all. The truth is, she's the one you should be warning. I suspect she's marrying beneath her, and all because I carried an antiwar sign." He winked at Sunny.

"It's her I'm thinking about as well." His mother didn't look convinced.

"Thanks for the warning then," Sunny said. "Maybe I can get him to go with me to California and start an organic gardening co-op, then sell our produce along the highway and live in a tepee."

His mom's look was half quizzical and half concerned, as if she couldn't tell if Sunny were serious.

Shane clarified. "She's kidding. I'm dropping out of school for now and cowboying in Montana. Sunny's all for it. She'll be able to finish her courses by correspondence if she wants."

Shane's mother's jaw now dropped, and she stared as if her son had just told her they'd bought a condo on the moon. Still, that was the last she'd said concerning the matter.

After the simple ceremony, with nothing more than a remote possibility of a job at a ranch, and lots of hugs and tears from Shane's mom, they headed north. Shane's pickup was loaded with the blue sofa and a few boxes of unopened wedding gifts, and their few material possessions, which were stuffed into two duffel bags.

* * *

In the café rest room, Sunny assured Kelli everything would be fine, but she was shocked by her pallid complexion. Sunny walked casually to the man who had shown Kelli the photo. "Sorry this took so long, the waitress got feeling ill, so . . ." Sunny set the soup down and another plate with cornbread on it. "Cornbread's on the house— make up for the wait."

"Thanks, no problem," the man said.

The photo of Mary sat on the edge of the table. "Is that a picture of the girl you were asking about?" In it Mary Rachel was standing next to a tree and squinting from the sun in her eyes. Her hair was longer than Sunny had remembered it being, but still it was her.

"Yeah, seen her?"

Sunny picked up the torn picture, pretending to examine it. "Looks like so many teen girls, doesn't she? Might've seen her, but I doubt it. Why are you looking for her? Runaway?"

"Actually, we think the woman who was with her abducted her. This girl wouldn't run away on her own, see." He took a bite of his cornbread. "Mmm. This is good. Anyway, I'm just trying to catch up to them before something bad happens to . . . to them. Just trying to protect the girls. This is the other woman." He put his hand inside his jacket and pulled out a small photo. "She'd be quite a bit older than this, twenty-four or so."

Sunny took the high school yearbook photo. "What was her name again—the older girl?"

"Kelli Carson."

"From?"

"Southern Idaho. Twin Falls area. Burley—when this photo was taken."

"If I see them, who should I call?" Sunny asked.

The man reached inside his jacket again and pulled out a card. "Private Investigator Fred Allred," he said and handed it to her. "Mind if I go back and ask the kitchen help?"

"I'll send Marty, our cook, out. Uh, who hired you, can I ask?" Sunny asked.

"You're asking quite a few questions for someone who hasn't seen the girls. You being straight?"

"Sure I'm being straight with you. It's just that a lot of people come through here, you know. How am I supposed to know who to trust and who not to?" Sunny gave him a shrug. "Besides, I don't always remember faces—the extra information might jog my memory if I'd seen them."

"Would this jog your memory?" The man placed a twenty dollar bill on the counter.

"Certainly not." Sunny responded indignantly, but then quickly caught herself and put on a worried look. "You know, if you're concerned for their safety, then I'll keep watching."

Sunny checked on Ned, who was just finishing up a piece of huckleberry pie. She leaned over and wrote on his napkin, "Don't say anything
about Kelli," and stood back up. "Enjoy the pie, Ned." Ned nodded his
head and took a sip of coffee. Then she stepped into the back kitchen.
Marty was pouring huckleberry muffin batter into oversized tins.

"Kelli running some errands?" he asked.

"No, she wasn't feeling too good and this guy's been asking
questions? Why?"

"Because I just saw her take off in your Bug is why. Emptied her
tip jar into her pockets and took off."

Sunny grabbed her bag and said quickly "Marty—I've got to run.
That man out there wants to talk to you. Remember, you haven't seen
either of the girls—now keep things running and I'm taking your truck."

Sunny grabbed the Dodge keys off the nail by the back door and
jumped into the dented blue '88 pickup. The truck jerked and spun
on the gravel in the parking lot. She pulled onto the main road and
drove north, to the edge of town, then on to her place. After a quick
glance around, she realized Kelli hadn't been there. Sunny pulled back
out and headed south, thinking she might still see the car somewhere.
But it was no use. Kelli had gotten a head start and Sunny didn't
know which direction she would've gone. After driving up and down
Main Street a few times, she went back into the diner. The "closed"
sign was in the window and no one was left except for Marty bricking
the grill. His grease-stained shirt hugged his protruding stomach.

"Flew the coop, huh?" he asked.

"Yeah." Sunny felt tears forming and blinked them away. She'd
allowed herself to get attached to this girl.

"Well, she was a good worker, but what did we know about her?
Must've committed some kind of crime or even kidnapped that girl,
like the guy said. Knew she was hiding something." Marty tossed his
utensils into the sink.

"Sure she's hiding something, but she didn't kidnap that girl. Did
he talk to Ned before he left?"

"Yeah, I saw him over there, but I don't think Ned said anything.
You tipped him off didn't you?" Marty asked.

Sunny went to the phone and picked it up to make a call.

"Reporting your car missing?" Marty asked.

"No." The phone rang at Jack's home. Sunny let it ring six times, then hung up and called his cell phone. He picked up after a couple of rings.

"Yallo."

"Jack, you seen Kelli?"

"No, why?"

"Seen my car?"

"Yeah, you ought to buy a new one, that thing is a piece of junk."

"You saw it then?"

"Sure. I saw it the other day when you and Kelli came by," Jack said.

Sunny felt her heart sink. "I meant today. Kelli just took off— stole it."

"She must be pretty desperate then, to take that thing. What can I do?"

"You owe me big-time, Jack, for stealing my diner and making a church out of it, so where are you anyway?" Sunny felt desperate.

"Working on a home down by Porcupine Creek."

Sunny could hear the whining of a power saw in the background. "Get over to the Lazy Moose and pick me up. And I mean now." Sunny hung up. *He's nervy, so I'll be nervy,* she thought.

"How far is it to Twin Falls?" she asked Marty.

"Follow me out to the truck, and we'll find out." Sunny looked over his shoulder as he unfolded the map and held it out. Marty whistled. "She's a long ways from home. You think that's where she went—back home?"

"I hope so."

By the time Marty folded the map back up, Jack had pulled in front of the diner, rolled down the window and said, "You called?"

Sunny jumped into his king-cab Ford pickup. She relayed what she knew about Kelli Carson, not Kelli Brewer, about the private investigator, and her own stolen vehicle. "I don't know what to do. I have a name to go on now, and know she hails from Twin Falls and Burley, Idaho. But— I don't know whether to call the police—since they could track the car down and her along with it, or since I don't—"

"Know what kind of trouble she was in. Yeah, that presents a problem." Jack was dressed in a red Pendleton shirt, Levis with suspenders, and black leather work boots. He drummed his fingers on the steering wheel. "Well, let's go back to my place, get on the Internet, and see if we can't track down . . . whoever it was she called the other night from my place. Her brother, you thought. Maybe we can get an idea of where to go from there."

When Sunny stepped into Jack's home, she was surprised. The front living quarters, as far as she could see, were very clean and tidy. "Whoa, wrong house, Jack. Better step back out and see if we made a wrong turn."

"No, no. This is the right place, all right," Jack said.

"You couldn't have done this by yourself."

"You don't think so?"

"Nope."

"Actually, you're right. I came home the other day from work and this is what it looked like. I thought you and Kelli did it, since you're the only visitors I've had all month, except for Dirk Barton. He's a buddy of mine, but he couldn't have done this. His place is a bigger mess than mine."

"I'm sure that couldn't be true, but you do have a mystery on your hands—not only who has the talent to do this, but who likes you well enough to do it. I really just can't imagine." She glanced at him as he sat at the computer to see if he was smiling. He was. "And I'm pretty sure it wasn't angels that did it, at least not in the heavenly sense."

"Just as I thought, you did do it. Thanks," Jack said smugly.

"I didn't."

"Don't be so modest. Anyway, let's get to business," he said. The computer was in another room, which also contained all the books, now shelved, that had been lying around the house just a few nights before.

"Okay. Whatever. But just so you know, I wouldn't lift a finger to clean the house of one of Mother Earth's enemies. Sorry to disappoint you."

Sunny plopped down on another chair next to the computer. They were able to find out Kelli's phone had been disconnected, and then, starting with Andrew Carson, began calling the thirteen Carsons in the Burley area, and the five in the outlying communities. Several weren't home, and for several they got answering machines. Samuel Carson was the last person on the list. "Hi. Sam here. Can't come to the phone. Please leave a message."

She left a message. "Hi, this is Sunny Day, and I'm looking for anyone related to Kelli Carson. Call if you can help at 408-221-8121 or call 408-760-2331. Thanks." She hung up. "Well, guess that's all we can do for the night. Let's sit back for a minute and hope some of those people call back, or at least the one we want."

chapter 16

baking cookies

Things had been going pretty well for the Carson children after the accident, until one day Sam had walked into the house and smelled something burning. He'd run to the oven and opened the door. Smoke poured out in black billows and sent him stepping backward, sputtering and coughing in search of fresh air. Then the remains of something cooking had burst into flames. He shut the door again, but not before the flames licked up the wall, catching a pot holder on fire. Sam grabbed the pot holder and stomped on it with his boots, burning his fingers in the process. "Kelli . . . Kelli!" he'd shouted down the stairs. "What're you trying to do here?"

Kelli appeared at the bottom of the stairs, with the phone pressed to her ear. She stopped chatting. "Yeah, Sam. What is it?"

"You darn well almost burned the house down."

Kelli dropped the receiver and ran up the stairs to the oven.

"Don't open it now. Whatever you had in there, you've got to let it burn itself out."

"My cookies. I forgot." She burst into tears and ran back down to her room.

Sam followed her but was met with a door that closed in his face. He picked the phone up from the carpeted floor. "Hello," he said.

"What happened? I heard yelling," a male voice said.

"Nothing much. I'll tell her to call you back." Sam hung the phone back up and went up to Kelli's closed door. He could hear her crying. "Kell, sorry I yelled. It's no big deal. Nothing burned down. Just try to be more careful, 'kay?" Sam paused to listen. "You okay?"

She continued to cry. He turned the door handle, tiptoed in, and sat on the bed next to her. "I'm so stupid," she sobbed. "I always do things like that. I'm horrible." She turned her face away from him.

"Everyone burns things, Kelli—even Mom. Remember that time she left the cake in the oven and went into town to shop? When I got home from school, the pan was burned all the way through and the cake was just ash. It was disgusting, really. The lady down the street—Mrs. Asbury—she'd called the fire department because there was so much smoke coming out of the house. When I heard the sirens, the smoke had cleared enough that I thought I could fool them. I ran outside and pretended I was playing basketball in front. You know, like nothing was wrong. 'Where's the fire?' they yelled from the engine.

"'Fire? Not here. But I thought I saw smoke down the street a ways,' I told them. Then I pointed at Mrs. Asbury's house. I don't know why I did that, but I thought it would be kind of funny—you know, the fire trucks pulling up to her house, all those firefighters jumping off the truck with a big hose in hand, squirting water into the house before she gets a chance to tell them otherwise."

"Really?" Kelli asked. She looked up at Sam, her eyes hopeful.

"Yeah, don't you remember?" Sam stroked her smooth auburn hair as he told the story. "And Kelli, you never do things like that. You are always so responsible. Hey, it makes me feel better to know you make mistakes once in a while. Now I know you aren't going to be translated and leave me here alone with Brandon," he laughed. "I couldn't stand it if that happened."

With that she started to cry again and he sat with her until she fell asleep. Then he took off her shoes and covered her with the crazy quilt Aunt Jenny had made for them after the accident.

* * *

Now on the pickup's bench seat beside Sam sat the double chocolate oatmeal cookies he'd baked and arranged on a china plate—the one adorned with blue periwinkle flowers. He pulled in front of the Grouse Creek church. He knew Stacey would already be there helping set things up on the lawn for the reception afterward. He carried the cookies in, and before he could even see who it was, someone grabbed the plate and disappeared into the kitchen. Bishop Jed Watkins greeted Sam. "Hey there. Ya ready for all this?"

"It's about time, right?" Sam asked.

"High time," the bishop said. "Stacey's in the Relief Society room, I suppose, but you can head into the chapel. I'll be in there to perform the ceremony in a few minutes."

When Sam entered the chapel he removed his hat, noticing about thirty people, give or take a few, dressed in their Sunday-best clothes. He took a seat in the front. He wore his nicest boot-cut slacks, vest, white shirt, and a black ribbon tie. An elderly woman with steel-gray hair played hymns on the organ without a hymnbook in front of her. A faint smell of spring flowers drifted through the air from the arranged bouquets decorating the front of the chapel.

Sam took his handkerchief out and wiped his forehead. It seemed warm. Finally, just before eleven, Stacey, wearing a simple black dress and a string of white pearls, slipped in next to him. His easy smile appeared and he put his arm around her and whispered, "You look great. I've missed you."

"I love you, too," she said. "Excited?"

"Sure, I think it's great."

Bishop Jed Watkins walked up to the pulpit. Sam turned around to see if he could see Herman and Maggie. He couldn't.

"We all know why we're here today. We're here to bring together two souls in marriage, and on a personal note, I say high time." The organ began to play a quiet rendition of the wedding march and Maggie walked out of a side door. She was wearing a white suit and carried a bouquet of flowers made with lavender rosebuds and baby's breath. A younger woman followed her, probably her daughter, then a small girl wearing a lavender dress and a white bonnet. The little one carried a basket brimming with dark purple pansies. A boy, not more than three, with his black slicked hair and a wide grin carried a small pillow with a gold wedding band on top. Lastly, Herman came out. His freshly shaven face wore a look of complete satisfaction. He smiled broadly and slowly walked to the front of the chapel. He wore a black suit, white shirt, black cowboy boots, and a gray tie. When he reached Maggie, he grabbed both of her hands. "Still time to back out if'n yer wantin'," he said.

"Not on your life, Herman Anders. Not on your life. I've had over fifty years to think about it and I'm finally ready."

A warm feeling engulfed Sam as the audience laughed. He was happy to have had a role in bringing these two together again. Bishop Watkins stepped down from the pulpit and stood at the front. "We are all here to see two fine people joined together. All of you are witnesses to this union. You are the choicest friends, the loved ones, and the family of this couple. You've seen their separate struggles, their sorrows, and their joys. Now they choose to share their lives with one another. Whether happy or sad, they'll be there from this time forth for each other. I pray with all of you that their union will be one of healing and of joy." Then he directed his comments to the couple. "Enjoy each other, laugh together, dance, work, cry, and pray together. Herman, don't let her get away again. And Margaret, hold on to him for all you're worth. May God bless and sanctify this marriage. Now get the ring, Herman, and put it on her left hand."

"What's that?" Herman tilted his ear toward the bishop. "Yer wanting me to bring her what?"

"The ring," Maggie said into his good ear. The little boy pushed the ring up toward Herman's face. Herman clumsily picked it up and put it on Maggie's outstretched hand.

"Did I get the right finger? All look the same to me." His eyes twinkled.

The bishop nodded and began again. "May the bonds be strong and enduring. Now by the legal authority that I hold, I pronounce you, Herman Anders and Margaret Miller Erickson, husband and wife." Herman put both of his arms around Maggie and kissed her. The audience oohed with delight. "I was going to say," Bishop Watkins began, "that you may now kiss the bride, but looks like as usual, Herman, you're an impatient man."

"Impatient, you say? I've a been a-waitin' fifty years too long for this day."

Stacey squeezed Sam's hand as they both laughed joyfully with the couple. Then she said, "I've got to head out and help with the refreshments. Meet me out there in a few minutes."

Sam pushed his way through the small group of people to the front lawn. It was nearly noon. Leroy's cows from an adjoining pasture bellowed a greeting to the wedding crowd and lined up at the fence, hanging their heads over and trying to reach the long grass that grew between the chain links. Sam, thinking the cows were not fitting guests at a wedding, grabbed a quarter bale of hay from a stack nearby and spread it along the opposite fence. "No one invited you all. Now eat in peace." The cows lumbered away from their outlook and began munching the hay. Sam knew it wouldn't last long, but it might get them a few minutes of peace. He watched from the distant view and could see Stacey going in and out of the church every few minutes, carrying plates of cake and refreshments. He felt a pang in his heart and wondered if this could ever happen for him. Would his life ever be stable enough to invite the woman he loved into it?

When Sam wandered back to the reception, Stacey was hugging Maggie and Herman. He walked up to Herman and put his hand out. "Congratulations Killer, you finally got what you deserved." He turned to greet Maggie with his hand out. Even with Herman in his mid-eighties and Maggie in her seventies, they made an attractive couple, and just like a couple of kids, they glowed with love in their eyes.

"Oh, no. Don't shake my hand—you give me a big hug. Sam, if it weren't for you, we wouldn't be here. And the alternative would be unthinkable." Sam hugged Maggie and wondered if she was thinking of prison. When he released her, he could see tears in her eyes. "Now don't take too long with Stacey," she continued. You never know what could happen that could whisk her away from you."

"Yeah." Sam turned to grab Stacey's hand but she was already carrying a bunch of dirty plates back into the church. With nothing else to do he glanced around at the crowd. He recognized some of the town's ranchers from the livestock sales, but knew very few of the women or children, and he guessed that many of the people there were Maggie's family. Sam sat down at a table as a young woman wearing a white apron set a plate with a cookie, a finger sandwich, and a small plastic spear with slices of fresh fruit on it down in front of him. Sam bit into the cookie he recognized as one of his own and watched the door, hoping to get a glimpse of Stacey again. His thoughts wandered between what the receptionist at the dentist office had told him, how to keep from losing his job, how he wished it were all over and Kelli were home safe, and how he could ask Stacey to marry him.

When Sam got home, it was after one in the morning. As usual, the first thing he did was check his answering machine. He listened to the message from Sunny and dialed the first number. The phone rang and rang. *Of course it is late, probably they won't answer*, he thought, but he let it continue to ring. When he heard a man's sleepy voice on the other end, he blurted, "Is Kelli there?"

"No, but who's this?" the voice slurred

"Her brother, Sam. Have you hurt her any?" Sam demanded.

"Whoa Sam, we want to find her too. She was here, but left."

"You disgusting piece of horse dung, you stole my sister's virtue, her house, and her money, and then have the nerve to act concerned."

"Sam, my name is Jack. I'm the branch president here. I don't have any idea what kind of trouble your sister has gotten herself into, but she has been with us, with a friend of mine, working here for over a month now."

"Call yourself a branch president? That's pathetic," Sam said.

"Well, I am a branch president. I didn't actually call myself that. The call came from the Lord through the stake president in Bozeman."

"Bozeman? So you aren't with the group in Idaho? Let me get this straight. Are you saying you're a real, LDS mainstream ward branch president?" Sam asked.

"We don't exactly qualify as a ward with only thirty-five members, twenty or so that show somewhat regular, but mainstream—yes. Guess we aren't as professional at Mormonism as Utahns or even Idahoans for that matter, and I don't actually feel like a real leader, but that's what they say I am."

Sam was confused. Was he really talking to a branch president and not some self-proclaimed religious leader of fanatics? "Wait, did you say she was there working?"

"Has been since mid-April."

That means she's been okay all this time, Sam thought. "Okay. I thought you were the dirtbag that duped her into getting involved in that rotten fanatical group."

"Serious? We had no idea. Knew something was terribly wrong, but she's been very closed about her past. In fact, the only reason we found out her real name was because a private investigator came through looking for her today. Did you hire him?"

"No." Sam's heart raced. "Hope you didn't tell him anything."

"Lucky for your sister, she's been staying with Sunny Day, who is just as warm as her name implies—at least to everyone except to me—and wouldn't tell a soul about Kelli. Anyway, she's very concerned for the safety of your sister and the other girl, Mary. Know anything about her?"

"No. So where are they now?" Sam asked.

"Don't know. When Kelli saw that a private investigator was looking for her she took off in Sunny's car. The other one left earlier. I know Kelli didn't have much money with her or anything. There aren't many people like Sunny Day to take her in, so I hope she finds someone who at least won't harm her. She seems vulnerable."

"Yeah, she's that." Sam sat on the kitchen chair and pulled off his boots with one hand. "Okay, sorry I called you names. Give me your address, and this Sunny woman's, and I'll get there as soon as I can." He wrote down "Lazy Moose Café, North Main Street, Trout Haven," and "Montana."

"Oh, and just so you know, we didn't report the car as stolen," Jack said.

"That's good. We don't know who we can trust, but obviously someone hired that detective, and it wasn't me. So we can assume that whoever hired him is someone from the cult, and the police report would lead him right to her." Sam hung up the phone and tried to digest what this new information could mean about Kelli's whereabouts.

chapter 17

on the run

Kelli knew that Sunny's car had the key permanently in the ignition. Sunny told her once that it had broken off there in a blinding snowstorm, and she'd never gotten it fixed since there was no need to. It just made things all that much easier. "Won't ever be late because I can't find my car keys," she'd said, "and someone would have to be crazy to steal it." Kelli headed north out of town, careful to not draw attention to herself. Within minutes, Sunny would figure out that she was gone and would most likely come after her, but Kelli guessed that Sunny would first head north, toward her house.

Highway 191 went straight to Bozeman. She could blend in with the college kids and maybe find a job. While her mind wandered, she hadn't noticed that she'd picked up speed. It was difficult to speed in Sunny's little Volkswagen, but she had managed it. Her foot had pushed hard against the pedal with the intensity of her thoughts. She heard the quick siren, and spotted the blue-and-black car with flashing lights in her cracked rearview mirror.

She pulled off onto the shoulder with the police car right behind her. She got her fake license out from her shoulder bag, which she'd managed to grab just before her escape, then opened the glove compartment and found Sunny's registration. Kelli hoped that Sunny hadn't reported the car stolen and she hoped that he would be fooled by her license. She knew both wishes were far-fetched.

"Going to a fire?" the police officer drawled.

"No sir."

"Got a college exam you're late for?"

"Something like that."

"Can I see your license and registration?"

"The car is my friend's," she said, handing the items through the window.

The officer examined the registration, "Debra Day. And you are . . . ?"

Kelli watched as he bent the license back and forth, then turned it over.

"By the looks of this I.D, you're not Kelli Brewer. Did you have this made so you could buy liquor or something?"

Kelli had her foot on the gas and quickly slammed the pedal to the floorboard. A dust cloud burst behind her and she sped down an exit ramp. She could see the police officer scrambling to his car in her rearview mirror. The distant but ever-increasing volume of the siren followed her. She headed south. Finally she saw a group of buildings surrounded by trees and huge parking lots. She parked haphazardly, left the door wide open, and sprinted toward an apartment building adjacent to what looked like the university. A couple was sitting on the upstairs porch of one of the apartments. The door behind them was open. She ran up the stairs, passed the gape-mouthed young people and flung herself into the open apartment, slumping down into an easy-chair. "I'm waiting for someone," she called out to them. "I'll just wait in here," she breathed heavily. Within minutes, she heard quick steps across the parking lot and then a man's voice hollering, "Seen a woman with curly brown hair?"

"Why are you looking for her?" a male voice asked.

"Speeding and possible stolen car, fleeing the scene—could be dangerous. Mind if I come up there and look?"

"No problem. Help yourself." Kelli could barely see the guy who was speaking. He was holding a guitar, sitting cross-legged, and had a fruit smoothie next to him.

Kelli was getting ready to run out the back door when she heard the sheriff speak. "Well, if you see her, mind giving the police station a call? Ask for Sheriff Maynard."

"Sure thing, Sheriff," the female voice said.

After about another minute, Guitar Man leaned his head back through the door. "You can come out now."

"I didn't steal a car—not exactly. I just borrowed it," she said, joining the couple on the porch. Kelli had intended to return the car when things settled down, when she figured out what to do.

"Hey, don't tell me. Tell it to the cop," Guitar Man said.

The young woman just laughed and Guitar Man went back to playing his music. The tune was a cross between a Spanish melody and a Monkees' song. Finally he opened his mouth. His sweet, soulful voice crooned a song that he made up as he went. "*And then I saw her face, now I'm a believer, I couldn't leave her if I tried. 'Cause she was out of breath with the law man just behind her, he couldn't find her if he tried. I believe her, she couldn't be a stealer, he must've lied. I see it in her face, that she must be my angel, sent to reform this forsaken place. Now I'm a believer, she won't leave here if she tried.*" He stopped strumming and looked at Kelli.

"Okay, what's the story?" he asked.

Kelli laughed. "Quite a song. I liked it." Kelli also liked him. How could she not?—he believed her. He had one of those half smiles; she wasn't quite sure if he was teasing or serious, but his blue-green eyes were inviting. His unruly blond hair was naturally wavy, and hung just over his ears.

"I don't really know where to begin. Let's just say I got myself in over my head and trouble is following me. I'm really not a thief, like you said in the song. But I am looking for a place to stay and I need to find a job," Kelli said.

Guitar Man slugged the girl next to him in the arm. "You're in luck. You can stay with Amber, can't she? You're short one roommate through the summer. Right?"

Amber was a thin girl with pasty skin. Short, dyed black hair with maroon highlights stood up in peaks on the top of her head. Her eyes widened at the suggestion, but she nodded. "Sure, I guess, long as you pay your share of things."

"Gladly, and I won't be staying long."

"On the run, right?" Guitar Man asked.

Kelli didn't answer.

"You've already been in my place—Amber's is right next door. I would've invited you to stay with me—I mean, it's not that I'm a selfish slug or anything—it's just that it'd be going against my standards to have a female living here. Don't laugh or anything, but I just don't feel good about that sort of thing. But come on in and I'll get you something to eat."

Kelli followed Guitar Man. "Let's see what we can come up with. Check out the cupboards and I'll check out the fridge." Kelli opened a cupboard door that was stacked with different flavors of ramen noodles. The next cupboard contained a jar of peanut butter and some boxes of no-name macaroni and cheese.

Guitar Man had pulled out one apple and a carton of milk. "This is it. What'd you come up with?"

"Noodles."

Guitar man laughed, "Yeah, I knew that's all there was in there. Okay, you slice up the apple, get out the peanut butter and spread it on the slices, and I'll make the macaroni and cheese."

The kitchen itself was U-shaped. Dark brown cupboards lined the walls, most of which, Kelli had noticed, were empty. It was small and she had to constantly walk around the card table set in the middle. There was just enough room at the table to sit on the chairs and not hit the cabinets.

"Cozy," Kelli said, spreading the peanut butter.

"Yup. Just the way I like it. Perfect for a single male living alone. It's cheap. This is a studio apartment. It's small, and has everything that you need right here. Amber's isn't, so there will be more room for you over there anyway." He stirred the macaroni.

"Why do you have two chairs at the table if it's just you here?" Kelli asked.

He set out two plates and dished them up with hefty portions of macaroni. "I knew you were coming. I have a crystal ball, and I was looking in it and saw a beautiful woman running into my apartment, but then . . ."

"Yeah?"

"I noticed that she was very sad, and even when she laughed, I thought she must be crying inside."

Kelli gasped and put her hand to her mouth. "Show me the ball."

"I was joking," he said.

"Of course. I was too." Kelli tried to smile.

They ate for a few minutes in silence. "Thanks for dinner," Kelli said, eating the last bite.

"Dinner? You elevate my offering." His tone was casual and easy.

"It was so much better than nothing. Can I ask you something?" Kelli said.

"Sure, anything."

"Why are you being so nice to me?"

"Let's just say—now don't take offense—but when you ran up those steps, I saw a look I recognized. I used to hunt deer with a bow. With a bow you have to get really close to your prey. Once, when I was seventeen, I tracked this buck in the Bitterroots—big rack, a four-point. I followed it all the way across the valley, through dense brush, and up the other side. Then I cornered it against the edge of a cliff. It knew that it could jump off the cliff or face me. I raised the bow and pulled back, and just as I did, he leaped off the cliff. The look in that buck's eye was similar to the look in your eyes. The buck broke his legs in the jump and I climbed down after him and finished him off. Anyway, it was the last time I went bow hunting. I didn't like seeing him with that kind of choice. You looked like your choice wasn't much better than his, so I gave you a way out. I couldn't actually lie to the police, but I wanted to hear what you had to say before I gave you away." He glanced at the clock. "Should we go over and get you settled in? And do you have anything we need to go get from that car you didn't steal?"

"I didn't have anything in it, and I'm sure they've impounded it by now."

"Oh yeah. By the way, what's your name?"

"Cindy, uh, Cindy Craw—son." Kelli said the first name that had popped into her head, and supermodel Cindy Crawford had been it.

"For a second there, I thought you were going to say Cindy Crawford. Crawson, huh. What kind of name is that?" he asked.

"Danish. What's your name?"

"Tony Stratton." He clenched his fist, knocked, on the wall and yelled, "Cindy's coming over now."

"No phone needed, right?"

"Right. Hey, listen, if you aren't too busy tomorrow, want to come to my church with me?" Tony asked.

Church. She hesitated. Since she'd been in Montana the days of the week had run together, one being just like the next, so she was always surprised when Saturday nights came around, and she'd need to help Sunny clear the floor for Sunday meetings. It wasn't so much that she didn't want to go to his church—it was that deep down she had the feeling that going to church was like standing out in the open—that not only could God see into her heart, but so could everyone in the congregation. Sitting in church, even in the Lazy Moose, had become almost unbearable. "I don't think so," she finally answered. "I'll probably be job hunting."

"Okay. But I'll be by in the morning, say, around nine-forty to see if you've changed your mind."

After Kelli went next door, Amber showed Kelli her room. It was just large enough for a built-in twin bed, a set of drawers, and a small closet. It looked like a dorm room, but at least she didn't have to share it with Amber. "I should've told you earlier," Kelli began. "I've only got a little money on me, so it will be awhile before I can help with rent—"

"Whatever, just as long as you pay it before you take off again." Amber's black, polyester-knit pants were cropped at the ankles, and she wore a thin black tank top. She had a tiny silver loop in her belly button and a stud in the side of her nose.

"So what do you do? Go to school?" Kelli asked, surveying her new roommate curiously.

"Yeah, but not the university. I'm in a beauty college near here."

"You're a hair stylist?"

"Yeah. Stuff like that. Hair, nails, makeup—you know—the works."

"Ever need someone to practice on?" Kelli asked.

"Who ya got in mind?"

"Me." Kelli closed her eyes. The only way she could think to hide from the detective, from the Church of Faith, and the police, was to start over again. If she had another drastic makeover, maybe she could make over her past as well.

"I'd love to do your hair. What's your natural color anyway? 'Cause I know that isn't it." Immediately she started running her hands through Kelli's springy hair.

"Auburn."

"And you changed it? I'd totally give anything for naturally red hair."

"Well, actually, I was thinking of going even darker—like your hair. Almost black, but no highlights."

"Totally awesome. Let's get started. I've got everything I need right here."

Kelli followed Amber into the bathroom and sat on a high stool by the sink.

"Best thing is for you to just close your eyes and relax, 'cause this is going to take awhile. Afterward, how 'bout we go to the body-piercing place. With your pale skin, you'd look really cool."

"I don't think so." Kelli shuddered at the thought.

"Okay." Amber shrugged. "First things first."

When she was finished, Kelli didn't recognize the image staring back at her. She faced short black hair styled to look messy, black eyeliner, and dark lipstick. No one would know her. "Perfect. Thanks."

"Really, you like it? I just didn't figure you for the type. I mean, come on, you're wearing cowboy boots. When I saw you running up those steps, I thought, 'Whoa, girl, where's your horse?' We both did," she finished.

Kelli turned away from the mirror. She now looked just like the kind of girl she would've avoided in the past. "Tell me something. You got something going with Tony?"

"He's my friend and my neighbor and that's it. Let me guess, he invited you to church tomorrow."

"How'd you know?"

"He invites everyone to his church. Trying to bring everyone to Jesus—that's Tony. Take some advice from me—don't go."

"Is he a born-again?"

"Something like that."

chapter 18

lost loves

When Shane and Sunny had arrived in Montana to start their life together, Shane had carried Sunny up the metal step and over the threshold of what would be their home for the next few years. The trailer was a Silver Streak. It wasn't a trailer house, but the kind of trailer a family would pull behind their paneled station wagon while visiting Yellowstone National Park. It had a built-in sofa that took up the entire width of one end, only three steps' worth to the kitchen area, a hall so narrow they had to walk sideways, and a tiny bathroom with a closet opposite. The back end of the trailer was their wall-to-wall double bed. Sunny squealed with delight. "It's perfect. Except where are we going to put my sofa?"

"Outside. Lucky thing for me that we got married. The rest of the guys on this ranch are all holed up in a bunk house, but we get this all to ourselves," Shane said, as if they'd rented the White House.

Since money was tight, they'd spent the night before sleeping, or at least trying to sleep, on the front seat of his pickup. So, in comparison, this was their honeymoon, even though Shane would have to report to work early the next morning.

* * *

Saturday night, Sunny sat at her booth where she'd usually smoked a cigarette before heading home. She looked out the window and watched lights flicker on in business windows. She took a stick of gum and put it in her mouth. *Finally!* she thought. Her craving for nicotine was almost completely gone. Her new calling as Relief Society president kept her on a constant run after work hours, and then Kelli's problems were stacking up like junk mail. She was beginning to forget why she'd liked to smoke in the first place, forgetting that cigarettes had been an escape for her. Sure she'd been edgy at first. The unsmoked cigarettes had nagged at her consciousness, like a fly in her diner, but she would forget what it was that was bothering her and would go about her business. Sunny blew a bubble with her gum, something she hadn't done since childhood. It felt good to sit again.

Marty had left his beat-up truck for her to drive, and his wife had already come to get him. *Lucky I have such good friends,* she thought. As she was concentrating on the twinkle of the light above Molly's Grill across the street, she noticed a familiar Ford truck pulling up. *Jack.* Irritated at his timing, she walked over to the locked door and opened it for him.

"Just thought I'd come by and see if you had the place ready for church tomorrow and—"

"Close enough."

"Also wondered if by chance you had any vegetable lasagna left over. I've been craving it," Jack said, patting his stomach.

"Those eyes in your head just for decoration or did you just not notice the 'closed' sign in the window?" She noticed he'd cleaned up after his workday. He wore jeans, gleaming white Nikes, and a black fleece vest over a turtleneck. "Yeah, I saw it." Jack sat in a booth. "Just hoping," he added. He pulled out his wallet and set a ten-dollar bill out.

"Oh, you think I can be bought?" she laughed.

"Hoping."

Sunny went back to the kitchen area and fixed a plate of lasagna and plopped it into the microwave. She brought it over to him and set it down with a small three-green salad and toasty garlic bread. "You'll do your own dishes when you're through."

Jack slid his hand over the ten-dollar bill. "Better replace this with something lower then."

"Oh, no you don't." Sunny grabbed it and stuck it into her shirt pocket, knowing that it would be safe.

Sunny was pleased to see his face redden and he stammered. His eyes flickered as if they had just been exposed to bright light. "Keep it. I was teasing," he said.

Sunny was amused by his discomfort, "Well, guess you'll want to know the latest. Got a phone call from the police. Kelli ditched my car near MSU. I told them I hadn't reported it stolen, so asked why were they calling me. Seems she got pulled over for speeding and tried to outrun the police. I didn't give them her name, just told them she was some homeless girl I was helping out, and that I had given her permission to use the car whenever she wanted. Which is true."

Jack took another bite of his lasagna. "True, except for the name part. We do know her name now." He wiped the corner of his mouth with the checkered napkin. "That girl never gets a lucky break, does she? Best thing we can do is help that brother of hers find her, and send her back home to Idaho. Did I tell you he accused me of stealing her virtue? And called me a piece of horse dung and lots of other not-so-nice things."

"Well, I'm sure you're used to people calling you names."

"Other than my ex-wife, you, and Kelli's brother, not really. Most people seem to actually like me."

Sunny liked him too. And she didn't understand why; he was rude, chauvinistic, anti-environment—the worst possible thing you could be in her mind—and probably even a Republican.

"Tell me, are you a Republican?" Sunny asked.

"I never mix politics with eating, especially in the company of a lady."

Sunny snorted. "Takes all kinds, I guess."

"Do you believe that?"

"No, actually, I just said that because I couldn't think of anything nice to say."

"When did that stop you?"

Sunny pulled another stick of gum from her sock and added it to the one in her mouth, then blew an extra large bubble.

He looked amused. "You probably ought to quit that. Blowing bubbles just doesn't seem fitting for a Relief Society president."

"Well, I don't think being a jerk is exactly fitting for a branch president either, but it doesn't seem to stop you." She started to giggle.

But, as usual, he wasn't fazed. He started to chuckle, finished the last bite of his dinner, then picked up his dishes and carried them to the sink. "I don't know why, Sunny Day, but I like you. Look, it's a

Saturday night. It's a little too late to head out of town for a movie, but I've got a great collection of videos and DVDs."

"Hot chocolate?" she asked.

"Sure, and I might be able to find some popcorn. Game?"

"What movie?" Sunny asked.

"I'll let you pick."

* * *

The house was still fairly clean, only a few books and a couple of days' worth of mail were stacked on the sofa. "The movies are in the cupboard there beneath the TV. Go ahead and pick one out while I make the secret recipe."

Only five movies sat on the shelf. "Thought you said you had a good selection. There's only five," Sunny said, glancing through the titles.

"Shoot. I forgot. My sixteen-year-old, Ashley, took them last visit. Those are the ones she didn't want."

"*Attack of the Killer Tomatoes, Building the Log Home of Your Dreams, Trophy Hunting in Montana . . .* Uh, Jack, there's nothing here that—"

"Never mind then. We'll do something else," he said.

"You must not watch movies much if you forgot."

"Not in the last year. We used to watch them together. I collected Cary Grant movies—videos mostly, since many aren't on DVDs yet. But since Kathy died, I haven't felt like watching much. How about a game of Scrabble?"

"You're on."

Jack opened another cupboard, stood on a footstool and pulled a worn brown box from the top. Sunny could see guns leaning against the side of the closet. She shuddered and sat down on the sofa. He opened the box and set it up on the coffee table in front of them, then jumped up to get the chocolate drinks.

He handed her the drink and then sat down beside her. Scrabble was something Sunny was very good at, and within the hour she had won the game by over a hundred points.

"You should've warned me," he said. "I would've suggested something else."

"I used to play with Shane. We didn't own a television—I still don't. Lots of long winter nights we played Scrabble. Don't be hard on yourself; you didn't stand a chance."

"Tell me about Shane. Was he like you?" Jack asked casually.

Sunny picked up the wooden tiles and put them back into the Scrabble box. "Shane was softhearted and a rough-and-tumble cowboy at the same time. He could spend a whole day branding calves with the toughest kind of men and love every second of it, then, when he came through the door and pulled his boots off, he would tell me funny things that happened, and we would laugh. Things like when they castrated the calves that the boss wanted to raise as bulls, and left intact the ones he wanted for steers. But he was also the kind of guy who would carry a half-frozen kitten in from outside and warm it with his hands. His hands are probably what I loved the most about him— big, strong, and calloused. But he could play a guitar like no one you've ever heard before. He's kind of a Leo Kottke–Jimi Hendrix mixture. I loved watching his hands when he played."

"That must've been difficult for you to be married to a cowboy. You know, the animal-cruelty-vegetarian thing." Jack stood up. "Can I get you more chocolate?"

"Sure, if you're buying." She held her cup out for a refill. "You're right, our lifestyles were a little incongruous, but with Shane it was never a big deal."

"He really does sound like a great guy. I'm sorry you lost him so young."

"Yeah, me too. Sorry about your wife, too. I'm sure you really loved her." Sunny felt her eyes mist up.

"It's been more difficult than I ever imagined."

Sunny felt herself sinking into despair thinking about lost love. "Listen I've got some stuff to get ready for Relief Society tomorrow, so I need to get going."

Jack looked disappointed, but stood up and stretched. "Yeah, well let me walk you out to your car—I mean Marty's truck."

chapter 19

joining forces

When Sam and Stacey pulled into Trout Haven, it didn't take long to spot the Lazy Moose. "There, I see it," Stacey said, pointing. "The Lazy Moose. It looks pretty busy."

Sam was tired. He pulled into the parking area in front and yawned. He had called Stacey right after his phone call from the branch president to tell her he'd be away for a while. Instead of asking for updates, she had insisted on coming with him. She'd driven in the middle of the night to meet him, and then they'd headed north together. Stacey had slept fitfully and spent most of her time telling Sam jokes to keep him awake. She'd taken a turn driving for a while, and Sam had fallen asleep for a few minutes, only to be jolted awake when Stacey swerved to miss an owl that had swooped in front of the windshield. Except for those few minutes, Sam really hadn't slept in more than thirty-six hours.

From the outside, the diner looked like a clapboard house painted a bright canary yellow. A large oval sign dangled from two chains, and it showed a moose sitting down with its legs sprawled out in front of it. The name "Lazy Moose, Vegetarian Cuisine" was etched into the wood and painted a deep mahogany color. "That's really strange. The window shades are drawn and there's a 'closed' sign in the window, but what's with all the cars?" Sam wondered aloud. He stretched and ran his fingers through his hair.

When they walked in, a half dozen men sitting around a table all turned in unison. One man, wearing a Disney tie, stood up and walked over to Sam. "Hello, you must not have noticed the 'closed' sign in the window. We're having a meeting here."

"Uh, yes I did, but I'm looking for Sunny Day," Sam said.

"This is her place, but she's engaged right now, so—" the man said.

Suddenly Sam recognized the voice. "Oh, you're the branch president, right?"

"Yes, and you are?" the man asked.

"Sam Carson, Kelli's . . ."

"Right. You're the one that called me names on the phone." He winked. "Pleased to meet you. Care to join us for the rest of the lesson?" He stuck his hand out to shake Sam's.

"And this is Stacey Willis," Sam put his other arm loosely around Stacey's shoulders as he shook the president's hand.

"So Stacey, I'm expecting you'll want to know where Relief Society is. Sunny is giving their lesson today, I believe. It's being held in the kitchen. Right through there," he said, pointing. "Sam, if you served a mission, maybe you can help us out on some doctrinal questions we're discussing."

"Uh . . . sure. So this is church? I'm confused. I thought the Lazy Moose was a café of sorts." Sam looked around. This certainly didn't look like any church he'd ever been to.

"Yes, that's right. Well, hurry and take your places, and after the meeting, we'll figure out a plan to find your sister."

Sam sat down around the table and watched Stacey as she walked through the kitchen door. She turned and gave him a little wave and a look of, *what are we doing here?* before disappearing. He wondered how he could have been so lucky to find someone who was okay chasing all over the country to find his sister, someone who accepted and gave so easily. Not sure he could handle the current crisis without her, he felt Stacey had graced his life at just the right time.

President Heath introduced Sam to the group. Brother Danielson wasn't much older than Sam but said he had five children. Brother Alder was an elderly man who looked a little confused but happy to greet a new face. The other three men stood and put their hands out to Sam in hearty handshakes but didn't say anything.

"So, let's get back to the lesson," President Heath said.

Sam tried to keep his eyes open, but the next thing he knew Stacey was waking him with a light kiss. He struggled for a second in that half-awake and half-asleep stage, and when he opened his eyes, her face was in front of his. Two others were there, looking on in amusement; President Heath, sitting at the table, and a woman, who he assumed to be Sunny Day. Suddenly, he felt like Dorothy in *The Wizard of Oz.*

"And you were there, and you were there too," he said groggily.

Stacey laughed. She was clearly the only one who got his joke.

A pleasant odor assailed his senses and he realized that along with going without sleep, he hadn't eaten anything since the tiny finger sandwiches at Herman and Maggie's wedding.

"Hi Sam, I'm Sunny. I've got some food cooking for you. Stacey informed me you haven't eaten in a while."

Sam tried to shake the sleepiness from his mind, a sleepiness that made him feel dull and thick, like he couldn't quite remember what he was doing in a café with strangers. But finally his head cleared and he found himself eating a wonderful meal of cornbread and stew, family style.

He remembered fully his conversation with Jack Heath from the night before. "Tell me everything you know about Kelli," he suddenly voiced.

"Well, look at that, my food's got him human again." Sunny began the story with finding Kelli and Mary by the white crosses and ended with the phone call from the police in Bozeman.

"She's desperate," Sam responded. "Whatever is going on in her mind has caused her to do things completely out of character. First the polygamy, now running from the police."

"Polygamy?" President Heath asked.

"Oh, you didn't know?" Sam asked.

"No, all she would do is cry when I tried to talk to her and say that she did unforgivable things."

Sam felt his heart breaking. If only she'd come to him, he could have helped her see that she had been manipulated in the worst way. "Now the most frightening question is, what will this group do when they find her? If they felt they had to hire a detective, and if they think Kelli actually kidnapped the younger girl, then Kelli could be in real danger."

"I don't know. There is a polygamist group down south of Big Sky. They've always seemed harmless to me," Jack said.

"Yeah, well, I know some groups are like that—just misguided and stuck in the past, but some use violence to control their congregations. Lots of murders have been committed by some of the more fanatical groups. Ever heard of the LeBarons or Laffertys? They killed because of supposed revelations. We can't assume this group has Kelli's best interests in mind," Sam explained.

"You're right," Sunny said. "We have to find her before they do."

"So we need to go to Bozeman and start looking, before they get wind of her run-in with the police." Sam looked intently at Stacey.

Stacey gripped Sam's hand and he gave it a tender squeeze. "Do you really think she'd stay in Bozeman? Realistically?"

"Probably not, but what else have we got?" Sam asked.

"Right," Sunny said, "and she did stay here with me for this whole month. I kind of got the feeling she knew it was dangerous to stay here, but she couldn't get up the gumption to go. She felt exhausted in a way, and must've needed someone to take care of her."

"And Sunny's the perfect one for that," Jack added. "So if she's lucky enough to find someone she felt safe with, she might just stay put for a while. And if she left Bozeman, she'd have to purchase a bus ticket or something, or hitchhike, so surely someone would've seen her."

"I don't think Kelli would ever hitchhike. 'Course I didn't think in a million years that she'd ever do any of this stuff," Sam said. "So what you think, President, is that for the time being she could still be in Bozeman. Right?"

"Oh, just call me Jack. Logically no, but probably yes."

"And that's not too far from here?" Sam asked. "Just over an hour, but we could get up there. Spend a few hours today talking to people—bus stations, college kids, grocery stores, or anyplace she'd have to go."

"We know where she abandoned the car, so we can start there. It was right near the college campus," Sunny suggested. "Or since we won't have much time, we can make some phone calls from here, and head up in the morning. I can get Marty and maybe his wife to run this place. And Jack could take off work, right?"

"Uh . . . uh . . ." Jack stammered.

"I mean, you can kill century-old trees any day of the week, can't you?" Sunny asked with a grin.

Sam looked at Jack and he was smiling. "Yeah, guess I could put that off for another day."

chapter 20

too many mormons, even in montana

Around nine thirty Sunday morning, Kelli searched Amber's apartment for something to read, anything, but didn't find any printed material except for a TV guide and some beauty-college textbooks. There was a television, but Kelli thought that might wake Amber, so when she turned it on, she kept the volume off, letting the images flash in front of her. She stared listlessly as an image of a golfer walking up to the green appeared. Suddenly someone knocked on the door, and Kelli jumped. She was about to hide, afraid of who it might be, when Tony, the guitar man, poked his head in. "Hey . . . Cindy?" he asked incredulously. "Is that you?"

Kelli automatically looked around the room to see if someone else was there before remembering that that was her name. She tugged at her new black hair.

"Oh, this?"

"Boy, you *are* trying to hide from something. I mean, no one would purposely do that to themselves if they weren't, except for Amber, of course, and her friends, but this just isn't you."

"That's the point." Kelli didn't budge from her seat.

"Oh yeah, right. Disguise. Well, anyway I was hoping you'd changed your mind and would come to church with me. Please," he added. He was wearing a white, crisply ironed shirt, a tie, and his hair was neatly combed.

"Well, I must say, Tony. That look just isn't you either. Your hair isn't even shaggy anymore."

"Sure it's me. This is me, too," he said.

"Well, then, *this* is me, too."

"Ok. Well anyway, you're all ready to go with that nice skirt and blouse on."

"The only clothes I have, actually," Kelli said.

"It'll be fun. And afterward, I think they're having a linger-longer. That means the bish—I mean our church leader's family—will have food at their house."

"Were you going to say bishop?"

"Yeah."

"So you're a Mormon, right?"

"Yeah. I thought maybe if you knew, you wouldn't come. But please come. I'd love to have you spend the day with me."

"Why?" Kelli couldn't believe that he was a Mormon.

"Because you're cute, even with that haircut, and seem nice, and maybe you'd feel some peace. I'm just trying to help."

The truth was that the idea of hanging out in this apartment all day, watching silent television, was disturbing to her, so Kelli went into the bathroom and washed her face. She had a little makeup in her purse—not the kind Amber wore, but the kind that looked natural with her fair skin. It didn't take her long to get ready. There was really very little she could do with her hair except wear it straight up, but she still wanted to make sure she didn't look like Kelli Carson, and she had to admit that, even with her regular makeup, she didn't.

"Okay, let's go. But promise me you won't make me say anything in your church, like answer questions about myself, or you know, other stuff."

Tony smiled, not a half smile, like the first time she'd seen him, but a full, I-can't-help-but-be-happy smile. "You look great, really. I guess I could get used to your hair."

It was late afternoon by the time the meetings, the dinner, and visiting were over. It wasn't as bad as Kelli had imagined. It was awkward at first, listening to lessons, speakers, and people who sounded so familiar to her, yet, at the same time, they didn't. There was one time when someone asked her name and she'd started to say "Kelli." The woman, dressed in a purple, floral-print dress, was big bosomed, and so much like the kind of woman who prompted warm feelings about her own mother, that Kelli hadn't noticed. But Tony had given her a sidelong glance. Now they were driving through town, back toward the apartment building.

"So, what's your real name? Starts with a 'K' sound right?" Tony asked casually.

It was then Kelli saw it, her car, sitting outside a 7-Eleven. "Stop!" she yelled.

"Boy, when you need to go, you really need to go. You mean here?" Tony pulled into the parking lot, and before he could even get the car to a complete stop, Kelli jumped out of Tony's car and ran up to her car. The license plates had been changed. *At least Mary Rachel has done that much,* she thought, but still it was easy to recognize. It had the exact ding in the front driver's side. Kelli was checking the doors to see if they were locked when she heard a booming voice.

"Get your hands off that car." She turned to see a man in his early twenties wearing a black T-shirt with the sleeves ripped off, ragged jeans, and boots. He was carrying a Big Gulp.

"Uh, where'd you get this car?" Kelli asked.

"And what's it to you?"

"It's my car. Well, or was my car until—"

"Until you sold it. Now it's my girlfriend's."

"Your girlfriend—is she really young, blond hair, a few freckles across her nose."

"No."

Kelli realized that she may not look that way anymore. "Well how long have you known her?"

"Another thing that's none of your business," he said.

By now Tony had wandered over from his car. "Look, you don't need to be hostile. She's just asking you some questions."

"And who are you—the police?"

"Look, this was her car—now it seems to be your girlfriend's. Just answer her questions for her."

"Or you'll what? Wrap that skinny tie of yours around my neck, huh?"

"You might be interested in knowing that your girlfriend is only sixteen years old. I think there's a law—" Kelli began.

"No she ain't. Known her since she was sixteen myself and now she's twenty-two." He took a sip of his Big Gulp and just realized he'd given Kelli the information they wanted. "Anyway, I know she's not sixteen. And this car she bought legitimate." The man started getting into the car.

"Please, let us talk to your girlfriend. I'm looking for the girl who sold her the car. It's really important. I won't try to take it back from her, really."

"Why should I believe you?" He started the engine and began to back out. "Get lost."

"Come on," Kelli grabbed Tony's arm and ran to the car. "Follow him."

"What? He could pummel us. He's bigger than . . ."

"Just do it," Kelli screamed.

Tony looked chagrined, but began to follow the blue Ford Escort anyway.

"Stay back just far enough so he doesn't notice us. Maybe he won't know we're following."

The man didn't seem to notice that they were following and headed east at an average pace. Tony looked straight ahead, determined not to lose sight of the Escort. After three blocks, the Escort turned south, then pulled in front of a small, frame house. The man got out of his car, placed the Big Gulp on the ground and opened the hood of the car. As he stuck his head under it, Tony and Kelli parked just out of sight.

Tony looked at Kelli. "Look, I'm sticking my neck out for you and you don't give me any explanations and won't even tell me your real name. Get my problem here?"

Kelli didn't even know how to explain her problems to herself, let alone to this friendly young man driving her around. "Yes, you're right. I've been very selfish to ask you to follow him. But please don't ask anything about me. It's better this way. I'm looking for a girl who drove that car. She could be in real danger—we both could be."

"The law?"

"Sure the law, but they aren't the ones I'm afraid of. Please don't," Kelli pleaded.

Tony leaned on the steering wheel and sighed. "Okay, now what do we do?"

"Just wait for a minute."

They sat in the car for close to a half hour before the man went into the house. "We've got to find out if there's a woman in that house."

"Let's just go knock on the door. If we're lucky, she answers, if not, we may see something." Tony drove the remaining way to the house and started getting out. "Come on."

"Tony, I don't want to involve you in all this, maybe we should just go back."

"A little too late. I'm involved. Coming with?" Tony asked.

Tony strode toward the house, and Kelli sprinted to catch up. She felt her heart pounding when Tony pushed the doorbell. She was scared, not just of the man and what he might do when he saw them again, but also of finding out something she wasn't sure she wanted to know.

Kelli didn't have to look twice to see that the woman who answered the door wasn't Mary. She was much taller, heavier, and older. "Look, we aren't interested. We've already got our own religion." She started to shut the door.

"Who sold you the car?" Kelli managed to blurt out.

"What?" the woman opened the door back up.

"The girl who sold you the car, was she young, about sixteen, freckles, short?"

"Sounds like her. Why?" the woman asked.

"You've got some nerve, following me here. Ought to call the police." The man appeared behind the woman and started to push in front of her.

"Don't think you should do that, considering you bought stolen property," Tony added.

"If that car was hot, I had no idea," the woman said.

"Look, we aren't here to get you into trouble or blame you for anything. I'm just looking for the girl. She's a friend of mine and there are people looking for her who want to harm her, that's all."

"People? What kind of people?" she asked.

"People-who-beat-her-up kind of people," Kelli answered.

"And you won't try and take the car back? 'Cause really it isn't worth much. On its last leg, Garth says."

"I won't try and take the car back. That would get my friend into trouble too, and I don't want to do that." Kelli looked into the woman's face. She'd had a hard life, she thought, but was caring.

"I don't know where she is now. We met her at a flea market out at the county fairgrounds last weekend. Everyone parks their cars to sell their junk, but when we asked to see her stuff, she said the only thing she had to sell was this car. Me and Garth needed another car. We'd been getting by on his '72 Chrysler. Garth's good with cars, so he keeps that thing purring, but still it's hard when we both work and have just the one car. We asked what she wanted for it and she asked what we had. Garth pulled out his wallet and had seventy-five dollars in it. He asked her if that was enough, didn't you Garth?"

"That was after I checked the engine over first and listened to it. Figured it was worth that, but not more, being dented and all."

Kelli cringed. The car was a '95, and although arguably a piece of junk, it was certainly worth a lot more than that. The new set of tires she'd purchased in January had cost her a hundred and fifty alone.

"The girl, your friend, she hesitated and said something like she needed more, so I got out my purse and pulled out every dollar I had—thirty-nine, I think. It was my mad money. I was hoping to find some new furniture, ya know? She still wanted more than that and so I gave her a coupon."

"A coupon?"

"Yeah, the coupon is worth at least fifty dollars. We sell them at the place I work, out on North Higgins, the Burger Barn. Anyway we sell them for thirty dollars, but like I said, they'll get you more than fifty dollars' worth of burgers and fries. Anyway, that seemed to clinch the deal and she handed us the keys, said the title and stuff was in the glove compartment, but it wasn't there. I guess I probably knew then that the car was hot, but . . ."

"No way, Tami, we did not know. No way," Garth said.

"Well anyway, I hope that helps you find your friend. I saw her eating just a couple of days after that out at my work. I could tell she was kind of embarrassed to see me, so I didn't say anything to her. To tell you the truth, that coupon excited her more than the money did. But, come to think of it, she didn't have blond hair. I don't remember what color, but I know it wasn't blond."

"Now what?" Tony asked when they got back in the car.

"Well, for now, let's go back to the apartment and then I've got to figure out a way to hang out at the Burger Barn until I find her."

chapter 21

curveballs

Sunny remembered when the doctor had asked that she and Shane come into his office. They knew then that something was wrong. Good news could be told over the phone. It seemed strange now that the office was permanently etched in her mind. Even the doctor's desk—it was large and walnut with double-beveled corners. And on the south edge of the desk sat the phone. It was vintage black with gold dials. There were four blocks of wood in a metal tray that made up his desk calendar, plus a family photo with five children and a lovely blond wife, posing in front of a studio background of autumn leaves. The doctor held Shane's folder in his large hands. He had a gold ring on his left hand and tiny nicks on his knuckles. He opened the folder, cleared his throat, and looked past them at some distant spot on the wall, maybe at the wallpaper of ducks with hunters in various poses. Occasionally he would glance back down at the folder, avoiding eye contact. Strange, also, that she couldn't recall the doctor's face. She knew he wore black-rimmed glasses and that he had a mole above the corner of his mouth, but his face was out of focus.

Walking back to the car, Sunny had willed her feet to move, willed herself not to cry, not to let Shane know that hope had just been sucked out of her. "We'll fight it together. What do they know?" she'd heard Shane say.

"Yes, of course. Lots of medical miracles happen every day. We'll get the best doctors, we'll . . ." but even before she'd reached the car door, her body trembled with sobs and tears flowed. How could she go on living without Shane? Shane had enveloped her in his arms then and she remembered the dampness her tears had made on his cotton shirt. "It could be worse," he'd said. "If it were you, it would be worse. If it had to be one of us, then I'm glad it's me. God knew which one of us could go on living without the other, which one of us could get past this and still be okay."

"Why either of us?" she'd asked.

"I don't know. Just the way the cards are stacked, I guess."

* * *

It occurred to Sunny that her life was made up of thousands and thousands of such snippets in time. Quick memories. She'd always thought that the really big events were the turning points that determined the thread one's life would take, but looking back, she decided it was actually the opposite. Seemingly insignificant acts had enormous consequences. When she walked away from her boyfriend's van, when the missionaries gave her a ride, when Shane had shown up at the antiwar rally bringing her a sandwich—these were little inconsequential things, but they'd set her on a certain path.

Life, she decided, was similar to those young adult mystery books that had been popular for a while. Choose your own ending, one, two, or three. But with life it was even more complicated. It wasn't one, two, or three, but more like if you chose to go to the antiwar rally, you'd meet a wonderful man to marry, but you'd lose the only child you'd have with him and he would die young. What if she had married someone else, lived not in Montana but in Florida, and he was a successful dentist and lived to be a hundred? That possibility could just as easily have happened. A thousand different lives were possible, but only one per customer. *You choose,* she mused. Still, when Sunny looked back on the snapshots of time, the vignettes that made up her life, she wouldn't trade them for any of the other possibilities. She wondered what would happen if she could get together with a whole bunch of people, everyone bringing their photo albums to the bargaining table. She imagined the conversations: "Here, I'll trade Susie's birthday party for your first ride on the Ferris wheel. Or, how about trading my trip to Japan for your ramshackle house in Montana, but only if you'll trade my alcoholic husband for yours dying of cancer at age thirty-one." Would she trade any of her snapshots? Sunny doubted that she would. She'd probably leave with the same photos in her album of life that she had brought with her. Sure, if she could erase some of them altogether—like that moment in the doctor's office—she would, but she was afraid erasing that moment would erase all the memories before that. Like the wonderful times with Shane—standing under a waterfall on the Clark's Fork River, hand in hand, mouths open, and tasting the water as it drenched their clothes, or riding horses with him in the Big Belt Forest on steep trails, or the party he threw for her thirtieth birthday, and surprised her with a visit from her mother and sister. If she traded the snapshot of Shane, his cancer, his death, she'd have to trade his life, too. This was her life, the good with the bad. And just when she thought she was getting the hang of living alone, with the routine of her daily activity, a young woman had shown up and thrown her a curveball. And this one didn't occupy just one snapshot, she took up a whole page, and who knew where it would end?

* * *

Marty's wife, Anne, agreed to help out at the Lazy Moose for a day or two while Sunny ran up to Bozeman to investigate. Sunny hoped not only to find Kelli, but also to get her car out of the impound lot. Jack would be along any minute to pick her up. She finished getting ready, then walked down to the end of her lane to meet him. It was a warmer day than they'd had in a long time. Sunny had previously planted wildflowers along her path and she noticed some green heads were pushing through the dark loamy soil alongside the dirt lane. Later, in June and July, the roadside would be bursting with an array of color. The sun was shining through the lodgepole pines, casting beams of light across her property. Since she had quit smoking, she'd noticed that her senses were more alive, and everything around her impressed her. Just when she was contemplating her peaceful surrounding, Jack's pickup came barreling around the corner. When he saw her, he slammed on his brakes and skidded, causing deep ruts in her muddy road and splattering his shiny truck.

"You should pave your lane, Sunny, or at the very least have it graveled," Jack said out the open window.

"I don't want pavement and I can't afford gravel either."

"Look what it did to my truck," he motioned to the mud-splattered sides.

"And look what that fuel-sucking monstrosity did to my lane. My car will high center on those deep ruts."

"Come on, get in. We've got stuff to do. I'll send a backhoe in, have your road fixed, and have them gravel it while they're here."

"I can't afford it," she protested.

As Sunny got in the truck and settled into its tan leather interior, Jack was already on his cell phone ordering the work to be done.

"Jack, I won't take charity, at least from you I won't."

He held his hand up to shush her, finished his phone call, then said, "You could afford it though, if it weren't for your causes. Saving Mother Earth can be expensive. Besides that, everyone in town knows that if you're down on your luck you can get a free meal at the Lazy Moose."

"They do?" Sunny asked, surprised.

"Sure, it's common knowledge."

She surrendered. "Well, thanks, it's very generous of you to do this for me."

"Think nothing of it," he said, grinning. "I thought it would make up for the great job of housecleaning you did for me."

Sunny sighed. He would never believe her that she hadn't done it.

Willie Nelson's voice, on the verge of breaking, serenaded from the speakers. "Is this a CD?" Sunny asked.

"Yes. Like it? If not, pick something else. The case is under the seat if you want to choose something else."

"Actually, I really like him. He was the one singer who Shane and I enjoyed together."

"Oh? What kind of music do you like?"

"I like most music from the '60s—Baez, Guthrie, Dylan, you know, the purists, but I also enjoy the Beatles, Grateful Dead, and others. How about you?"

Jack laughed. "Could guess those. But no, I guess I'd have to say I'm sort of a purist as well. Pure country."

Sunny was thinking that Jack's first wife leaving him the way she did was just like many country songs, but of course she didn't say anything. He'd been through enough.

As if reading her thoughts, Jack suddenly said, "You know, I just got an idea. Remember when I told you about my first marriage? The whole pork-chop scene would be a great country song. Maybe I'll play around with some lyrics and come up with something." Jack smiled.

"You write music?"

"Sure, a little. Just to play and sing on my banjo or guitar. I'm in a little band. You might have heard of us—The Cattle Rustlers."

He glanced at her when he said it. Was he trying to impress her? Even if he wasn't, she was impressed, but tried not to show it. "I don't know, where do you play?"

"Unfortunately, besides the county fair and a few other gigs, mostly bars all the way up to Whitefish. I guess I ought to quit the band, you know, now."

"Now what?"

"Now that I'm a branch president. Doesn't seem quite right, playing in bars I mean. I don't drink or anything of course, but the atmosphere isn't the best."

"Yeah, I can see your dilemma, besides it being kind of hard to explain to your flock," she agreed.

"I wouldn't feel too bad about leaving if I weren't the lead singer."

Another surprise. Sunny looked out the window at the passing scenery. By now they were out of the forested area and in the open. "Life is complicated."

"How's that?" Jack asked.

"Complicated, I said. Your band, your marriages, kids, the diner, the church, and then to really make things difficult, Kelli 'Brewer' Carson."

"And technically she's not even part of my flock, so to speak. Really, Sunny, both of us should be taking care of the Danielsons, Edna, and Brother Bradford. But we just can't leave well enough alone, can we?"

"Still, aren't we obligated to do what we can when we know someone needs us? '. . .The least of these'?" Sunny asked.

"We could've left it for Sam and his girlfriend. What's her name?"

"Stacey. Could we though? In good conscience? When I stopped at those crosses and took Kelli home with me, from there on I had to follow it through, and you, Jack, you asked her to help out with the branch. Don't forget those goodwill runs she did with us. You can't just forget about her."

"I know." Jack nodded.

They exited off the highway and into Bozeman. "Sam and Stacey are going to canvas the apartment buildings around the university and go out from there, and they'll check the homeless shelter, cheap motels, and so forth. We're supposed to check all the transportation centers, grocery stores, any other places she might have gone. And we know where to begin—a block away from the university."

Jack nodded. "One problem, though, is that photo Sam gave us. It really doesn't look like she does now with her curly brown hair."

Sunny looked at the photograph again. "No, but it isn't just the hair. It's the look on her face. Sam said this photo was taken at his brother's wedding a couple of years ago, and in this picture, she looks happy, hopeful. She doesn't look like that now, does she?"

"One good thing we have going for us is the clothes you said she was wearing when she left. She'll stand out in those clothes." Jack pulled into a grocery store parking lot.

"Funny though, she said she bought them because she wanted to blend in."

"All right. I'll head over to the Laundromat there and you take the grocery store and meet me back here in ten minutes."

chapter 22

good news and bad news

Sam and Stacey began where they knew Kelli had left Sunny's car. Sam drove the pickup and parked it in the parking lot. "Okay, here's where she left Sunny's car. She would've been in a hurry—so which way would she run?" Sam thought aloud.

Stacey began to walk toward some low-lying shrubs that surrounded an apartment building. "My guess is that she would hide in those bushes until the coast was clear. Either that or head right into the middle of campus, hoping to blend in with the students." Stacey had a shoulder bag and inside it her cell phone began to ring. She grabbed it. "Hello? Yeah, he's right here. It's Mel."

"Uh-oh," Sam said, grabbing the phone. "Yeah, Mel, how are things?"

"Not good. I've really tried covering things for you the best I could, but now the owner says he's had it up to his eyeballs in your not being responsible anymore. Look, I had to come right out and tell him about your sister missing, trying to win sympathy for you. And he just said for you to turn it over to the police and you'd better haul buns back here quick. He said if you aren't back to work by tomorrow morning, you'll be back to being a yard man, mucking out stalls. He's serious, Sam." Sam let the words sink in.

"Thanks for the warning, Mel."

"What are you going to do?

"Pick me out a good shovel and leave it by the stalls."

"Sam, you'll be back to minimum wage. Look, there's more. He's giving me your job," Mel continued.

"Hey, congratulations." Sam glanced at Stacey and winked.

"It's not the way I'd wanna get it," Mel said.

"Don't worry about it. Look, gotta go." Sam handed Stacey the cell phone back.

"Bad news, huh?"

"Looks like I suddenly have a lot more time on my hands." Though outwardly optimistic, Sam sighed inwardly, realizing that there was no way that he could now ask Stacey to marry him. He had nothing to offer.

After a discouraging morning of finding very few students home in their apartments, being finals week, Sam and Stacey headed to the library on campus. Sam approached some students studying and showed them the photo he was carrying, explaining that Kelli would have a different hair color. Everyone glanced at it and shook their heads no. Stacey had a separate photo and did the same thing on another floor. When they had covered all five floors, they met in the downstairs lobby.

"Any luck?" Sam asked.

"None for you?"

"No, and I have the feeling even if they did know they wouldn't tell me. Do you get the feeling that because they aren't sure why we're looking for her, they aren't talking?"

Stacey slipped her arm into his. "Kind of seems like it. Why don't we go check out the eating areas and get something to eat?"

They strolled across the beautiful campus and found a student eating area called Union Market. The gold-and-brown booths and tables were filled with students. Sam couldn't help but be frustrated when he saw how many more people they still needed to talk to. While Stacey picked out some lunch for them, he walked around talking to students in the cafeteria.

"Hi, I'm Sam. This is my sister and she is missing. She's been seen in this area and I was wondering—"

A young man grabbed the photo and examined it. "Same girl that other guy is looking for. Photo's different, but it looks like her. No, haven't seen her."

Sam assumed he meant Jack Heath. "Uh, about fifty?"

"Nah, I think this man was younger, maybe thirty-something. He was dressed in a grayish suit, I think. Asked about another girl, too."

"When was this?"

"Yesterday. I was at my apartment. He was knocking on doors. I thought he was a salesman, but he said he was a private investigator."

Sam felt sick. "Okay, thanks." He could see Stacey motioning to him. "Do me a favor," he told the boy quickly. "If you see the private investigator or my sister, will you give me a call at this number?" He handed him a card with Stacey's cell number. "And don't tell the detective anything. He's working for someone who could harm her."

"How do I know it's not the other way around?" the student asked.

"You don't, but—"

"Okay—I believe you for some reason. Good luck finding her. I'll spread the word around my apartment building."

"Bad news," Sam said, sitting down in the booth with Stacey. "The detective's already been here."

"Well, here's some good news for you. Jack just called and said they stopped at a 7-Eleven store where a guy witnessed an argument yesterday between a guy and a girl who thought he was driving her car. The store clerk there said that even though the girl's hair was short and black, she was wearing the kind of clothes Kelli had on. He said he really noticed the girl because she had a punk haircut and dressy western clothes. The contrast struck him as odd."

"Where'd she go? Did he see?"

"Said she got in a car with a guy wearing a shirt and tie. He couldn't describe the car, but said the car they were arguing over was a blue Ford Escort."

Sam's spine tingled with the news. "That's it. That's Kelli's car. That means she was here yesterday, and that if we drive around we may find the car and can at least talk to the guy." Sam reached over the booth table and grabbed Stacey's hand.

"We'll find her," she said.

chapter 23

accidents waiting

Kelli cut through campus on Tony's black bicycle. It was Monday morning and she would spend the entire day at the Burger Barn waiting for Mary Rachel to show up. May in Montana was so beautiful. The air was crisp, but brimming with the promise of warming up as the day wore on. She passed next to a little duck pond and paused to watch mallards disappearing into the dark water, then bob up. She rode up a sidewalk flanked with maple trees.

"Hey, you. You aren't supposed to ride bikes here," someone warned her.

"Oh, sorry." Kelli jumped off of her bike and walked alongside it. Amber had let Kelli borrow some clothes, so she wore a tight black body suit and a long top with metal studs decorating the top and fringes on the bottom. She felt ridiculous, as if she were dressed for Halloween, but no one paid any attention to her.

She was just about to pass the library, when, in the distance, she noticed a guy with a cowboy hat on. Kelli giggled to herself. She had always been a sucker for any guy in a cowboy hat, but knew that a cowboy wouldn't give her a second look the way she was dressed. She watched the cowboy sitting on the front steps of the library, and every time someone stepped out he would stand up and talk to them. There was something familiar about the way he bobbed his head when he talked and stuffed his left hand in his front pocket. Being in a disguise gave her confidence, and she decided she had nothing to lose by striking up a conversation with him, something she never would have done in Idaho. She would tell him how she noticed the survey or something he was taking and that maybe she could help out. When she was just about close enough to say something to him, a cute girl joined him. Kelli suddenly realized that not only did she know the girl, but the good-looking guy was her own brother. An array of emotions assaulted her. She ached to run to him, give him a hug, and feel his strength, but restrained herself. Then, pausing just long enough to etch his image in her mind before turning away, she jumped on her bike and rode quickly out of sight.

It was difficult to see as she rode her bike down Main Street with hot tears running down her cheeks. She kept wiping her eyes with one hand and steering with the other. Near Lindley Park, still a block from the Burger Barn, the front tire dropped into a chuck hole. She lost control and sprawled onto the road. She felt the asphalt rip through her leggings, skinning her knees. Before pulling herself up from off the ground, she allowed herself to cry for a few more seconds. Then Kelli picked the bike up and slowly walked it the rest of the way, feeling the blood trickle down her legs. When she reached the Burger Barn, she parked the bike out front and limped inside. She grabbed a handful of napkins out of a dispenser, and found a table where she could keep an eye on both doors. The blood had congealed, and now the leotard stuck to the sores. She dabbed at the wounds anyway and winced from the pain. A quick glance around the room let her know Mary Rachel wasn't there.

"If you want to order something, come up to the counter. We don't wait tables," a voice said. "Oh, it's you. You look different in those clothes."

Kelli looked up to see the woman who had purchased her car. Tami, she remembered. Kelli stood up, glanced into the parking lot, and could see the Escort she once owned parked on the far side.

"I hurt my knees. I thought I'd just hang out here for a while."

"Uh, I can't really let you do that, at least, not if you're not ordering anything. Policy, you know. I haven't seen your friend yet today."

Kelli limped to the service counter. "Could you please give me a hamburger and small fries, but first the fries, and then when I'm all done with those, then I'll have the burger and when I'm all done with that, maybe some water. I need to make this meal last as long as possible."

"Well, okay. I'll find you some bandages, too," the woman said. "That comes to $2.65, okay?"

Kelli knew that at this rate, she'd be out of money in a few days, and since Sam was in the area, heading out of town seemed imperative. With good luck, she would find Mary, and the two could figure out what to do together. Kelli took her fries and sat back down. Before each bite, she would dip them into the ketchup. It took her a whole hour to eat the fries. People stared at her with the Band-Aids on her knees, and she imagined her face was streaked with dirt from the fall. She didn't dare go to the rest room, for fear of missing Mary. Kelli listened to people scold their children for playing with their food, or talk about how nice the weather had turned, or discuss what they'd seen on television the night before. The Burger Barn was a little out of the way to get a lot of business. Most of the tables were empty, but a small crowd of people managed to eat their meals and leave, only to be replaced by others. When Kelli finished the fries, Tami brought out a burger. Kelli managed to stretch the burger through another hour. She was on her last bite when she saw a young woman come in by herself. She was carrying a large backpack and her hair was short, reddish brown, and wavy. Kelli looked down at her food, not wanting Mary Rachel to notice her yet. She watched how Mary avoided eye contact with the woman she'd sold Kelli's car to. Tami raised the volume of her voice, trying to make sure Kelli noticed who had just come in.

Mary had her tray in her hand and was trying to decide where to sit when Kelli stood up and motioned for her to sit by her. Mary Rachel smiled, looked confused, then started toward her. Mary was about to set the tray down, when she suddenly recognized Kelli. For a second, Kelli thought she would drop the tray and bolt, but after hesitating, she sat down.

"How'd you find me?" Mary asked.

"Lucky break. Found the couple you sold my car to," Kelli said.

"Sorry about that. I needed money."

"I know, so do I."

"I figured you were fine staying up there with Sunny."

"Yeah, well, your father hired a detective. He showed up at the diner . . . uh, Sunny's place."

Mary's face turned rigid. "I was afraid of that. I keep thinking I should just go back . . ." she started to laugh nervously.

"No. It isn't safe for you."

"Oh, they'll just beat me again. It's no big deal. It used to happen a lot when I was little, but then my father quit beating me once I was a teenager. After that, I finally learned obedience. Until, you know . . . You look weird—just so you know. What's with the clothes, hair, and the dirty face?"

"Disguise."

"It works. I didn't know you until I was about to sit down. I get tired of eating by myself. That's why I started over here, thought you might be a friend—you know."

"I am." Kelli put the last bite of the burger in her mouth. "So where've you been hanging out?"

"Just around, you know, the bus station, all-night cafés—I move around."

Mary chomped down on her food as if she hadn't eaten anything all day. *Probably, this is her only meal of the day*, Kelli thought.

"I've got a place to stay and you can stay there too, until we can figure out our next move. Nice people, but I feel bad because I haven't paid any rent yet. But at least let's stay there tonight and then we'll go somewhere else in the morning."

Mary Rachel looked uncertain, so Kelli continued to talk. "After you left Sunny's, I started working as a server for her. I wish we could go back there, but now that's out of the question. But what a great woman. And President Heath, he's pretty cool too, sort of crazy and all. He's single and I think he'd be a great match for Sunny if she can ever figure out what a great guy he is. It's strange to think people their age have romantic feelings, but Sunny thinks Jack is a jerk, so I don't know. Actually, he is in a way, but I think she's sort of interested in him, too. She talks like she can't stand him, but when he comes into the diner, I notice her face lights up like a Christmas tree for a second, and then she gets this angry look just as quickly." Mary Rachel didn't look interested, but kept watching the door as she ate. "This guy that lives next to me in the apartment. His name is Tony, and would you believe he's LDS too? I was shocked. What are the chances of running into so many Mormons in Montana? Anyway, he doesn't know that I'm one. And he thinks he's teaching me the gospel. I went to church with him and that evening he bore his testimony to me. He's so sweet you wouldn't believe it. He makes up songs, and has a great voice, and plays the guitar."

Mary finished her food. "We were taught from as long as I could remember to hate Mormons. You know, because you let the government tell you what to do and gave up the principle of polygamy."

"Really? Kevin never mentioned he was supposed to hate me. Do they ever tell you that in the early days of the church only some were called to live polygamy? That you didn't just decide for yourself. And the women weren't coerced like you would've been. And the Lord revealed to a prophet that it was no longer needed."

Mary wiped her mouth with a paper napkin. "Yeah, well—no. But you don't have to tell me. With my father beating me and giving me no choice, I gave up the last thread of belief that it was right. I didn't think it was anyway. It felt sick to me. You're the one I can't figure out. You were on the outside. Life had to be good for you, and then you join. What on earth for?"

"It's a long story. Basically, I liked being around Kevin, and somehow, in all our long conversations, it started to make sense to me. And I thought I could escape my past by living the minimalist lifestyle in some out-of-the-way community. I also thought that by joining, I'd be forgiven of all my past sins. It seemed like the answer. But by the time I found out that I was going to be required to marry Richard, your father, I felt more or less trapped. Even then though, I still had this thread of hope that it would turn out right. I kept trying to convince myself, you know." Talking about her experience brought tears to her eyes and she felt her throat feel tight. "I just want to feel whole."

"Yeah, me too. When did you come to your senses?"

"When I saw your father beat you. It wasn't the first doubt I had. There had been lots all along, and if I had been paying attention, I would never have been there in the first place you know? But then to hear Richard announce what an honor it would be for you to marry the prophet. I thought, 'No way. She's too young.' That was the last straw."

Mary sighed. "This life on the outside is hard. Sometimes I think I ought to go back. I miss them you know—even my father."

"Yeah, I know. I miss my family also. But after what . . ." Kelli let her words trail off.

Mary looked out the window. "My father says guitars, drums— any kind of instrument used in rock bands—are of the devil. So I've never really heard someone play the guitar, like your friend."

"Oh, well I'm sure you're unlearning a lot of things. I know I am."

"I'm confused I guess. I mean, I keep running into people who seem to be good, like Sunny, you, and a few people I've met since then. And I was always taught that outside of our family compound, the world is an evil place, you know?"

"Yeah, I know." Kelli watched as Mary Rachel took a sip of her water. "What about Kevin though? Why did he have so much freedom? He danced with me you know."

"The men all have more freedom, but he was sent out to recruit someone. I imagine you appealed to him."

After finishing their meals, Kelli coaxed Mary outside. "Think we can ride double on a bike for eight blocks?"

"Sure, but I'll do the pedaling. By the looks of the holes in those tights, you can't ride a bike at all."

Kelli sat on the hard narrow seat, while Mary stood up as she pedaled. When Kelli was little, she'd often ridden this way with either Brandon or Sam doing the pedaling, and sometimes she even sat on the handle bars. Once, she had been riding on the handle bars with Brandon and, because he couldn't see where he was going, he ran smack into the hood of a slow-moving car. Kelli's body was hurled onto the hood of Mrs. Weston's blue Cadillac. The woman leaped out of her car, screaming hysterically. Then when she saw that Kelli would be all right, she fainted right on the street, slumped over like she'd been knocked out. The whole thing happened less than a block away from their house. Neither their mom nor dad had been home, so Sam, barely fourteen, but old enough to drive in the state of Idaho, took all three to the hospital. With nothing else to drive, he'd driven Mrs. Weston's Cadillac. Kelli sat in the back with Brandon, holding blood-soaked napkins to her chin as blood oozed out the inch-long gash. Mrs. Weston sat in the front, pale and trembling.

Thinking about the memory, Kelli ran her finger along the old scar. "Listen, I'll get down and jog beside you. I'm afraid you'll have an accident this way."

"Well, whatever," Mary Rachel said.

When they got close to the apartment building, Kelli could see Tony out front playing his guitar and Amber sitting cross-legged filing her nails.

"Hi guys, this is Mary Rachel. Mind if she hangs with us for just a while?" Kelli asked.

"Just Mary, please. I'm dropping the Rachel."

"First of all, what happened to you?" Amber asked.

Kelli looked down at the holes in her leggings. "Oh sorry Amber, I ruined your clothes."

She waved a dismissive hand in the air to signify that it didn't matter and said, "What kind of trouble are you both in? I don't mean to complain, but if they get to digging too deep, they're going to find a couple of things they can hang me out to dry on. Today some guy comes looking for the both of you. He showed me a couple of photos that looked nothing like you do now, but then he explained you'd probably look differently, so I took a second look."

Knowing how Sam could sweet-talk women, Kelli knew she would've probably given her away. "Good-looking cowboy?"

"Not this dude. He looked more like a CEO than a cowboy. Longer, blow-dry styled hair. I always notice the hair. Actually, I thought a better haircut would've taken ten years off—it dated him."

"Forget the haircut. What'd you tell him?" Kelli asked.

"Nothing," Amber said.

"You didn't say anything that would give us away?"

"No. I was real cool like. I'm like, 'let me take a good look at those photos, 'cause I do hair, so maybe they came into our place to have their hair done, you know.' Then I looked closely and said something like, 'I'm real good with faces. If they'da come in I'd remember.' Really, he won't be back here."

Kelli felt relieved. Amber was convincing.

Tony started strumming his guitar again and sang, "*Young girl get out of my life. My love for you is way out of way out of line—better run girl—you're much too young girl.*"

"Do you ever listen to anything besides the oldies station?" Kelli asked.

"Oldies? I thought he was making all these songs up," Amber said.

Tony laughed. "I mix in some original stuff. Anyway, how old are you Mary? You really do look young."

"I'm eighteen," Mary said.

Close enough, Kelly thought.

"Guess this one doesn't have any money either, right?" Amber asked.

"Right. But we'll work on that," Kelli said.

"Don't worry about it. No skin off my nose." Amber pulled herself up off the cement and leaned against the wall.

"So is your real name Mary, Mary?" Tony asked.

"Yes."

"And are you two drug dealers or . . . ?" Tony trailed off.

Mary laughed, "You want to know the truth, huh? Okay this is it. Kelli here—"

"Kelli?" Tony interrupted and glanced sidelong at Kelli. "So that's your name."

"Yeah. Kelli joined our polygamist church awhile back, but then saw my father beating me because I don't want to become the fifth wife of our prophet. She got scared and ran away. I knew she was running away, so I hid in her car and came with her. Then Kelli panicked because of some white crosses on the side of a road. I still don't know why, but this nice woman took us in for the night. I stole a little money from her—borrowed really—and left Kelli there with her. But then Kelli got nervous when some guy, probably the same one with the styled hair, showed up in, what's the name of that town—Trout something?"

"Stop, Mary. You're saying way too much," Kelli said.

"Look, I'm tired of all this running. I feel like I have to go back, like I'm supposed to go back. I've broken too many promises, and besides, I'm about out of burger coupons."

Kelli glanced at Tony. He had been laughing, probably because he thought it had all been a joke, but now his face turned serious as he intently studied Mary.

"No kidding? Now that is something I couldn't have guessed." Tony began to pluck a tune out on his guitar. *"Blackbird singing in the dead of night. Take these broken wings and learn to fly . . . blackbird fly."* He stopped playing and cocked his head as if listening to something. Somehow none of them had noticed the ordinary green sedan in the parking lot, hadn't noticed the blond man with styled hair walk silently up the stairs. Now they were startled by a smooth, low voice.

"Mary Rachel, come with me and no one will get hurt." The man pointed a gun right at them.

Kelli was about to scream as Amber did, but stopped when the man threatened again to shoot if anyone made another peep. Mary was stoic. If she was frightened her face didn't show it. *A poker face,* Kelli thought. It was impossible to guess what she was thinking. Mary stood up from the porch and stuck her hand out to Tony. "Thanks for the guitar music and the singing. You're the best guitar player I've ever heard."

Kelli knew that he had been the *only* guitar player Mary had ever heard but she didn't smile at the joke. Kelli didn't know whether to run or try to knock the man down or what, but when the man spoke again, she realized he hadn't even recognized her.

"I'll be back for the other one. You can count on it. If you see her, tell her," the man said in a low, threatening tone.

Kelli shot a frightened look at Mary. Mary winked at her and allowed the man to lead her away.

"Hey, the police will be here any second," Tony shouted.

"We'll be long gone by then, but thanks for the warning," the man said.

Amber had already disappeared into her apartment to call the police. Kelli was trembling and couldn't believe how brave sixteen-year-old Mary had been even while walking away with a gun on her. Now Kelli was worried for her own safety. She figured that even though she was able to fool the investigator, she didn't want to take her chances with the police officers again. Tony seemed to be able to read her thoughts.

"Come on," he said.

"Where?"

"Just get in my car."

chapter 24

sunny's big shock

Since Sunny had started going to church again, stopped smoking, and become Relief Society president, she thought back to why she'd quit going to church in the first place. *Distance, that was it.* The ranch Shane had worked on was fifty-eight miles from the nearest Mormon church. They had tried to go a couple of times, but getting Sundays off when Shane was just a ranch hand was next to impossible. Finally, when Sunny started feeling nauseated in the mornings, they had given the idea up altogether. Once, some home teachers had come out to see them. They'd all crowded together in their tiny living room while an older man, his wire-frame glasses resting on his red bulbous nose, read a story from a Church magazine. He continually cleared his throat and glanced up nervously as if expecting them to disagree with something. Why he was uncomfortable, Sunny couldn't imagine. Shane didn't seem to notice. Shane's smile was as big as Montana itself, and his personality just as inviting as the morning sun. Shane laughed and nodded and asked the man questions. The other man said it was time to head back and stood up to leave, but Shane sat him back down and handed them each a piece of Sunny's cornbread with honey, and topped with pats of butter. The warm cornbread seemed to warm the men with each bite they took, and eventually they were swapping stories and laughing as if they'd known Shane all their lives. Sunny was the odd one out, but she didn't mind. Her bulging stomach occupied all her thoughts, and she knew she hadn't been the best of company for Shane lately. She was glad someone from the Church had come to visit, and now she hoped they would come often.

But they hadn't. If Shane had been disappointed he hadn't shown it. He was willing to wait until after she had the baby, after things settled, after calving season, and then they would go back to church together.

* * *

Sunny was glad to have her Volkswagen Bug back. It suited her— the torn upholstery, the temperamental radio with the songs fading in and out, the put-put sound Volkswagens made, and best of all the forty-something miles to the gallon she got. Just as she entered town again, she noticed Jack standing out by the "Heath" sign marking the entrance to his place. His truck was still running and he held a cell phone to his ear. She thought of driving by without stopping, but then realized he was waving for her to pull over.

His vehicle irritated her. It was too big. It polluted and used much more natural resources than was reasonable, and Jack himself cut trees down and built rustic shopping centers with no more thought than she took to swat a fly at the diner. He was the enemy—so why was she happy to see him waving her down?

She stopped her car, shut off the lights, and unrolled her window. "Trouble in the branch?" she shouted.

He held his hand out as if to hush her and continued to talk into the phone. Deciding to tease Jack, Sunny started her car up again and began to back up, then noticed him chasing her down. She stopped again, but he continued to talk on the phone, so she backed up again.

"Just wait. Please," he shouted.

She ignored him and he finally yelled out, "It's about Kelli."

By now he'd put his cell phone back into his pocket. She waited for him to walk the short distance to her window. He leaned in and she could smell his cologne. *Expensive probably, like everything about him except for that Disney tie he wears to Church*, she thought.

"Sunny Day, I didn't think you'd make it back in this rolling death trap, but here you are, looking every bit as beautiful as our sunset." The sun had lowered. A big ball of orange hung above the thick forest west of the road, and the sky was washed with blended pale pinks and warm yellows.

Sunny felt herself blush at the compliment, then inwardly chided herself for being so vain after all these years. He was just flattering her. It had been ages since any man had called her beautiful. She was fifty-two, and beauty had long since been replaced by a more durable look. Crow's-feet fanned from the corners of her blue eyes, and she was softer—everywhere. She guessed that Jack was just buttering her up so she would stop harassing him about his developments. Still, she could feel herself hoping he really meant it, and her girlish dreaming annoyed her most of all. "So what about Kelli?"

"Marty spotted her, at least he thought it was her. In a car with a man. Said he saw the car stop at the diner, then it pulled away again, like maybe they'd changed their mind or something. I was just trying to call Sam and let him know, but Stacey's not answering her cell. Oh, and I have to apologize."

"Anything in particular bothering your conscience, or just everything in general?"

"My house, it's been cleaned up again, and since you were with me, I'm going to have to assume now that it wasn't you taking care of my place. I was kind of hoping it was—you, I mean."

Sunny laughed. "Apology accepted. Anyway, now what?"

"I'm going to follow you up to your place and we'll decide," Jack said.

"Do I have a choice?"

"No, I'm hungry."

"Oh, you mean the diner?"

"No, your place."

Just when Jack was starting to melt her cold feelings toward him, he would jolt her back to reality again by doing something like inviting himself to dinner. They were from two different planets. How could she possibly ever think otherwise?

When she pulled into her lane, she was amazed. The entire quarter of a mile from the main road to her bungalow had been graveled and graded. Her Volkswagen putted evenly along her new smooth road. Jack was just behind her. Now she could see lights flickering in her house window. Although it was unlike her, she must've left them on.

"Surprised." Jack said flatly when he got out of his truck.

"The road? Yes, thanks so much again."

"No, I'm surprised. At you I mean—wasting electricity seems a little out of character."

"Yes, I must've been distracted, but let's go on in and . . ." It was the smell that stopped her from continuing on. It smelled just like her stew, the kind she cooked whenever life wasn't going well, or whenever someone else's life wasn't going well. It was the stew that made her diner famous. "What the—"

"Surprise!" A light was on above the stove, and Kelli was silhouetted as she stirred a pot. The butcher-block counter where Sunny prepared meals looked like vegetable confetti covered it.

"Kelli, I'm so glad you're here. We've been up in Bozeman all day looking for you." Sunny felt such a warmth for Kelli that it startled her. She decided not to say anything about the altered appearance.

A young man with shaggy blond hair stood up from the sofa. "I've heard all about you. You must be Sunny, and I take it you're the branch president, right?"

"Right, and you are?" Jack asked.

"Tony. I met Kelli in Bozeman and today things got a little hairy, so I brought her back to her friends in Trout Haven."

"Tricked me, is what he did. I thought he was taking me to friends of his in Laurel, but anyway, here we are."

"But where's your car?" Sunny asked, "Or did you hitch rides?"

"Parked around back, didn't know who might be following, you know?" Tony said, his face on the verge of a smile.

"By the way, I'm starved. Think there's enough of that stew to go around?" Jack asked.

"Made enough for ten, I think."

"So how did you know how to make that?" Sunny asked. "It's my secret recipe."

"I'm a fast learner and I watched you a couple of times," Kelli said.

"Write it down quick before you forget, and maybe I can post it in the Church newsletter," Jack teased.

"Oh, no you don't, Jack Heath," Sunny warned.

They all crowded around Sunny's small table, their elbows nudging each other as they ate.

"I have a question," Kelli said.

"Yes, what?" Sunny asked.

"By any chance has a cowboy been asking about me?" Kelli asked.

Sunny swallowed the stew. It wasn't quite as good as hers. The herbs were a little off; still, it was good. "Dark hair and eyes, easy laugh, big heart?"

"That would be him. Is he mad at me?"

"Not this cowboy. This cowboy seemed like he wanted nothing more in the whole world than to find you and take you safely home. Seemed like the kind of guy who would only feel anger toward someone who'd talked his sister into giving away their childhood home and marrying into polygamy, but not angry toward her, not his sister," Sunny said, then watched the tears form in Kelli's eyes. "So what do you say? You willing to give him a chance? I think he'll be calling here soon. He and Stacey were going to stay on in Bozeman and look for you longer."

Kelli stopped eating. Tony took her hand and held it. Sunny could tell by the look in Tony's eyes that he was interested in Kelli, but Kelli didn't seem to notice, didn't even seem to notice that he was holding her hand.

"They've got Mary," Kelli said.

"Who has got Mary?" Jack asked.

"A man showed up with a gun and took her. None of us got a chance to see the license plate or anything. We called the police, then we took off to here—didn't want to see if they could figure out it was Kelli they were looking for," Tony answered.

After dinner, they waited around hoping Sam would call. Tony taught them a card game, something he called "Spit." The game was too fast for Sunny. She was feeling a little strange anyway, so she wandered to the window and listened to their laughter. She stepped out on the porch, sat down in her porch swing, and thought about her day.

"Mind if I join you?" Jack was suddenly standing in the doorway.

"Yes, I do mind. I'm thinking," Sunny said.

But he ignored her and sidled up next to her. "Beautiful night. I was just wondering how the no smoking is going?"

"Okay, now that I'm past the worst of it."

"I really can't figure out why you ever smoked in the first place: vegetarian, environmentalist, smoker. Remember that tune from Sesame Street? Used to watch that with my kids: *'One of these things doesn't belong here, one of these things just isn't the same,'* or something like that, and they'd show maybe a fork, a butter knife, and a saw. The idea was—"

"Never had kids, Jack, or a TV. I don't know the show."

"But you see what I mean, don't you?" He put his arm around her, and she felt her entire body shiver. It had been twenty years since Shane's death, and even longer since she'd really been touched by a man like this.

"I do see what you mean. It doesn't fit, I know, me and smoking. It never did. After my baptism, I've always eaten healthily, avoided pills of any kind, taken really good care of myself."

"Yeah, so why did you start?"

"I didn't care much about my life after Shane died. I'm not the type to put a gun to my head—don't own one, even if I had wanted to. Besides, Shane would've been so let down if I hadn't even made an attempt to go on living and loving. That's what he told me, 'You go on living and loving. That's what you do best, Sunny. Don't stop loving the world and loving people. Don't let this get you down.' But of course it had gotten me down. So even though it wasn't a conscious thought exactly, I just decided to shorten my time here on earth, one cigarette at a time. Later, when I found that I could still go on, when I found this diner and finally snapped out of the deep funk I was in, I couldn't stop smoking. Believe me, I've tried often enough. This time though, it worked—a miracle."

Jack smiled. "Well I'm glad you quit. This feels good, doesn't it?" "What?"

"Rocking back and forth on your front porch. Being together."

"The only thing greater than your presumptions is your obvious disregard for the Earth. I don't know which I find more distasteful at the moment."

He had the nerve to ignore her. She couldn't believe it.

"The stars are enchanting tonight aren't they? See that little grouping?" He pointed just above the tip of the largest pine in her yard. "That's Draco, the dragon. If you squint you can imagine his tail."

She squinted and could imagine it. On a clear night in Montana, the stars were endless.

"Ever see the northern lights?" Jack asked.

"Yes. While we worked on the ranch, Shane and I did a couple of times, then once while I lived here. Amazing. A natural fireworks display."

"You know, I'd really like to kiss you except I've never kissed a Relief Society president before. I'm not sure if—"

"Don't then." Sunny stood up abruptly, the swing shifted backward and Jack stood up too.

"I've never dated since Kathy . . . Maybe another time then?"

Sunny looked at his hopeful eyes and laughed. "The whole thing is ridiculous, you know. Too incongruous."

"I don't think it is. I could congrue. Is that a word?" Jack shifted his weight and leaned against one of the slivery pillars that held the ramshackle roof up over her porch.

"No, I don't think it is a word, and even if it is a word, I don't think you could. Congrue, I mean." In that moment, seeing his body tilt with his weight on one leg, the way his jeans bunched at the bottoms above his athletic shoes, his large calloused hand holding onto the post, she felt an attraction for him. Why, she wasn't sure, but just as quickly the moment passed, and she looked away from him and up at the stars. Clouds had already moved in, nearly obliterating Draco, only the tip of his tail visible.

Now she could hear the rumble of a truck and lights pierced the black night. As she peered at the lights, trying to guess who it was, she was overcome by a sudden dizziness and felt a little nauseated. Maybe she was still suffering from withdrawals. Sunny leaned over and felt her chest tighten. In her mind she had an image of a rubber band windup toy and someone was turning and tightening the band, tightening, tightening, tightening. It would snap if they kept on tightening it. She was sweating now, she knew. In fact sweat was drenching her body. Her knees buckled beneath her and she felt her face hit the wood planks of the porch. *What is happening?* She could hear footsteps running on the new gravel path, could feel Jack carrying her, and then she could feel her own bed. Car doors slammed and voices were all around her. The voices finally faded with her consciousness.

chapter 25

healing

Sam now remembered another time when he'd been really worried about Kelli. Life was divided for him—for all of them—into two parts, before the accident and after. Everything was measured either before "it," or after "it." Within a few months of the accident everyone thought Kelli was doing remarkably well, considering what she had been through. She'd kept up with her schoolwork and continued with her extracurricular school activities, even basketball. Life had continued on for all of them. But one day Lisa Lynn Staples, Kelli's best friend, came looking for her after school.

"I thought she was with you," Sam said. It was nearly 5 P.M. by now. If she wasn't with Lisa, where was she?

Lisa shuffled her feet. "Okay, well, see ya. She'll be home soon, I'm sure."

"Lisa."

She was already halfway down the sidewalk, like she couldn't get away fast enough.

"Lisa, get back here!" Sam shouted.

She turned and slowly trudged back to the porch. While she stood there, he noticed how she towered above the shrubs; he remembered when she and Kelli were shorter than the tops of those bushes. "You know something you aren't telling me. What is it?" Sam asked.

He thought she would cry. "I promised I wouldn't tell."

"Tell what?"

"Sam, you know if I told you, I'd be breaking my promise."

"Well, come on in and I'll make you a cup of hot chocolate and you don't have to tell me anything. No harm in that, is there?"

She'd looked uncertain, but stepped through the door and followed him into the kitchen. He hummed while he filled the kettle with water and then set it on the stove. By the time the kettle whistled, Lisa was wringing her hands and glancing at the door, waiting for Kelli to walk through it.

"You said she'd be all right. You seem pretty sure about that," Sam said.

"Yeah, she's all right," Lisa mumbled.

"How come you're so sure? Did she stay after school for something?"

"Not really," Lisa said.

He measured some chocolate powder into two ceramic mugs, poured hot water in them, then stirred the liquid and watched as they turned a creamy brown. He set the cup in front of Lisa Lynn. Her head was bent and he couldn't see her eyes, but guessed she was avoiding him.

"I just don't want you to be mad at me."

"And why would I be? You're Kelli's best friend."

"Because you all are Mormon and . . ."

" . . . And?"

"I just thought it would help her, you know. She's so sad sometimes," Lisa said.

"What would help?"

"To talk to a priest, you know. He's really nice and I told her about him. She doesn't even have to see his face if she doesn't want to. It's easier that way."

"Let me get this straight." Sam smiled. "You sent her to talk to the Catholic priest in Burley—your priest, right?"

"Don't be mad, Sam."

"Now why would I be mad? I would've taken her there myself if she'd just asked me to. I hope she has a ride back home though."

"Oh, she does. My brother was going to pick her up. I just thought they'd be here by now. You know, because she—"

"Didn't want me to know." Sam took a sip of his hot chocolate. Lisa was such a cute girl, and so much fun. He'd loved teaching her and Kelli how to ride horses and barrel race. Lisa had a natural flair for horses. "Tell me why Kelli needed to talk to a priest. Does she think she has something she needs to confess? Is that it?" What that might possibly be Sam had no idea; she was as close to perfect as any fourteen-year-old could be. But then the phone rang and he leaned back on the metal kitchen chair and reached for the receiver.

"Uh, Sam?" the voice asked.

"Yeah?"

"This is Bishop Hansen, is Kelli there yet?"

"No she isn't."

"I think she'll be there in a few minutes. I just wanted to let you know that I'm on my way over. Thought I'd pay her a visit tonight."

"Well, okay. Can I ask why?"

"It's a private matter—you understand that. Someone informed me that she wasn't handling everything as well as we thought she was. By the way, how are you holding up? You and Brandon?"

"We're doing okay. Thanks." Sam hung up the phone. "Well, looks like it's Kelli's night for spiritual guidance. That was our bishop and he seemed to have the idea that Kelli is on her way home." Sam figured the priest must have called him.

Lisa sipped her chocolate again. "Maybe don't tell her I came over. She's probably forgotten by now that we were going to ride horses. I don't want her to guess . . . you know, that I told you." She slipped out the door and he watched her run down the street toward her house.

* * *

Stacey and Sam drove every street in Bozeman looking for the blue Escort before giving up and heading back to Trout Haven. Just as they pulled in front of Sunny's house, they saw Sunny buckle over, clutching her chest as she fell. They parked and ran toward the house, then followed Jack carrying Sunny through the door.

When they bolted through the door, the small house seemed to be bursting with people. Too many people for this cabin that was no larger than Sam's living room. He heard a sharp gasp and some sobbing that he couldn't quite make out. The sound didn't come from Sunny. She was as still as death. Jack was doing CPR on her. Now Sam noticed a woman standing with her back to him in a shadowy corner, giving directions to someone on the phone—probably an emergency crew. The gasping sound he heard might have come from her direction. She was sobbing between her words. She was dressed in some kind of punk clothing, all black, or was it the gothic look? He couldn't keep up. Maybe she was Sunny's daughter. Of course she would be distraught at seeing her mother's apparent heart attack. Sam moved to the bed. Stacey had disappeared from his immediate view, but there was also a younger guy in the room.

"What can I do?" Sam asked the branch president.

"You know CPR?"

"No, but Stacey does. Stacey?"

He turned and saw Stacey talking to the punk girl, and then he noticed them hugging each other. Why was Stacey hugging the punk girl and crying? "Stacey!" he shouted. "Jack needs help doing CPR."

Stacey ran from the girl now, and confidently helped Jack, who was now shouting, "Where are they? They should be here by now." Jack was counting in time with Stacey as she pushed Sunny's chest, then he placed his mouth over Sunny's and blew life-giving breath.

"Dispatch says they will be here any second now. They want to know if she's breathing on her own yet?" Sam could barely understand the punk girl; her sobbing was louder than her words.

"No," Stacey shouted.

The girl with black spiky hair had the telephone cord stretched as far as it would reach, but he still couldn't see her clearly in the shadows.

When the emergency workers flew through the door, carrying a stretcher, Sam heard the phone drop to the floor and the punk girl stepped out of the shadows.

She had short black hair, pale skin with dark circles around her eyes, wore a strange outfit adorned with metallic studs, and had stockings with holes ripped in them. He was staring at the bandages peeking out of those holes, trying to figure out how this young woman had hurt herself. The girl didn't say anything, but was walking toward him, and was crying hard with her face turned down. He noticed her shoulders shaking, indicating that she was out of control and couldn't stop crying. Sam automatically went to the girl to comfort her. She let him hug her. "She'll be all right. Don't cry. They're here now to take her to the hospital."

"But—"

He could feel her small frame shivering. He held her tighter, trying to stop the tiny spasms of her body. What was it about crying women that made him feel as if he had to help them, was *required* to help them? It had always been that way for him.

"I'm so sorry. I'm so sorry," the girl gasped.

"It'll be all right."

"I love you," the girl sobbed.

What? Why is this girl telling me she loves me?

"Tell me about Brandon, is he mad?" she asked.

Finally, it slammed into Sam's mind.

"Kelli?" Sam asked, incredulously.

Sunny was now being loaded into an ambulance. Everyone including Jack and Stacey disappeared with them, and he was left with his sister and some other kid, who seemed about as confused as Sam had felt.

"Are you okay? Are you okay? What did they do to you? Tell me everything." Sam blurted questions and led Kelli to the sofa, pulling her down next to him.

She was sobbing and her shoulders continued to shake. Sam grabbed the quilt and carefully laid it over her. Kelli leaned her head on his shoulder. Sam couldn't believe Kelli's appearance. She looked like some homeless person. Her face was drawn and tired. Her eyes looked hopeless. He tried not to stare, tried to avert his eyes from her so she wouldn't suspect how terrible he thought she looked.

"Look, I've got one more final exam tomorrow, so I'm going to head out," a young man said, after a moment of awkward silence.

The young man was now standing next to the table. "Uh, you are?" Sam asked.

"Tony. I brought Cindy—I mean Kelli—here."

Sam stood up and walked Tony to the door. Kelli seemed oblivious to her surroundings, and hadn't even acknowledged that the kid had spoken. "Look, I get the impression you helped her out when she needed it. Thanks for everything. She really is a great girl."

"Yeah, I've guessed that. Listen, will you call me and let me know how things turn out? You know, if you're able to find Mary, and if Sunny lives, and just whatever else. Here's my phone number." Tony ripped off a scrap of paper from something in his wallet and started writing.

"Tony." Kelli stood up suddenly and ran over to him. "Are you leaving?"

"Yeah, final tomorrow."

Kelli threw her arms around him. "Thanks for everything, and good luck. Maybe I'll see you sometime."

"I hope so." Tony just stood there shifting back and forth on his feet and staring at Kelli. Finally, he stepped out the door.

"Oh, and tell Amber thanks too. Tell her to keep the clothes for rent payment. Those boots were fairly expensive and she'd look good in them."

"Well, okay. I'll tell her, but I doubt she'd wear them. Maybe you ought to come by and get them. Better yet, I'll bring them by sometime. You're going to need them."

"Okay," Kelli said.

They sat on the sofa and then Kelli lay down with her legs across Sam's lap. "Remember how Mom would read to us like this? I miss that," Kelli said.

"I miss that too."

"There's so many things I miss about Mom and Dad. How would life have been if it hadn't happened?" Kelli began.

"I wonder all the time. But we both know we'll see them again. Anyway, I want to know about that scummy cult. What did they do to you? Did they hurt you? How can I help you now?"

"Sam, no one hurt me. But I need to go back there to find out what happened to Mary."

"Whoa! You aren't ever getting near that group again. And you need to start from the beginning. You gotta remember, Kell, I haven't been privy to anything."

Kelli only got to having met Kevin before she started to cry, and by the time she got to driving out to the compound and meeting the group for the first time, she was asleep. Sam tucked the quilt around her chin. He pulled his cowboy boots off and fell asleep on top of Sunny's bed.

chapter 26

baggage

When Kelli had been invited to join the Church of Faith, she began to pack her things. Even though she still wasn't positive that she would join, she thought she should pack for an indefinite stay—just in case things worked out with Kevin as she hoped. *Socks,* she'd thought. She would need lots of socks. She was busy trying to find the mate to her favorite fuzzy knee socks when the phone rang, and even before she looked at the caller ID, she knew it would be Sam. A quick glance had confirmed it. She would let it ring as she had done with all of his calls the past couple of weeks.

She'd wanted to talk to him; she loved her brother more than she could possibly love anyone else, but she was about to do something that she knew Sam would try to talk her out of, and no matter how well she explained it, he would never understand her decision. The phone had rung more than a dozen times before he'd given up.

Kelli had planned on filling all three black canvas suitcases (Sam's from his mission), but now realized that all she needed was the large one. In this one, she'd already packed clothes for a variety of seasons, and shoes for walking, working, and church. She would also need winter boots. She tossed in a pair of insulated duck boots, the kind ranchers wore. Then she pulled another boot box out from under her bed. She lifted the cardboard lid and put her hands on her favorite black leather boots. They sported a long zipper that kept them snug against her legs. Holding them to her nose, she could still smell the new leather. In these boots she felt glamorous, chic. When she wore them with her plum skirt, showing off her long legs, she turned heads. It had taken her three paychecks to save enough to buy them.

Kelli had slipped her jeans off and put the boots on. She'd stood in front of the mirror wearing an oversized IFA Feedstore T-shirt and her black boots. Her legs were among her better assets, but now, remembering how important the boots had been to her, she felt foolish—shallow. She unzipped the boots, placed them back in the box, set them on top of the bed, and scrawled on the lid in black magic marker, "For Stacey." Stacey had admired the boots when they were all together at Christmas. Kelli also remembered Stacey joking that maybe she'd move to Twin Falls, just so she could borrow them.

Kelli finished packing, zipped the large suitcase, slid it over by the door, and sat down to write Sam a letter. She set the letter on the bed next to the boots.

The suitcase wasn't very heavy considering that it contained everything she might need for the rest of her life. She'd heaved the bag into the trunk of her Escort and headed away from Twin Falls. It had been the middle of the day, and she knew Sam would be gone, so she'd taken a detour to drive past his house one more time. But immediately after passing, she'd backed the car up, pulled into the drive and gotten out. Walking into the house and looking around, she'd breathed in deeply, hoping it would still smell like grandma's dusting powder, but it hadn't. The house Sam had inherited from Granny five years ago smelled more like a montage of fried food and Sam's aftershave. She walked into the living room and selected a family photo off the rolltop desk. The photograph had been taken just days before Sam left to go on his mission. The whole family stood in front of the lilac bushes at their house, just blocks from this house.

She'd set the family photo on the front seat of the car and continued the drive. When she crossed over Goose Creek, she began to count the telephone poles. Just as she reached twelve, she saw the faint road she'd been on several times before. She turned east. After five miles she came to the commune—a grouping of singlewide trailer houses encircling a double-wide trailer home. The trailer village was nestled in a small valley surrounded by close hills. Jagged cliffs, the color of a burnt-sienna crayon, rose up from the valley floor on the south side. Junipers and sagebrush dotted the dusty hills. As she'd stepped out of the car, she noticed a pair of turkey vultures flying above the cliffs. It was quiet for the middle of the day. She'd walked toward the main house, her heart pounding, but was surprised when the person who answered it was Kevin himself. She had expected he would be away until evening, so when he opened the door, she felt reassured to see the young man who had persuaded her to give their lifestyle a try.

She was introduced to a woman bouncing a baby with downy-yellow hair on her lap. Kelli was surprised by how young she looked; not more than eighteen. Another woman, well into her forties, stood at the kitchen sink peeling potatoes. She stopped, dried her hands on her apron, and reached her hand out to Kelli. "Welcome to the fold. I'm Andrea." She put her ample arms around Kelli and drew her into her bosom. She did it with so much warmth and spontaneity, that Kelli felt her eyes swim with tears. She was about the age Kelli's parents had been when they died. She blinked away the tears and smiled.

Kelli had then turned to the young woman. She might have been a beautiful woman once, but her eyes were tired and seemed blank. Her stomach bulged with another baby on the way, or maybe she still carried the extra weight from the last one, Kelli wasn't sure. The woman didn't smile, but simply put her hand out. "Excuse me for not getting up. I'm Sarah." Kelli took the sticky hand in hers and shook it, but dropped it quickly. It seemed completely without warmth, a stark contrast to the greeting from the older woman.

"Didn't I tell you she was beautiful—glowing from the spirit within her?" Kevin had whispered as he motioned for Kelli to follow him out the front door. "Let me show you around." He grasped her hand and led her to a clearing. Benches formed a kind of amphitheater. "When weather permits, we hold our daily worship services right here. And this is where the Prophet Daniel will marry us after a brief courtship. But, of course, that can only happen after I get permission."

Kelli had breathed deeply. She really liked Kevin. The thing she'd liked best about him was that he was so easy to talk to, and even when she asked many pointed questions about his faith, he explained it as if he were talking to an intelligent adult, a peer, instead of treating her like a child. He'd take her hand and look into her eyes when he spoke. She would be honored to be his first wife.

"We can ask permission tonight if you're ready."

She had been anxious, ready to begin, ready to unburden her life—but she wasn't quite ready for that.

* * *

The morning after Sunny was taken to the hospital, Kelli woke up and couldn't remember where she was. It was dark, but she could make out that she was lying on a sofa in a small building. She pulled the blanket around her face and fingered the hand-stitched quilt. Then she remembered Sunny, Sam, and Tony. She sat upright and looked out the window. She could see that it was early in the morning. The sky was a chalky gray. It was freezing. Even though it was the end of May, it was still cold enough in Sunny's cabin for Kelli to see her breath. She started a fire, then searched Sunny's drawers to find some of those thick socks Sunny wore, and for something else to wear. Kelli was tired of these black clothes. Besides, the leggings were still stuck to her sore knees where the blood had dried. She warmed up in the bathtub, then came out dressed in her own clothes—the ones she'd left in her rush to flee Trout Haven earlier. Sam was still asleep on top of Sunny's bed. He had to be freezing, Kelli thought, since he wasn't even covered. She got the quilt and laid it carefully over him, trying not to wake him.

"Stace, is that you?" he asked sleepily.

"No. It's me, Kelli. Go back to sleep."

He bolted upright and looked around the room; taking it all in, Kelli figured.

"Good, you're still here. Where's Stacey? Sunny—is she all right?" Sam asked.

"I don't know. They never called. It's still really early in the morning. They'll call. Go back to sleep."

But Sam was already pulling on his boots. He checked the phone. "This is why they haven't called, it never got hung up last night in all the commotion. Let's get down to the hospital."

"Okay, but do you know which hospital they took her to?"

"No. I don't even know where one is. Guess we'll wait a little while and then start making phone calls."

Kelli sat on a bench by the woodstove. She pushed her feet straight out until they were almost touching the black belly of the stove. Heat radiated toward her body and she felt better. Sam sat on the bench with his back toward the fire. "I feel like a Popsicle."

"Sure makes me a believer in central heat," Kelli said.

"Yeah. Listen, last night you started telling me about Richard Ellstrom, some guy named Kevin, and you only got to when you got to the compound, but it was over a month before we heard from you again. What happened after that?"

Tears stung Kelli's eyes. "I'm just so ashamed of it all. I don't want to talk about it. You'll be—"

"What? I'll be what?"

"Disappointed in me."

Sam turned himself around now on the bench and put his arm around Kelli. She curled up in a ball and laid her head on his leg. "You just don't get it, do you?" he asked.

"What?" Kelli thought she got it. She knew Sam loved her, knew that his love for her was forever, so what was it she didn't get?

"When I got the word about the *accident*, it changed something inside of me. Sure I cared about you and Brandon before then, but you didn't occupy my thoughts all that much. I mean I had my own dreams, still do, but all of a sudden I felt a shift up here," Sam said pointing to his head. "And in here." He patted his heart.

It had never really occurred to Kelli before—the enormous responsibility that had suddenly become Sam's all at once. "I'm sorry, I never thought about how it had affected you. It seemed so easy for you. All I thought about was my own pain, my own guilt."

"No, don't be sorry. I didn't tell you about me to add to that pain. I'm trying to get you to understand that you matter to me—more than you can possibly imagine. You can't be a disappointment to me, can you get that? I remember once, Mom and Dad saying something I didn't understand at the time. It was when I'd shot out old Willie's windows in his trailer house. Remember that?"

"I was only around five."

"But you remember."

"Yeah, no one could believe anyone would do such a thing to such a nice old guy. People were blaming town kids from Burley. No one suspected it was one of the Brokely kids." Brokely is what the Carsons had dubbed the few scattered houses between Oakley and Burley, to not only designate the location but also the financial situation of many of the farmers there. "And Sam, you stood right there when the bishop called our parents and said you didn't know anything."

Sam laughed. "Dad knew it was me right away. He told me he could tell by the way I was so quick to point my finger at someone else, and because I wasn't very good at lying. I knew Mom and Dad would be disappointed in me, so I kept right on denying it tooth and nail, even after Dad stood there with my smoking gun, so to speak, in his hand, and noticed the pellets scattered in the yard where I had loaded it before heading over to Willie's. He then said I should never be afraid of telling him anything, that although he and Mom could be, and were, very disappointed in what I had done, they weren't disappointed in me. I never understood the difference until after the shift in my mind took place, you know."

"But why did you shoot out the windows?"

"Oh, Willie got after us for cutting through his yard. We figured since he didn't have any grass, we could just cut through, but he yelled at us and said he'd just planted the whole thing in barley and we'd just trampled the tender plants. I just wanted to show off to my friends, so I told them he'd be sorry for telling us what to do. Okay, now I've confessed to you, so it's time for you to confess what else happened to you.

She finished telling Sam about everything that took place at the compound; taking care of the children, helping the sister wives, not getting permission to marry Kevin, being chosen to marry Richard Ellstrom, getting sick and the postponed wedding ceremony, witnessing Mary's brutal beating, and the escape at the dentist's office. She had avoided Sam's face, and instead focused on the sound of the popping fire in the black woodstove and the smell of the pine burning. Finally, she glanced at Sam's eyes. If he had been disappointed in her, he didn't show it. Instead, she saw tears in his eyes.

"The sham marriage never took place," Sam stated.

"No, I guess not." Kelli hadn't let herself think about it. She had never allowed herself to feel the enormous relief that now filled her.

"Wow. Does that mean that you never . . . this is embarrassing to ask my own sister, so if you don't want to answer—"

"I never slept with him and he never hurt me, at least not physically. I feel pretty wounded, but it's all my own fault."

"If I could get my hands on him I'd like to—"

"Sam, it isn't over. We need to find Mary." The realization of the danger Mary was in sent Kelli's mind racing again.

The phone rang and Sam jumped up to get it. "Yeah, uh-huh, okay. See you soon then." He hung up the receiver. "Ready to go up to the hospital? That was Stacey. Guess they've been trying to call us most of the night."

Kelli looked at Sam's face. "She's dead, isn't she?"

"No. She'll be okay."

chapter 27

peace, be still

After her heart attack, Sunny woke up to see Jack sleeping in a teal-colored vinyl chair, his legs sprawled out in front of him. She didn't feel good. In fact, she felt terrible. An IV machine was hooked up to her arm and she watched a little bubble in the colorless liquid. Something was across her face and she realized after some thought that it was an oxygen mask. *Why is Jack sleeping in the corner?* He was really the only thing she could look at without the excruciating effort of turning her head with the mask strapped to her. His chin was resting on his chest, and she could hear his breath escape slowly. The door was closed and she longed to see outside it. Outside her door people were talking—laughing even, while she lay in a world between life and death.

What was she doing here? She had only a vague memory of standing on the porch with Jack, gazing at stars, and of a huge pain gripping her chest and dropping her to her knees. She moved one of her legs. Jack must have heard the rustling material because he lifted his chin, then smiled broadly when he noticed she was awake.

"Hey, beautiful. Welcome back." He walked over to her and she tried to talk, but her voice came out garbled under the mask. He lifted it up for her.

"You allowed to do that?" she asked.

"Yeah, for a minute," Jack said.

"What happened? I remember being on the porch with you and being irritated about something you said, and that's it."

"Darn," he said.

"What?"

"I was hoping you'd remember how good it felt to be together, you know—not irritated."

"Oh."

A woman in a white coat stepped in. "Awake now? Great. Things look really good," she said in an overly cheerful tone. "We'll continue to monitor the situation to see how much damage was done to the heart. But I have to say, you are one lucky woman." Sunny realized the woman was her doctor—just who she needed to talk to.

"Uh, what happened?" Sunny asked her, as Jack laid the oxygen mask aside.

The woman tapped the clipboard in her hand. "Heart attack. We'll keep you around here for a week. Make sure you're on your feet, then send you home. We'll let your, uh, pastor take care of you for a while, and gradually you can resume your normal activity." She had short loose hair, blond. Sunny liked her. Another person, presumably a nurse, stood at Sunny's side, took her pulse, strapped a cuff to her arm, and took her blood pressure. "How are you feeling anyway?" the doctor asked.

"Like a giant pine tree fell on me. Can you get rid of the oxygen mask? It's uncomfortable."

"Soon. You know, often people who suffer from first-time heart attacks die because no one recognizes what is happening to them. Symptoms differ so much, people usually don't realize they're having a heart attack. Luckily, Jack here knew what was going on. He saved your life. He and the young woman."

"Really?" Sunny glanced at Jack and he was smiling. For once she didn't have a snappy comeback. What did she say to someone who'd saved her life?

"Yes, really," the doctor answered.

Sunny felt her mind race. Jack had saved her and . . . who else was there? And why had she had an attack in the first place? "But why? I quit smoking. Why now?"

"Hasn't it only been a few weeks since you quit?"

"Yeah, but it does seem a little, you know—ironic or unfair or . . ." Sunny glanced at Jack. She hoped to see something in his face to help her sort out what she was feeling. She'd done what was asked of her: quit smoking, accepted the position as Relief Society president, and she'd still had the heart attack. She felt cheated.

Jack seemed to understand what she was thinking. "Life isn't fair, is it? Sometimes we never know . . . the reasons things happen the way they do."

No, life is definitely not fair. Sunny's mind raced back to nearly thirty years earlier when she was expecting her baby. When Sunny had felt her uterus tighten over and over in a regular pattern, she hesitated to relay the message to Shane. He was right in the middle of calving season; besides it was too early—almost two months too early—to have the baby. She eased herself onto the built-in sofa, and propped her feet up on a pillow, hoping the pains would go away. The sun was peeking in through the drawn curtain and she watched the dust particles dance and sparkle in the shaft of light. As luck would have it, Shane had had one of his feelings. He'd just gotten through pulling a breach calf when he knew something wasn't right. He'd made some excuse to the crew boss and ran home, poked his head into the trailer, and, before Sunny knew it, they were on their way to the hospital in Billings, fifty-eight miles away. She'd stretched out the best she could on the bench seat of the pickup with her feet jammed up against the door. Shane gripped her hand with each pain, and they flew along the road as fast as his old pickup could go. Whenever Sunny opened her eyes, she could see the tops of the mountains whizzing past through the windows.

Even though the doctors had assured Sunny and Shane that the baby wouldn't have lived even if they had made it sooner to the hospital, Sunny couldn't help but blame herself. She didn't know why it was her fault, but for some reason their baby was born premature, and she knew she must have done something to cause it.

* * *

This time Sunny could easily make the connection between what had happened and why, it's just that she'd believed that if she did the right thing, God would bless her for it.

"By the way," the doctor said, interrupting her thoughts. "I'm the cardiologist who'll be seeing you through this thing. I'm Doctor Dennehy. Just so you know what you're hooked up to, we're running a continuous EKG, and in a few minutes a technician will come in and draw some blood samples. And I'll be back at the end of my rounds to see how you're doing. Also, I'm limiting your visitors for today to only family. There are several friends who are concerned about you. Can I relay any message for you to them?"

"He's not family," Sunny said weakly. She felt so tired that it took too much effort to point at Jack.

"No, but he informed us that he is your spiritual leader." The doctor nodded and turned to leave.

"Hah," Sunny mumbled as Dr. Dennehy and the nurse walked out the door, setting Sunny's chart in a clear holder. Sunny wondered if doctors, technicians, or even nurses had any idea who she was until they read it on the chart.

Jack scooted a chair next to the bed so he could be closer.

"Guess I should say thanks, but I can't help but think if I hadn't met you, this wouldn't have happened," Sunny said.

He placed the oxygen mask back over her face. "You need to quit talking. But I just want to know one thing. Why do you blame me for this? You heard the doctor, you wouldn't be alive if it weren't for me." He removed the mask again so she could speak.

"You told me you'd pray for a miracle so I could quit smoking, and by hook or crook you got one, didn't you? The problem is you forgot to inform the Lord that I'd quit. But no, it wasn't good enough for you—too easy maybe. Maybe you thought I needed a firm reminder to never smoke again."

"I hope you're joking. But just in case you aren't, you give me far too much credit with the Lord. I wouldn't wish or pray for this. A miracle, yes, and that happened, but not this. Sunny, I thought you were dead, and you were briefly, if the truth be told. You can't blame me for this." He tried to pat her hand. "It might be God's will or it could just be the consequences that come from not taking good care of yourself for so long, or maybe it's genetics."

"So you really didn't ask the Lord to do this to me?" she asked mockingly.

Jack just shook his head. "You just be quiet for a while. Let that oxygen do its stuff."

"Tell me one more thing," she said.

"What's that?"

"Why do you keep calling me 'beautiful'?"

"Are you kidding? I mean, you don't look that great right now," he teased, "but on better days, don't you ever look in the mirror? I mean, if you didn't try so hard not to be, you'd be stunning."

"What do you mean 'try hard not to be?'" she said indignantly.

Jack swallowed hard and Sunny could see the bob of his Adam's apple. "I mean you downplay your assets, with clothes you must've worn in the '60s, and no makeup. You know what I mean. But then, you don't need to do anything. You're beautiful anyway."

"Bad attempt at recovery. Besides, fashion goes in a cycle—my clothes should be back in style by now," Sunny said.

"That only works if they were in style in the first place. Anyway, I have to say, I thought you were a strange choice for a Relief Society president, but after working with you this past month, seeing the miracles you've already performed, the people we've invited back to church, I've realized the Lord knew just who He needed. Everyone seems to have fallen under your spell . . . even me."

Sunny didn't know what to think, what to say. Jack then opened the drawer by the hospital bed and pulled out a palm-sized green book, and thumbed through it. "You need to rest and not try to talk too much. As your spiritual advisor, I'm going to encourage you to do just that by reading to you as you go to sleep. Gideon's Bible to the rescue. 'And he arose, and rebuked the wind, and said unto the sea . . .'"

Sunny gently lifted the oxygen mask off her face, careful not to let the needle inserted in her arm move. Jack stopped reading and looked at her.

"So can you promise on that Gideon Bible that it was inspiration to call me for Relief Society president and not because you needed a place to hold church?"

"Inspiration, I swear."

"Well, don't swear, Jack. It really isn't proper for a branch president, a man of God, or my spiritual guide," Sunny said.

"Give me a break. Please."

"Give yourself one and go call people and tell them I'm all right." Suddenly she remembered Sam and the whole reason Jack had been there that night. "Hey, did Sam and Stacey ever get back from Bozeman?"

"Yeah, but the reunion between Sam and his sister was overshadowed by someone very dear nearly dying."

Jack continued to read. "'. . . Peace be still. And the wind ceased, and there was a great calm.'" Sunny closed her eyes. In her mind she saw Jesus walking on water with His arms outstretched toward her.

chapter 28

getting ideas

True to his word, when Sam got back to Burley, the owner of the livestock auction had demoted him to a yardman. Overnight, his salary had been cut in half. While cleaning out the stalls in preparation for auction day, it didn't take Sam long to figure out that he didn't want to do this the rest of his life. Sure, he did it even as the manager, and he'd cleaned plenty of stalls at his own place, but this was different. Now would be a good time to pursue the dream he'd had ever since he was a young kid helping his grandpa. He would train horses. He'd always trained horses and was good at it. He even turned down several opportunities each year because he didn't have the time. It might take a few years to be able to make a good living at it, but it was now or never.

Sam set the shovel against the wall and searched for his boss. He found the man in his office. "Don't take this personally or anything, Rich. I appreciate your being so good to me over the years. I mean, taking me on so young, taking me under your wing, and really teaching me the business, but I'm quitting."

Rich had been going over some papers at his desk. He looked up, taken by surprise. "Now hold on, son. Just wanted you to take a few days to figure out that you can't leave people hanging over a barrel. I'm sure we can work things out—get your old job back. I didn't know all that stuff that was going on with your sister. Now sit down here and let's talk this out. I'm sure Mel would understand—you're better at most things than he is, even though he's older."

"Well, besides the situation with my sister, I'm going to start my own business as a horse trainer. I'll help out until I can get things going, but Mel can probably handle the whole thing. I know you'll run into plenty of ranchers who could use my expertise, so if you wouldn't mind sending them my way, I'd sure appreciate it."

Rich sighed and sat back. "I'll let you go on one condition—help out on auction days."

"It's a deal."

After nodding, Rich started to chuckle. "Samuel Carson, horse trainer. Got a nice ring to it, don't it? Well, if there's one thing I can understand, Sam, it's pursuit of a dream, 'cause I'm living mine, and I have to say I hoped to turn it over to you one day. That kid of mine, he knows more about feeding programs into computers than which end a cow eats from, but maybe Mel will be interested. I don't know."

"Thanks again, Rich." Sam touched the brim of his hat.

"Wait a second." Rich stood up and held his arms out. "I know you're tough, but give an old man a hug before you go."

Rich's belly hung over his belt like a sack of grain. Sam hugged him around the obstacle, then Rich sat back down at his desk, opened a drawer, and held out a pair of spurs. The polished metal was silver, etched with a pattern of running horses, and the leather was hand-tooled.

"Wow, those were made by a real artist. I've never seen anything quite like them. Mind if I take a closer look?" Sam reached for them and could feel Rich's eyes on him as he examined them closely. He handed them back.

"Keep them." Rich said. "I was always going to give them to my son, but you know that wouldn't work too good. He wouldn't be able to appreciate them like you can. Made them myself, when I was about the age you was when you started working here."

"Rich, I couldn't possibly. These are priceless."

"Take them. I want you to have them."

Sam put his hand out to the old man again. Rich's leathery hand grasped Sam's. "Thanks, I'll treasure them."

"Use 'em. And you can bet I'll be sending work your way. Put up a shingle in the café if you want, and bring me in a stack of business cards. You already have a reputation, 'specially since your old grandpa was legendary. He was known for some pretty innovative stuff. A lot of traditionalists still wouldn't agree with his breaking technique, but few could argue with his success. After a few years, you'll be able to name your price."

"I appreciate your vote of confidence, and for—you know—understanding. Sure you don't need me until Thursday then, auction day?" Sam asked.

"Nah. Mel can do it. I've probably never given him enough credit."

Sam searched the yard until he found Mel and told him what he'd decided. The spurs dangled from his hand.

"Guess he took it pretty well, seeing how he gave you his prized spurs."

"Yeah." Sam grinned.

"Well, I'll miss you. Anyway, best of luck." Mel put his hand out and gave Sam's hand a quick jerk. "How's your sister doing, anyway? You going to be able to get back your house or anything?"

"She's having a real tough go of it, but she'll be okay. And I don't know about the house yet. Kind of doubt we'll ever get it back."

"Well, that's a shame, isn't it. Don't be a stranger now, hear?"

* * *

When Sam pulled up to the house, he felt a little worried about cutting back on his hours, especially when Kelli wouldn't be working for a while. He'd be supporting both of them now. Maybe he'd jumped the gun. But his savings would last awhile, he figured.

"Hey, squirt," Sam said.

Kelli was lying on the sofa with her hand in a bag of potato chips. "Stacey's on her way over. Called from her cell. She ought to be here any second. Said she had some ideas to discuss with us."

Sam's mood brightened at the thought of seeing her. It had been a week since they'd left Montana together.

Kelli started giggling.

"What's so funny?" He hung his hat on a rack. "What should we have for dinner?"

"I just noticed the grumpy look on your face when you walked through the door, and as soon as I mentioned Stacey's name, your face just lit up like a Roman candle."

"What is a Roman candle anyway?" Sam asked. "I've never figured that expression out."

"I think it's those things they light on the Fourth of July that spurt sparks into the air."

"Oh."

"Anyway dinner's all made. Some casserole dish that Sunny makes. I tried copying it."

"Sunny is a vegetarian. I don't know how good it'll work if we turn into vegetarians. I mean, we raise our own beef here."

"Don't worry. Sunny wouldn't approve, but I altered the dish. I used a pound of ground beef instead of eggplant."

Sam smiled. "Well, I can't wait to have it. I might get used to having you around, Sis. You sure you don't want to stay here?"

"I have to for a while, since I lost my apartment."

"Guess your neighbor had all your stuff put into storage. We'll go get it whenever you're ready."

"I tried calling Justin today, to apologize, you know. Anyway, by the sounds of it, he got over me pretty quick. Said he'd love to see me, but he's dating someone. Anyway, Sam, why don't you just marry her? You know you want to. You've always been a little moony-eyed, but I swear Sam, your eyes never leave her whenever she's around."

Sam laughed. "You see right through me. But first things first. Let's get you on your feet again, make sure the police find Mary, and—"

"But not in that order, Sam. We need to find Mary, but I don't see why you have to be single to do that. It'd certainly be more convenient for both of you if you were married. I mean, the two of you traveling that long bumpy road between here and Grouse Creek. It's ridiculous. Think of the tires you'd save, not to mention the gas and the time." Kelli pulled out the casserole from the oven and set it down in the middle of the table.

"I really should run out and check the stock and—"

"I did that already. Just sit down here. Stacey said on the phone she'd already eaten, so let's get to it."

"You could spoil a man."

"Don't get used to it. I just want to earn my keep while I'm here."

After a blessing on the food, they heard Stacey knock and then walk in.

"This looks good," Stacey said, surveying the meal.

"It is," Sam said, standing up and meeting Stacey with a hug and kiss. "Join us."

"Thought all this establishment knew how to make was steak and potatoes."

"Well, this establishment got a new cook," Sam said.

Stacey sat at the table and began, "I've gotten some leads on where the compound was moved to. Well, not where exactly, but I think I can find out."

"How?"

"By a stroke of luck. A man came in today. He was kind of abrupt at first, wanted to set up an account at the co-op to buy his milk every week. He ordered enough for around fifty people. About then he noticed that I had my scriptures open on the counter. I was preparing for a Sunday School class Bishop Watkins asked me to teach. Anyway, he started asking me all kinds of stuff about my beliefs. At first I was kind of defensive, and then I decided he might be the polygamist we're looking for, so I started softening my tone."

"What did he look like?" Kelli had now finished her dinner and was rinsing her plate off in the sink.

Sam scooped up another helping. "Last chance to have some of this . . . what do you call it, Kell?"

"It's sort of a moussaka."

"So anyway, he was probably about fifty, thin brown hair, nice eyes," Stacey said.

"Did he wear an expensive suit?" Kelli asked.

"No, actually, he wore jeans and a flannel shirt. Looked too warm to me."

"Well, it could still be Richard, or one of the others."

"Anyway, he asked me if I was married, and when I told him no, he turned on the charm like a snake. I was absolutely grossed out. I can't understand why anyone would fall . . ." she glanced at Kelli. "I mean, why he thought I would be interested. I looked out the window and saw two women waiting in the car."

Kelli smiled as if she knew Stacey hadn't meant the way she'd said the words. "If it's him, they are both really nice, especially Andrea. I miss her."

Sam felt the familiar gnawing in his stomach and took another bite of casserole. If Stacey was leading up to what he thought she was, he didn't know what to do. It would be dangerous.

"So," Stacey went on, "I ignored my gut and started to really show interest—lots of eye contact, nodding, you know. Finally I said something like, 'You make a lot of sense. Are you some kind of preacher? Because to tell you the truth, I'm a little disillusioned by my church. It seems like they've lost some things along the way.'"

"I don't like the sound of this," Sam said.

"Anyway . . . jackpot! He invited me to a meeting. I gave him my phone number and he's going to call and give me directions."

"Shoot, Stacey. Are you out of your mind? Haven't you learned anything?" Sam counted in his mind and realized it had only been nine months since Stacey had been attacked and nearly killed. "You can't. Look, I know you're strong and that you've come a long way, but you can't possibly put yourself in that kind of danger . . ." He grabbed her hand across the table.

Stacey was quiet for a moment. "I'm not as strong as you think I am, Sam. I doubt I ever will be. But after months of counseling, more self-defense courses, lots of midnight prayers, I am dealing with it. I've thought about this a lot today, and how I've chosen to deal with what I went through is to turn my nightmare into someone else's victory. I need to face my fears head-on and maybe help someone else along the way."

Sam was frustrated. "Look, Stacey. We've given the information to the police and they're looking into it. Let them handle it."

Stacey stood up, clearly frustrated and hurt. "Let them handle it?" she asked. "How are they going to find them? I doubt they have any young females who can walk in and sign on as polygamists."

"Well, you certainly aren't going to do that. I won't let you sign on as you say—"

"You, 'won't let me'. . . ? I can't believe what I'm hearing. Besides, I have no intention of actually signing on—at least not when it comes down to it. But what gives you the right to tell me—"

"Nothing gives me the right, except that I love you, and won't stand for you putting yourself in jeopardy like that. And if you love me, like you've told me often that you do, you won't even consider it," Sam's voice rose. He glanced at Kelli and she was still putting dishes in the sink. "Maybe we ought to stop this conversation."

"Conversation?" Stacey asked angrily. "This isn't a conversation. When people converse, they chat, they discuss—they don't tell people what to do. In case you don't recognize it, Sam, this is an argument." Stacey picked up the remaining dishes and carried them to the sink. She grabbed a washcloth off the metal rack above the sink, wet it, and slopped water around the table.

In all the time Sam had known Stacey, he'd never seen her react like this. "You're right, Stacey," he said in a calmer voice. "Sit down here and we'll discuss this like two rational individuals."

Stacey dried the table, then sat down. "Okay. That's better. I know you're scared, and you don't want anything terrible to happen to me again. Believe me, I don't either. And I'm scared too. But, as I was saying, you know how it was for me. I couldn't even socialize with people at first, especially men. Lately though, I've felt like the whole thing, as awful as it was, has given me an inner strength I didn't have before. I don't think I'm supposed to get over it completely, not really. I think I'm supposed to make sure things like that don't happen to other women. I feel compelled to help other victims. Look, Kelli told us about Mary. Surely there are other young women beaten, coerced, married off young. I want to do something about that."

"Look, it can't be you. Someone, but not you," Sam said calmly.

"Then I was wrong about you. I thought helping girls like your sister was important to you, too. Sounds like there's nothing to discuss here," she said as she picked up her keys off the kitchen counter and walked out the front door.

Sam went after her, but before he could get to her car she'd gotten in, started it, and backed out of the driveway.

What in the world happened here? he wondered to himself. When he got back in the house, Kelli was curled up on the recliner with the remote in her hand. She flipped off the TV. "Boy, you always know just the right thing to say, don't you?"

"Where did I go wrong?" Sam asked, confused and hurt that Stacey would walk out on him.

"Probably back there where you said something like, 'I won't let—'"

"Did I say that?"

"Yeah. Why don't you call her on her cell phone?"

"Good idea."

Sam picked up the telephone and pushed the buttons. Her voice answered. "You've reached Stacey . . . " He hung the phone back on the wall. "Figures. She won't answer."

chapter 29

changes

Kelli stared at the digital clock next to her bed. It was nearly 7:30 A.M. and Sam would be gone to work by now. She loved sleeping in this room. Sam hadn't bothered changing it, and it was exactly the same way she remembered it when her grandparents were alive. The built-in bookshelves were painted a robin's-egg blue, and the books that lined its shelves were old. She doubted Sam had ever pulled one out. He liked to read, but mostly horse stuff and a few John Grisham novels, or other mysteries. But here were all her grandfather's history books, old *National Geographics,* classics, and a few ledger books. The closet was small—one door wide. When Kelli opened the door, her grandpa's coveralls still hung on a hook and her grandmother's shoes, pumps mostly, lined the bottom of the closet. A writing desk sat under the window, and Kelli could still see some of Grandpa's stationery in the slots. It'd had been years since he'd died, and she was surprised to see everything the same. She wasn't sure if Sam was just too busy to change it, or if the room brought back memories for him as well.

Kelli pulled herself out of bed, grabbed her grandmother's robe, put it on, and went into the kitchen. She filled the teakettle with water to boil for hot chocolate, and looked out the back window. She was surprised that Sam was still out in the yard and hadn't left for work yet. He had a lead rope on the colt that had been born a couple of months earlier. Sam kept draping the rope on the colt's neck and then taking it off. He repeated the process several times before Kelli sat down to eat.

After she ate breakfast, showered, and dressed, she walked out to Sam's arena. "What are you still doing here?" she hollered from the pole fence.

"I quit my job."

"You what?"

"You heard me," Sam said calmly.

Now Sam clasped the rope around the colt's neck. It kicked its hind legs and began to whinny. Sam's voice soothed it, finally calming it down, and then he repeated the process. Kelli understood that she needed to be quiet, so she walked away from Sam and over to one of the brood mares, Starlight, or something like that. She stroked the horse's nose. "What will we do now, pretty girl?" The horse whinnied and nodded its long face. "I don't have a job, or a house, I gave my money away, and now my sweet brother says he doesn't have a job anymore either. What shall we do, huh?"

"You talking to me?" Sam said.

Kelli jumped, not having heard him step up behind her.

"No, to Starlight."

"Oh. Starlight's gone, Kelli, sold her to a ranch in Almo. This here is Nodra."

"What kind of name is that for a horse?"

"Watch," Sam said. "Do you love Sam?" he said to the horse in a singsong voice. The horse whinnied and nodded.

"And do you think Sam is the most intelligent person you've ever known?"

Nodra nodded her head once again.

Kelli tried, "And do you think Sam is an idiot for letting Stacey get away last night and possibly forever?" she singsonged the way Sam had done.

Right on cue, Nodra whinnied and nodded her head.

"There are some problems with the system," Sam said. "So you think I'm an idiot?"

"Hey, not me. It was Nodra. She thinks you're an idiot," Kelli teased.

Sam stroked the mare. "Just so you know I tried calling about ten times this morning. She isn't answering. And at the co-op, she must have caller ID, because she didn't answer there either."

"You don't have a job. Drive over there."

"Actually, I do have a job. I'm a horse trainer and part-time auctioneer."

"Well that's great, Sam. But that means you still have time to drive over there, since I don't see any extra horses around here, which means no one is actually paying you money to train."

"Not right now, that's true." Sam paused, thinking, and stroking the mare's mane.

"Then what are you waiting for?"

"You know, you seem pretty feisty right now. Maybe you're going to be okay after all."

"I will be. I am." Kelli felt okay as long as she forced herself not to think about how guilty she felt about everything she'd done. "Sam, when I get money though, I want to pay you and Brandon back for losing the house."

"Look, the house was yours. And I almost forgot. Brandon wants you to call him at work. He's happy you're home."

"I can't talk to him yet. I feel terrible about the house. Plus running away from everything, and your having to come look for me." Then a thought occurred to her. "Wait, did you lose your job because you came up to Montana to find me?"

"First things first, Kelli. You're carrying around way too much guilt. Let go of it." Sam moved over to her and gave her a hug. "I've got some savings—enough. Plus we have lots of things we can sell. Make an appointment with a good mental-health physician. I'll pay for it. And about the job, you did me a favor—this is something I should've done long ago."

"Since when did you use words like 'mental-health physician' instead of 'shrink'?"

"Since my sister needed one. Anyway, guess I'll go in and get ready to drive to Grouse Creek. Want to come along?"

"I don't think so. I've got some stuff I want to do, like head to Twin Falls and get my things out of storage." *Plus,* Kelli thought to herself, *I have an appointment to talk with our bishop.*

chapter 30

seeing signs

After Sunny and Shane had lost the baby, Sunny started working with Shane on the ranch. She did great with the calving season, and didn't even mind staying up at night for their turn to ride through the herd to check the calving cows. For endless days and nights from February to the end of March, calves were born. Most of the cows didn't need help with the birthing, but occasionally, they would have to pull one. It was then that Sunny saw Shane come to life. Usually, he managed it himself. After slathering his hands and arms with a lubricant, he'd reach inside the cow's uterus. Then he'd turn the calf until he could get a grip on both its feet, and he'd pull back, the calf eventually emerging. Sometimes all Shane needed to do was unlock the calf and it would slide out easily. Occasionally they had to use a puller, a heavy chain device. Other times it took both of them pulling back with all their strength. She would then wipe the membrane off the calf's face, and, if it was a cold night, which it always was that time of year, towel dry the animal while the mother licked it. Most of the cows, even the heifers who were first-time mothers, were good nurturers, but occasionally, they got one that had rejected its own, and Sunny was good at bringing out the mothering instinct in the animals.

Once, she'd found a new calf that had been neglected among the heifers. It was feeble and struggling for life. Shane had packed it into the trailer house, and they kept it in the playpen they'd bought for the baby. The pen took up all the space in their living room. Sunny stayed up with the calf the whole first night and tried to get it to suck from a bottle, but it seemed to be too weak. She left it for a minute and snuggled next to Shane, then woke with a start. A whole hour had gone by. She jumped out of bed to check the calf and found that it had stopped breathing, but just barely. Shane had told her once about saving a calf by using artificial respiration. Why not? If it worked for people, it could work for an animal. She fought back her own repulsion, put her mouth over the calf's terra cotta-colored mouth, and blew air into it. After a few minutes, and repeated tries, it started breathing on its own. She screamed out loud for joy. Shane stirred in the bed, then shouted, "What's going on?"

"I just saved this calf. I used artificial respiration, just like you told me you could."

Shane laughed. "You are truly a remarkable woman. I knew there was a rancher hidden in there. Now come back to bed. In less than an hour, I've got to be to work."

The calving season was all about life, and Sunny found it invigorating. She could work as hard as the men, and had more stamina when it came to keeping long hours. But shortly after calving, the branding began, and she found that less tolerable. It was her job to take hold of the red hot irons and sear the calves with the Bar-W brand while Shane tackled the animals and held them still for her. The mournful sound of the bawling calves and the smell of the burning hair and hide never left her. But in all honesty, the calves' pain seemed to subside as soon as they were finished. The calves would struggle to their feet, then lope off to pasture or back to their mother. So Sunny endured it as a necessary part of the process.

But when it came to taking the animals to the sale, things broke down for her. These were her babies. She'd taken care of them since birth and there was no way she was going to participate in their demise. It was then Sunny learned how to cook, and was soon the official ranch cook.

Not working alongside Shane was hard at first; she missed his crooked grin and the way he'd wink at her when she caught his gaze. She especially missed seeing how much he loved the cowboy life, but it was his life and she needed to find her own niche.

* * *

Sunny had been home from the hospital for a few days. Jack had been spending almost all of his spare time in the diner, pretending to eat, but really, Sunny suspected, to keep an eye on her. It was irritating the way he fiddled with his huckleberry pie for a whole hour, all the while she'd feel his eyes follow her as she moved around waiting on people, and chatting with them about how nice the weather was getting.

She sauntered over to him. "Aren't you finished torturing that pie yet? You've got to be the world's slowest eater. If you worked as slowly as you eat you'd never get any building done." Glancing around the diner, she noted that everyone seemed to be taken care of for a few minutes, so she took a seat across from him.

He smiled and stopped eating. "Just want to make sure you don't overdo it."

"I don't need you for that. Doctor Dennehy said I can do anything I feel up to."

"Yeah, but that's the secret isn't it, knowing what that is. I had an interesting call this morning."

"Oh?"

"Kelli called. You know, that girl—"

"Jack, I certainly know who Kelli is. So what did she want?"

"She wondered how you were, and wanted to know if she could come back to work for you."

"Why did she call you?" Sunny grabbed a fork and took a bite of the pie.

"I was curious about that too. So I asked her, and she said she figured that since I saved your life we'd be together by now."

"She did not say that," Sunny said, shocked.

"She did."

"Don't go away. I've got to take care of someone, but I'll be right back." Sunny walked to the kitchen window and grabbed the two plates of eggplant parmesan and took them over to Ned and someone she didn't recognize. "Enjoy your meal, boys," she said.

"Hey Sunny. How does it feel to be back among the living?" Ned asked.

"Great."

"Heard you quit smoking and everything," Ned said.

"Yeah, well I sort of had to, now, didn't I?" Sunny said.

Jack was chuckling to himself when she sat back down.

"You were saying," she said.

Jack was wearing a plaid green Pendleton shirt. She swore the green was the exact shade of his eyes. She quickly averted her own eyes when she found herself staring at his, and was afraid that he'd noticed.

Jack picked up the menu from behind the napkin dispenser and studied it while he continued, "She said she'd tried calling you once, but then thought, 'Surely she'd be with the branch president. He saved her life. It's obvious Sunny liked him even before that happened. By now they're probably hooked up!'"

"She said 'hooked'?"

"Well, it's certainly not my word. Yes, she said 'hooked.'"

"What did you say?" Sunny glanced out the window and noticed a boy stomping in a leftover puddle from the previous night's storm.

"I said that I figured if I hung out often enough at the diner, that you'd see me for who I am, and that we would be hooked up before she could get back up here and claim her job as your assistant."

"Just who are you, Jack Heath?"

"Just a man falling for a lovely woman with a big heart and great personality."

"Why?" She turned away from his gaze.

"I just told you."

Sunny looked out the window again and could see the same boy now peering into Molly's Bar. This distraction from Jack's words had no effect upon her—she still felt her heart jump. Since her heart attack, she seemed very aware of her heart; its every beat. It was strange, but she felt as though she could feel her life unfolding now, moment upon moment with her heartbeat. She wanted to hug Jack. He was so—what's the word she wanted?—adorable. He was adorable. But how could she love someone who didn't care about nature? How could she look past that? It was simple, she couldn't.

"Jack, I'm flattered. I really am, but . . ."

"So you know—remember that deal I've got going outside of town? Tourist and recreation center, lodges, golf course—the works. The one that would take out one thousand acres of forest? 'Course the whole thing wouldn't have been built on. I would've staggered the development—you know, left green space. In all only about 100 acres would've been buildings, concrete, and asphalt."

"Would have? What do you mean 'would have'?"

"The owner just wanted to sell. He doesn't care what I do with it. I decided to put in a government conservation easement."

"You mean you signed papers so that it can never be developed?" Sunny was hopeful.

"Yeah."

"What possessed you to do that?" she asked incredulously.

"I told you I could congrue. It's a win-win situation. I still get some money, not nearly as much, of course, but the land is saved from future development virtually forever."

Sunny clapped her hands and stood up. That land bordered Trout Lake and was pristine wildlife habitat. In the summer the mountain meadows were carpeted with wildflowers—Indian paintbrush, white daisies, and lupine. She felt like kissing him right on the spot.

He seemed to sense that, stood up, embraced her, and kissed her before she could do it.

She felt tingly and warm. It felt good to be in his arms, and just for a second, she allowed herself to enjoy it, then stepped back away from him. "I've got to get back to work."

"Hey there, Sunny! This new religious awakening must be working pretty good, eh?" Ned hollered.

Sunny blushed. *I honestly can't believe that I feel like this. I'm fifty-two. When do you stop feeling giddy when a good-looking man kisses you? Never*, she hoped. She was startled to hear the roar of Jack's diesel pickup and watched him back up, exhaust smoke billowing from the rear. *Polluter*, she thought, then went back to work, smiling.

On her way home from work that night, Sunny decided to take a walk down Main Street. She had to do something to replace her evening smoke, and tonight the stars were bright in the clear sky. Grabbing a jacket, she stepped outside and felt the night air on her cheeks. Across the street there was a new flower bed planted in front of Molly's bar, and she wanted to see what the bright orange splashes of color were that she could see from her own window. *California poppies, of course*, she thought. She leaned down to smell their sweet fragrance. As she looked up, a sign on a telephone pole caught her eye. It was yellow with bold, black print. A picture of a band was in the center.

Friday Night, 8 P.M., June 20th, The
Cattle Rustlers will be playing at the
Lazy Moose Café. Free Admission.

She read the poster again. Right in the middle of the five-man band was a picture of Jack, smiling broadly and holding his guitar. She read the poster again and again and again. *Where will the nerve of this man end? He is actually advertising to play in my café, and doesn't even ask me!*

"Heard you an' Jack Heath the lumberjack hooked up."

Sunny jumped and turned to see Shauna Summers. "What?"

"You and Jack. I think that's great."

Shauna wore a snug black T-shirt that stopped a good inch above her silver cowboy buckle. Sunny didn't know anyone who wore hip-huggers paired with a stamped cowboy belt. But then she didn't pay much attention to fashion. "Uh, we aren't, yet." *Had she said the word "yet" out loud?* She didn't think so, but just in case she tried again. "No, we aren't."

"Oh, that's too bad. For you I mean. Good though for the rest of us. I mean, have you noticed the size of that man's chest and his deep green eyes? Whoa." She fanned her face as if she had suddenly become very hot.

"How old are you? Jack's old enough to be, well, not your father exactly, but almost."

"Who cares? When you've got it, you've got it. Besides that, he's loaded."

"So they say." Sunny watched Shauna step into Molly's. She thought about Jack. Shauna was right—he did have nice green eyes, money, and more. And although Sunny could have cared less about his money, she had to admit that she was starting to think about him more all the time. His goodness was starting to overshadow his obvious flaws.

chapter 31

dogged determination

Sam knew from the very beginning of their relationship that Stacey wasn't one to be told what to do. She had a mind of her own. And often her confidence preceded her ability, but he also knew that her confidence was the reason she was such a quick learner. He remembered trying to teach Stacey how to ride a horse the year before. First he showed her how to properly mount. But even though she nodded as if she understood, she stepped into the stirrup with her hand on Sam's shoulder instead of on the saddle horn. Blue Moon had stepped away, and for a second Stacey's legs were straddled between Sam and the horse. Had he used one of the more skittish horses, she could have been hung up and dragged around the arena. As it was, Blue Moon just whinnied, and when the stretch between Sam and the horse grew larger, Stacey fell into the dirt. Sam had tried to help her up, but she had yanked him into the dirt, laughing. Blue Moon took the chance to escape out an open gate, and it had taken Sam and Stacey two hours to corral him again. The next time Stacey mounted the horse, she did it with more skill. She was a quick learner, and by the time it was dark, she was maneuvering the horse around the training arena as if she'd done it a dozen times before. The next time, he'd figured they would do a trail ride and he'd be able show her how to cut cows and move a herd. Something else she would probably do with surprising ease.

* * *

This had been Sam's first real argument with Stacey. He had to admit she was a strong-willed person. Size had nothing whatsoever to do with dogged determination. She was back to herself: defiant and confident. Still, he couldn't let her put herself in danger. Besides apologizing, he needed to talk some sense into her. *These people Kelli got involved with carry guns.* Sam laughed to himself at that thought. *So does ninety-five percent of the population in southern Idaho.* But this group was dangerous; he knew it. After all, Kelli had witnessed a brutal beating and had been coerced by manipulative—albeit charismatic—men.

When Sam passed the house Stacey had been living in, he could see her car wasn't there, so he headed on down to the co-op. He pulled up next to the small white clapboard building and went inside.

"Hey Sam, what can I do for you?"

Sam touched his hat, "Welcome home, Jean." Sam was surprised; Stacey hadn't mentioned that Jean had come home, and Stacey had been working as Jean's replacement and living in her house for the last nine months.

"You look like you're surprised to see me. Didn't Stacey tell you I'd returned from my extended holiday?"

"No, she didn't mention it. Where is she?"

"She didn't tell me. 'Course she's still stayin' in my house. We both are for the time being, but she did mention that maybe now that Herman and Maggie have officially tied the knot that she might move into his back cabin. Maybe she's gone up to their place to see."

"But she doesn't have her job here then, since you're back. Why would she stay in Grouse Creek?"

Jean put her paperback novel facedown on the counter. "I told her she could keep the job as long as she needs to. I don't need the work particularly—just gives me something to do. I think she likes it here, for a while yet anyway."

Sam shifted his weight, removed his hat, and ran his fingers through his hair. "Guess I'll go see Herman then."

Sam could see Herman leaning against his pole fence before he got to the house. Herman's house had been painted with a fresh coat of white paint and the trim was an even darker blue than the last time he'd been here. His heart sank when he couldn't see Stacey's car anywhere. "Seen Stacey?" he hollered as soon as he stepped out of the car.

"Well, look what blew in on the expressway. How ya doin' stranger?" Herman asked.

"Not so great." Sam put his hand out to the old man, and firmly pumped Herman's up and down. "I'm looking for Stacey."

Herman tilted his head back as if in thought, and rubbed his chin. "Now what did she say she was doin'? Came here first thing this mornin' and asked about rentin' our place. Told her we'd be more'n pleased. Then she went on in and visited with Maggie for a bit, and took off down the road—headin' north. Go on in. I'll be with ya in a piece."

Sam knocked on the door and waited for Maggie, noticing that the half-barrel flowerpot was brimming with purple and yellow pansies. Maggie's influence was already obvious.

"Sam Carson, come on in," she said, smiling. She put her arms around him and gave him a quick hug. "Make yourself at home." She motioned to an elegant leather armchair.

"This place has changed," Sam observed. "Wow, it's nice." Sam sat down and held his hat on his lap.

"Just had a few of my things sent in. You like it then?"

"Sure, but Maggie, I'm actually here looking for Stacey. Herman said you might know where she went."

"Did you two have a fight?" Maggie sat down in a rocker and moved in closer to Sam. "When I asked how you two were doing, she wouldn't look me in the face and quickly changed the subject."

"I didn't think we were having a fight exactly, but maybe it was. She has a half-cocked idea of running with the polygamist group that Kelli got entangled with so she can save other young women from being victimized."

"And you don't approve?" At Sam's hesitation Maggie jumped up. "Let me get you something to drink—soda, juice, water?"

"Water's fine. And no, I don't think she should. She wouldn't know danger if it hit her in the face . . ." Sam remembered the attack on Stacey and how beat up her face had been afterward and realized the dark irony of his statement.

Maggie handed Sam a glass of ice water. "She wouldn't? Stacey strikes me as a very astute person. I didn't know her before her horrible attack, but especially now, she seems reasonably cautious."

"Yeah, I thought so too. But Maggie, these people use guns to threaten people. They force their own daughters to marry old men and—"

"Just what Stacey wants to do something about, I think. And she has the intelligence and looks, I might add, to get in and stop it."

"It's that last part I'm worried about. They'll want her, all right, to add to their entourage of gullible women. But she could get killed, especially if and when they figure out what she's up to."

Maggie set her own water down on the end table between them. "Well I don't know if she's gone off to join up with them yet. She loves you, Sam. If you really don't want her to do it—she'll listen to you."

"She told you about it then?"

"Not exactly. But she did tell me about the man who came into the co-op and invited her to a . . . cottage meeting, I think she called it. She told me she planned on going to the meeting to gain information."

"Where's the meeting?" Sam jumped to his feet.

"Hold your horses, cowboy. If you show up there, half-cocked as you say, then you're very likely to upset the whole thing, and really put her in harm's way. Sit back down."

Sam nodded, realizing she was right. "Got any ideas?"

"She won't do anything rash. If she did they'd be suspicious anyway. She'll meet with them today, and at least a few more times to try to find out where they are located. And then, as far as I know, she'll turn it over to the police."

The idea made Sam shudder. He closed his eyes and could feel the thump in his chest. Almost from the first time he'd talked to Stacey, he'd fallen for her, and the thought of her getting hurt again was more than he could stand.

"It's just about dinnertime. We'd love you to join us, and by the time we're finished she might be back. She was planning on moving her things over from Jean's tonight."

After dinner, Sam stood up to help clear dishes off the table when he heard a noise behind Herman's house. It sounded like a car door slamming. He stuck the dishes into the sink and bolted out the back door.

Stacey was struggling to balance a large box as she backed through the cabin door. She had to have seen his truck parked out front. Her purposeful avoidance of him stung. He pulled two more boxes out of the open car trunk and carried them into the cabin.

"Thanks, just put them down on the bed," Stacey commanded in a dispassionate voice.

Sam set the boxes down. "Stacey, I'm really sorry."

But she was out the door again and was rummaging through the trunk.

"Good thing I didn't move much out here. Just my cameras, a few books, clothes and stuff. This is all of it, so you can head back. I've got it."

"Stacey, are you kidding me?"

She hurriedly closed the trunk and walked away, and he thought he heard her lock the cabin door before he had a chance to follow.

There wasn't really a porch to stand on, just a brown spiky mat made to pull dirt off shoes. Sam clenched his hand into a fist and pounded on the door. "Stacey. Come on. Let me in. I didn't drive all the way over here just to help you carry two boxes in. Now let me in." He was shouting when he got to the last few words. He waited. He expected to hear her come to the door, laughing at her joke, but there was only silence. Then he could hear hangers rattling against each other, as if she were putting clothes away. He couldn't believe it. "Stacey," he pleaded. "You know, whatever it is you're upset about, I'm sorry. Come on."

Behind him he heard Herman's door shut and he turned around to see Maggie tiptoeing toward him. She put her finger to her lips.

She slipped a key into his hand and then disappeared back into the house.

When Sam bolted into the cabin, Stacey turned, surprised. He could see tears in her eyes. He was so confused. *Why is she treating me like this?* he wondered. "What is it you want me to say? I'm sorry."

"And just what are you sorry about? Are you saying you didn't mean what you said?" She turned back around and continued to hang her clothes up.

Sam scooted up behind her and put his arms around her. He felt her shiver with his touch. "I don't know—I'm just sorry for whatever it was I said that made you so angry. Probably I'm sorry about saying, 'I won't let you.'" *Wasn't that what Kelli said he should be sorry about?* He tried again. "I shouldn't tell you what to do."

"So it is okay with you, then?" She turned around, her eyes hopeful.

"Well, no, it's not okay with me. I don't want you to get hurt again. Shoot, Stacey, they carry guns and threaten people."

"You carry a gun and threaten people."

"I do not," he said, remembering how he'd threatened Stacey's ex-boyfriend and beat him up after suspecting his involvement in her attack. "I didn't use a gun on Dave; wouldn't have even if I'd had one with me. Besides, that's different, and you know it."

"Why? Because you know what's good for everyone else?"

"Come on. Dave was a jerk. These guys are jerks—they marry underage girls, and beat them, for Pete's sake. I just don't want you involved. I can't stop you, I know that, but I'm pleading with you. Just let the cops handle it. Like I said before."

"That's just what I'm doing. After I left your place I talked to the cops. Today even, right before I went to the polygamist meeting, and they told me if I could find out where they're located, they could go in and at least arrest that Richard guy on Kelli's testimony. I think it will snowball from there. My part is minimal really." Her tone was softer.

Sam suddenly felt sick to his stomach. He grabbed his midsection and reeled. It didn't sound minimal to him. "Those idiots," he blurted. "They can't ask you to do that."

"I volunteered. And all I'll be doing is going to a couple of cottage meetings until I can find out where they are located. I'm not going to the compound. I don't even want to."

Sam sat down on a wicker chair in the corner, took off his hat, and tossed it across the room. Visions of Stacey's crumpled body flashed through his mind, then of her lying in a casket, then of him standing at her grave placing a bouquet of yellow daisies on it. He groaned.

"Stacey, I know I'm probably overreacting. It does sound reasonable." But his throat felt tight as he said it. It didn't sound reasonable, not to him, but he could tell he couldn't talk her out of it. He remembered sitting across from his mission president in Germany and hearing of his parents' death. *I'm sorry to tell you this, Elder Carson, but your parents . . .* He couldn't take losing anyone else. He'd just gotten Kelli back after nearly losing her as well. Not again could he stand to let someone he loved slip away from him.

Finally Stacey quit shuffling her clothes and came over to him. She looked puzzled. "You're really scared, aren't you?"

"Yeah. I am," he said quietly.

"Sam, it's the right thing. Trust me on this. I know what I'm doing."

He got up to leave. "Just promise to call me as often as possible."

"I'll try, Sam. I promise. And thanks for, you know, trying to understand."

He thought he should go in and tell Herman and Maggie good-bye, but didn't feel like it. He turned the key in his truck and started backing out the driveway, but was startled by a tapping on the truck window. Stacey stood there, holding his hat in her hand. He rolled down the window.

"Didn't think you'd actually leave without it."

"Forgot. Thanks."

He looked away. He hadn't thought she would actually do something he'd begged her not to. It surprised him, and wounded him as well. He started to roll the window back up.

"Sam." She had tears in her eyes again. "And I'm sorry. Really sorry. But I need to do this."

"Why you? She's *my* sister. I just don't get it."

"That's why I need to—exactly why. You of all people should understand why I need to do this, to help her. I love you, so I love your family as well, sister and all. It has to be me. I know what that feels like. I really don't want Kelli or anyone else to go through that ever again."

Sam knew he should say something again, tell her it was okay, that he knew she would be okay, encourage her, tell her he was proud of her for her bravery, but he didn't feel any of those things, so he didn't say them. "See ya then. Remember to call." He looked behind him, backed out of the gravel drive, and when he turned his head forward again, she was gone.

chapter 32

false sincerity

Stacey told herself that Sam needed this time away from her to get his horse-training business off the ground, but she knew the main reason she didn't want him hanging around was that whenever she saw his eyes, she felt herself weaken, felt herself thinking he just might be right after all—that it was too dangerous, and that she should just let the police handle things without her. So instead of letting him break down her resolve to get information on the group, she'd told him that it would be better all around if they stopped seeing each other while she was working on the case. "I think we need a little space—some time apart," she'd said. She could see how hurt he was at the suggestion, but also felt the pain herself. Thoughts of Sam lulled her to sleep at night and got her moving in the mornings.

And now, listening to this blue-eyed man with luxuriant blond hair claiming to be a prophet in these last days, all she could think about was Sam, his dark mischievous eyes and crooked grin, and his deep spontaneous belly laughs. He was the exact opposite of this man who mesmerized people with his words. The main difference was that while Sam was a born optimist, Daniel—Stacey refused to add the title "prophet" in her thoughts—was all about destruction, doomsday predictions, and inciting fear. But his way of speaking bound people into a spell that was hard to resist. The group listening was made up of the "chosen flock," as they liked to call themselves, and a few young women—"recruits."

Polygamy was never mentioned, and Stacey was beginning to wonder if she'd ever find out anything beyond that much of the cult's doctrine was based on the fact that they felt the world would be coming to an end soon. It was difficult for Stacey not to react like she normally would. She had to stifle her personal feelings. She believed in modern prophecy, believed in the modern prophets and in priesthood authority, but this blond man's whole purpose, it seemed, was to incite fear among his followers and show them that only through him would they find salvation from the mass destruction of the world. Stacey wanted to raise her hand and mention that he was forgetting Christ, the true Savior of the world. The self-proclaimed prophet said that only his chosen flock would rise from the ashes of the destroyed world, like a phoenix, to start the world anew with a pure race. Although scripture was often quoted, Stacey noticed few actual chapter and verse citations were made, so it was difficult to look them up afterward to check the context. But lots of scriptures were mingled with the blond man's own "List of Commandments." Furthermore, for security reasons, and to make sure they could enjoy the "full spiritual experience," note taking was forbidden. Tape recorders were also out of the question, and recruits were carefully searched before entering the tent meetings. It was explained to those in attendance that they regretted the inconvenience, but since "enlightened groups" were being closely watched by the federal and local law enforcement—Satan's warriors—they were forced to take the precautions.

After the cottage meetings, the church's leaders would visit with the recruits. Stacey thought this was probably where the careful screening process was taking place, in the private conversations. But somehow, even though she had tried to seem eager, so far she had been ignored by the higher-ups and Prophet Daniel.

At the third meeting Stacey attended, as the blond man spoke, she let her mind wander back again to Sam and the last encounter she'd had with him. How he'd stormed from her cabin forgetting his cowboy hat in the process. Leaving the hat behind signaled that he was more upset than he'd let on, and then she'd heard his voice crack on the phone as she explained the break they needed from each other. Her body ached with missing him. The sudden tears in her eyes surprised her and she automatically blinked, and put her hand up to wipe the tears away.

After the Prophet Daniel finished speaking, Stacey heard him announce that everyone was welcome to stay and ask more questions afterward. Stacey jumped up from her seat, feeling she couldn't face the fanatical conversations she was destined to feign interest in. She stepped away from the small crowd, committing herself to doing better next time, and walked toward her car. Just as she reached her hand out to open the door, a firm hand came down over hers.

She jumped and felt her heart race. Not having heard him come up behind her, the man had frightened her. "Oh, I'm sorry. I didn't mean to startle you. I don't know if I ever introduced myself when I met you in Grouse Creek. I'm Adam. You're not leaving so soon, are you?"

"Uh, yes. I have to get back—appointments pressing."

"But don't you just work at that little store in Grouse Creek?"

"Yes, but I'm looking for other work. I'm just . . ." *How stupid am I? This is just the opportunity I've been waiting for.*

"So you need the work? Things aren't going well financially? I don't mean to be nosy, its just that if things progress the way God wants them to, you won't be needing another job. We are a self-sufficient group." Adam looked eager and smiled expectantly.

Yeah, sufficiently reliant on conning people out of their money. "It's not so much that I need the work. My father left me a pretty good sum when he died, socked away in stocks and properties in Burley, but working in Grouse Creek is getting dull." Stacey felt funny about lying, but knew it would make her sound more appealing. "I really need something more in my life. That might be why I became interested in your . . ." Stacey didn't know what to call the group; knowing 'cult' sounded offensive, she finished, ". . . spiritual guidance."

Stacey had watched the man's eyes and noticed a slight flicker of interest when she'd mentioned the money her father had left her.

"I noticed how moved you were by the prophet's words today. You seem to be the kind of person who could benefit from and be a real asset in what our church can offer. I feel inspired to tell you that you're ready for the next step."

It took Stacey a second to realize Adam must have noticed her tears and mistaken them for her being spiritually moved. This was the chance she had been waiting for. "Oh, I'm embarrassed that you noticed my tears. It was something he'd said about eternal life, and how your group could offer salvation. I can't remember what now, but at that instant I thought this is what I've been searching for in my life. I had such a warmth come over me. I can't really describe it. It's something I've never felt before. If I could just have what *he* has." Stacey hoped her words sounded sincere.

"You're ready then. And your name is?"

"Stacey." Stacey didn't want to use her real name, but knew he could easily find it out by calling the co-op. "I'd like to keep coming to your meetings. They make me feel hope for my future," Stacey said.

"There is much more to us than these meetings. These meetings only scratch the surface of what we can do for you."

"Oh?" Stacey stepped away from the car. "How can I learn more?"

"I need to talk to some of the other brethren. If they feel you're ready for the next step, I'll get in touch with you. Can I have your phone number?" He opened a small black address book and pulled a pen from his jacket.

"The number is 435-747-1212. I'm usually home in the evenings, but you may call me at the co-op if you have something important. I'll be there for a while yet until I find something else. I have a feeling I'll be moving back to Burley soon."

"I have a feeling that you'll be with us soon. I sincerely doubt you'll need anything else. We can offer you everything you'll ever need or desire."

Stacey forced herself to smile again and wondered if she could manage a tear or two for effect, but finally just settled on grabbing his hand. "That would be so wonderful. You can't imagine how I've been praying for something like this."

"I'll be calling you."

After she watched the man walk away, Stacey automatically wiped her hand several times on her jeans, trying to wipe away the disgust she'd felt when she touched his hand. The evil in the man reeked. She found it hard to believe that Kelli had been conned into nearly marrying one of them. She shuddered at the thought, but if she were honest with herself she could see how persuasive the impassioned speech by the prophet was. It could definitely allure someone who was struggling with self-esteem and guilt.

chapter 33

moving on

The ten years following her parents' death hadn't all been terrible
for Kelli. She'd had good friends and family. Sometimes she was
almost able to forget her guilt and pain. Sometimes she even thought
of herself as a person who deserved happiness. Sometimes she was
able to focus on her talents. She was smart, especially in math. Her
sincere ability to make others feel good about themselves kept her
surrounded by friends. And she had a strong desire to learn all she
could and do the right thing. At age twenty-one she'd thought about
going on a mission, but at the time she was in a serious relationship
with Zach.

Once Zach had asked her to go waterskiing on the Snake River
nearby. Kelli had packed a lunch to take. She hadn't felt like cooking,
so she ran down to Price's Café and ordered roast beef sandwiches for
two, threw in some apples and drinks, and sat down on the front
porch and waited for Zach to pick her up.

He drove up in his parents' brand-new, green Ford F-250 detailed
with stripes resembling a Nike logo, and he was pulling a water ski
boat. She liked Zach a lot, and he managed to make her feel beautiful. Another couple was already in the backseat of the club cab:
Zach's cousin Joe, visiting from out-of-town, and his fiancée Ashley.
Kelli had discovered on earlier trips with Zach that she was a natural
at waterskiing. Kelli was able to get up on her second try and was
skiing slalom by the end of the day.

The outing went well until they docked their boat in a cove and Joe
began rambling about a tragic accident he'd heard about. A father and son

were going hunting together and when they got into their pickup, the son carelessly tossed the rifle in, causing the gun to fire and kill the father.

"I mean how would you feel if you were that son? I swear, if I caused someone else's death, I'd kill myself for sure, wouldn't you?"

Zach, right in the middle of a bite of sandwich, interrupted. "Didn't I tell you Kelli was something on skis?" he said with his mouth full. "You wouldn't believe that up until a few weeks ago she'd never even been on skis before."

But Joe just kept talking "I mean, think about it. Because of your stupidity, a whole family has lost their father, a slew of kids are left on their own—"

"Joe, this isn't good lunchtime conversation," Zach had interrupted, slipping his arm around Kelli and giving her a slight squeeze. She had a towel draped over her shoulders and felt the cool dampness on her skin. She realized painfully that Zach had become aware of how difficult the conversation probably was for her.

"Well, anyway, they're deciding whether to press charges— manslaughter or something. I think they should too. I mean, everyone knows you shouldn't throw around loaded guns." Joe took a bite of his sandwich.

"So what makes you think it wasn't the dad's fault?" Zach asked. "My guess is that the dad loaded the gun before the trip himself, making it virtual suicide, and the poor kid has to live with that the rest of his life. They shouldn't charge the kid, no way." Zach jumped up and started the motor.

Joe quit talking and finished his lunch in silence. Kelli appreciated Zach for essentially sticking up for her, but what Joe said never left her mind. She was guilty. And if she was to be forgiven, she should pay a price. Later that year, when Zach had hinted that he hoped he could have a future with her, she'd crumbled and broke off their relationship. It wasn't that she didn't want to continue seeing Zach, but she was scared to get too close to anyone. Afraid if she allowed herself to love someone that they could be ripped away from her again, and even worse, that she could be the cause of it. She had decided it would be easier for her to keep her distance.

* * *

When Kelli got to Trout Haven to reclaim her job as a server, she had to park her car a block away from the diner. Something big was going on, and she wondered what it could possibly be. When she opened her car door, her ears were attacked by the booming twang of country music. As Kelli walked toward the Lazy Moose, the sound became louder, more distinct. Finally, she could see people standing in front of the diner laughing, sipping drinks, and eating at small tables in front of the café. A few people were dancing in the middle of the street. Kelli had to push her way through the crowd until she could spot the source of the music. At the front of the café a five-man band played, and much to her surprise, President Jack Heath was singing into the microphone and plucking the strings on a guitar. She had expected him to be there; that wasn't the surprise, but she hadn't known he was in a band. Kelli smiled to herself and found a just-vacated bar stool to sit on. She pushed the dirty dishes aside on the counter, resisting the urge to clean up, and let herself enjoy being a customer for a change. A young woman with her hair pulled back in an untidy ponytail carefully stacked the dishes into a rubber tub. "Be right with you," she said.

When she appeared again, she was breathless. "Sorry, it's not usually like this."

"I know. I used to work here."

"Oh, you're Kelli then?"

"Yes, and I'd like the lasagna with an extra-large portion of salad."

"Sorry—out."

"Hmmm, how about the eggplant?"

"Out."

Kelli took a sip from the glass of water the waitress had put in front of her.

"Why don't you tell me what you do have?" Kelli asked.

"The only thing we have left is the Sunny Day Stew."

Kelli laughed and wondered why she hadn't told her that already. "Okay, bring me that then, with salad."

"There isn't—"

"Just the stew will be fine. Oh, and tell Sunny I'm here."

Jack Heath's deep smooth voice sang about loafing in a natural spring after a long day of riding the range. It was sometime between

ten and eleven o'clock, and Kelli knew that normally the diner would
be shut down by now, but just as on Sundays, the tables were pushed
together at one end, only this time it was to clear a dance space. She
was just finishing her stew when she heard a familiar voice. "Kelli?"

Tony stood with his usual half grin, his hands jammed into his
jeans pockets.

"Tony!" Kelli jumped from the bar stool and threw her arms
around him, surprising herself at how happy she was to see him.

"Good to see you too. You look . . . wow, great."

"What do you mean? I've been traveling nine hours and . . ."

"Last time I saw you your hair was black, not this nice auburn
color, and . . . well, your clothes were . . ."

Kelli pulled at her hair, pleased that he'd said auburn. "It still has
a ways to go. I got a stylist to match the color, but, I mean, it used to
be long and straight."

"Yeah, well, I like it. It suits you."

"And I've never seen you dressed like a cowboy. What's up?" Kelli
asked.

"Didn't you see me? I'm in Jack's band now, the Cattle Rustlers,
playing backup guitar. I saw you come in."

"Since when have you played with Jack?" she asked.

"Since he started playing here. Jack asked me a few weeks ago.
We've been here the last two Friday nights. Now we've got restaurants
all over wanting us. It's been great for Sunny's business, and even
though she won't admit it, she seems to enjoy it. Anyway, let's dance.
That's what I came out here for." Tony led her around a few old men
with their feet propped out in front of them, then to the middle of the
cramped dance floor. They did the western swing and then a slower
dance. She leaned her head on his shoulder as President Heath sang
". . . my pork chops he was eating and with my wife he was cheating."
The song was meant to be funny, but it brought tears to Kelli's eyes.

"Let's go sit down," she whispered in Tony's ear.

He escorted her back around the old men and heard them
shouting to each other, trying to be heard over the music. "No, no,
no. Now the way I heard it, his wife left him and took everything in
the house 'cept the pork chops."

"Why are you so melancholy?" Tony asked.

Kelli laughed and wiped a tear from her eyes. "The song. I just think it's so sad."

Tony laughed. "It's not sad. Listen to it. It's funny. Really."

"Breakups are always sad. Sad for someone."

"Yeah, well." Tony jumped behind the counter and grabbed some muffins, and as he took a bite of one, crumbs spilled out his mouth. "It's just a song. A moving-on song. Jack says that's what he does. He takes the everyday sorrows and joys of life and writes lyrics about them and then sets them to music. Music explains, he says. He says that if you write a song about something that's troubling you, it doesn't trouble you anymore. And if you write about your joy and sing about it, then the joy spills over into the trouble and pushes it out, leaving room only for the joy."

Kelli moved behind the counter and filled two glasses with milk and brought them back. "I wish I could write music then."

"We'll do it together. You going to be in town for a while?"

"Rest of the summer at least. I called ahead and got my job back," Kelli said.

"I'll be here too. Working for Sunny and Jack as well. Now that business is booming, they need all the help they can get. I'm helping Jack build an addition for more seating and a dance space."

"What do you mean, 'Jack'?"

"Didn't Sunny tell you? The two of them are partners now. Signed the papers last week. I guess he's got some recipes for hot chocolate and the only way he'd give them to her is if she let him buy into the business."

"Are you serious?"

"Serious."

"It really is great hot chocolate. But I can't imagine Sunny letting anyone come in with her."

"Actually, I think there's more to it than that. She says the reason she let him join her is that ever since she got out of the hospital, she couldn't get rid of him. He planted himself in here day and night, and hardly let her out of his sight. She said she may as well put him to work because she just couldn't stand to see him twiddling his thumbs and pushing huckleberry pie around with his fork. And since he put a halt to that resort west of town—"

"You aren't serious?" Kelli's jaw dropped.

"Serious."

"And since he got her to quit smoking . . ."

"You mean Jack . . . she and Jack . . ."

"Are the talk of this small town, anyway. Nothing's been set as far as a date or anything, but that's just a matter of time."

"I thought it would happen." Kelli took a bite of a lemon poppy-seed muffin and closed her eyes, savoring the delicious flavor.

Tony nodded, "Guess I'd better get back to the band. I think we quit at midnight. You still be around?"

"Guess so. I need to talk to Sunny about a place to stay. Where are you staying?"

"At Jack's."

Kelli had hoped to just sit and listen to the band play, but every time she sat down, someone would ask her to dance again, and being her usual polite self she didn't want to turn anyone down. By the time the band finally announced their final number, her T-shirt felt damp with perspiration. She yawned as an older man with gray, grizzled hair and a gold-capped tooth stepped up. Suddenly she found herself being twirled in the cowboy swing by her best dance partner so far. She didn't recognize him from town and wondered if the café was actually attracting out-of-towners. When the music wound down, she found herself shaking his hand and thanking him.

"Pleasure's mine, miss." He touched the brim of his hat, smiled, and sauntered out the door. As she watched him leave, she realized he was just like all the other old men in the diner, out-of-towner or not, in that he reminded her of her grandpa—he reminded her of home. This felt like home. Kelli smiled at the realization.

chapter 34

jealousy

What worried Sam the most was that Stacey hadn't noticed him yet. He'd been following her around for the last two weeks, ever since he'd last seen her in Grouse Creek. If she could be so easily pursued, then wasn't she vulnerable? He told himself that he was different than her ex-boyfriend Dave. After all, Dave had stalked her out of jealousy, he rationalized. What Sam was doing was different—he wanted to protect her. The first week it had been easy to convince himself, but this week, weary with exhaustion from sleeping in his car, the thin line between the two blurred. He felt like he might be turning into Dave—desperate to keep his relationship with Stacey going by keeping his eye on her. Daily, Stacey left overly chipper messages on his machine, telling him that everything was fine and not to worry and that she'd talk to him soon. If he happened to be there, which was almost never now, she'd keep the conversation short and breezy.

Driving back to Grouse Creek, an extra fifty or sixty miles depending on where the meetings were held, must have proved too difficult, because now Stacey was staying with someone in Burley. Which also meant she wasn't working at the co-op anymore.

It was late afternoon and Sam was following Stacey's car when he noticed the red Nissan turn on Malta Avenue and then onto 16th. He hung back just far enough so that he wouldn't be conspicuous. He had resurrected his grandmother's luxurious pale yellow Lincoln because Stacey would be less likely to recognize it.

His routine was simple. He kept his sleeping bag in the car, and after falling onto the floor the first couple of nights, he'd adjusted, finding it almost comfortable. Then he'd eat a bagel and a pint of juice purchased from the grocery store the night before.

Stacey would emerge from the house, usually around eight in the morning, looking every day less like herself. Her clothes became . . . he wasn't sure what exactly, but definitely less modern looking each day. Instead of her usual jeans, she now wore simple skirts and blouses. And her hair went from a loose natural look to being pulled up in a tight bun on her head. She would then head to the police station where she would usually stay just over an hour.

Sometimes at that point Sam would hurry home, take care of his animals, clean up, and then hurry back, hoping she hadn't gone anywhere yet. Today he waited, feeling sure things were starting to happen. He'd parked across the street from the sheriff's department and half a block away. She came out again after an hour. He followed her car to First National Bank. After a few minutes, she emerged again, and he saw her walk directly to another vehicle, a gray Isuzu Trooper.

Sam held the binoculars to his eyes. The glasses were small, but powerful. Through the lenses, her beautiful face was so close he thought he could touch it. She smiled and he felt a familiar tug at his heart. Then she leaned her head through the window and got very close to the man behind the wheel, maybe to whisper something. He saw the man—receding hairline, graying brown hair, forties or fifties, put his arm on her back. Sam's first impulse was to jump out of the car and run down the street, but he didn't. Instead, he found himself outside of his yellow car pounding his fist on the hood. She handed the man something and, as she did, she turned her face toward Sam. Afraid she'd see him, he ducked quickly and pretended to be checking the car tires.

"Shoot," he said aloud.

"Hey, cowboy," a smooth voice responded. "It's been awhile. Car trouble?"

Sam looked up to see someone he recognized but couldn't place right away. "Uh, actually . . .who—"

"Don't tell me you've forgotten me already? I'm Angie Baker from the real-estate office. I met you there awhile back."

"Oh, sure." Sam put his hand out to shake hers, then glanced back to see if Stacey was still there.

"Saw you out here lurking in this car with binoculars pressed to your face. Whew, what a car. A Lincoln Continental. Leather upholstery, I bet. I noticed you banging on it with your fist. Now why would you be doing that?"

Sam tried to ignore her and kept his eyes on the red Nissan that Stacey was stepping back into.

"Got to go." He jumped in the Lincoln and turned the key and at the same time, Angie leaped into the backseat.

"Don't even mind me. I'm just checking this thing out for the ride—see if they're as smooth as they say they are," Angie said.

"What the heck?" Sam slammed on his brakes, pitching Angie forward.

"Not so smooth, it seems. Guess I'll have to put my seat belt on."

Sam turned around. "Do you mind? I'm in a hurry."

"Now, last time we were together, you were ever so polite—a gentleman, if I remember. So what's this attitude you have all of a sudden? Just curious to know whatever happened to your sister. You were supposed to call me."

The red Nissan turned a corner. Sam had no recollection of ever telling her he'd call her. Maybe he'd said something about calling her for information, but he couldn't remember. "Hold on!" Sam hollered and pulled out onto the highway, flooring the pedal to catch up. Again he saw the red car turn and he followed. It was heading out of town now, toward Rupert. By now, Angie had crawled over the high seats into the front and started to scoot next to him, but he put his hand out in protest. "Don't mean to be rude, but I need full access here. If you're coming along, sit over there."

"Not nearly as friendly when you aren't after something, are you, cowboy? Whole different thing going on here." Angie laughed. "You know, I might could help you. I saw you spying on that dark-haired chick. I mean, if she's dumping you for that guy, than she's one psycho woman."

"She's not dumping me. She's sort of working undercover."

"Hmmm. Then what are you doing? Are you under-undercover?"

"Huh?"

"I mean, you say she's working undercover and yet you're following her. So what are you doing?"

Sam looked sheepishly at Angie and shrugged his shoulders.

"I get it. You don't trust her. That it?"

"I trust her. It's them I don't trust—the Church of Faith. That guy or someone like him conned my sister."

"And just how does your girlfriend fit into the picture?"

"I don't even know how to explain that," Sam said as he continued to follow the car all the way through Rupert and to an outlying area.

Stacey pulled off and got out of her car. The Isuzu was already there, parked in front of a sprawling brick rambler surrounded by trees and an immaculate yard. Just over a half dozen cars lined the street, and Sam pulled behind the last one. He took his hat off and combed his hair. Then he opened a tin of Altoids and popped one in his mouth. He pulled the car door handle.

"Whoa. Hold on to your horses, cowboy. You can't follow her in there if she's undercover."

Sam hesitated. She was right. What was he thinking? He looked at Angie.

"What are you going to do? Confront the old guy, get him in a headlock, and then knock him dead with your, uh . . . you got a gun?" she continued

"Not on me."

"Then you've got nothing. They're after young girls, right? You wait right here and keep out of sight," Angie said. And before Sam could say anything, she was out the door and sashaying right up to the front door.

By the time she returned he'd fallen asleep on the spacious passenger side of the front seat. He jumped when the car door slammed.

"Stay down," she whispered, climbing behind the wheel. "I don't think they should see you. And I'm driving."

"What time is it? You were gone forever." He felt the car pull out into traffic.

"You're in deep, cowboy. That wasn't an Amway meeting. Just relax and stay low until I tell you it's safe."

"Did you see Stacey? What happened?" Sam asked, waiting for the answer as the car made several more turns.

"You can sit up now," Angie said.

It was hot. Sam pulled his sweaty shirt away from his skin and turned on the air conditioner. "Well? How'd you get in?"

"It was strange. I'd planned on pretending like I'd lost my cat in the neighborhood. That was something I'd seen on Oprah—a technique that kidnappers and pedophiles sometimes use to lure their victims. It's very effective. But at the last second I changed my mind and decided to just act like I belonged there. That turned out to be the right thing. Everyone just assumed I was one of them. Guess you have to be invited special to this thing, you know. But it seems no one knows who invited who for sure, so I walked right in. The meeting was in this guy's backyard. They had an enormous barbecue first—roast beef, pork, chicken, even roasted fresh pineapple. Now that was fine-tasting fruit."

Sam's stomach began to rumble and he opened the glove compartment and took out a granola bar.

"Oh, yeah, you must be hungry." She jerked the car into a drive-thru at a Burger King and slammed on the brakes.

Sam grabbed onto the door for support. "Watch it."

"Uh . . ." she said into the microphone. "The cowboy will have a double burger, fries, and . . .What kind of drink, Sam?"

"Root beer."

"Root beer. Yes, that's it. Got cash on you?" she asked Sam.

Sam pulled out his wallet and handed Angie a five-dollar bill. "Now who's that a photo of? You got more than one girlfriend?" she asked, pointing at the picture of Kelli.

"No, this is my sister, the one these guys conned into giving them her house. I think I told you at your office."

"Anyway—" Angie handed him the sack of food and the drink. "First thing is they search me. I couldn't believe it, but I acted nonchalant like I didn't expect less. And then I just start walking around, chatting and eating the food. I saw your girlfriend right off. She kept standing next to Trooper man and she'd give him these big eyes like she thought he was the next best thing to Joe Millionaire, if you know what I mean."

Sam didn't know what she meant, but nodded anyway.

"She's good at undercover. So I watched her and I did the same thing—not with him, though. I chose this other man, and I just gave him these big moony eyes and it worked. He says, 'I haven't seen you here before. How did you become involved?' And I said a girlfriend of mine told me about it and he said, 'Oh? Who was that?' and I pointed at Stacey. 'Oh, you know Stacey, then?'

"'Yes,' I said. 'We're acquaintances.'

"And he said, 'Well, she's a full-fledged member of the order now. Are you thinking of becoming one with us?'

"I thought 'with us' was a strange way to put it, but I said yes, and somehow he started telling me how Prophet Daniel can work miracles for those who show enough faith, and for those really interested in the principle, and in being saved during the apocalyptic destruction in the end. I mean he was seriously freaking me out. He said Stacey has already shown how she can really sacrifice for the cause. 'Oh, yes,' I said. 'She gave up quite a bit.'

"And he said something like, 'Not when you think about what she'll get in return. Eternal joy and unimagined wealth that we can't even comprehend here on Earth.'

"Then I threw in this line I'd heard at church once for effect: 'God helps those who help themselves.' Really, it didn't have anything to do with the situation, but he seemed to like it. I had him—hook, line, and sinker. 'Course, he probably thought he was about to reel me in too. Then he asked if I'd be willing to do what she did, and I wasn't exactly sure what Stacey had done, but I sort of nodded. So he said 'And she's planning on giving up *all* her worldly possessions, just like all of the believers, and like you'll do when you're ready to become one with us.' I put on this look of true spirituality, like this." Angie looked at Sam, and he had to admit, that the way she held her eyes and the way her lips formed an innocent smile, she truly looked angelic. "What do you think?" Sam winced and felt his foot hit the floorboard as she swerved to miss a bicyclist.

"Watch the road. Let me drive now?"

"Not until you finish your burger, cowboy. Anyway, I hoped that he wouldn't say anything to Stacey, you know, not knowing how she'd react to the news that she knew me and all, but she is good. Really good. You should be proud. This man who I was talking with, his name was Riley or something, anyway he walked over to Stacey and I said— right off so she'd know something was going on—'Thanks so much for asking me to come,' and I grabbed her hand, shook it, and gave it a knowing squeeze, hoping, praying actually, that she'd catch on."

Sam didn't like that Angie's eyes were on him instead of the road. He couldn't look at her, feeling like he had to watch the road for her.

But Angie just kept talking despite his nervous hints that she should be looking out the windshield. "And she did catch on. She's like, 'So glad you could make it,' and then for a second the two men disappeared, and I was able to clue her in that you had brought me. I know she wanted to ask me who I was, but she didn't. She just chatted on about how great the spirit is in the order and how much happier she is now that she's put herself in line with the will of God. It was creepy hearing her talk like that, and I wanted to tell her she could drop the act, but then I thought it was smart of her not to. She almost fooled me, really. She is really good. It was awesome. If you hadn't told me she was undercover, I never would've believed it."

Sam crumpled his empty sack and tossed it in the backseat with the rest of the two weeks' worth of garbage. He didn't know whether to be relieved or more worried. But he was a little irritated with Stacey still. "Pull over so I can drive. We're almost home."

"Home? Oh yeah, I forgot. By the looks and smell of this car, you've been living in this thing. My car is parked another block away in the office plaza parking." After a moment she pulled into the lot. "I don't see it anywhere. It's a midnight-blue Honda hatchback."

Sam pointed to a sign. "Could that be the problem? 'Employee Parking Only. Violators Will Be Towed at Owner's Expense.'"

"But I always park here," she whined, pulling out a cell phone. She began pushing numbers. "Anyway, so after the barbecue there was this meeting with some blond guy who everyone seems to practically worship. He has the most incredible blue eyes I've ever seen. What color are your eyes?" she asked, squinting at Sam, but her squint was interrupted by someone answering her call. "Yes, I need to find out what brainless imbecile towed my car away, " she said into the phone.

Sam thought that *brainless* and *imbecile* were redundant, and might have told her, but she continued.

"Uh-huh. Midnight-blue Honda. Uh-huh. Okay, I'll hold." She held the phone to her ear, then looked back at Sam. "Brown, aren't they? So anyway, this man with the eyes—I mean, he could talk me

into anything. He's beautiful. A true Adonis, if you know what I
mean. And he has this deep resonating voice . . . Seventy-five dollars!
You've got to be kidding? Who has that kind of money? I know I
don't. And yes I can read just fine!" Angie shouted into the phone.
Then she listened, grumbling under her breath, before pushing the
off button. "Problem with cell phones is you can't really slam down
the receiver. Notice that? You can be furious, but how will the other
person know it?"

"I think they knew it."

"You got seventy-five dollars on you, cowboy?"

"Do you even know my name?"

"Uh, sure, Samuel L. Carson."

Sam wondered how she knew the middle initial since it would
never have come up in conversation. "No, I don't have seventy-five
dollars on me," he answered.

"Can't get my car out of impound, then. Want to drive me to my
apartment? It's in Twin. You can stay there, if you'd like."

Sam laughed. This girl was unbelievable.

"Thing is, I have a futon you could stay on. Beats sleeping in this
car, even with leather upholstery."

Sam switched places with her and pulled onto the highway.
"Where's the impound place? I'll write a check for it," Sam said in
surrender.

"Now I couldn't let you do that." Then, without missing a beat,
Angie continued, "It's two blocks, then turn south, for one block."

Sam laughed again. "Anyway, so the Adonis . . ."

"Oh, yeah, so this blond man—he's the whole reason your sister
joined up for sure. He's probably only about thirty. Little goatee. I
think he's going after the Old Testament-prophet look. And on him it
works. He's . . ."

"I don't think she'd even met him until later maybe, from what
she said."

"Oh, well there's a couple of other cute guys, but not many. Most
of the men are older than my grandfather most likely. Anyway, I
honestly had to remind myself several times that these guys were
crooks; that even the blond beautiful man—as honest as he looked—
was probably after my money. He would've died if I'd shown him my

bank balance, died right on the spot. So anyway, I kept pinching myself until I got tears in my eyes. The pinching was, you know, so I'd remember why I was there, which actually—now why was I there?"

"To see if Stacey was okay."

"Oh yeah. Anyway this Riley guy came to me afterward and asked me if he could contact me again. And I found myself willingly writing down my phone number. It wasn't until I got back in this car that I remembered, you know, that I'm not a bit interested in that cult thing. I mean, I'm telling you. I got involved with Amway once, and that was bad enough—the recruiting, the—"

"He's interested in you as a wife. Another wife and your money. They're polygamists."

"Hmmm. Really? No one has wanted me for his one wife yet, let alone his one wife of several. This could be interesting."

Sam pulled up to the gated, locked impound yard. A young man with black glasses and curly hair was silhouetted in a lighted booth with his nose in a book. Sam jumped out of the car, wrote the check, and within minutes the man had Angie's car for her. Still, she stayed in his car.

"Okay—it's been nice seeing you again." Sam put his hand out to shake hers.

"What, no kiss?" Angie asked.

"No kiss," Sam stated firmly.

"You're going to let me help you out on this thing, aren't you? Riley will be calling me—I saw to that. I forgot to tell you that I sort of let it slip that I owned quite a bit of property in Montana. I don't really own any, but I said Montana because I went there once with this boyfriend of mine. Tristen was his name, but he turned out to be a jerk, like all guys, 'cept you of course. When I said, 'Montana,' Riley said that they have another branch of believers up there, and that my land could be a real contribution to the furthering of their movement to save souls from apocalyptic destruction. So I said I'd have to see if things worked out and all. So anyway, Sam, after this guy gives me a call, you want I should get hold of you, or . . . ?"

"Yes. Here." Sam fumbled in the glove compartment for a pencil.

"Oh, I'll just look your number up in the phone book, and then I'll keep an eye out for this yellow banana. Call me at work if we miss each other."

"Okay, and thanks," Sam said, wondering why she would be willing to help a near stranger.

"See ya, cowboy. I'll be waiting for your call," she said.

* * *

When Sam pulled up to his house, all he could think about was a bed with sheets and a hot shower. But Stacey's car was there. He ran to the house. She was on the phone, laughing when he entered, but as soon as she saw him, her face turned sober. "Sam's here, you want to say hi?" she said into the phone. She handed him the receiver.

Sam wasn't interested in who was on the phone, but took it anyway. "Hello."

"Hi, Sam. I've been trying to reach you for days. Just wanted you to know everything's going great up here in Montana. Sunny's expanding and . . ."

After a minute of nonstop chatter, Sam thought he'd better give his attention back to Stacey. "That's great, Kelli," Sam cut her off gently, "but would you mind terribly calling me back in about an hour or so?"

"Oh, well, okay. Talk to you later, then."

Stacey's hair was down now, the way she normally wore it, and it was so great to see her again he was beside himself. But the look on her face was emotionless. "Stacey, everything okay?" he asked. He hugged her nervously, but she didn't reciprocate. "What's wrong?"

"Sam, are you following me?"

"Well—"

"I can't believe it. You are."

"Stacey, I just had to see if you were okay. I—"

"Where'd you find the cute little bimbo?"

"She isn't a bimbo. She's smart, funny, definitely not—"

"I was this close to getting what I needed out of that group—this close," she said, her finger and thumb pinching the air. "And then your friend shows up and now I'm back to square one. Sam, I wasn't authorized to invite people to the cottage meeting. Now they are questioning my loyalty. What could you possibly be thinking?"

"Stace. . . I don't know what to say. I've been so worried about you. I really care about you." Of course she was right. But her words stung. He put his hat back on. "I've got to check the animals and then clean up," he said as he stepped out into the yard to think.

"I'm cooking us some dinner," she hollered from the door, frustration starting to leave her voice.

"Don't bother. I ate at Burger King," he mumbled. But as he said it, he realized he was still hungry even though it had only been just over an hour since he'd eaten. His horses whinnied when they heard him coming. "I've missed you too," he said. He patted Nodra, then pushed the hose nozzle into the horse trough and turned the water on. The new colt racing next to his mother was taller than her underbelly now and couldn't slip in and out between her legs as he once did. Sam looked at the sky and wondered if a storm were brewing. It smelled like rain, but the night sky was clear with stars glimmering against the darkening backdrop.

When he returned to the house, Stacey had the table set for two and had broiled a couple of small steaks and boiled some potatoes. "Not much food in the house, so . . ."

"It's great." Sam hung his hat on the hook and pulled his muddy boots off.

"Kelli has lots of news from Trout Haven. Sounds as though the branch president up there has quite a country band. Remember Tony?" Stacey began.

Sam cocked his head. "No. Can we not talk about Montana? I may be stupid, like you said, but—"

"I didn't say you were stupid. I would never say that," Stacey said.

"But you implied it, and you have no right to call Angie names."

"I'm sorry. I was upset, okay? Well, I'm saying a blessing on this food." Stacey silently bowed her head for a moment, then started cutting her steak. "So just what were you thinking?"

"That I can't stand another day without you. That's what I'm thinking."

"And if you hadn't shown up there, that would have happened sooner than later," she retorted.

Sam changed the direction of the conversation. After all, he didn't want to fight on their first night together in weeks. "She said you were great. A very convincing polygamist." Sam tried to smile.

Stacey smiled and scrunched her nose. Her eyes widened. "It's kind of fun. I think when this is over, I'll see about maybe going into law enforce—"

"Oh no. Don't even think about it."

Instead of getting mad, she smiled at him, clarifying that she was teasing him. When they finished eating, Sam and Stacey went into the living room and Sam pulled her down next to him on the sofa. "Can we just spend a little time pretending you aren't angry with me?"

She leaned her head on his shoulder and slipped her hand into his. "I'm really not. I wish like anything that you could be there with me."

"Why can't I be? They've got men in their group."

"Don't even consider it. There's no place for a jealous boyfriend in this kind of an organization."

"Jealous? Me? I could control myself long enough to—"

"And what would you do if you saw me with another man?"

"Absolutely nothing," Sam said, remembering banging his fist on his grandmother's car.

"Or when you hear them saying the prophet of our Church is spawn of the devil? That's what they teach, Sam. Could you listen to that?"

"Of course. You need to remember I served a mission. I've heard worse."

"Well anyway, I found out they are taking lots of extra precautions. I tried to buddy up to one of the women and found out things are a lot tighter now than they used to be. They aren't taking any chances. Nothing was said to me specifically about Kelli, but . . . I get the impression she's really got them worried. And of course, in Utah, several polygamists have been charged with crimes. That's got them really paranoid, I think."

"You aren't going to actually pretend to join are you? Do not under any circumstances go out to that compound. It sounds like Kelli thought she was just going out there to check things out, but that's where the brainwashing really took place."

"I could never be brainwashed."

"That doesn't sound like a firm resolve to stay away from the compound." Sam's voice rose slightly.

"Well, I'm not going to do anything foolish. I promise. I already promised that. And unless I'm absolutely sure, and can take my own car out there, and feel good about things, I won't go there. Really."

She sounded so sure. Sam could only hope for so much cooperation on her part, so he tried to believe everything would turn out okay after all.

"Anyway Sam, you put me in an awkward position with Angie showing up."

"Sorry."

"Actually, it might be okay. I think I got them convinced that I was inspired to invite her. Her quick thinking about mentioning property she owned helped. It seems that is mostly what this cult is about—acquiring money, property, and power. Power is a big thing, and the way they ensure strict obedience is through fear."

"See, Angie's not an airhead."

"Oh, I know. She's just so cute. I guess I felt a little jealous. I figured if she was helping you out, she must like you a lot."

Sam laughed. "It's the hat. And you know I have eyes for no one but you."

Stacey smiled.

"Oh, I've missed that smile." He leaned his head down and kissed her. He held onto her tightly, not knowing when he'd see her again.

chapter 35

living and loving

It was the Sunday before Independence Day, the Lazy Moose Café's busiest week of the year, so it was nice to take a break from the hectic activity to enjoy Church meetings. And this Sunday, all Sunny needed to do was find someone to take a meal in to the Jamisons. They were a new family in town with a new addition—a little boy. Today was taken care of, but she was hoping to get someone else for the following day and was just wondering who to ask when she suddenly became aware of the entire Sunday School class looking at her. *Okay, Jack must be up to his old tricks and has announced something I should've caught.* She glanced up at Jack, who was teaching the class and standing at the makeshift podium with a huge grin on his face. "Will that date work for you, Sister Day?"

Sunny looked around the room, and every single person was staring at her with expectant looks and huge grins, except for three-year-old Chandra Danielson who was lying under her chair sucking her thumb.

"Excuse me, President Heath. I must've been thinking about something else. Could you repeat the date and time?"

"The morning of September fourth at the Idaho Falls Temple."

"Well, if you think I'll be ready by then." Sunny thought that even for President Heath, this was a little too casual an environment to be asking her if she would be ready to go back to the temple. After all, it hadn't been very long since she'd quit smoking, and less than a year that she'd been attending church again. But then, he was Jack, and you could never outguess his sometimes outlandish boldness.

"Great. We'd like to extend the invitation to our marriage ceremony to every temple recommend holder and then, when we get back to town, we'll have a big party for the whole community. It'll be right here at the Lazy Moose with the Cattle Rustlers playing—minus the lead guitarist for at least a few of the dances."

Sunny gasped out loud. And even though it was entirely inappropriate in Sunday School, Brother Calder started applauding, and a handful of others followed suit before President Heath held his hand up to hush the gathering. Already everyone around Sunny was leaning toward her and whispering their congratulations. She felt faint and slid out of her chair, then headed outdoors into the open air. A sudden urge to smoke overcame her, and her hand automatically jerked down to her ankle socks, fishing for a cigarette. Instead of finding any, she took her hand up to her face and twirled a strand of hair that had escaped from its bun. Tears sprang to her eyes and she longed more than anything for Shane.

The street was bustling with holiday activity. Flags lined the street. SUVs with bicycles ornamenting the roofs passed by. Beat-up Subaru wagons and VW vans with stickers like "Earth First" or "Mean People Suck" were parked in front of Molly's Bar and Grill. *The '60s and '70s all over again,* Sunny thought. On normal days these tourists would've been parked in front of her café, but the large "closed" sign that hung out front sent them across the street. Wallace Bruner had thanked her on a daily basis for closing down on Sundays. "Funny thing," he'd said, "You get religion and I get blessed for it." But the blessings had been hers as well; countless blessings she couldn't begin to number, but a good many—she had to admit—were because of Jack. If she were honest with herself, she would have to admit that she hadn't stopped smiling since the day he'd walked into her café and asked her to be Relief Society president. And except for the heart attack, everything in her life was better now. Even the heart attack had allowed her to reflect on just how good it was to be alive, so it might be one of those blessings in disguise. And now, somehow, it seemed Jack wanted her to marry him. What would Shane think? If she could only ask him.

Without a backward glance, she hopped into her VW Bug, and with skillful maneuvering, quickly unblocked herself from behind the Danielsons' orange-and-white Suburban. Within minutes Sunny was on the highway. It took her five hours to get to the cemetery where Shane was buried. It was one of those forgotten settlers' cemeteries, overgrown with tall grass. Most of the headstones were no longer visible from the road. Shortly after they were married, they'd been traveling and had noticed the weathered pole fence from the highway. It was in a peaceful spot outside what had once been a thriving mining community. Now the area boasted just a handful of summer homes and decaying remnants of its glory days. Scars over a hundred years old still cut into the mountainsides, and old trestles, buildings, cables, and carts littered the area. Sunny had told Shane she wanted to move there and plant seedlings to repair the damage from the earlier era, and start an effort to clean the streams of the mining tailings that polluted and left the water rust-colored and devoid of fish. They'd never moved there, but as they'd walked through the picturesque cemetery—and even though dying seemed as remote a possibility as a trip to the moon—they'd decided to be buried there. From his hospital bed, Shane had reminded her of their pact, just days before he lapsed into a coma. She'd sat by his bedside and listened to his breathing; it was quiet, rhythmic, and reassuring. Then, gradually, the breaths became sporadic, then almost nonexistent, and she would lay her head on his chest to feel the eventual gentle rise and fall. For days he clung to life, and finally she took his hand, still warm, and whispered into his ear, "Go, I'll be all right. I promise." He left Earth life as gently as a ripple of water dissipates after a pebble is tossed into it.

Bright blue flax and red Indian paintbrush were splashed like paint dots among the abandoned graves. The lodgepole pines had encroached on the tiny untended cemetery, and Sunny was pleased to find that a new sapling had pushed up at the foot of Shane's grave. She pulled some of the grass away from the headstone so his name was visible, then sat cross-legged on the ground and began to talk.

She often talked to Shane, usually just in her mind, but sometimes when she had to face a big decision, she would talk out loud, not intimidated by what others might think. Marty at work was used to it, and had stopped answering her when he noticed her mumbling.

Today, she cut right to the chase about Jack. "Shane, someone wants to marry me. He's insufferable in so many ways, and yet for some reason I smile every time I see him. Is that enough to build a marriage on? More than anything, I want you to be a part of this decision. Of course I've never stopped loving you, not even a millisecond, it's just that I never thought I could find room in my heart to love again in this way. You know that when you died my heart withered so much I didn't think I could ever feel anything again. And yet I do. But a part of me feels guilty about enjoying someone other than you. I wish you were here to help me decide what to do—"

Then Sunny started laughing. "Do you realize how ridiculous that is?" she asked Shane. "If you were here, I wouldn't have this decision to make and that would be so much easier. So what do you think?"

Sunny stopped talking, hoping to hear something—maybe his voice whispering on the breeze. Instead she noticed a mountain blue-bird fly from a nearby branch, then a burst of iridescent blue exploded from the nearby tree as a small flock of birds took to the sky. The forest was filled with sounds—trees creaking, birds singing, insect noises. Every rotting log and growing tree and shrub teemed with activity. She sat still and listened to the forest din, cried, and remembered how good it felt to jump into bed and cuddle next to Shane. She thought back to the day they'd been told the heart-breaking news of his having cancer, and how he'd told her not to let his death get her down, that she had too much to give, that she should always go on living and loving. She sat there for an hour in the shade of the tall pines and felt peace. Her answer didn't come from any perceptible voice or sound; she'd had it even before she left Trout Haven. Shane had given her permission to be happy even before he died. He had reminded her of it again before slipping away from her.

It was after 11 P.M. when Sunny returned to Trout Haven and knocked on Jack's door. She felt faint from lack of food, but was anxious to tell him what she and Shane had decided. He was still dressed in his Sunday clothes when he answered the door. A quick look of relief crossed his face and he invited her in.

"What a day," he said. "I've been running around this town putting out fires all day."

"Really? What started them? Fireworks? Do you have something to eat? I'm starving," Sunny babbled.

"Sure, someone brought a casserole over and put it in my fridge. I'll warm some up for you. I think it's the same person who's been cleaning the place up—Sister Danielson, I think. Her daughter Jennifer sort of spilled the beans in church, asking me if I like the way my house looked lately. Then she giggled and covered her mouth. I'll have to thank her mother. It sure looks nice." He walked to the kitchen and went to work. "I didn't mean actual flaming fires, and where were you? I sure could've used some help. 'Course, Kelli was glad to help, but my counselor is out of town for who knows how long."

Sunny was confused. Had she completely misunderstood his proposal? "So what's been going on?"

"For starters, the Jamisons' baby is jaundiced. Then some Fourth of July revelers drank a little too much at Molly's and the county sheriff had to be called in to break up a brawl. Guess one of the guys was an inactive Mormon—don't know how they knew that, but they thought I ought to go and talk to him. Then Brother Calder's got a kidney stone, and you know how painful that can be—"

"Actually, I don't know. I've never had one."

"Oh. Well, they say that it's as bad as the pain of child bir—"

"Jack, was I wrong about today? I thought I heard you propose marriage."

"Of course you weren't wrong. I said it and I meant it. Why would you doubt that now?" He dished the unrecognizable conglomeration onto a plate and handed it to her.

She sat down at the kitchen counter. "It's just that you haven't even heard my answer yet, and you're talking about all this stuff that seems strangely not as important as one would think my answer should be to you. I've been consumed with this all day, and you obviously haven't given it a second thought."

"I didn't give it a second thought because I thought you agreed—you said that date was all right." Jack knitted his brows and bit his lip.

"I told Shane you were insufferable, and this is a perfect example of that. I can't believe that you think you could propose something as important as marriage over the pulpit. And it wasn't even a proposal. It was—"

"I'm such an idiot, aren't I? I just assumed that because I love you, and I know you love me, that we had an understanding."

"How do you know I love you? I've never told you."

"I guess I just assumed that too. I'm such an idiot."

"You already said that."

"I know, but it's true." He got down on one knee and took hold of Sunny's right hand. "Sunny Day—by the way, I think you should keep your name, it's such a great name—"

"Shane thought so too. But go on."

"You will make me the happiest man in Trout Haven—no, Montana—no, on the face of the Earth, if you'll be my wife."

"I'd love to." Sunny felt herself overcome by a rush of giddy excitement. Love—being in love, knowing someone loved her the same way back—was overwhelming.

Jack got up. He wasn't smiling and Sunny thought his eyes looked moist. "I'm so happy," he said.

"I am too," she said, and she meant it.

He gave her a hug and a peck on the lips.

"Surely you can do better than that."

"I can—but it can wait. And again, may I ask where you were today? I didn't even see you leave church, but then I couldn't find you anywhere."

"I went to see Shane."

"Shane?"

"At the cemetery."

"And?"

"And he approves."

"Good. I didn't have anyone to check with except for my kids and the Lord."

"And?"

"And they approve. He approves."

"Good."

chapter 36

out of focus

Stacey was finally invited to visit the compound. If things worked out, she could take a quick peek around and be back to Burley by dinnertime. She'd stop at the police station, give them a location and a rundown of how things looked, and then leave the rest to them. Things were starting to get too sticky anyway. She didn't know how much longer she could feign interest without arousing suspicion as to her real motives. Now she longed to put it all behind her and get back in with Sam's good graces. How much further could she push their relationship before he'd call it quits? This polygamy thing wasn't worth losing him over—that much she knew.

When she pulled into the Smith's parking lot at 1:00 P.M., she could see Adam's gray Trooper parked on the far west end. Stacey parked next to it, thinking he would now pull out and she would follow him, but instead a young woman in her late twenties got out of the Trooper and demanded Stacey's keys from her. She was a pretty woman, with her hair in a braid that fell down her back.

"Leave everything in your car and get into the Trooper," the woman said dispassionately.

"I planned on driving my own car out there." Stacey felt a surge of panic. This wasn't what she had planned.

"Sorry, we can't take those kinds of chances. You'll be brought back here if you don't want to stay."

Stacey reassured herself, then got in the vehicle with Adam. He immediately apologized, but said he was forced to take extreme precautions. She assumed he meant taking her car from her, but as soon as they were out of town, he handed her a blindfold and asked her to put it on. Another feeling of panic gripped her. On the drive, Stacey tried to memorize the direction, but quickly lost track and felt her heart race with a fear she hadn't felt since the year before. Now she wondered if Detective Hacker was right to warn her not to get too involved and not to let them really know anything about her. After what Stacey guessed was close to an hour, she felt the Trooper stop.

"Ready to begin your new life?" Adam asked as he slipped the blindfold off of Stacey's eyes. He patted her hand and smiled.

"Look, I don't know where you got the idea that I was ready to commit to something. I just thought I was checking things out, you know, before officially becoming a member. This is a serious decision, not one I can just—"

"Sure, I know," he said. She felt a little relieved, believing he truly didn't mean any harm to come to her. "It's just that it might be awhile, a day or two, before anyone can take you back. You understand. Besides, you'll get here, fit right in, and won't want to leave anyway. We've got all kinds of things happening this week. The Prophet Daniel is here."

Stacey felt the blood drain from her face and tried to give herself an inner pep talk. *You're okay. Nothing can happen. Stay focused.* But she felt a sense of dread, a warning that she was in danger.

The settlement looked like a typical ranch nestled at the end of a windy dirt road. It consisted of a modest, cedar-sided home, a couple of house trailers, and a few outbuildings and corrals. There weren't any other ranches or roads in sight. Desert hills covered with dense juniper trees and sagebrush surrounded the ranch. It reminded her of Grouse Creek, but they hadn't driven far enough for that. Stacey glanced quickly around. If escape became necessary, she had no idea which way to head. The desolation only increased her feeling of panic, and again she wondered if she'd be able to get out of there unscathed.

After being at the compound for a day, she asked Adam if he could take her back, but he said things were too hectic. She also hadn't seen any sign of anyone named Mary, her main reason for coming in the first place. As difficult as it was, Stacey tried to free her mind from her fears.

To really give the group a chance, the leaders had insisted that Stacey needed to experience enlightenment, and the only way was to begin fresh. This included a purification phase. After Adam promised to check on her often, she agreed to the experiment. Stacey was afraid that if she showed any fear or didn't go along with them, they might become suspicious of her motives, putting her in more danger. For three days she lived primarily in a room smaller than her bathroom had been in her Salt Lake City apartment. It was bare except for a thin mattress and a toilet. For the first two days, she was given only water, the third day allowed fruit nectar. The nectar tasted amazing after the starvation period. She let it drizzle down her throat. She begged for more, but was told by the woman bringing her the juice, Sarah, that it was strictly regulated for a reason she would understand by the end of the training period. Stacey hardly had a minute to herself, as her days were completely regulated from five in the morning on. Kelli hadn't told Stacey anything about this, so she wondered if it was something new. Three times a day Stacey joined the group for prayer, chanting, teaching, and confession. Twice a day, Adam, or another member, would come into the tiny room and "unteach" her, as they called it. Three things were to be accomplished by this: "We are purging your soul of evil influences, purging your mind of all preconceived ideas, and purging your body of impurities that can negatively affect the mind and soul. When these three things are accomplished, you will enter the next phase, a birthing into a new spiritual awareness so thorough you'll be completely transformed by the end of the week. Only when you've learned to abandon your own will for the good of the group will you be ready to fulfill your destined purpose for the furthering of our mission."

The only thing greater than her feeling of misery was her fear for her own life, and the fear that she would never see Sam again. *This is crazy,* she thought desperately. *Sam was right, I should've let the police handle it.* During the unteaching, Adam would walk her through her childhood and "undo the damage" others had inflicted on her. Lights were on constantly in the room, bright and buzzing. A tape was playing from a speaker constantly, teaching her doctrines of salvation, and how to survive the upcoming apocalypse. Stacey was finding it more and more difficult to block the constant onslaught to her senses. Her physical being was weak. It was difficult to think with the constant noise and light. She wanted to scream. She wanted to cry. She wanted to sleep. She wanted some relief. She wanted Sam.

"Stacey." Someone knocked on the door.

"Yes," she forced herself to speak calmly.

"It's me, Adam." He opened the door after she heard the click unlocking it. "You can come out for group teaching."

"Adam." Even though she vowed not to let him see her cry, tears sprang to her eyes. No matter what he believed, she thought there was a chance he would feel compassion toward her.

"Stacey? What is it? You look so distraught."

"I just hadn't expected this. I'm really miserable. I don't know if—"

"You don't know what? Are you having doubts? Of course you're miserable now, but after this phase is over, you'll be so grateful to have gone through it. You'll be truly ready to put your will into the hands of a higher power. It's the only way to get your heart and mind in complete compliance with a higher power. You'll feel—"

"I'm just not sure I'm strong enough yet to go through this. Could I just go back home for a while and prepare?"

Adam took her hand and held it tight. "In time, you'll see that your old friends and family stood in the way of your progress. In time, you'll see that everything and every person you need is offered within the society. Outside groups don't have your best interests in mind. Only we can offer you salvation. I was really hoping you were ready for the next step, but I can see you need a few more days of purification."

"But you promised that I could go back whenever I wanted. Please," Stacey pleaded.

"You are past the point of just walking back into the world. But now it's time for teaching, so you'll be allowed to join the group."

"But you lied to me. You promised." Stacey realized she really was a prisoner. For the first few days, she'd believed that all she had to do was tell the leaders she'd had enough, and that someone would begrudgingly put the blindfold on her and take her back to Burley. Stacey felt so exhausted all she wanted to do was lie down on the mattress and disappear.

"Stacey, you are so young. You have no idea what you need. I can see your needs far better than you can. Did you honestly think that with all the opposition to our way of life that we can just bring people out, put them up as if they are on a holiday, and then take them back? The world is an evil place and we certainly can't take risks to our safety. What we do here is too important. But I have to say I'm surprised at you. I thought I recognized in you a strength much greater than you're showing now. When I first saw you reading your scriptures, even though you were misled, I thought I perceived someone who was seeking to improve the world, and seeking God's will. Now these selfish thoughts emerge. I hope you won't prove to be a disappointment." Then Stacey watched the demeanor on his face soften and a slight smile emerged. "In time you'll see that I'm right. Now let's go join the group and put on a happy face. Kevin will be there. He seems interested in you."

Stacey had noticed Kevin as well. He didn't seem to belong here any more than she did. Maybe he would befriend her.

The group sat in a large circle on the floor. In the past, Richard Ellstrom had done the teaching. Even though Stacey still hadn't met Mary, she found herself hating the man who she knew had beaten the young girl. Stacey glanced around the group of believers. No one was allowed to talk to those in the purification phase. Everyone else looked so much better than Stacey felt. Maybe it was because they hadn't been duped into joining. Stacey had expected the children to all have a shell-shocked look, but she had to admit that they looked like typical children. They giggled, hit each other, and had to be hushed before the meetings. Their clothes weren't unusual. The boys wore jeans and T-shirts, and the girls, although very conservative, wore skirts and blouses not much different from school uniforms. The women, who were obviously the mothers of the more than thirty young people of various ages, didn't look abused or coerced. *Most,* Stacey thought, *seem happy even. Is it possible that Kelli is wrong about Mary's being beaten?* Today's teaching was being done by Uncle Riley, whom she had met for the first time in the backyard barbecue outside of Rupert. Stacey noticed that "Uncle" seemed to be more of a title.

During the teaching, Stacey focused on her own feelings and needs instead of listening to the brainwashing around her. She forced her mind to disengage from the messages being taught and thought about more pleasant times. Today her mind wandered to the time Sam had shown up in Grouse Creek at 6 A.M. on a Saturday with two horses in tow. He'd told her to get ready for a ride and then he'd made breakfast for the two of them—bacon, scrambled eggs, and French toast. Sam was the first boyfriend she'd ever had who cooked anything besides noodles. Hands down, he was a better cook than she was. When she came out of the bathroom wearing the outfit he'd given her, a cowboy hat, boot-cut jeans, long-sleeved western-style shirt, and boots, he'd whistled and said, "Aren't you a sight for sore eyes?"

She had laughed, remembering that her first college boyfriend had used the same expression once, only they had been going to a dance. She had been wearing a formal gown and her hair had been styled professionally at a salon. "Last time a guy said that to me, I had spent a hundred and fifty dollars to look that way," she'd said.

"The boots alone cost that much," Sam admitted, "and I'd say this money was better spent, wouldn't you?"

After breakfast they'd ridden into the hills and up a narrow canyon with gnarled mahogany trees sprouting from sheer rocky clefts and ledges. The geology had changed in the ascent. Instead of gray soil, the cliffs were rusty oranges, yellows, and reds. Large boulders looked like they'd been tossed haphazardly across the hills by a giant hand. *Boots to make me beautiful.* The thought made her smile.

Stacey caught herself smiling and remembered something else from her past. She'd once had a lead role in a high school play, acting as the blind woman in *Wait Until Dark*. Portraying a convincing blind person, although extremely difficult, was simple compared to convincing the leaders of the Church of Faith that she was completely in tune with this bizarre lifestyle. She would have to try harder if she meant to escape.

* * *

By the seventh day at the compound, the line between reality and acting had blurred and she felt completely broken in body, mind, and spirit. She was no longer able to focus outside of the immediate situation and think about Sam, her own spiritual beliefs, or her purpose for being there. Eventually she couldn't tell when one day ended and the next began; she was only aware of a constant light in the room and voices reverberating in her head. It seemed that every time she slipped into gratifying sleep, something or someone would jar her awake and then the voices would start again in her head. She had cried so hard that her tear ducts no longer produced tears, and she simply heaved in sporadic miniconvulsions.

chapter 37

an angel

Sam drove straight to the realty company where Angie worked. When he entered, he removed his hat and leaned on the counter.

"I don't even have to look up to recognize that hat."

"You owe me seventy-five dollars," Sam said.

"Yeah, so? Would you be wanting that in cash or—?

"Wondered if you've heard from the Church of Slimeballs yet," Sam said, trying to ignore that her shirt was a bit too tight for office attire.

"Yes. In fact, you're on my list to call. See here." She pointed to his name in her appointment book. "I've got a 'cottage meeting,' with them right after work."

"Okay, great. This is the deal. Stacey hasn't contacted me and it's been longer than a week. I checked with the police and found that they haven't heard from her either and were also concerned. I've reported her missing."

The smile on Angie's face vanished. "Oh, I'm sorry. You must be really worried then."

"You have no idea. They think you're friends with Stacey. See if you can't bring her up in the conversation. Without causing suspicion, find out anything you can. And you can forget the money you owe me. When this is all over, I'll owe you."

"And to think I was just going to do it because things were getting a little boring here. But I like the sound of you owing me."

"And I don't think you should wear those clothes to the meeting," Sam smiled.

"Be serious, cowboy. No one wants to buy without inspecting the goods first, and you said yourself they wanted me for a wife."

"Believe me—just wear something more, uh, frumpy." Something troubled Sam. He closed his eyes for a second and thought, remembering that someone from this group had more or less abducted Mary at gunpoint. He knew he had no right to ask others to put themselves in danger with this group. "Listen, on second thought, I don't think you ought to get involved. Don't even go to that meeting tonight. It really could be dangerous," Sam warned.

Angie smiled. "I'll call you when I get home from the meeting."

Sam sighed and glanced at the clock. "You have a cell phone, right?"

"Yeah, but I can't take it with me into the meeting."

"I just want you to call me right before you get there and let me know where the meeting is being held. And then call immediately when you get out. If, by chance, Stacey is at the meeting, make some excuse, and get to your phone and call me. I'm going to park about a block or two away and will somehow come and get her out if she's there." Sam clung to the unlikely hope that she was perfectly fine and that he could just march in there and get her.

"Okay." Angie scribbled an address on a piece of paper, stood up, and handed it to Sam. "Be near this place, but not too close. I know you're nothing but a lovesick cowboy and it's hard for you to think clearly. But still don't do anything if I don't call you."

Sam felt morose but tried to smile. This girl had been so nice to him. *Why is she helping me? She has nothing to gain by doing this.* Still, he trusted her sincerity.

Sam walked toward the door. "By the way, Angie, you're an angel."

"I know," she replied.

* * *

Later that evening, Sam returned to his home disappointed. Angie had called him right after the meeting, sometime after eight. Stacey hadn't been at the meeting, and whenever Angie had tried to bring her name up, she was only told that Stacey was a role model for her to follow. "Give up everything and join us," she kept being told. Sam started to worry about what Stacey had been forced to give up.

chapter 38

bad vibes

Even at the height of tourist season, the man stood out from the average person on the street of Trout Haven. Probably because he looked *too* alone. The locals by now were familiar to Kelli, and tourists tended to travel in clumps—family clumps or friend clumps or as couples. And another thing was that the man didn't seem to be doing the typical vacation things. She noticed him from the window of the Lazy Moose while she waited the tables. He was just sitting in his car in front of Molly's. That wouldn't have been too strange, had he been waiting for someone, but he was still there at lunchtime. A couple of times when she looked out, he'd be standing outside of his car, but he'd always drift back into it. It really hadn't occurred to her that the polygamist group would still be searching for her, but now she realized how premature that feeling of safety had been. For some reason when she was back in southern Idaho, she had wanted to be back in Montana, close to Sunny. Sunny's ability to nurture her was what she really needed if she was going to put the nightmarish experience with the cult behind her. Jack also saw to it that Kelli got professional counseling, and every day Kelli seemed to relax and feel more like herself—even though she wasn't sure what *self* she was trying to get back to. Would she be better off as the pre-cult Kelli or the pre-accident Kelli? Her counselor, a caring woman at the university in Bozeman, tried to convince her that neither would do. She had to become a new Kelli, free from the unnecessary and harmful guilt she had burdened herself with, and less naïve than the Kelli from before the accident. Only a totally new perspective on life would do. Each day Kelli felt she was closer to remaking herself, and she felt happier all the time.

"Marty, see that car across the street?" Kelli asked.

He wiped his hands on a towel. "Which one?" He stood in front of the large window.

"Back up," Kelli whispered. "Don't let him know we're looking at him."

"Oh, you mean the red Nissan with the Utah plates?"

Stacey has a red Nissan. Lots of people drive red Nissans, Kelli reminded herself. But still, Kelli stood as close to the window as she dared and peered again, wondering if the car could possibly be Stacey's. "Yeah. He's been there all day. I'm a little nervous about him."

"Okay, maybe I'll head over there and talk to him," Marty said.

"What would you say?"

"Just remind him that the town of Trout Haven has a two-hour parking limit, and say I wondered if he was aware of that law. I'll make it sound like I'm just trying to save him from getting a ticket."

Kelli remembered something that would identify it as Stacey's car. She'd laughed when she first read the sticker and thought how it fit Stacey's independent nature. "When you're there, try to get a look inside and see if there's a sticker on the dash that says something like, 'Well-behaved women seldom make history.'"

Marty looked confused. "And why would it say that?"

"It probably won't—just checking a hunch."

Only a few customers were in the place, ordering Sunny's specialty fruit drinks. Business was way down while Jack's crew had been working on constructing the addition. At first, Jack tried to work around the dinner hours, but finally he and Sunny had just decided to get in there, work hard for a couple of weeks, and be done with it, instead of stretching out the din and dust all summer. Kelli waited for Marty behind the counter, organizing glasses and wiping smudges off the drink machine.

She watched from just behind the machine, hiding from the man's view. Marty seemed to be engaged in a conversation with an old friend instead of a stranger on the street, gesturing at the different buildings as if he were conducting a tour of the town. Finally, the man got inside his car, and Marty opened the Nissan's hood. *Car trouble, that's the reason the man is there. That's all it is.* Now Kelli felt embarrassed. The loud whining of electric saws sent the last two customers out the front door. "Come back soon," Kelli hollered.

Marty closed the hood, then leaned into the car window and appeared to be shaking the guy's hand. When he stepped back through the café door, he looked serious.

"I'm just being paranoid, aren't I?" Kelli asked hopefully.

"Not unless you're a psychic."

"What do you mean?" she asked.

Marty walked over to Kelli. "I'm going to get Jack and Sunny in here first. We've got a major problem." Marty disappeared into the construction area and returned with the others, including Tony. They all squeezed into a booth away from the front window and Marty motioned for Kelli to join them. "Kelli, tell us who the owner of the car is and what it means."

"You mean he isn't just having car trouble?" Kelli asked.

"He said he was, but it started right up. The guy laughed and said something about me having the Midas touch, but there's a sticker in the car, and it's been ripped. It now reads, 'women seldom make history.'"

Kelli felt the blood drain from her face. "I don't know what it means for sure, but it can't possibly be good. Remember Stacey? Sam's girlfriend? You all met her last month."

"Of course, she did CPR on Sunny," President Heath said.

"That's her car."

"But—" Tony began.

"She was pretending to be interested in the Church of Faith to try to find Mary."

Several moments passed before anyone said anything. They were trying to process information that didn't quite fit.

Finally, Sunny stood up. "Call your brother, Kelli."

chapter 39

new surroundings

It was night when they led Stacey to the back of the van. She wasn't blindfolded, but she didn't need to be. The cargo area was dark, with no windows. But that didn't matter either because Stacey had finally convinced the leaders that she was obedient, willing, and eager to be one of them. She figured the sooner she acted completely converted, the sooner she'd be able to wake up from the nightmare that had become her life. Several others were also chosen to be transferred to another complex, and Stacey was pleased that she was selected to be included. Often the members talked about the other group, the other followers, or the other fold, and since she hadn't seen Mary yet, Stacey knew she must be with this other group. She couldn't make out the faces of the others in the van, but knew Kevin was there. She was glad. He seemed somehow different. Probably he'd been caught up with the church simply because he didn't know anything else. Kindness seemed to emanate from him. Stacey hoped so. She'd tried to gauge who she'd be able to turn to for help when the time came. Another young girl was there. Maybe she, too, hadn't been fully indoctrinated. Stacey hoped to take the young girl under her wing, and be a kind of mentor to her.

Three weeks had gone by since Stacey had been coerced into leaving her car and joining the commune. Once the ten-day purification had ended, Stacey found it easier to think clearly. But she still felt weak, even though she was now allowed simple meals to eat. Her already small frame was even smaller; her skirts fell around her hips instead of fitting snugly around her waist. Stacey found herself praying and silently talking to herself often, just to keep her thoughts straight. Usually she was successful at pushing out the teachings, but occasionally she noticed herself listening to Prophet Daniel. When he spoke, if she wasn't careful, she found herself riveted by the sound of his voice, his eyes, and even his unusual doctrine.

When the van finally stopped, two men opened the back doors and Stacey squinted when the dusky light hit her eyes. She struggled to pull herself up and out of the van. Her body was so extremely cramped from sitting on the hard van floor. Besides that, she was starving. She stepped out to see the mountain peaks highlighted with a golden hue. The scene before her looked vaguely familiar, like any of the mountains east of Salt Lake. But even though she'd managed to sleep part of the way, she was sure they'd driven farther than that. The mountains were carpeted with pines, and the valley floor surrounding the ranch house was lush with green grass and wildflowers. It was beautiful.

Stacey was led into a spacious room in a log home with cathedral ceilings. There was a sunken meeting room with a kitchen adjacent, where several women were preparing food. She put her hand to her stomach, feeling the rumbling of having gone so many hours without food. It was hard for her to get used to the minimalist lifestyle she was now a part of. When she joined the already-congregated group, she was brought a meal to eat. It was simple, but nutritious. Stacey immediately scanned the faces of the group, and her eyes fell on a young woman who matched the description Kelli had given of Mary. It must be her.

chapter 40

interrupted

It had been days since Sam had shaved. He rubbed his face, feeling the bristly stubble with his open hand. He rummaged under his bathroom sink, found shaving cream and squeezed a ribbon of it into his hand. The investigation had reached a standstill. He'd hounded the sheriff's department, but they hadn't had any luck locating Stacey, the church, or even Stacey's car. Not knowing what else to do, Stacey's parents had organized a special fast for her safe return. And Sam hadn't made up his mind whether it was good or bad, but Angie hadn't been invited to any more meetings. The days rolled into each other, unfolding in yet another phase of an extended nightmare.

He lathered the cream on his face, then slowly dragged the razor across his jaw. Sam shaved the same way he mowed the lawn, in long parallel stripes, careful to just overlap the pass, so as not to miss anything. He had completed three stripes when the phone rang. It rang a half dozen times before he was able to get to it.

"Yeah," he said, his face smearing shaving cream on the receiver.

"It's Kelli. Sam, when was the last time you heard from Stacey?"

"It's been three agonizing weeks. Why?"

"There's a guy parked across the street from the café here."

"Yeah?" Sam wondered where this could possibly be going.

"He's in Stacey's car."

"What? You sure?" His voice was frantic.

"Yes, I'm sure. It's hers."

"Then she's got to be up there somewhere."

"Not necessarily. The cult probably seized her car, same as they did mine at first. And the guy driving the car must be with the cult, and he's almost surely looking for me. Sam, now I'm worried for Stacey, too. Something could've . . . I mean, she'll be okay. Don't worry."

Sam tried to laugh, but it caught in his throat. "Yeah, that's like telling me to stop eating. Is the branch president around there anywhere, or Marty, or Sunny?"

"Yes, they're all here. Who do you want the most?"

"Jack."

"Hey, Sam. What do you think?" Jack asked.

Sam could feel the quickly liquefying lather slide down his neck in tiny rivulets. He tried to wipe them with the back of his hand. "I don't want Kelli involved in this thing. She's been through so much already. And she needs to be under close protection," Sam said.

"I couldn't agree more," Jack said. "But it's impossible to keep her out of it entirely—I mean, they're looking for her."

"Do the best you can. You have to follow that car. Find out where he goes. Wherever that car ends up might lead us to Stacey. I'm coming up, but of course it'll be at least eight hours before I can get there, and that would be if I left right this second. And don't let him see you." Sam knew he sounded abrupt and demanding, but under the circumstances he didn't care.

"That's what we're planning on. I already have my truck ready to go. It says Superior Log Construction on the sides—it'll be a good cover in case he spots us."

"Good. What about Kelli? If he's waiting there for her . . ."

"We'll figure out something. Don't worry," Jack said.

Not worrying wasn't possible, but he would try to stay level-headed so he could at least think this through. "Okay, just find out where that car goes. Don't do anything beyond that until I get there."

chapter 41

telltale lies

It might have been Kelli's red hair, the way it had looked the first time Sunny saw the girl's huddled mass by the white crosses, that had made it impossible for Sunny not to be involved in Kelli's life. Her own little girl had had red hair, and that image still stuck with her. The tiny infant—too tiny to live—had a startling shock of red fuzz on her head. The image still brought tears to Sunny's eyes if she let it seep into her consciousness. Or it could have been seeing how badly Kelli needed a mother—her frantic running from her past, her lost look, or her overburdened soul; all these things about Kelli made Sunny want to reach out to her. She was only a couple of years older than Sunny's own girl would have been, and Sunny imagined that Kelli embodied just what her daughter would have looked like. Gratefully, Sunny could tell that in the last few weeks, Kelli had started to be truly happy. Her smile was quick and her eyes had gone from being constantly frightened or sad to gazing out almost in a relaxed manner. Just when everything seemed to be going better for her, the trouble with the cult had returned. Of course, it was overly optimistic to have ever thought she was completely safe. And then there was the danger both Mary and Stacey were in. Well, it was Sunny's nature to reach out whenever needed, and clearly she was needed. Sunny decided she was in this to the end.

Just before five that night, about an hour after they'd talked to Sam, Tony and Kelli strolled out and climbed into the borrowed Toyota Camry that Kelli was driving. Kelli sat in the passenger seat, leaned the seat back, and pretended to be engaged in animated conversation with Tony. Sunny doubted that the two had to feign interest in each other, even though it was part of the plan. Sunny had noticed the extra sparkle in Kelli's eyes whenever Tony was around, and most likely the real reason Tony was pounding nails for Jack was to be close to Kelli. She questioned whether Kelli was ready to have Tony as anything more than a friend; still, one couldn't have too many friends. And Tony certainly had been a good ally.

Right on schedule, at 5:00 P.M. sharp, a tour bus pulled up in front of the café. People streamed out the bus doors onto the streets, some into the café. With the bus effectively blocking the Nissan driver's view of the café, Kelli slipped back inside. Then Tony took off in the Toyota. Sunny watched as the Nissan immediately backed out of its parking spot and began to pursue the Toyota. Sunny breathed a sigh of relief that the first part of the hastily conceived plan had worked, and crossed her fingers that everything else would go well.

She felt Jack's arms around her waist and his breath on her neck. "It worked," he said. "Now, we'll just wait right here until he figures out that Kelli isn't the one driving the car and when he does, he'll be back. Maybe, just maybe, he'll give up on Kelli quickly, and we'll be able to follow him."

"And to think I'm marrying you for your money, and then to find out you're smart, too," Sunny said.

Jack laughed. "And don't forget the hot chocolate recipe."

"Triply blessed."

Jack headed for his truck to wait while Sunny kept a close eye out the window as she waited tables. She listened for the signal from Tony: three telephone rings, meaning the man was on his way back. Before long, Sunny could see the man's car parked again a little farther down the road, but still in plain view of the front window. She made a point of passing back and forth in front of the window often, so the man could see that she was the only one waiting tables. He couldn't know that Kelli was still in the building. The man stood outside of his car with his head buried beneath the hood. After a while, he closed it and got back in the car. A tiny burst of exhaust escaped from the tail pipe when the man started his engine. Sunny bolted to Jack's truck, leaving Marty to handle the café.

It was hard to hang back far enough in such a small town, but they figured he had no reason to be unduly suspicious of them. The

Nissan headed north of town, then turned into Sunny's drive. Jack and Sunny continued past on the highway.

"So he knows where Kelli's staying," Sunny said.

"Which puts you in danger also. Maybe we should find both of you another place to stay," Jack suggested.

"I don't think that's needed. He's probably just checking to see if Kelli's there."

Jack pulled the pickup off the road, jumped out, and grabbed a chain saw from the truck bed. "This is no time to start butchering trees," she shouted. *What is he thinking?*

Jack stuck his head in the window. "I've got to look like I've got a reason to be here."

In a few minutes, the Nissan appeared again, and this time headed north. Jack tossed the saw back in the truck and followed the Nissan. It slowed when passing the café. Sunny noticed that Marty had shut the blinds and put out the "closed" sign. She felt bad that she'd been dumping more and more on him lately.

They followed the Nissan onto the freeway and past Bozeman toward Livingston. Finally, it turned onto a minor road before vanishing from view in dense forest land outside of the national-forest boundary.

Jack and Sunny slowed, trying to figure out where the car had gone. They were looking for a road of some kind. It wasn't that there wasn't a road, but there were several dirt roads forking off, and they couldn't see which one the car had taken, so they pulled off.

"Now what?" Jack asked. He looked at Sunny expectantly.

"Take the road *more* traveled—it could make all the difference," Sunny grinned.

"And which is that?"

"The one on the left," Sunny pointed to a narrow road edged with tall grass and scrubby bushes.

They'd only driven a short way when the man from the Nissan appeared out of the trees and stood in the middle of the road with his hand out in the traditional "stop" signal. The barely visible Nissan was tucked into a thicket of scrub. Jack rolled to a halt and pushed the power button to open the window. Sunny opened the glove compartment, pulled out a map, and buried her head in it. It took several seconds for her to realize that the map was upside down, and a map of southern California besides. The man was too far away to notice anyway.

"Hey mister," Jack shouted out the window. "I've got a work order for somewhere in the area. Uh, I'm looking for John Parson's ranch. He said it was one mile off of the state highway, then—"

The man stepped up to the window. He was fortyish with a large frame, and thick straw-colored hair. Pushing his sunglasses up on the bridge of his nose, he announced, "This isn't it. All this is a private ranch."

"Not John Parson's place?" Jack questioned.

"No. I've never heard of him."

"You must have. He owns a good chunk of the valley west of the forest boundary. You probably bought your land from him, if it's in the area." Jack motioned with his hand to indicate the vastness of the Parson ranch.

"If you know so much about him, then how come you don't know where it is you're going? It looked to me like you were following me." The man scowled.

"Yeah, you got that right, yours being the only car down this way, figured you would know something, but as luck would have it, you don't seem to."

"Didn't I see this truck in Trout Haven, parked outside of the café there?" the man asked skeptically.

"Oh, you know the place. Great food. It's my wife's café. She and I often scout around the countryside, scoping out my work sites. I help her. She helps me. Great life, we have. Me and my wife, Sunny. Listen, we've taken loads of your time, and you've saved us from heading down the wrong road, so I tell you what. Next time you're in Trout Haven, stop in at the café and we'll treat you to a nice meal. You and your uh . . . are you married?"

"No. Okay though. Maybe I will. And your name is?" The man's face softened.

"Now I probably won't be there. You know, got to keep the saw blade going. But my wife, she's there most of the time. Then we hire help, so we'll let them know about the free meal too. They're all used to that sort of thing, so no one will think anything of it. In fact, bring whoever with you. It'd be fun to meet some new folks, wouldn't it Sunny?"

Sunny caught on to what Jack was doing. She folded the map back up. "Sure, but just in case I'm not there, what name should I tell our help? We're in the process of hiring right now. Our best waitress, Kelli, quit today to start work elsewhere. You can't hang on to the good ones. They've always got bigger fish to fry." Sunny watched the man's face to make sure he knew who she was talking about, and thought she detected his interest pique at the mention of Kelli's name. She hoped this would encourage him to stop looking for her.

"We can leave your name up by the register. If you're a fish lover, we've just added trout to the menu. Before now we were pretty much a vegetarian place, but we go with the flow."

The man fidgeted and finally said, "Hank Smith. But I'm pretty busy. Not even sure if I'll be able to make it in."

"The offer's good whenever you pass through. You must have business that takes you there every now and again, if you were there today. What line are you in anyway?" Jack asked.

"I'm just sort of a handyman. Do whatever the boss needs doing." He reached to open his car door.

"Would I know your boss?" Jack persisted.

"Doubt it. Listen, I've got to go." Hank's car started up.

"Thanks again," Sunny shouted, but doubted he heard her over the roar of the engine. She looked at Jack, raised her eyebrows, and grinned. "Where'd a branch president learn to lie like that?"

"I haven't always been a branch president. How about you? What experience in your life taught you to think that quickly?" Jack started the truck up and began backing up.

"That was new for me, and I was following your lead. I was always taught not to lie, but I was also taught to follow my religious leaders," she said with a mischievous grin.

Jack bit his lip. "Hope that's okay with the man upstairs, under the circumstances and all. Guess we found our cult, or at least have a pretty good idea where this road leads."

"Think he suspects anything?" Sunny asked, stuffing the map back in the glove compartment.

"Nah, the guy's dumber than a post."

"What makes you think so?"

"He practically led us to the front door."

chapter 42

recruiting

Stacey was disappointed that Mary Rachel wouldn't be allowed to participate in the recruitment effort with her. She had hoped that Mary would be allowed to go with her, so they could make a break together. But after Mary's runaway attempt, Mary had been denied most privileges. Stacey felt drawn to Mary, probably because she could see her younger self in the girl, and because Kelli had told her enough about Mary that Stacey knew she could be trusted.

Today a few of the more trusted in the society were going into Bozeman to invite people to a cottage meeting at the ranch. Stacey was honored that she'd won the admiration of her superiors so quickly and was being asked to participate. Stacey and a couple of young members of the society would work the college campus. Even though it was summer and fewer students were attending classes, the leaders felt summer would be most profitable since the students who were on campus were extra dedicated, just the kind the church was looking for.

Stacey was hoping they trusted her enough to let her do it herself, but soon realized that her participation was just another test of her obedience to the group. Although she hoped to sneak away so she could call Sam for help, she knew that she couldn't do anything that would put her in more danger. She was relieved at least that Adam wasn't chosen to be her supervisor. Instead, Jared, college age himself, was her companion.

Jared wasn't any older than Kevin, but he was different. Kelli had told Stacey that she felt as if Kevin were a victim himself, and that he questioned the prophet's authority. Stacey had tried to get to know

Kevin more, but realized he was no longer allowed privileges. Jared, however, didn't seem like much of a victim. He didn't smile very often and his devotion to the faith was unwavering. Much to her chagrin, he hadn't left her side since the van dropped them off. Stacey wondered how she could possibly get a message to Sam with this guy breathing down her neck every second.

It was the middle of the day when they entered the university library. Stacey and Jared each grabbed a couple of books and walked around the various study areas to get a feel of the place and the people. At a training session, she'd been told to look for people alone, not in groups. She saw a guy studying with a stack of books next to him. He was by a window, far away from some of the tables where several people studied together. She looked toward the young man sitting alone.

"Go ahead and give it a go," Jared whispered.

Jared pretended to be searching the shelves, but stayed within listening distance. "Hey, looks like you're really studying hard. Do you have a big exam coming up?" Stacey asked.

The young man looked up at Stacey, confused. He ran his long fingers through his curly blond hair. "Do I know you?"

"No, just thought I'd come talk to you. School can sure be tough sometimes," Stacey tried to sound sympathetic.

"Are you hitting on me?"

"Heavens no." Stacey sat down. "I'm Stacey, what's your name?"

"Look, I've got a lot to do here." The guy didn't give Stacey a second look. She tried to think of another approach, but finally gave up and looked around the library some more. She was surprised by how much weaker physically she felt since she'd been involved with the cult. Her body ached most of the time, probably because she was eating so much less and not getting any exercise. She spotted another kid and noticed he was studying Gardner's *Art Through the Ages*. His hair, the color of margarine, hung in his face. His bare feet were propped on a chair in front of him. Stacey could see his Teva sandals under the chair. She walked over to him and sat down in the cushioned chair next to him.

"Art major?" she asked.

He jerked his head back in an effort to get his hair out of his face. "Yeah, got a test tomorrow. Professor wants us to have the whole section on the High Renaissance period memorized. Like knowing what year Michelangelo's *David* was carved makes any difference." His voice rose. "We're forced to memorize and regurgitate meaningless facts upon demand. I don't know why we can't focus on what mattered. Michelangelo was so visionary, so ahead of his time. He was an absolute genius. Trying to glimpse his dream—just trying to understand his intellect—is mind-boggling. Anyway—"

"I totally agree. Michelangelo was definitely a genius. I'm Stacey. You are?" Stacey noticed Jared hovering nearby in an effort to hear her approach. They would indubitably talk about it afterward.

"Traden."

"Well Traden, you seem pretty visionary yourself. The kind of person who is concerned about important, world-changing issues." Stacey watched his face. He put his finger in the enormous red book to hold his place and looked up at her.

"Yeah. Of course."

"I belong to a discussion group, Traden, with people just like you. We talk about important things and how we fit into this crazy world. We're having a get-together tonight. It'd be fun if you'd come with me." Stacey felt guilty trying to talk this kid into coming, but planned on somehow letting him know later what was going on.

"With you?" he asked. Stacey could tell he was looking her over. She pretended not to notice.

She knew she had a pretty smile, so she smiled. "Yeah, with me. Lots of good food, too."

"Well, if it were any other night besides tonight, but—you know—Gardner's comes first." He patted the massive book with his hands. His fingernails were long on his right hand, short on his left. *Guitar player*, she thought.

"I don't know. You just don't seem like the type that would put "trivia" first. You said it yourself Traden. Besides, what's one night out of your life? Lots of people in the world are starving. Wars, poverty . . . it's a mess. You'd be with people who, just like you, care about these things. You can even bring your guitar along. Play us a few tunes. I bet you're really good."

Traden looked confused, then glanced at his hands, piecing together how she knew. "And you'll be there?"

"Yeah, and if you want, I'll meet you and we'll go together."

"Okay Stacey, but it's not long, is it?"

"Oh no. It's just a quick get-together tonight, so you can see what you think." Stacey made arrangements to meet Traden outside of the library at 5:30 that afternoon.

She tried a few more people, then went to the drinking fountain.

Jared followed. "You did great with Traden. You flattered him, made him feel guilty, and even flirted with him when you noticed that's what he was going for. Just right. But the others didn't really spark. That's okay, though. You aren't going to be successful with everyone, of course, nor would you want to be." She knew now that Jared believed she was sincere, and that he would pass on that information to their superiors. She hoped that the next time she would be allowed out by herself. That had become Stacey's new plan. She'd get them to trust her, then she'd escape with Mary and anyone else who wanted out.

This time, though, Jared dogged her every move, and she was beginning to think she wouldn't find a way to sneak away and place a collect call to Sam. They stepped outside the library and started walking along the sidewalk, the same walk she'd taken with Sam just a couple of months before in an attempt to find Kelli.

It was hot. "Let's take a break," Jared said. He sat down on a park bench under a linden tree. Stacey joined him.

"Why did you join the group, Jared?" Stacey asked.

"I was born into it."

"So when did you know for sure it was right?"

Jared looked thoughtful. "I've never had time to even wonder about that. It's just all that I've known. There has been no question."

"Oh."

"How about you, though? You joined, right?" he asked.

Now Stacey regretted that she had started this conversation. Jared couldn't know her true feelings and she didn't feel like lying to him. "Yeah, I joined," she said. "Adam found me. I started attending meetings, and eventually knew I had to join."

"Oh. Well, I wish I'd found you first."

Stacey was confused by that statement. "Because?"

"Then maybe you could be my wife instead."

"I'm not anyone's wife, yet."

"I know, but Brother Adam has claims on you. And of course, that's the way it works."

Stacey felt slightly nauseated at the thought. She couldn't let that happen. "Do you mind my asking how many wives you have?"

"I'm only seventeen."

Stacey was surprised. He looked quite a bit older and had a mature quality to him that made him seem older as well. "How old do you have to be?"

"Eighteen usually, for the men anyway. Girls, usually fifteen or sixteen. It works out better if the man is a little older. Then the women are more willing, you know. There's a girl who's promised to me."

"Do you love her?" Stacey asked.

"Love isn't important in marriage. As long as we're both committed to the church, that's the main thing."

Stacey felt sorry for Jared. Given the right chance, he could have been a normal high school senior. Instead, he was talking about getting married to a young girl he didn't love.

The campus was quiet. The summer environment was so much more laid back than when Stacey had been there in the late spring. A perennial flower garden caught Stacey's attention and she automatically went over to it. She loved flowers, especially perennials and wildflowers. Among the tall pink echinacea, she could see yellow daisies, her favorite. Stacey picked one and tucked it behind her ear. A memory suddenly came to her. Just before she'd investigated the Church of Faith, she and Sam had a dancing date at the Desert Dog in Malta, Idaho. When he'd picked her up, he had a bouquet of yellow daisies interspersed with blue forget-me-nots and baby's breath. He had picked one of the largest blossoms, pushed her thick hair back, and tucked the flower behind her ear. The memory made her smile first, then it tugged at her heart. She missed Sam more than she had thought possible.

* * *

The recruiting party hadn't been quite as successful as the society had hoped. Traden had ended up being Stacey's only recruit, and she could tell that it probably wasn't the society he'd been interested in at all, but instead only in her. That was just as well, since Stacey really didn't want any new people to join the group. Only a few others attended the cottage meeting. Richard Ellstrom, who she had finally met, spoke instead of "Prophet" Daniel, who wasn't there, so even that wasn't too successful. Whenever Daniel spoke, the ratio of repeaters to the next meeting was sometimes as high as seventy-five percent. When anyone else led the discussions, it dropped to less than fifty percent of repeats. Eventually it dwindled down to one or two people. And that was just what the society wanted; one or two joiners to keep the order growing. Stacey kept thinking about Sam and how worried he probably was about her. She watched Traden's face during the meeting and could tell he thought the whole thing was crazy. He had to be wondering why she'd gotten involved in all this, let alone why she had invited him, but she didn't dare tell him too much. When she was sure no one was watching her, she managed to get close enough to whisper an apology. "Sorry to drag you here, I had—" Then she noticed Jared staring at them. She quickly changed the subject. "Anyway, Traden, if you want to know more we'll meet again next week." She held her hand out to shake his and slipped him a note, a tiny piece of paper—the only thing she had been able to find, with Sam's number on it. Fearing he might glance at the note before it was safe, she gently pushed his hand toward his pocket, and was relieved when he stuck the note into his jeans pocket. She whispered, "Please tell him I'm okay and tell him—" She stopped again, noticing other members close by. She'd wanted Traden to tell Sam she was stuck somewhere close to Bozeman, Montana, but was happy that she had at least managed to pass the phone number along.

After the barbecue was over and the prospective members had gone home, the leaders encouraged Stacey and the other recruiters not to be disappointed. They were in uncharted territory and it would take awhile to find those truly sincere individuals who would best be an asset to the society.

That evening, when they returned to the ranch, a prayer meeting was being held. A little girl, Jenny, had become sick. Stacey could see a group of people encircling Jenny. Jenny was lying on the floor and looked very pale and weak. A few days earlier, Jenny had been playing, climbing some of the rock ledges on the ranch, and had gashed open her arm. Stacey had attended to the wound. Although she thought then that the girl needed stitches, she was told matter-of-factly that such was out of the question. So Stacey had pulled the skin together the best she could and bandaged it.

Over the past year, the church had become more and more suspicious of any outside influence. At one time they had routinely sought medical help, but recently a revelation to the prophet had prohibited it. Instead, some of the members trained in first aid treated any who were sick. This basic treatment, combined with prayers and faith, would be the only medical help the girl would be allowed. Now the girl was shockingly incoherent. Stacey felt determined to see the leaders, and if need be, "Prophet Daniel," to try and convince them to seek medical attention for the girl. Stacey realized her influence might be Jenny's only chance of survival.

chapter 43

don't worry

Sam had a hard time keeping out the negative thoughts that constantly bombarded his mind. Instead, he reminded himself that Stacey was a strong person. He thought back to the day he'd first met her at the Burley livestock auction. Her fire and determination had immediately attracted him. He chuckled, remembering how she'd called him a jerk within moments of their introduction. She wasn't one to be easily manipulated.

There is no way the most persuasive Kirby salesperson could even talk her into a vacuum. I can't believe that these spiritual doomsayers could get control of her. But Sam's next thought scared him. *That means they must be holding her against her will.* Hating that thought, Sam reconsidered, recalling Dave, Stacey's ex-boyfriend. *He was a manipulative jerk, and Stacey dated him for months—even considered marrying him.* This thought wasn't any more comforting than thinking Stacey was held against her will, though. A brainwashed Stacey would be in even more danger.

It was a little after one in the morning when Sam showed up on Sunny's front porch. He knocked and Sunny opened the door, her terrycloth robe pulled tightly around her small frame. "Come on in," Sunny said.

Kelli peeked her head around the bathroom partition. "Hi, Brother." She came out and gave him a hug and a tense smile.

"We're keeping Kelli out of sight, just in case," Sunny said. "We made the sofa up for you. Kelli and I are sharing my bed while you're here. First of all, you aren't to worry. Things are looking. . ." Sunny seemed to be searching for the right word. "Hopeful. Definitely hopeful."

Sam took his straw cowboy hat off and glanced around the room, looking for a hook. Finally, he set it on the kitchen counter. He was anxious to hear what they'd been able to find out. "So did you find them?"

"Sit down first." Sunny pointed to the sofa made up with sheets, blankets, and a pillow. Sam sat down, wondering how soon he could slip off his jeans and slide under the blanket. He was exhausted from the long drive. Kelli snuggled back under the covers in Sunny's bed across the small room, and Sunny got in next to her. *Kelli found herself a mother,* Sam thought. *It's what she's needed all along.* Then Sam glanced again at the pair and was reminded of his childhood. Sometimes when his father had been out of town for the night on business, their mom would let all three children squeeze into their queen-sized bed with her. It was too tight to sleep that way, but for an hour or so it was always fun. When Mom was in a really good mood, she would drag the TV in and prop it on top of the dresser. Then they'd watch shows and even eat popcorn. "Don't leave any kernels in my bed. That would spoil our secret," she would always say. Sam smiled to himself at the memory.

Sunny interrupted his thoughts. "We think we know where they are. It's about an hour from here. We were able to follow the Nissan that far," she began, continuing until she had explained everything that had happened. Finally she said, "Get some sleep though. Can't do anything tonight."

"Okay." Sam tried to digest the meaning of everything Sunny had told him. "Do you mind first if I check my messages? I keep hoping Stacey will call."

"Sure, help yourself."

The first message was from a man who wanted him to train a six-month-old sorrel. He saved it. Then it was another male voice. "Hey, uh, yeah . . . I met this chick, Stacey. Anyway man, she told me to tell you she's okay." Sam was relieved that she was alive. *But why didn't the guy leave his name?* Sam's thoughts raced. *Why didn't she tell him where she was? Does she know where she is? Still, this guy met her, so does that mean she could leave if she really wanted to?* In the morning, Sam decided, he would get the kid taking care of his stock to go in the house and see if the guy's number was on the caller ID; until then he'd try to get some sleep.

Sam slept fitfully, then at daybreak fell into a deep sleep. He was awakened by the midmorning sun streaming in through the window. He sat up. He realized he was still wearing his clothes from the day before. Kelli sat at the kitchen table, dressed and staring at him.

"Why didn't you wake me?" He pulled his boots on, stood up, and smoothed his wrinkled shirt with his hands.

"Relax. I've made some cracked-wheat cereal and orange juice. I'll dish it up for you," Kelli said.

Sam sat down at the table. "Where's Sunny?"

"Work."

"What are you going to do?" Sam asked.

"I'm supposed to stay out of sight, but I want to go with you."

Sam remembered the message from the night before. He wolfed down the hot cereal. "Remind me to leave some money to pay for my long distance calls," Sam said, picking up the receiver and pushing the buttons to call Derrik, the young man working for him. Derrik didn't answer. Sam glanced at the clock on the wall and realized Derrik would already be at his regular job by now. "Dang!" He banged his fist on the table, then got control and began planning his day.

chapter 44

loyal friends

Shane's boss at the ranch had taken out a ten-thousand-dollar life insurance policy for Shane, with Sunny designated as the beneficiary. Even though she hadn't wanted the money, she socked it away in savings and nearly forgot about it. For a while, she continued on at the ranch as the cook and all-around manager of morale. "Just keep everyone happy with your cooking and your smile, and I'll keep paying you the same wage as you and Shane had together," the boss had said, standing on her small porch holding his cowboy hat, nervously bouncing on the heels of his boots with each word.

It was a generous offer, far beyond what she expected. Of course, he'd always gotten both of them essentially for the price of one anyway. When she started cooking for the crew and helping out in other ways, it had just been understood that wives did those kinds of things. Now, she realized, her services really were valued. She thought she would be able to do it. She thought that being around the other cowboys would help her keep Shane alive in her mind. Instead, his absence hovered over every aspect of ranch life like an ominous cloud. No one cradled a new calf quite the way Shane had, like a human infant. She hadn't known that his method was different until she watched the others carry calves over and over, and no one did it the way he did. Other things too were different, like the way he branded, with the smile that emerged only after the calf was back on all four legs and running off. Even the way he brought his fork to his mouth at lunch and would wink at her, just as he took his first bite. All these things haunted her—not the reminders of him, but the total absence of reminders. If just one of the cowboys had been even remotely like him, she could have stayed on.

Eventually, she drove to the bank, took out the ten thousand dollars in cash, crammed it into the glove compartment, and headed for somewhere else. Anywhere else. After years of working odd jobs in Great Falls, then Butte, then back to Bozeman, she happened upon the small tourist town of Trout Haven, less than an hour's drive from Bozeman. There were two bars, one gas station, a half dozen gift shops and galleries, a couple of motels, a grocery store, and a fishing-guide service, but not one single café. She stopped in front of an empty building for sale. It had once been a realty office, then an art gallery, then a tanning salon. After the salon failed, the building had sat empty for nearly a year. In the instant Sunny saw the "For Sale" sign, she envisioned her café and living in this town. She grabbed her envelope of money, still after all these years in the glove compartment of her car, found a pay phone, and called the number on the sign. When she got to the agent's office, she followed a couple into the building. The man, she quickly learned, was Marty. He and his wife Anne were just passing through on their way to Kalispell hunting for jobs, and mistook the Realtor's office for a coffee shop since the name of the Realtor, "Maxwell," was emblazoned across the picture window. They'd stepped inside and were trying to figure out where they were. Sunny, enthusiastic about her idea, blurted it out to Marty and his wife Anne, even before the Realtor had a chance to invite them to sit down. After a quick consultation with Anne, Marty asked Sunny if he could cook at her new café. He'd cooked in Vietnam, and even for the family of the governor of Colorado, so he was well qualified. By the time the three walked out of the office, they were already fast friends.

* * *

Now, years later, Marty still worked with her and was still a good friend. Sunny watched Jack and Tony put up a piece of Sheetrock for the interior wall of the new addition to the café. Jack's face twisted in concentration as the nail gun blasted nails into the wall. Because of the deafening noise, Sunny had given up trying to open the café today. Sam and Kelli walked through the back door just as Sunny put the finishing touches on the trout-and-mushroom bisque to serve to the workers.

"Kelli, you're supposed to be keeping out of sight," Sunny shouted to be heard over the clamor.

"I've got my bodyguard," Kelli shouted back happily. She grabbed Sam's arm and they took seats at the counter where they could still talk to Sunny. Even with this latest trouble, Kelli was looking more radiant and more relaxed all the time, Sunny thought. It was hard to believe the changes in her since they'd first met. But Sam's countenance seemed to have darkened and he was looking more troubled all the time. Sunny wondered how he managed to keep going. After sprinkling a little tamari into the soup, and then setting the heavy stock pan onto the stove, she turned it to low. "Well Sam, I know you've got to be awfully worried. Have the police heard anything?"

"No. I did let them know about Stacey's car. From what I heard, they've canvassed the area and haven't found anything matching the description."

"What about the people themselves? The compound couldn't be too far from where we spotted the man in Stacey's car who called himself Hank Smith."

"The whole mountain is apparently dotted with cabins and homes. The police are going door-to-door to talk to people. Of course, they have a photo of Stacey to show, hoping they'll happen upon her or someone who's willing to talk," Sam said. "I'm just not willing to wait long enough for them to find her. I know with some help, we could find her faster than they can. For one thing, their uniforms alone will alert anyone on the inside of the cult. No one who has actually seen Stacey is going to talk to the police. And since they have no proof that she's not just on vacation or something, they can't just storm in there."

"And you're thinking?" Sunny stirred the bisque.

"I think we should gather up everyone we can, give them all tools so they'll look like construction workers, and just show up at the place ready to work. Jack's pretty sure he knows the location, having done work in that area. We can catch them off guard. If we're lucky, and we see Stacey and Mary and anyone else who wants to leave, they simply come with us. If we can't see them, we look around the best we can without arousing suspicion, see what we can see, and then figure out something else." Sam took off his hat and set it on the stool next to him.

By now, Jack, Marty, and Tony had set down their tools and joined them at the counter.

"Suppose they carry guns? Would it be too dangerous?" Jack asked.

Kelli turned on her bar stool to face Jack. "I never saw any guns, except for the time Mary was abducted. I don't think the men normally carry guns at the compound. I know the women and children don't."

"But they might have guns," Jack said.

"It's a chance we have to take," Sam insisted.

Jack pulled off his safety goggles. "Sam, it is a chance you have to take. And I'm willing to join you."

"And so am I," Tony said.

"And of course, so am I," Sunny said.

Marty, who was helping out with the construction, wiped his brow with a paper napkin. "I'm sure in on this thing too."

"But," Jack continued, "we can't ask other people to put themselves in danger."

"How are we supposed to overwhelm them with just five people?" Sam asked.

"And me." Kelli said. "I'm going."

Sam shook his head. "No, Kelli."

"You can't tell me what to do," she said defiantly.

"Well, I am telling you. You can't go."

Kelli abruptly stood up and strode over to the jukebox. Sunny guessed it was so no one would see her face; either tears were forming, or she was angry. Soon the '50s tune, "You Don't Own Me," filled the café. Tony's face broke into a smile. Sam didn't seem to catch on.

When Kelli returned, she seemed to be deep in thought. "I'll stay out of sight, stay in the truck even, but I'm going. Stacey wouldn't even be in this mess if it weren't for me." Kelli put her hand over Sam's, then continued. "The best time of day—that is, if they are still following the same schedule—is midmorning. The male leaders control everything to that point, then for a while, around ten, they disappear to some meeting of their own. In the compound I was in, the men had a special meeting room away from the group. While the men are meeting, the children are given academic lessons by some of the women while others prepare food, and others clean and take care of laundry. There is likely to be some kind of room where the children are taught. Stacey, given her age and education, would probably be teaching. Mary, I'm not sure."

"Well, sounds like we need you," Sam said reluctantly. "Okay, so tomorrow morning let's meet here at nine and maybe we should take guns along, just in case."

"We're not going to shoot anybody. As soon as we're sure that's where Stacey is, we hightail it out of there and call the police. Let the police bring their guns. The last thing we want is to start a shoot-out with innocent people," Jack said. "We won't do anything besides check the place out and look for Stacey."

Sam looked thoughtful. "You're right, of course. My brain is a little cloudy these days."

"The bisque is about ready, so why don't you eat," Sunny suggested. "And I'll mix up one of my specialty drinks, guaranteed to cure the thickheaded. No offense, Sam."

"None taken. Besides, anything you make, I'm eating," Sam answered, cheering up a little now that they had a plan. "Then, maybe for today at least, I could help you with this construction project."

"Good deal," Jack said. "By the way, did you hear? Sunny and I will be getting married in a few weeks—you can bring Stacey to the wedding party."

"Congratulations. I'll plan on doing that."

Sunny glanced at Sam's expression. *How much more can this kid take?* she wondered. She wasn't sure a wedding was the best thing for Jack to bring up. It seemed to have brought another cloud over Sam's countenance.

chapter 45

you're next

Richard and Adam brushed aside Stacey's concerns about little Jenny. "Her pallid appearance is a reaction to her being possessed. Eventually, she will be healed if the group as a whole shows more faith. If she isn't healed, then it's simply God's way of chastising us for not being more obedient," Richard said.

Stacey was confused and surprised that something as simple and miraculous as medicine was no longer accepted here. "She just needs antibiotics. Her wound was infected. The infection has spread. People can die from infection."

"Oh ye of little faith," Adam said, not even glancing up from his studies.

The rebuke angered and frustrated Stacey, and she felt tears well up. "She needs—" Stacey broke off. She could see it was futile to talk to them. "Could I make an appointment to see the prophet?"

"Stacey, Stacey." Richard rose from his office chair and touched her face lightly with his hand. "How easily you vacillate back to the world. Antibiotics are of man, not of God. The prophet won't tell you any differently. Why show him your weaknesses?" Richard glanced at the clock on his desk. "It's time for group teaching. Prophet Daniel will be teaching us before he heads back to Idaho."

Stacey walked back to the conference room. It was already full. People sat cross-legged in a large circle on the floor. Prophet Daniel was already in front. Stacey could feel the prophet's gaze following her while she searched for Mary and sat down.

"You're next," Mary whispered.

"What do you mean?"

"Prophet Daniel has chosen you to be his next wife."

"No, I think I'm intended for Adam."

"I don't think so." Mary nudged Stacey and nodded toward the front of the room.

Stacey glanced back at the prophet and his eyes were on her. "I don't understand."

"It doesn't matter who chose you already. If the prophet wants you, he'll get you. It wouldn't even matter if you were already married to someone else. Prophet Daniel only has to say, 'I've received a revelation' and that's that." Mary's volume dropped even lower. "Don't let on I told you—I don't want to be beaten again for subversion."

Stacey felt a sudden knot in the pit of her stomach. Things were reeling out of her control. She should have made a run for it when she was at the college. But at the time she'd been sure that, if she were patient, a better opportunity to flee with Mary would arise. By now she'd started to feel that such an opportunity might not ever come. She leaned over to ask Mary a question, but Mary jabbed her and nodded to the front. The prophet had begun to speak, and it was wrong to whisper during his teaching time. He spoke with such power, such magnetism, that Stacey wondered how Mary had grown up in this society and still found the strength to resist it. Today Stacey ignored Daniel's words by silently praying about sick little Jenny, and by dreaming of escape. She had to find a way to talk to Mary.

After the meeting, Stacey scanned the room for Jenny. She couldn't see her. "Do you know where Jenny is?" she asked Mary.

"She's in a room upstairs. Her mother is worried sick, but can't do anything about it. Everyone has gotten so paranoid around here lately. They don't want to seek any outside help. Things are much tighter now than before I ran away."

Stacey could see one woman who seemed to be crying, and guessed it was the girl's mother. "What will happen if the girl dies?"

"I don't know. This hasn't happened before. My guess is that she'll be buried quietly. No one ever asks questions." Mary put her fingers to her lips.

"How have you resisted all this? You seem so strong," Stacey whispered.

"I haven't resisted. I'm in complete compliance. I'm now one of the prophet's wives. What else could I—" Mary broke off and became very quiet.

Prophet Daniel was standing next to Stacey and Mary. "Mary Rachel, I need to talk to Stacey now. Will you please take care of the children in your charge?"

Mary nodded.

"Stacey, follow me outside. I want to take a walk with you."

Stacey followed Prophet Daniel away from the ranch. Every instinct urged Stacey to run in the opposite direction, but she knew that would be futile. They walked until the forest became dense. The ground beneath them was spongy with overgrown moss and decaying logs. Finally, he stopped in a small clearing and sat down on a rock. "This is where I like to pray. Would you like to pray with me, Stacey?"

"I'm concerned about the girl, Jenny." Stacey said her words softly, hoping he would listen to her.

He looked confused. "That shouldn't concern you. Sit down on this rock next to me."

Stacey sat down and she felt the prophet take her hand in his. She spoke again. "But I *am* concerned. Why won't you accept that modern medicine is part of God's miracles? The girl will rebound with antibiotics, I'm sure," Stacey said.

"Medicine is just one of Satan's many tools to take us away from relying on God. When someone gets better, who do they give the credit to? Not to God, no; they give credit to the doctor or to the medicine. It's a trap we've learned in time to avoid. Recently it has been revealed that the medical professionals are simply carrying on the work of Satan. Simple faith is all that's required."

There wasn't anything she could do. She'd already stepped far beyond what a woman should do. She'd actually questioned a man— even worse, the accepted prophet of the society. Her hand felt sweaty in his. He tightened his grip and began to pray. He prayed for Stacey's soul and for her willingness to accept God's will. When he was through, he looked Stacey in the eyes. His eyes were like sapphire jewels, so intense that Stacey felt herself blushing. "God has spoken," he said. "You're to be my wife."

Stacey felt her heartbeat quicken with panic. She glanced around quickly, avoiding his eyes. She felt her head moving back and forth. "I can't," she heard herself say. "I can't," she said again, now clutching her nauseated midsection.

For a brief second, anger passed over the prophet's face. Then Stacey watched it soften. "I think you've misunderstood. No one defies my authority. You will marry me. And we will do it right now."

Stacey stood up abruptly and looked around the forest. They were about a fourth of a mile from the house. She could run there, and then what? *Find a telephone.* There weren't any phones. Daniel had stood up immediately after she had, and now grasped her tightly. What was she thinking? She had to do what he said. She had no choice. Stacey closed her eyes and sighed, then felt Daniel's hot breath on the back of her neck. *Is he nuzzling my neck?* she wondered in disgust.

"Who will marry us then?" she asked weakly.

"The same being that married our first parents, Adam and Eve. God will marry us, right here, right now."

The panic that Stacey had momentarily been able to dispel hurtled back. She'd always dreamed of a different kind of marriage, with someone she loved—Sam. His image popped into her mind. She saw their first kiss at Winfred's field at the Labor Day barbecue. How perfectly happy she'd felt at that moment.

Daniel lifted her face to meet his. He smiled. Daniel now held Stacey and began to kiss her.

"Wait," Stacey said. "What are you doing?"

"We're already married, Stacey."

"What?" Stacey backed away and felt Daniel push her against a tree. Her back hit the trunk and the impact sent shock waves through her body.

"I'm a prophet. No one has to marry us officially. I say it. It's done." His voice had a calming quality. "No one defies me, Stacey."

When her back hit the tree, it was like hitting a replay button in Stacey's head. Instantaneously she relived her attack from the year before. Daniel's face became the face of the gap-toothed man with steely-gray eyes who had nearly raped her at the rodeo grounds.

"Come now," Daniel said. "God wants us to consummate our sacred union." Daniel began pushing Stacey to the ground.

"No!" she shouted. She pushed Daniel back with as much strength as she could muster. "No!" she shouted again as she began to run wildly into the dense forest. She heard him curse behind her and she ran faster.

chapter 46

in the door

They divided themselves into two pickups; Sam's and Jack's. Unable to dissuade her from coming, Sam insisted that Kelli stay out of sight in the backseat of Jack's club cab. The road Sunny and Jack had driven earlier passed a few small summer cabins, but Jack was sure they should keep driving, and eventually the road ended at a larger ranch house nestled in a forest meadow.

When they pulled up to the house, no one was in sight. Dressed like construction workers with tool belts strapped to their waists, everyone except for Kelli stood on the front porch. Kelli did as she was told and hid in the truck. Sam knocked on the door. They waited. Sounds of people shuffling around drifted from the house. Sam knocked again. There was a peephole in the door. The house became quiet, then a baby cried.

"Superior Log Homes, here to work on the house," Jack shouted through the door.

Sam looked around at the beautiful area. Behind the ranch he could see a dense forest. Cliffs rose up from behind the trees, forming a natural amphitheater. A pasture of wild flowers spread out from the front of the house. If circumstances were different, Sam might like to bring Stacey to a place like this and start up their own horse business. *Maybe someday it will happen.* A woman, dressed simply in a brown jumper and an apron, cracked the door. "Can I help you?" she asked nervously.

Sam resisted the urge to just push through and see what was on the other side of the door. Instead, he said, "Hi, we're here to see to that room addition you ordered."

"May I ask who you spoke to? I'm unaware of any construction." The woman stepped out onto the porch and closed the door behind her.

Sam flipped open a notebook as if reading a work-order form. "I think it was a Richard Ellstrom," Sam said, using the name Kelli had told him. "Is he here?"

"Oh. Well . . ." the woman still hesitated. "I guess if he sent for you, come in."

Sam wanted to know if Richard was in the area, so he tried again, although if he was there, Sam had no idea what he would say. "I was hoping to talk to him. Is he here?"

"Uh, no. Not right now," the woman said.

"Well, that doesn't matter," Jack said. "We can get started without him."

The woman opened the door for them. "It's so strange, he didn't say anything to me," she said as Jack stalked into the main room of the house. It was a spacious room with a vaulted ceiling. He laid a blueprint out on a table and pretended to study it.

"Now what he wants is to open the north room, ma'am. We're going to have to take a look around the entire house to see how we can best tie this room together seamlessly."

"Go ahead. I'll be working in the kitchen." The woman disappeared and waved her arm wearily, indicating the house was theirs. A group of women of various ages was in the kitchen preparing food. While Jack, Tony, and Marty began measuring around the kitchen walls, Sam and Sunny began searching the house—measuring tapes in hand, just in case. Sam opened a door and peered into a small room. He noticed a sleeping child. The child didn't stir, and they continued down the hallway opening doors. Most rooms were small, containing only a bed. Several doors were locked, and Sam leaned his head against those doors and said as loudly as he dared, "Stacey?" No response. Finally, they found a large room. A sign taped to the front of the room said, "Keep Sweet." Over thirty children of various ages were in the room and several young women were in the room teaching. *She has to be in here,* Sam thought and quickly scanned the faces. *Where is she?*

Sunny entered the room, looking the part in her carpenter coveralls. A rubber mallet hanging from a loop on her pant leg swung rhythmically as she approached a young woman teaching in the room. Sunny whispered, "Mary, it's me, Sunny."

Sam watched the lovely girl. She smiled at Sunny first, and then he saw fear in her face. "You've got to get out of here," Mary whispered.

"Where's Stacey?"

Mary looked confused. She glanced around the room at the other women. The children all stopped working and stared at the intruders. A child tugged on Mary's skirt. "Who are they?" the child asked.

"Just a minute. I need to talk to these construction workers," Mary said loudly, for the benefit of the other women teachers. "They're working to make our schoolroom better. Isn't that nice?"

The other women watched the three step to the side of the classroom. Sam could tell they were suspicious. Mary whispered. "It isn't safe. You'll put us all in danger. Just leave."

"Where's Stacey?" Sam whispered again.

"I don't know. Our prophet came running back from the forest. All the men took off on four-wheelers. My guess is she bolted. When they find her, they'll—"

She didn't need to finish. Sam was already out of the room. It took him a second to find the rest of the group. He noticed Sunny had disappeared, but didn't think he had time to look for her. Marty, Jack, Tony, and Sam, with Kelli still waiting, squeezed into Jack's truck. They left Sam's truck behind and followed a four-wheeler trail where the meadow grasses were bent. It led to the edge of a dense forest. They skirted the forest perimeter, windows down, listening for the sound of the vehicles or any clue to Stacey's whereabouts.

"We can't get anywhere in this big truck. Let's ditch it and go on foot. We'll have better luck," Sam said, anxious.

Jack parked his truck under a canopy of trees, hidden from view of the trail. They visually divided the sections of the mountain, and took two-way radios so they could stay in touch. Sam had packed rifles and hunting jackets in Jack's pickup. He took one and handed Jack and Marty guns. "So we look like hunters," he said to Jack's skeptical expression. "Lose the tool belts and take these." They agreed to radio each other only if they were in danger, or if they saw some sign of Stacey, and to meet back at the truck in one hour, with or without Stacey. Kelli would stay out of sight, but be ready to drive the truck at a moment's notice.

Sam looked for any traces of passage, foot or otherwise. Other than the creaking and moaning of the tall pines, swaying at the slightest breeze, the forest was eerily silent. The sound of Sam's own boots breaking twigs with each step seemed like gun blasts in the quiet. Not being able to hear even a distant hum of four-wheelers, Sam figured it was safe to shout. "Stacey?" he started. "It's me, Sam!" He paused and listened, then called again with every few steps he took.

chapter 47

lost

The Montana sky was vast, living up to its moniker. White wisps of cloud stretched like cotton candy across an azure-blue background, a watercolor-painting sky. The sun was like a fixed spotlight, a giant eye in the sky that Stacey needed to avoid.

Eventually, the footfalls behind her stopped, but she continued running, thrashing through the shadowed forest. She held her hands in front of her face to protect it from grabbing tree branches. Avoiding the clearing, the bright sun, and the jeep roads branching out into the forest, she went the opposite way.

Stacey felt like a failure. She had neglected to bring with her even one piece of definitive evidence against the group. And now she'd had to escape without Mary or the sick girl. Jenny would die without medical attention, and then Stacey's suffering would have been futile. But she had witnessed abuse, at least—if only she could get back to civilization that might be worth something.

Nothing in her life had prepared her for this. She prayed and thought aloud with each step. When she finally could hear her own voice, she immediately silenced herself, afraid that someone else might hear her. Keeping track of the direction she was going was difficult in her nervous state. She planned to skirt the edge of the forest as far as possible, and then turn back toward the clearing, but only when she was sure it was safe.

Stacey looked at the soft ground and noticed her shoes were leaving imprints. She took off her shoes and threw them as far away from her as she could.

Stacey had only been lost once in her whole life, but even though she was surrounded by people then, she'd been frightened. She was four years old and her family had gone to Sea World. She remembered standing pressed against a rail, watching a tank of colorful fish dart through dark waters in a huge glass aquarium. Her parents hadn't noticed that she wasn't following and had continued on without her. She was watching a starfish pressed against the side of the glass, creeping almost imperceptibly. Her mother had recently taught her how to draw a star, crisscrossing crayon lines in such a way that the magical shape would appear. Stacey was transfixed to see this same shape alive. It was only when she reached up to grab her mother's hand and it wasn't there that she discovered she was alone.

She had run frantically through the crowds of tourists, a mass of swinging legs and arms, moving past the aquariums. Faces were too far up, and she couldn't find any that were familiar. Finally, she turned her face against a candy machine and began to cry. Twix bars, M&M's, and Doublemint gum swirled together in her tears and then she felt someone grab her hand. She looked up into the face of a grandfatherly man, who from her child-size perception seemed to be all nose and huge eyes magnified by thick black-rimmed glasses. He led her to a structure where a young woman wearing a red T-shirt with a Sea-World logo asked Stacey her name and age.

"Stacey Willis, four years old, wearing pink shorts, can be found at . . ." blasted across an intercom system. It must not have been much longer, but it seemed like forever to her before her dad had come. It wasn't until Shamu, the beloved killer whale, had drenched her family, that they'd noticed Stacey wasn't with them. Mom and the new baby had stayed put while Dad had begun a frenzied retracing of their steps. Then, hearing the announcement, he'd found her wailing, still hand in hand with the man with the prominent nose and thick glasses.

* * *

The adrenaline rush Stacey had first felt started to subside and she slowed her pace to catch her breath. For the last month while she'd been living with the Church of Faith, she hadn't been able to exercise. Probably the extensive fasting had also weakened her physically. A sharp pain seized Stacey's side and she felt as if she might collapse. Pushing the pain in with her hand, she moved on. She doubted she'd gone even a mile yet, not far enough to turn toward the clearing.

Suddenly the wind in the trees wasn't the only sound Stacey could hear; there was something else. *What was it?* She stopped to listen, thinking at first it was a chainsaw, then realized it was the noise of four-wheelers. She could identify three different directions they were coming from. One of the four-wheelers sounded too close. Stacey quickly examined her surroundings, searching for a hiding place. A ravine banked to the left and Stacey stepped lightly toward it, so she wouldn't displace any earth. She couldn't take the chance that they'd see her footprints. She followed the ravine through dense underbrush until a rocky cleft hung out over it. The four-wheeler rumbled nearby. Stacey squished herself back under the ledge until the dark shadows hid her completely. Then she heard the four-wheeler in the same ravine coming toward her. As the sound became louder, she willed her body to stop panting. The sound of the engine idled every couple of minutes. Stacey guessed the rider was stopping to listen, maybe even checking the bushes on foot before continuing.

Suddenly the motor stopped right next to her. Stacey automatically put her hand over her mouth, then stopped herself from even taking a breath or moving a muscle. She prayed silently as she heard the man's feet on the gravelly bottom of the dry creek bed. *Can he see my footprints?* Then she heard the man thrashing the bushes. Finally, he leaned over and peered into the darkness right at her. She doubted he could see her in the blackness, but he paused for a long time. Then she heard a new noise— the static of a two-way radio. A voice began whispering. It was Richard's. "I think I've found her. I'll wait for backup before flushing her out." To her horror, she heard him describe the location of her hiding place.

Stacey knew it would take only a few minutes for the others to arrive. She couldn't roll out of the crevice and run past him, so instead she stealthily crept deeper into the blackness, dragging her body forward in tiny increments, following the back wall of the over-hang away from the man. The hole was getting deeper. It wasn't just a crevice, she realized. She was in a cave. She wasn't sure where the cave would lead, but anywhere would be better than being outside with Richard and the others.

chapter 48

taking a stand

Sunny was bothered by her impressions of the little girl sleeping alone in the cell-like room at the ranch house. Why was she there in the middle of the day when everyone else seemed to be busy with other things? While Sam was talking to Mary, Sunny had stolen out of the schoolroom back to where the girl was. This time, she'd glanced around, then slipped into the room and closed the door behind her. She tried to sit on the edge of the bed, but discovered it was merely an army cot. She dropped to her knees next to the blond-haired girl and felt her forehead. The girl was burning up with a dangerously high fever. Alarmed that no one was paying any attention to her, Sunny threw the covers off the girl and her nose was assaulted with smell of urine and soiled clothing. She ignored the stench and leaned her head over the girl's chest. The rise and fall of breathing was slow, even irregular. *What is going on here? This girl needs immediate medical attention!* Sunny had scooped the tiny, limp form in her arms and run back to the schoolroom. "Mary, quick. Come with me," she commanded.

Sunny sprinted down the stairs to the main floor with Mary following, protesting.

"No, you can't take her. Stop."

Sunny ignored the warnings, the gasps, and shouting of the women in the kitchen as she ran past them. She didn't know what she was going to do. It wasn't until Sunny reached the main door that she realized the rest of her group were gone. *They left me!* she thought in panic. *Now what am I going to do?* Mary made a show of blocking the front door, but moved away slightly so Sunny could open it. Sunny balanced the sick child in one arm while she struggled to turn the door handle. The women in the kitchen seemed frozen in place. When Sunny stepped outside, she couldn't believe her luck. Sam's truck was still parked right where he'd left it earlier. "Please let the keys be in the ignition. Please let the keys be in the ignition," she chanted as she struggled with the extra weight of the girl on her way to the truck.

Mary jogged alongside her. "You're going to get us all in trouble," she whispered.

"Come with me then," Sunny said.

Mary looked like she wanted to, but stopped. "I can't. Next time they'll kill me."

When Sunny made it to Sam's truck door, the women seemed to finally figure out what was going on and ran frantically toward her in an attempt to stop her. Sunny opened the passenger side, slid the girl onto the bench seat, then climbed in and locked the truck doors behind her a split second before the women reached her. A couple of women tugged on the door handles, but Sunny suspected that most of them did it merely for the sake of appearances. These were women, mothers themselves mostly. Sunny felt that deep down some of these women, not able to admit it even to themselves, were rooting for her. One woman held her hands to her face as if trying to stop tears.

The keys were not in the ignition. Sunny rummaged through the glove compartment—nothing. Then she felt under the seat and the visors. She pulled out the ashtray drawer. *They must be in Sam's pocket,* Sunny thought. She sighed. Then a sudden thought struck her, almost as if someone had whispered it to her. *Some people hide keys on their vehicles, just in case. Sam is the type who would be prepared.* The thought calmed Sunny. The little girl moaned. Sunny noticed Sam's water bottle sitting on the front seat. She pulled off the bandana scarf she'd used to pull her hair back, soaked it in the cool water, and gently bathed the girl's face with it.

Sunny would wait until the women left to find help, then she would look under the hood and the tire wells to see if a magnetic hide-a-key box was anywhere. One by one, several of the women eventually headed for the house, except for Mary and two others, including the woman who was sobbing. Sunny didn't know for sure where any of the men of the compound were, but they didn't seem to be around. Perhaps the women had gone back to get them out of their meetings.

Sunny glanced around the interior of Sam's truck. If only she had something to protect herself, or threaten the women with, just to get them to stay back. A metal rod stuck out slightly from the under the seat. It was a crowbar. When Sunny pulled it out, she knew she could never hit anyone with it, not in a million years, but she gambled that the women wouldn't know that. She opened the door and shouted. "Back away from the vehicle, or I'll hurt you!" Sunny's legs felt wobbly when her feet hit the ground. She swung the iron around to show she meant business. Mary nodded in understanding and backed away. The other women hesitated, but when Sunny swung her weapon wildly again, the women backed up.

"Farther," Sunny demanded.

They took a few steps back. Sunny knelt by the tires and ran her hand under the wells. Nothing. She walked backward to the front of the truck, watching the women with every step. When Sunny tried to open the hood, she discovered it was the type that only opened from a knob inside the cab. He probably wouldn't hide it there, she realized. Retracing her steps, while waving the iron bar in the air, she walked alongside the truck, feeling around the edges of the truck bed. Finally, she felt a small metal rectangular case. Sam was a good Boy Scout after all, she thought jubilantly. Sunny reached for it and ran back to the truck cab. She slid open the tiny metal lid, fished the key out, and started the engine. Then she had one more thought. She put the truck in park, jumped back out with the crowbar, and bolted toward the women, grabbing Mary by the arm. "I'm taking this one with me—just so you won't . . ." Sunny didn't know how to finish the sentence. "Just don't try anything or I'll . . ." She left the last word dangling, letting them imagine the worst, then swung the crowbar one more time, dragging Mary to the truck. Mary pulled and screamed theatrically. The other woman spilled out of the house again, shouted for help, and soon all half dozen of them began chasing Sunny as she drove down the dirt road.

Mary hugged Sunny and burst into tears. "Now you'll be in danger too."

"I'm not worried," Sunny assured her.

But she was worried. She nervously watched her rearview mirror, hoping no one would follow. She just had to make it to the hospital in Bozeman to get help before it was too late for this little girl.

chapter 49

hunting

The afternoon sun streaked through the pines like long sparkling fingers. Normally Sam would have been struck by the beauty. Instead he cocked his head in the direction of a sound—the four-wheelers. He guessed that there were four or five roaring along the mountainside hunting for Stacey. He searched the ground, looking for broken twigs, footprints, bent grass, or anything that would show where Stacey had gone. The four-wheeler trails were easy to follow. They left wide paths, destructive to the plant growth and probably to evidence of Stacey's trail. Sam could hear the four-wheelers frequently stop and start. He realized the drivers were on foot nearly as much as he was. Sam heard a four-wheeler coming in his direction. He thought about ducking into some thick growth, but knew if they found him that would be hard to explain, so he continued walking at a normal pace.

The motor idled behind him and Sam turned to see a man with long blond hair riding it. He stepped off the machine. "What are you doing?" the man asked.

"Hunting," Sam answered.

"Hunting what?"

Sam could only hope this man didn't keep current with the hunting season and regulations. "Elk."

"Any luck?"

"No. You?" Sam asked, pretending the man must be hunting also.

Sam wondered if this was the "blond Adonis" Angie had talked about. He did seem to have the good looks that could attract women.

"I'm just checking on my property. You're trespassing."

"Oh, I'm sorry. I thought this was public forest."

The man seemed to be mulling this over. "Well, unfortunately, it isn't," he said in a lighter tone. You need to head about a mile north before you get to the boundary." He got back onto his four-wheeler. When the man lifted his leg over the seat, Sam noticed the bulge under the man's shirt. He was armed.

"I have a few friends hunting as well. Did you see any of them?"

"Not yet, but you'd better warn them that the whole lot of you are trespassing. I don't want to sound threatening, but if you don't gather your friends up and leave, I'll have to call the game wardens. They'll fine you and—"

"Don't worry," Sam said. "We'll be on our way as soon as I locate them."

A voice came over the man's radio and the blond man grabbed it off of his pants. He held it to his mouth and turned his back. Sam heard him say something into it. Then the man hopped back on his four-wheeler, turning around in the opposite direction. He waved to Sam in a friendly gesture.

Sam tuned his radio to different frequencies until he heard the blond Adonis's voice. "It's Daniel," the radio voice said. "Message received. Stay with her. I'm on my way."

They had her. Sam knew they did. He hid from view of the four-wheeler and ran full speed through the brush. He followed the sound, trying to keep up with it. He stopped, hid behind a huge boulder, and watched the four-wheeler drop down an incline and out of sight. Sam edged along the rocky ledge until he could look over. Now he could see three four-wheelers, all parked in a dry creek bed at the opening of a hollow in the limestone cliffs. Three men, including the blond man, dropped to their bellies and disappeared into the opening.

chapter 50

hiding

As Stacey inched her way forward, pulling herself on her stomach deeper into the cave, she heard the four-wheelers' engines stop one by one. She heard footsteps, then grunting noises as the men dropped to their stomachs to slide beneath the overhanging ledge. She had expected the crevice in the cliffs to dead end, but it hadn't, and she kept crawling deeper into the mountain. She heard the men's voices shout in dismay that she was missing, then she heard a man creeping up behind her—his exertion evident with each groan he made. He couldn't make it much farther, she knew. Stacey herself barely fit through the narrowing cold chasm, her size an advantage to her now. She could slither along like a snake in the narrowing black tunnel. Finally, the grunting noises stopped. "You fool!" Daniel shouted to her. "There's no way out. You're stuck. You might as well crawl back. This cave dead-ends. If you come back now, I'll forgive you." Stacey hesitated. She wanted to believe him. "Come back now, Stacey! If you do we won't . . . punish you." At those words she took a breath and pushed on with firm resolve. She would rather die in the mountain than remain any longer in the hands of these men. The tunnel kept going deeper, and even though Stacey was afraid that it would eventually dead-end, just as Daniel told her it would, she had to try. She pulled herself along on her forearms, feeling the sharp rocks bite at her flesh. It was completely black; not even a glimmer of light pierced the total darkness.

At times the burrow narrowed so much that, even on her stomach, the top of her head scraped on the jagged ceiling. Then the tunnel nearly closed so that she became stuck, unable to inch forward or back. Her heart raced in sheer terror. She let out her breath to make herself as small as possible, adjusted her angle, and eased forward again. Eventually the passage widened slightly and Stacey dragged herself along more quickly.

Panic and the will to live drove her deeper into the cave. When the cave forked, she always veered to the right, knowing she might have to find her way out again, but eventually she lost track and she realized that if the cave did dead-end, she'd never make it out alive. She couldn't tell how long she'd been in the narrow cave. It seemed like hours, but Stacey doubted that in reality it had been more than thirty minutes. Then she had a new sensation—she could hear a tiny trickle of water. She had no idea if that was good, but took it as a positive sign. When the water touched her skin, she dropped her tongue onto the wet floor, sipped the cool liquid, and let the water seep around her face. It rejuvenated her spirits.

Now the passageway turned up at nearly a ninety-degree angle. It took all of her strength to pull herself up the steep incline, and then the tunnel became even steeper before it leveled out again onto a shelflike ledge. On the rocky ledge, she was almost able to stand up, but had to keep her head bowed; the roof of the cave still wasn't tall enough for her to straighten completely. She felt with her hands above her head for a continuation of the cave, but couldn't find one. Then she felt along the back wall again—nothing. The opening had dead-ended. She sat down on the ledge, cried, and prayed for strength.

For a second, Stacey's mind raced to the worst possible endings. She wondered if the cult would dynamite the opening so that she'd be forever enclosed in the cave. She wondered if they would stay, guarding the opening until she was forced to come out for food. *How many days would that take?* She knew people could go a long time without food, and she had a little water in the cave. Maybe she could outlast them. Again she started to sob, knowing how determined they were to find her. Besides, she doubted she could ever make it back out of the maze anyway. When she sat back down, putting her face in her hands, she noticed something distinctly different. The air was different. . . no longer stagnant. She felt as if the frigid air were moving around her. *What does that mean?* she wondered with excitement. Something else was different as well. The light. When she put her hand in front of her face, she couldn't discern its shape, but she could detect movement. Light was finding its way into the tunnel.

Stacey stood up as straight as she could and tried to feel for the source of the light. Finally she located a breeze at the back of the enclosure at the highest point. The hole was small, but she could feel the air moving. She felt renewed energy and began to excitedly pull rocks away from the opening, widening the hole one rock at a time.

When the hole was wide enough for Stacey to put both arms and her head through, she grabbed hold of the more solid edge of the hole and pulled herself as if doing a pull-up in gym class. Her feet fumbled beneath her until they found an edge to give her added stability. When she had squeezed her body into the hole, she saw a tiny shaft of light. She scrambled up the craggy rock tunnel toward it.

In just seconds, another surge of adrenaline fueled her effort to push one hand out of the mountain. She felt like she'd been buried in an underground tomb. Her fingers groped outside of the hole until she felt some brush. She grabbed onto it with one hand to try and pull herself out of the opening. It was then she heard the noise. Footsteps. Someone was standing there waiting for her. They'd found her. They would take her back to the compound, and then what? Beat her? Kill her? She pulled her hand back into her burrow. She heard the person step toward the hole. She could barely make out a man's shoe. Not a shoe, she realized—a boot. She could barely make out the pointy toe of . . . Sam's scuffed black cowboy boots.

She pushed her hand back out and clutched onto his boot as she let out a sob of relief. She felt him jump away from her grasp. Then he gasped her name and bent down, grabbing her hand and pulling her through the narrow opening. The earth had swallowed her whole and now released her into the light again. He tugged her to her feet and embraced her. Stacey had never felt so much relief, joy, and fear in her life. *How did Sam find me? Where are the men?* Her thoughts jumbled about in her head. It would only be a matter of minutes, maybe even seconds, before they'd hear them and pursue. Sam held his finger to his lips to tell her to be quiet. He picked up the rifle that he'd dropped by the nearly invisible hole, then they backed quietly into the woods. When they were a few steps away, Sam whispered, "Run full speed to the clearing. Jack's truck is there."

Sam and Stacey ran hand in hand. They made a good deal of noise breaking though the shrubs and trees, and the skin of Stacey's bare feet tore open from the twigs and rocks on the ground. Now they could hear the rumble of the four-wheelers behind them, but Sam and Stacey ran through dense brush where the machines would have a hard time following. She heard the machines stop, then running footsteps, branches breaking, and shouting. Then a gunshot. Running faster now, they leaped across small hollows, over rocks and fallen trees. Upon reaching the clearing, Sam directed Stacey west until she could see Jack's truck. They were only about fifty yards from it when they could hear the men right behind them. They ran faster, but their pursuers were gaining on them. Marty, Jack, and Tony were standing behind the truck pointing rifles toward the men bearing down on Stacey and Sam. Of course, that meant they were pointing guns right at them as well, and Stacey had to force herself to keep running straight for the long gun barrels.

When they got closer, Kelli, who was behind the wheel, started the engine. Just then the men from the compound reached the clearing, shooting. Sam and Stacey scrambled into the back of the pickup bed and ducked. Jack and Marty fired a couple of warning shots into the air, then jumped in almost on top of them. Kelli floored the truck and flew along the bumpy meadow road. Stacey flattened herself across the ridged metal bottom of the truck bed. Again the men in Jack's truck fired rifles, in an attempt to dissuade the pursuers from continuing their attack. Jack's truck weaved wildly and Stacey wondered if Kelli had been shot, but after the truck continued forward, she guessed Kelli must be trying to make them a more difficult target. Sam slammed his fist on the back window and shouted, "Just go faster," as the truck hit a huge bump and they were airborne. Stacey felt her body slam back into the truck bed as it came back down. She reached out to hold onto something and found Sam's booted leg again.

Finally they reached the highway and drove straight to the Bozeman police station. With Stacey's battered and bruised body, and her testimony that a girl was still in the compound in dire need of medical help they figured there would be enough evidence to warrant a search of the compound.

When they reached the parking lot of the police station, Jack looked apprehensive. "I hope Sunny got out of there okay. You left your keys in the truck for her, didn't you, Sam?"

Sam's face turned ashen. He reached in his pocket and pulled out his keys.

"More reason to get the police out there immediately," Jack said in a shaky voice, as they all went into the police station. The officer behind the desk took one look at the bedraggled Stacey and ordered that she be whisked away to the hospital.

chapter 51

anniversary

Stacey was put under close observation. She suffered from mild dehydration, exhaustion, and had lost some blood from her numerous cuts. Sam sat by her bed and held her hand. She smiled weakly. "I don't need to be in here. I'm perfectly fine."

"Considering." Sam winked. He looked at her. Her already-thin body was even thinner than the last time he'd seen her. Her normally beautiful olive skin was the color and texture of sun-bleached bone. Besides the numerous cuts and bruises on her body and face, black shadows encircled her brown eyes. She looked almost as bad as she did after her attack the year before. In some ways, worse.

"How'd you find me, Sam? I mean, when I heard someone outside the cave I knew it was the end for me—I didn't stand a chance. Your being there was nothing short of miraculous."

"I know." Sam gently stroked her face. "I came across the blond Adonis—

"Blond Adonis?"

Sam smiled. "That's what Angie called him. Anyway, I knew they'd found you, so I followed the sound of the four-wheelers. From where I hid above the ravine, I could see that they had you trapped inside the cave. I was sick. It looked to me like there was no way out, and I knew I couldn't take on four armed men. I was trying to figure out what to do, praying with every step, hoping that Jack and the others would come along so all of us together could do something. Then I remembered that since our time limit for searching was past, the others would be back at the truck. Then I heard the blond man and the others with him shouting, and I realized they couldn't get you out, that you'd gone deeper into the opening. At that point I noticed the limestone strata, seeing how the rock rose up from the ravine." Sam cleared his throat. "I know a little about caves and could tell by the strata that if there was another opening, even a small one, chances are it would be higher up, at the other end of the strata and away from the men and the opening. I just followed the limestone. Then, sometimes I get these feelings, and I got one."

"What kind of feelings?"

"Well, like, one time I knew I had to get home, and Kelli called right then. Another time, I knew I should turn left, and I found this guy that needed an ambulance. I get a tingle at the back of my neck, and then an urge to do something. I'm pretty sure it's how the Lord knows I'll listen. But anyway, this time I felt like I had to keep moving up the mountain. When I did, I couldn't see anything, but I could hear you coming up. I was just searching for the hole when you grabbed my boot. It scared me to death."

"I did feel you jump," Stacey said smiling. Then she sobered. "What's disturbing is that, even after all that, I didn't get Mary or Jenny out, or get evidence of abuse. It was a waste. I should've listened to you. And you and the others could've been killed."

"Well, you should've listened—yeah. But you're wrong about it being a waste, Stacey. They've got them nailed. Jack called and said a SWAT team is on their way to the ranch house now."

Sam watched Stacey's face. She shivered and tears welled up in her eyes. "I hope they don't . . . they can't hurt . . . I mean, a lot of nice women and children—and even some of the young men—live there. Lots are victims, themselves. I hope they know."

Television images of the burning inferno that was David Koresh and his followers flashed in Sam's mind. Sometimes the best of intentions went wrong. He knew that. "Kelli's told them all about the women and children. They'll be careful. I think they've learned some lessons over the years." Sam hoped he was right.

"And Sunny—what about Sunny?" Stacey asked.

"What about Sunny?" interrupted a loud voice from the doorway.

Sam turned and there she was—Sunny Day—still in her striped denim overalls, ready to work construction.

"How'd you get here?" he asked.

Then both Sunny and Mary walked into the room together. Sunny strode to the window, pulled the blind up, opened the window a crack, and fluffed Stacey's pillow. "Got to get some air and sunshine in the room so this girl can breathe."

"Mary. Oh, I'm so relieved. I can't tell you how horrible I felt about leaving you there," Stacey said.

Sam too felt a rush of relief. "Sunny, I was sick to death when I realized I didn't leave the keys in the ignition. Force of habit. I meant to. So how . . . ?"

"You should've seen her," Mary began. "She threatened to kill us with a crowbar, then found your spare key."

"I took a chance that you're a trusty Boy Scout, Sam, and figured you might have a hidden key. I also had a little help figuring all that out." She indicated heavenward with her eyes.

Sam shook his head. "Amazing. And you just came with her?" he asked Mary.

"No, I'm an unwilling hostage." Mary grinned. "And Sunny has something else to tell you."

"Wait," Sam said. "Does Jack know you're here? We left everyone else at the police station."

"I doubt it." Sunny answered, "I don't know how he would."

"You need to call him at the station. He's worried sick. And the police need to know you two aren't there so they don't search the area for you."

"Good idea. You tell them the news, then, Mary. I'll be right back." Sunny headed for the door.

"What news?" Stacey asked.

"Jenny. She'll be okay. We brought her here."

Stacey closed her eyes and said a silent prayer of gratitude. Everything was going to be okay.

* * *

When Stacey opened her eyes again, she realized she'd been asleep.

"How long have I been asleep?" she asked, realizing Sam was still in the room.

"Just long enough that everyone else has gone downstairs to raid the vending machines." Sam was still in the chair near her bed, but now a bouquet of flowers arranged in a vase sat on the table next to her. Stacey smiled, sat up, and reached for the card as she smelled the daisies, forget-me-nots, and baby's breath.

"Happy Anniversary," she read. "What does this mean?" Stacey asked.

Sam cocked his head. "It's been a year since you showed up at the livestock auction. One year ago, today, I laid my sore old eyes on the woman of my dreams."

chapter 52

balm of gilead

Kelli enjoyed living in Montana. The Big Sky Country seemed to be as healing as the balm of Gilead. It had been a month since Stacey's escape from the compound. Kelli had learned that most of the men of the group got away; they disappeared on foot, or on four-wheelers, or in their cars, leaving the women stranded to face the men swarming in with bulletproof vests, guns, helicopters, handcuffs, and demands. Richard Ellstrom, "Prophet" Daniel Beekers, and Adam Riley were arrested, however, and faced charges in four states: Montana, Idaho, Nevada, and Utah. They were charged with child abuse, child endangerment, child rape, and numerous counts of assault with criminal intent, as well as federal fraud and tax evasion. A few of the women were charged with child endangerment as well, although most were let go. Kevin had worked out a plea deal and would be testifying for the prosecution. Kelli wondered what would become of them after the society was dissolved. For now Kelli would put the trial, months away, on the back burner. Then she would testify as to what she had witnessed.

When Kelli arrived for the day, Tony was already at the diner, standing on one of the booth tables washing windows. School was back in session, so he'd driven up from Bozeman for the weekend. Kelli was pretty sure the only time Tony combed his wash-and-go hairstyle was on Sundays. He wore casual jeans and a T-shirt with a picture of some guy with dreadlocks. Probably a famous guitarist, she realized, though Kelli didn't recognize the silk-screened face.

"Hey," he grinned and saluted her.

"Hey, Tony, how's it going?" Kelli asked. "What do you think I should tackle first?"

"Marty and his wife are in the kitchen making doodads to eat. You can help me with the windows, and then we ought to clean up the new addition before we get the tables set up. Jack left instructions to leave space for a dance floor again. Guess who the lead singer is tonight?"

"I don't know—that guy on your shirt?" Kelli guessed.

"This guy?" Tony pulled at his T-shirt and looked down on it. "Nah, he's dead. Don't tell me you don't know who this is?"

Kelli twisted her face in consternation. "Should I?"

"Yeah, you should, but that's not the point. I'm the lead singer tonight." He pointed to himself proudly. "Jack wants to spend the evening greeting friends and dancing with Sunny."

Kelli climbed onto the table with Tony. She grabbed a squeegee out of the soapy water and slicked the window clean. "So who gets to choose the songs? You or Jack?"

"We compromised. He wrote down ones he wants sung specifically. He wrote one for Sunny and he'll sing that one. And then we'll do our usual set, along with some of my oldie originals." He dipped the sponge in the water and wiped the next window.

"Well, I can't wait to hear you, and the song Jack wrote for Sunny. That's so sweet. I can't think of any nicer way to tell someone you care about them than writing a song just for them," she said, nudging him in the ribs lightly.

Tony looked deep in thought. "But I already wrote you a song, remember?"

"Yes, I remember," Kelli said, shuddering at the memory of running from the police. "And on the spot, even."

Then Tony grinned his easy, natural smile—the one that turned Kelli's legs to jelly. They were still standing on the booth table when he put his arms around her and pulled her close for a hug. She felt the wet sponge drizzle soapy water down her back, but she didn't care.

When she was ready to get into a relationship, she hoped Tony would still be around. But for now, she was content to have him for a friend.

chapter 53

tender mercies

It was a picture-perfect September day along the banks of the Snake River in Idaho Falls. The wedding guests would be arriving shortly, but Sunny needed a few minutes to herself to gather her thoughts. She sat on a park bench and gazed at the man-made falls. *Appealing, nonetheless,* she thought, mentally forgiving their unnatural state. She watched a pair of geese glide in across the smooth water above the falls, honking, feet outstretched for the landing. They skied across the pond, an arch of water spewing from behind their webbed feet as they touched down.

Sunny wore a simple azure-blue cotton dress. Her long, straight hair was gathered on top of her head in a casual bun. The new heels she had bought for the occasion made her feet ache, reminding her why she hadn't owned any previously. She couldn't help but tug at the uncomfortable panty hose she was wearing. The only other time in her life she'd worn them was for Shane's funeral. Across the river, a demonstration was taking place. A dozen or so people marched, pushing their handmade signs up and down so passing motorists would pay attention. So little had changed. Sunny almost felt compelled to walk around to the other side and join the group, to talk to them and find out what they believed in so deeply.

Joining demonstrations would have to wait until another day, she realized. Jack was waiting for her in the temple across the street. In a few minutes she would vow to be his life partner. She admired him, and she loved him for how easily he'd put aside their apparent differences and envisioned the reality that they could be happy together. Someday maybe she could get him to join her in her causes, but for now she would accept him the way he was; and if he didn't become an Earth First spokesperson, then that was okay too. She could "congrue." In her heart, Sunny thanked God for His tender mercies, and walked across the street toward the temple.

chapter 54

detour

It looked as though they might be able to get their house back, after all. Sam had met with an attorney. "The wheels are in motion," he'd told Sam. Life had begun to settle into a comfortable routine since Montana. Sam had several clients he was training horses for. He spent most of his hours working with the animals, but today Stacey was coming over and they would head back up to Trout Haven for the wedding celebration. In a way, he had dreaded going back there, back where he'd felt like he might break. Life had a way of piling pain on, one disaster at a time. He knew that people thought he rode life's ups and downs as easily as he rode a bucking bronc in a rodeo. The truth was that at times he felt as though he couldn't face one more day. Responsibility reined him in and controlled his life, and sometimes he hated it. Today though, things were looking up again, and he knew he could make the trip to Trout Haven. He also knew he could face one more responsibility.

Sam finished getting ready; he combed his hair, brushed his teeth, knotted his nicest silk scarf around his neck, pulled on his best polished boots, then grabbed the morning paper and waited by the picture window so he could see Stacey pull in the driveway. He'd only made it halfway through the second article when the red Nissan pulled up. Her car had been damaged a little by the cult, but it still ran well. He watched her step out the car door. She wore jeans and a white blouse. She was still rummaging through her trunk to pull out her suitcase when he surprised her, hugging her from behind.

Within a few minutes they were on the highway, heading north, but then Sam turned the truck off of the main road.

Stacey looked confused. "A new way to Montana?"

"Just a little detour. Some of the aspens have turned already."

"Do we have time for this?"

"On a day like this, we make time." He winked but tried not to give away the excitement he felt.

The road wound around the mountain like ribbon candy, and the aspens shimmered like gold coins in the morning sun. At the top of Mount Harrison the road dead-ended at a parking lot and a fire watchtower.

"Come on." Sam grabbed Stacey's hand and led her up the steep narrow steps of the building on stilts. Then they stood on the landing and looked out over the huge valleys below. They gazed at thousands of patches of farmland, pieced together in a multishaded quilt of greens and yellows. Sam opened the door of the tower and they went inside a room surrounded by glass windows on all sides. Sam had been here many times just to sit, think, and talk things out with the man who ran the place and who had been his friend for many years.

"So, how you folks?" the old man inside asked.

"Great," Sam answered. "Jim, this is my—uh, Stacey."

Jim winked at Sam, but Sam hoped Stacey didn't notice. Jim took Stacey's hand and pumped it up and down. "Stacey, you look like an awfully sweet girl to be tied up to this wild man."

"Don't let Stacey's size and looks deceive you. She's as tough as a two-dollar steak," Sam said. Stacey smiled, and Sam finished, "I came up to show Stacey the sights."

"Grab yourselves a cookie first. Made 'em fresh today—raisin oatmeal." Jim held a plastic container in front of them. "Bet I'm the oldest forest service employee to give you cookies that good."

"You're the only forest ranger to ever give me cookies," Stacey said, reaching for one as she grinned.

"And how old are you now?" Sam asked the man.

"Eighty." Jim held large binoculars to his face. "You want to show Stacey your place, Sam?"

"Sure, let's take a look at it from way up here."

Jim led Stacey and Sam to a large instrument in the center of the room. "Now, if I remember right, Sam, your place is south of Burley . . . about . . . right . . . there." He lined up the eyepiece on the circular instrument that helped him pinpoint exactly where fires were so he could relay the coordinates to firefighters.

Jim continued, "Well I'll be . . . what the sam hill? Is that smoke I see rising from your fields? It's something. Definitely something black and sooty! This is terrible, terrible!" I need to call this in on my radio. If you'll excuse me . . ." Jim disappeared down a circular set of steps, shouting, "Take a look through that scope and see for yourself!"

chapter 55

smiling

Stacey had thought it strange for Sam to detour in order to see the fall colors. He wasn't the kind to just let his responsibilities go like that. Usually he'd be anxious to get going where they were going. But she was happy that he thought sharing beauty with her was a good enough reason to throw caution to the wind. On the way up the winding road they'd stopped at Lake Cleveland, a glistening turquoise jewel surrounded by pines and aspens. They watched someone fly fish, the rhythm of his hand flicking the rod, letting the fly momentarily lie on the water before snatching it off the surface again—the wet line catching the sun's glint and arching across the blue cloudless sky. Then Sam took Stacey's hand and led her back to his truck, and they'd continued up the drive to a lookout tower. There he introduced her to an old man, Jim, dressed in standard forest-service khaki. She was surprised to learn that this spry, fit man, who didn't look over sixty, was actually eighty years old. Even more delightful was his great sense of humor, and that he actually baked cookies right in the lookout tower so he'd have something to offer visitors.

But then Jim had bolted down the stairs in a mad rush to call in a fire at Sam's place. Sam seemed nervous about the fire, but not like what you'd expect from someone whose place might be in the process of burning down. Stacey felt sick. One more tragedy in Sam's life. How much could he take? Sam peered through the scope. Then he stood up. "Want to take a look? It's my place all right," Sam sounded disheartened.

Stacey didn't need to bend over to look through the scope, it was at her eye level. She expected to see billowing black smoke, but instead she saw something else. *What is it?* They were black curving shapes. There wasn't any smoke. Instead, letters were blackened into Sam's fields. "Marry me," Stacey read aloud, her heart pounding.

Sam dropped to one knee. "Please."

Stacey laughed, then blinked away the tears. She couldn't think of anything else she'd rather do. In all her life, she'd never met anyone that made her feel the way Sam did.

Sam stood up and pulled Stacey in, hugging her for several seconds. Finally Sam cleared his throat. "Stacey?"

She tried to answer. The events of the past year rushed through her mind. Meeting Sam for the first time and thinking he was a jerk, being stranded with him in his pickup, the attack on her and Sam's attentive kindness, their first kiss and dance together, him saving her from the cult, and then his bringing her a bouquet of flowers at the hospital. Tears rolled down her cheeks and she wiped at them with the back of her hand.

"Stacey?"

"Yes. Yes. Of course yes!"

"Hear that, Jim? She said yes!" Sam yelled.

"She sure had to think hard on it though, didn't she? Can I come on back up now? A real fire may've sprung up by now—with all the time she had to think on it. Ya never know, dry as it is. So when's the big day going to be?" Jim appeared from downstairs.

"We've got plenty of time to figure that out on our way up to Montana. All I know is, I hope it's soon. I don't know how many more days I can stand," Sam said. "That road to Grouse Creek is long."

"Who said I wanted to move out of Grouse Creek?" Stacey said in mock outrage.

But Sam was ready to compromise on anything to have her. "Well, one way or the other, we're going to be together."

"Have I ever thanked you for finding me?" she whispered, suddenly grateful she had an opportunity to choose anything at all—to be alive, even.

Sam pulled her in for a kiss and whispered back. "Not in so many words, Stacey Willis from Salt Lake City, but yeah, you have."

about the author

Carole Thayne Warburton was raised in Orem, Utah. She is the youngest child and only daughter of Jeanne Anderson Thayne and the late Stan Thayne. She and her husband Mick Warburton live in Paradise, Utah. They are the parents of two wonderful children, Trevor and Ginger. Carole and Mick taught school together in the K–10, two-room school in Grouse Creek for five years, where much of the material for her novels was acquired.

Carole graduated from Utah State University in art education in 1980, then magna cum laude in English in 1999. Besides her new career as a writer, Carole is also a respected potter in Cache Valley. She is an avid lover of the outdoors, where she spends as much time as possible skiing, hiking, riding bikes, walking, and enjoying God's creations.

False Pretenses is Carole's second published novel; it is the sequel to *A Question of Trust*. Carole would love to hear your comments. Please contact her via Covenant Communications, P.O. Box 415, American Fork, Utah 84003-0416, or through e-mail at info@covenant-lds.com.